RECKLESS SKYE

SLOANE FLETCHER

HQ

ONE PLACE. MANY STORIES

HQ
An imprint of HarperCollins*Publishers* Ltd
1 London Bridge Street
London SE1 9GF

www.harpercollins.co.uk

HarperCollins*Publishers*
Macken House, 39/40 Mayor Street Upper,
Dublin 1 D01 C9W8
This edition 2026

1
First published in Great Britain by HQ,
an imprint of HarperCollins*Publishers* Ltd 2026

A catalogue record for this book is available from the British Library.

ISBN: 9780008834609

Printed and bound in the UK using 100% Renewable
Electricity by CPI Group (UK) Ltd

MIX
Paper | Supporting responsible forestry
FSC® C013604
FSC www.fsc.org

For my husband.

Yes, your karma for that one stupid mistake is that you have to hear me threaten, 'If you hurt your back again . . .' anytime you try a new activity. For the rest of your life . . .

Trigger Warning

Reckless Skye includes recurring themes of abuse, chronic pain, and depression, as well as reference to suicidal ideation, risk and treatment. Please take care while reading.

Important Note for Rodeo Girlies

While I've done my best to accurately create Skye's world and portray the necessary elements of dairy farming, rodeo (specifically, barrel racing), and life on the road, please note that certain elements of this book, including Skye's racing schedule, the details of the rodeo events she attends, each rodeo's performance date/schedule, trade deadlines, horse change rules, and prize money amounts have been tweaked (. . . okay, heavily adapted) to create a more enjoyable read for horse and non-horse girls alike.

Irrespective, I hope you enjoy *Reckless Skye.*

— Sloane

P.S. If this is your first rodeo, then head to the back of the book for a glossary of rodeo terms.

RECKLESS SKYE

Prologue

Odessa, Texas – January 9, 2027

The moment she opened the trailer door, Skye stopped dead in her tracks.

Because there, leaning against the piped arena fencing, a box of to-go coffee and a bag of bagels in his hands, was TJ, the man she'd tried so hard to forget.

For one awful moment as their eyes met, Skye considered running. She could lock herself in the trailer and pretend that he wasn't there. As appealing as the thought was, Skye didn't dare retreat. She had always promised herself that when she saw him again, she'd act indifferent. And after the previous night's drunken escapade, she had some major ground to recover.

It didn't help that her heart was tapping furiously against her ribs or that, despite everything, TJ was as handsome as ever – maybe, she thought bitterly, even more so. He'd changed in two years. But his longer hair, leaner body, and hard green eyes, absent of his signature laughter, only made him look more dangerous, more appealing.

As if her thoughts weren't treacherous enough, Bandit – the traitor – ran to him instantly. The dog yipped with excitement and wagged his tail a million times a minute.

TJ pinched the bagel bag in the same hand as the to-go coffee so that he could reach down to welcome the dog, but he never took his eyes off of Skye.

She stepped out, closed the door behind her. 'What do you want, TJ?'

'Can't an old friend stop by for a catch up?'

'We're not friends.'

TJ just nodded. 'No. I don't suppose we are.'

Feeling tired and vulnerable, Skye stuffed her hands into the pockets of her jacket. She walked to where he stood, mimicked his lean against the arena, as if to say: *See, you don't bother me.*

He didn't try to touch her, didn't so much as shift closer or angle his head to look down at her, just said, 'Last night wasn't how I imagined it would happen.'

Skye hated that she wanted to poke at that, wanted to ask how he *had* imagined it happening and how often. 'Look,' she said instead, 'we had a fling ages ago. It ended. We both moved on. There's nothing to talk about. And there's certainly nothing to rehash.'

'Glad we agree on that,' he replied casually.

Skye ground her jaw as her anger bloomed. 'Yup.'

'I half expected you to be pining after me all this time.'

Fury burst through her instantly. She tipped her head back to glare at him. 'Do not fucking push me.'

TJ's eyes glinted with a dark and twisted triumph. Leaning close, he whispered, 'There you are, my reckless Skye.'

PART ONE:
RUN

Chapter 1

Highland Park, Texas – December 13, 2024

Skye saw the slap coming.

But then again, she always did. Holden Beauford Marchant would never use his fists on a woman. Fists left obvious bruises, whereas an open-handed slap with a good wind-up could spread that pain over five points, delivering a stunning strike – but leaving very little evidence of physical damage.

The force of it sent her to the floor.

Skye landed awkwardly, her right hand spread, her left hand twisted beneath her body. She refused to cry out when her middle and ring finger gave beneath her weight.

Blood trickled from her split lip, staining the white tiles.

She instinctively tried to swipe it, to clean it up, then stopped. *Not this time*, she reminded herself.

Her father came to stand over her, the disappointment on his handsome face backlit by a streak of lighting that illuminated the foyer of the Marchant's immaculate Highland Park house. 'You know I don't enjoy punishing you, Skye. But if you think you can come into *my* house after leaving the way you did and try to pollute my own wife against me, you have another think coming.'

'She's *my* mother,' Skye dared to snap back.

Holden crouched down on the floor – an agile man despite his sixty years. When she refused to look at him, he fisted one hand in her hair and forced her head back, his movements controlled and calm, almost gentle.

Skye's hands rose instinctually, gripping his wrist, and although she used her nails on him, digging them into flesh, her father just sighed sadly. 'You're no longer welcome in my home.'

Even lying broken on the floor, Skye was manic enough to grin. She couldn't help it. The words 'my home' were comical for so many reasons.

The beautiful house, with its twelve-foot front doors and wraparound porch, had never been a home, only a showpiece: a gilded cage for Skye and her mother to preen and hide in.

And it wasn't even his.

Skye's grandmother had owned the house, but since Grandma Jo's death six months prior, the taxable monstrosity was *technically* in trust – and Skye would become the trustee on her twenty-fifth birthday in a little over two years' time.

The note that had accompanied Grandma Jo's will had read: *I've grieved for the daughter who wouldn't accept my help, but I'll be damned if the same happens to you. Get out, Skye. Live your life. Do what you can for your mom. Love you always, Gran.*

It was the only power Skye had over Holden.

But it was mighty.

Because the money and all it could buy – the prestige, the show home, the cars – were *everything* to him.

Holden had waltzed into her mother's life with his salesman's smile and wooed her – a woman barely eighteen to his thirty-six – with false promises and lies. He'd charmed her, despite her family's hesitations, and once he'd had her in his grasp, he'd slowly tightened that grip.

Skye's birth had been nothing but a minor inconvenience to her father, so that, throughout her childhood, she had learned to mimic her mother. She had kept her head down and her smile soft. She'd been careful to be friendly and polite but never *too* friendly. Acquaintances didn't ask questions; friends did. And Skye had learned the hard way that she would be the only one to suffer if those questions were asked.

But not anymore.

She'd left, and even though she'd known she'd risk running into Holden if she returned, Skye couldn't leave without trying to get her mom out one last time.

Now, the knowledge that she'd failed consumed her. Her grief grew. And it turned to hate. She let her lips peel back, revealing her blood-covered teeth. 'What will you do without Grandma's money to fund your lifestyle?'

Holden might have been partner at a successful law firm, but he still lived well above his means through his wife's generous allowance.

But not for long.

'As soon as I turn twenty-five, I'm going to turn off the tap,' she taunted.

Holden's calm façade flickered.

He released her and pushed to his full height.

Skye took a deep breath of relief – one that was cut short by his sharp, vicious kick to her ribs.

A gurgled sob left her lips as fire spread through her side.

Skye curled into the foetal position, as much to protect against the next blow as to try to contain the pain. When she opened her eyes, all she saw was her father's snakeskin boot hovering above her face.

Tired of always being *so much smaller*, of always fighting, of always losing, she said, 'Do it. I dare you.'

'Holden.'

They both stopped at her mother's voice, unusually firm.

'Go back upstairs, Caroline. This has nothing to do with you.' Holden's voice was back to cool and calm. 'I will not be disrespected, nor taken advantage of, in my own home.'

For the first time ever, her mother refused to do as she was told. She took two shaky steps before stopping and looking down at Skye. Her blonde hair, always so pristine, made her pale face look sickly. 'Get out.'

'Mom—'

'I said, get out, Skye.'

The pain that came with those words was far worse than any physical blow. Still, seeing an escape, Skye painstakingly crawled, first to a kneeling position and then to her feet.

She turned, facing the mirror image of herself if she didn't leave for good, and she smiled at the irony. A mother reduced to childlike dependency. A child forced to grow up as a result.

'I meant what I said,' Skye told her mother. 'If you ever want to leave, I'll help. But until then, I won't see you again.'

Caroline didn't react. If anything, her blue eyes – eyes so like Skye's – were dead.

Skye looked at her father one last time. 'Under the terms of Grandma Jo's will, you have use of this property until I take over from Mr Simcock as trustee. From that moment on, I'll expect rent.' Although she couldn't look at her mom when she said it, Skye added one last jab. 'I'll also be dissolving Mom's allowance. While I'll guarantee that she'll be looked after, any expenses that I deem not directly for her benefit will be denied.'

Holden's knuckles whitened as he clenched his fists together, wanting, she knew, to take all his fear and rage out on her. After all, what would he do without the Highland Park home, the spiffy cars and the country club membership? How would he suffer the humiliation of being so reduced in the eyes of all his acquaintances?

Time would tell.

Skye would have access to the trust in just a few short years, but the money meant nothing to her when compared to the new taste of freedom.

She was a caged bird set free, and while her wings were still so weak and untried, she was wild with it. Leaning forward, she whispered, 'Tick-tock, Holden,' and snapped the air in front of him with her teeth.

Skye didn't take the car she'd once driven, a sporty little Porsche 911. While the trust had paid for it, Holden had bought it for her.

She huddled in her jacket as the December storm raged, soaking her through, washing the blood from her face, cleansing her. She limped the mile to her best friend's apartment, crossing the tollway, leaving the little hub of Highland Park for Dallas's less insulated world.

While she walked, she planned. For the first time in her life, she had nothing to tie her down: no mother to protect, no classes to show up to, no social obligations to make an appearance at.

So, she would travel, maybe pick up a second-hand truck and hit the road, staying far out of Holden's reach while she could.

He wouldn't kill her. Certainly not before she turned twenty-five and took control of the trust. Still, Skye wasn't an idiot. Her father didn't have to kill her to control her. The year of her adolescence she'd lost to the Hamburg Treatment Center had taught her that.

So, for the next few years, she'd keep a low profile and stay off his radar. She'd see the United States, forgoing Holden's preference for five-star hotels to sleep under the stars in all the state parks. She'd get lost and – just maybe – find herself in the process.

The world was her oyster.

When Skye let herself into Andrea's apartment, her friend was anxiously pacing her living room, waiting for her.

Andrea looked up when she heard Skye's footsteps. 'Oh my God. What the fuck happened?' She pulled Skye into her arms, squeezed her tight, before setting her back and scanning her face closely, looking at the extent of her injuries.

'He came home unexpectedly,' Skye explained. 'But I'll be okay.'

'We need to go to the police, Skye.' Andrea spun around. 'File a formal report.'

Skye shook her head. 'No. My mom . . .'

'Skye . . . *Please*, don't let him get away with this. If he were locked up, we could start helping your mom.'

For the first time that night, panic slashed through Skye's calm resolve. Still, she kept her voice steady. 'He already has gotten away with it, Dre. He'll have had my mom clean up the blood. If we do get the cops involved, he'll make her lie for him. And she will. He's done it before – and I ended up institutionalized.' She sighed deeply – and regretted it instantly when her ribs protested against even that slight movement. 'I can't put her through it. She's not capable. And Holden . . . He'll paint a perfectly detailed picture of a bitter daughter with a history of mental illness.'

Andrea crossed her arms. 'I don't agree with you.' She sighed. 'But I'll trust that you know what's best for you.'

'We document. Again.'

'I'll text Stevie.' Andrea ran one hand tiredly through her chestnut hair. 'Why don't you change while we wait for her?'

Skye nodded, relieved that this wouldn't be another battle. It was so simple with them. Her girls.

She'd met Andrea and Stevie in her freshman writing class at SMU, the college just down the road from her parents, the school Holden had insisted she go to so that she would *be close to home.* On the first day, Stevie had plonked down in the seat next to her and started rambling as if they'd been best friends for years. Minutes later, when the professor had split them into groups of three, they'd both met Andrea.

Although Skye had tried to avoid them outside of class, they'd made it difficult for her. They'd pulled her into group lunches and then girls' nights in their dorms. They had slowly peeled back her layers until they'd realized that something wasn't quite right. And still, it had taken Stevie and Andrea a year to get the truth out of her, another year to convince her to speak to a therapist at a women's shelter.

Skye winced when her smile pulled at her split lip. 'Today's the day, Dre. I can't . . .' She trailed off as the immensity of it overwhelmed her. 'I can't stay for her anymore. My mom's never going *t-to leave . . .*'

Andrea nodded. 'We've known that for a long time.'

'I guess I just hoped I could change her mind.'

Despite graduating almost seven months prior, Skye had waited to move on in the hope that she could convince her mom to come with her. She had turned down every entry-level law clerk job offer she'd received. And with Holden Marchant's name paving the way, there had been many. Several, she hadn't even applied to.

Eventually, Holden had caught on. He'd told her in no uncertain terms what his expectations of her were.

Skye had refused.

He'd kicked her out, expecting that she wouldn't be able to rough it without the lavish lifestyle she'd grown up in. But what Holden couldn't have known was that all those things had just held her down.

Skye had stayed on Andrea's sofa for months, broke but free. She'd picked up night shifts at the local dive bar on Lemmon Avenue. She'd worked hard, slinging cheap drinks for less than minimum wage and hefty tips. She'd slowly and consistently added to the small pile of savings she'd accrued and waited for the right time to speak to her mom.

All for nothing.

'Where will you go?' Andrea asked.

'I don't know.'

Andrea followed as Skye limped through to the bathroom to strip her soggy clothes.

'I just need to *move*, you know. Maybe head west to California. Work my way across the country. There's a place my mom took me once – Hunt Ranch.'

Andrea rubbed at her nose. 'A *ranch*? Like with cows and stuff?'

'It's technically a resort – a luxury one. But maybe they could use my business degree? Or I could get a job with the horses?'

Skye gingerly tugged her shirt up over her head. She inhaled a broken breath when rivulets of pain funnelled down her torso.

'Hunt Ranch is the only place that's ever really felt *safe*, I guess. Maybe it was only an illusion. It was one of the rare occasions my father wasn't with us. It was just my mom and me.' The memory had that grief rising, but Skye slowly, systematically forced it down. 'It's as good a place to start as any.' She shrugged, too afraid to let her excitement show. 'Hopefully, they'll hire me. If not, I'll move on until I find a place that will.'

Andrea didn't reply.

Skye looked up and saw Dre's eyes fixed on her purpling ribs.

'Skye . . .'

'It won't happen again,' Skye assured her.

'Do you think he'll follow you?'

'No. He won't know how to find me, and as long as I don't cause any waves, he probably won't try. Not yet . . .'

'And your grandma's will?'

'Holden's not an idiot,' Skye replied. 'Even if he was a danger to me, my grandma didn't trust him. If anything happens to me prior to my twenty-fifth birthday, the trust is dissolved and the money is dispersed to pre-selected charities. So, I have over two years before I can access the trust and start legal proceedings to cut him off. That buys me time. The most he'll do before then is try to contest the will. But he won't get anywhere. Grandma Jo was remarkably sharp until the end, and everyone knew it.'

'But—'

'I'll handle it, Dre.' Skye didn't know how. But she would find a way. She had two years to plan.

She pulled on a loose-fitting cotton top, one that wouldn't squeeze her ribs.

Her broken fingers, she'd tried to force straight on the walk home. Now, they were still slightly crooked, angry red, and hugely swollen. 'Can you grab me two plastic knives and that medical tape?'

'Yeah. No. How about we go to urgent care and get some X-rays?'

Skye shook her head. 'Mandatory reporting.'

Andrea rubbed both hands over her face, clearly overwhelmed. 'Okay. What do you need?'

'I need you to withdraw my cash.'

Andrea had saved it in her own bank account, because there was nowhere else for Skye to hide it.

'And then drive me to the used car dealership off the 45 by Wilmer first thing in the morning.'

'The one that looks like a car graveyard?'

'Yes.'

'Why don't we just go to the dealership off Lemmon?'

'I need somewhere that'll let me pay cash for something cheap. It doesn't matter if it's on its last legs, so long as it gets me the fuck out of Texas, and a Ford dealership isn't going to give me that.'

Andrea pulled out her phone. 'Okay. I'm making a list. We'll stock you up on food. Maybe get you a gun.'

Skye laughed. 'Ah, Dre, while I appreciate the sentiment, there are dozens of places to eat on the road and no shortage of grocery stores. And the last thing I need to worry about is learning how to use a gun.'

Andrea rubbed her chest. 'Oh, God. I'm panicking.' She swung around. 'Why aren't you panicking?'

Skye lowered herself down onto the closed toilet seat. How could she explain to her best friend that, after looking at the sole of her father's boot hovering over her face, nothing would ever scare her again?

'I'm free.' The words were so simple but so true.

Andrea knelt on the floor. She took Skye's uninjured hand in hers. 'I don't know if running is freedom, Skye. It's going to catch up with you eventually. *He* will catch up with you eventually.'

'Yes. He will.' As true as those words were, Skye knew that there was no point trying to explain to her friend that running *was* freedom, so long as you never looked back for long enough to see what was following you.

'Okay. Fuck. Um, so . . . the list is: splint flingers, withdraw cash, buy a car. What else?'

'Will you cut my hair?'

Andrea raised one hand to tug at a long strand of Skye's hip-length blonde hair. 'Why? You love your hair.'

'Time for a change,' she replied. Because the truth – that no man would ever incapacitate her with her own fucking hair ever again – was too hard to voice aloud. 'Cut it all off.'

Andrea paled. 'What?'

Skye grinned as the impulse solidified into something that felt beautifully reckless. 'You heard me. Get rid of it.'

Andrea plonked onto the floor. 'Ah, okay. Are you sure?'

'Yes.'

'I think we'll wait for Stevie to help with that one.' Andrea held her hands out, showing Skye how they shook. 'I'm kinda freaking out.'

'Let's do the video while we wait for her.'

'Yeah. Okay.' Andrea pulled her phone out of her back pocket. She shimmied until she was sitting against the opposite wall and could fit Skye's entire body in the frame. 'Ready?'

Skye took a deep breath. She looked into the camera. 'My name is Skye Marchant. Today is December thirteenth, 2024. The time is 8.05 p.m.' Taking out her own phone, she pulled up the calendar app and showed the date and time to the camera.

She painstakingly detailed the timeline of events, from arriving at her father's house intact to leaving battered and bruised. She repeated what had been said, word for word. She leaned forward, showing the camera her split lip. She raised her shirt so that her ugly bruises were documented too. Finally, she lifted her hand, showing two swollen fingers that still skewed slightly in the wrong direction.

Andrea's sniffles punctuated the video.

But Skye was oddly at peace.

'I'm leaving,' she said, and smiled *so brightly*. She felt it rise from within her before it broke over her face. 'I'm starting over. And I'm not looking back.

'But I wanted to leave one last video, because in just over two years' time, I'm going to have control of a lot of money – money my grandmother left in trust for her family, money that I will guarantee my father loses access to. On the off-chance that anything happens to me before my twenty-fifth birthday, I would like my grandmother's attorney, Mr Simcock, to continue in his role as trustee until the terms of the will have been met.'

She powered on. She had one last thing to say.

'If anything happens to me *after* my twenty-fifth birthday, I want it on record that my father, Holden Marchant, was probably the one who had me killed.'

Chapter 2

'This place is freakin' terrifying,' Stevie stated the next day as she pulled up to the rusted wire gate that contained Jim's Used Cars. She somehow managed to look stylish dressed in baggy sweatpants and a cropped sweatshirt, with platform Uggs on her feet. Her black hair, long and curly, waterfalled to her waist in a thick mass. With her pale skin and dark eyes, Stevie could have played a live-action Snow White – until she opened her mouth. It was all downhill from there.

Skye, dressed in leggings, sneakers, and a baggy sweater, leaned forward in the passenger seat so that she could take a better look.

Behind the rusted gate, used cars lined up like cattle going to slaughter, headlights covered in dust, paint chipping, tyres flat. In the middle of the morose gathering, an ancient trailer sat. And in front of the trailer, a hulking giant stood by a drum fire, warming his hands.

'Stay in the car,' Skye instructed her two friends. And because they both looked terrified, she added, 'Just in case he's a serial killer and you need to go get help.'

'Wait, what?'

Skye hopped from the car before Andrea could hold her back, and because that new wildness was dancing through her, she spun in a circle and blew them a kiss before approaching the gate.

In the frigid morning, frost still clung to the scrap metal. At the fence, Skye called, 'Hi! You must be Jim!'

The giant didn't speak, only started towards her, his heavy boots scraping over the gravel.

Skye watched him approach cautiously, because she was a woman who had learned that size did, in fact, make a difference. But the moment she saw his face, her smile grew. He was younger than she'd expected, maybe thirty-five, with shaggy brown hair and brown eyes that were warm and kind despite his size.

'I'm Jim,' he replied. His gaze settled on her split lip. 'You looking for a ride?'

'I am. Something cheap that'll get me across country.'

'What's your budget?'

'Honestly, Jim?' Skye gripped the chain-link fence, wincing when her newly splinted fingers pulled painfully against their constraints. 'As cheap as possible. I'm willing to drive with no windows as long as the wheels keep spinning for long enough to get me out of Texas.'

Jim missed nothing; his eyes flickered to her wrapped fingers. 'Come on in. I have a few options for you.'

He pulled the gate open with one arm, waved Stevie and the car through.

The moment Stevie had parked, the girls got out. They huddled together, watching Jim mistrustfully.

He didn't seem to mind. 'If you're looking for something *official*, something that will have a title to transfer, you're gonna be looking at five k *minimum*. And it's gonna have miles on it.'

Skye's smile was wide and a little unhinged. 'Show me what you got.'

He led them around the back of his trailer. From inside, a dog barked wildly, prompting Jim to say, 'Ignore Roscoe. He doesn't like strangers.'

Behind the graveyard of vehicles, tucked away from view, Jim had quite the operation: everything from second-hand Priuses to like-new Ford trucks, even a sparkling Jeep Wrangler in glossy black. A dilapidated barn structure sat at the end of the line, and although Skye wouldn't ask, she wouldn't have been surprised if a trio of Ferraris were stashed there.

She sighed and moved past the newer vehicles, making her way down the line to ancient trucks and mommy vans.

Next to her, Stevie was eerily quiet.

Andrea whispered, 'Skye, these aren't going to get you far.'

Jim heard her. He didn't get mad, just slapped the rusted hood of an old blue Ford F150. 'The only reason this beauty is listed at four k is because she has two hundred thousand miles on her and a rusting paint job. But the thing with the Fords, especially these older models, is that they'll drive forever. They're low maintenance, and any grease monkey in any shop could service one for you. The tyres have a lot of life in them yet.' He kicked one to make his point.

'Four grand?' Skye chewed her bottom lip. It wasn't that she didn't have the money, but every penny she spent was a penny she didn't have until she could settle for long enough to find a job. 'What year is it?'

'2002.'

'Fate,' Stevie whispered. Because that was their birth year.

Skye peered in the window. The off-cream leather seats were cracked and torn, the stuffing popping through. The carpets were browned with age. The steering wheel was peeling. Skye looked at the shift stick and sighed. 'It's manual.'

'You mean it's a shit stick?' Andrea asked.

Stevie slowly turned her head to look at Dre. 'It's called a *shift* stick.'

'Oh.' Andrea flushed. 'Well, how the hell am I supposed to know that? I don't think I've ever even seen one.'

Jim stood by silently, looking concerned for the first time.

Skye was going back and forth on the pros and cons of buying the truck when she heard it: a low nicker, coming from the dilapidated barn. Her gaze flickered in that direction. 'You have horses?'

'One. My girl left it here when she lit out a few weeks ago. I'm having a bitch of a time trying to look after the damn thing.' Jim's eyes narrowed on her face. 'You a horse girl?'

'Used to be.' Skye had started horseback riding at ten. It was the one thing she and her mom had been allowed to do completely alone. They'd drive out to the barn, groom and tack Skye's lesson horse, a big chestnut gelding called Rollo.

For two beautiful years, she had taken dressage lessons. She'd been good for her age, but she'd missed her first show for a social engagement that her father had insisted they attend, and when Skye had dared to argue, Holden had punished her by ending her lessons completely.

Looking back, that might have been the first time she'd realized that something wasn't right in her home. Her dressage instructor, Jill, had called and messaged, but Caroline had ignored her. When Skye had answered the home phone by chance, Jill had asked, 'Skye, I just need to know what happened? You're doing so well, baby. And I see your face when you ride; I know you love it.'

Skye had cried. She'd said, 'I do. But my dad . . .'

Jill had gotten very quiet.

'He says I can't anymore because of my attitude problem.'

Jill had sighed. 'Baby, you don't have an attitude problem. You're the sweetest, kindest kid I've ever met. Okay?'

'I'm not. I'm stupid. And I have a problem with discipline. But I'm trying really hard to be good, Ms Jill,' she'd promised.

'Baby, I'm going to give you my number. Skye . . . If there's anything you ever want to tell me, anything you ever need, you call me. Promise?'

'I promise,' Skye had said. But at twelve, she'd wondered what Jill meant. What could she possibly need that her father didn't already provide?

'My number is two-one-four—'

The line had cut.

Skye had looked up to see Holden at the house phone's answering system, his face cold with fury. Skye had seen the look and known what was coming, even then, but all she'd been able to think was: *I didn't get the number.*

Now, she shook the memory off with practised ease.

At her side, Stevie asked, 'Can we see the horse?'

Jim shrugged. 'Sure.'

As Andrea and Stevie walked towards the barn, Skye stayed behind, even though her feet itched to follow, to touch that soft nose and feel the horse's hot breath blow against her palm.

She forced her attention back to the truck, listening to Andrea and Stevie's excited chatter with one ear. 'Will you take three-five for it?'

'Four.' Jim was firm. 'But if you take the horse and her trailer, I could be persuaded to settle on three-five.'

Skye's brain flatlined. 'Ah . . . What?'

'She's sick. And my only other option is to send her to auction.' He kicked at a loose stone and sent it flying. 'I can't do it. I might get a grand for her, but she's young still. Doesn't deserve to hit the pipeline just because my ex is a shitty person.'

That reckless and wild part of her, so newly free, started rising. And even though the rational part of her brain screamed, *Food, vet bills, farrier fees*, Skye couldn't quite grasp them when faced with the alternative: living that little girl's dream.

She knew she'd say yes. But sensing an opportunity, she acted long-suffering. 'Jim, do you know what it costs to feed a horse?' Although she didn't say it, she thought: *because I sure as shit don't.*

'Three grand. Final offer. Truck, horse, and trailer.'

Skye pretended to think it over – for about one second. 'Throw in a lesson on how to drive shift stick and you have yourself a deal.'

Jim held out a hand. 'One lesson in shit stick included.'

As she sealed the deal that surge of freedom rose again. For the first time in her life, Skye was well and truly independent. And it didn't scare her. She had been through too much for it to scare her. Instead, it *thrilled* her.

'Let me get her fuelled up and check the oil and water for you.' He shucked a thumb in the direction of the barn. 'Go on. I can see you're dying to take a look.'

Her act at nonchalance officially blown, Skye gave an excited squeal and ran in the direction of the barn, making Jim laugh.

She slid open the barn door and stepped inside.

It was dark and damp and smelled mouldy. She squinted until her eyes adjusted and then walked to where Andrea and Stevie stood in front of a single roped-off stall.

The horse inside was fuzzy with her winter coat, but even beneath her thick hair, her ribs were visible, and when Skye chanced a look down at her hooves, she saw the way they spread with overgrowth, well past a trim. The mare's colouring was beautiful, almost an ash grey. She had a black stripe down her back and matching ones on her legs. Her eyes were alert, her ears pricked forward.

Skye ducked beneath the rope and stepped inside.

'Ah, Skye. Maybe we should check with Jim first?' Andrea suggested.

'Why?' Skye approached the horse with confidence, something she remembered from those early lessons. 'She's officially mine.'

She ran one hand down the horse's neck, laughed when the horse rubbed a broad cheek against her torso.

'Excuse me?' Stevie asked. 'Could you repeat that? It sounded like you said you bought the friggin' horse . . .'

'Jim gave her to me for free and knocked a grand off the truck for sparing him the inconvenience.'

'Skye . . .'

Hearing the concern in her friend's voice, she turned to meet Andrea's eyes. 'Yeah?'

'I get that you need this – to make decisions for yourself. But *this*' – she waved a hand at the horse – 'feels a little irresponsible. I mean, how will you transport her—'

'Jim threw in her trailer.'

Andrea blustered. 'How will you feed her?'

'I'll work.'

'Where will you keep her?'

Skye grinned. 'Haul her to a new state park every day. I have Google, so I can check which ones have horse trails. Ride, camp, rinse, and repeat.'

Andrea clapped her hands with each word. '*Stop. Making. It. Sound. Romantic.* I mean, do you even listen to those true crime podcasts you're always playing?' She looked to Stevie for help. 'Tell her this is crazy.'

Stevie nodded seriously. 'This is crazy.' Her grin was slow but wicked. 'And I am so fucking excited for you!'

Skye turned to look in the mare's eye. 'Whattaya say, girl? You wanna hit the road with me?'

The horse snorted.

'Sounded like a yes to me,' Stevie observed.

Andrea sighed. 'This is so stupid.'

'I'll check in with my location every night,' Skye promised. 'And send you my destination and ETA before I leave each morning.'

When the horse put her big head over Skye's shoulder, Skye leaned back, drawing strength from that solid contact, that *warmth.*

Andrea refocused on Skye and the horse and then immediately softened. She let her head fall back and said, 'Shit,' on a long-suffering sigh.

'What?' Skye asked, confused.

Stevie snapped a picture of Skye and the mare on her phone and then passed it over.

Skye knew what Andrea had seen instantly: a battered girl and a battered horse, both bruised by the world through no fault of their own, recognizing one another, leaning *into* one another.

Skye didn't believe in fate or fairy tales. Life had never given her that luxury. But for the first time ever, she felt like she had a purpose. And it wasn't grand or laudable. If anything, it was embarrassingly simple: learn how to care for a horse.

Jim opened the barn door and stepped inside. He glanced at where Skye stood with the horse, smiled. 'So? What do you think?'

'I think I got the better end of this deal, Jim.'

'Glad you think so.' He handed her a piece of scrap paper. 'I'm going to give you my number. If you need to take the truck into a shop, you call me. Put me on the phone with the mechanic so I can check he's not taking you for a ride.'

Skye's eyes burned. It still took her by surprise to know that strangers could be kind. 'Thank you. I really appreciate it.'

At her side, the mare snorted.

'Almost forgot.' Jim fished around in his pocket for a second piece of paper. He handed it to her. 'Horse's registration with the American Quarter Horse Association.'

Skye opened it. She traced the mare's bloodlines, and even though it meant nothing to her, she promised she'd research every horse in the lineage. When she came to the mare's registered name, she laughed aloud.

'What?' Stevie demanded.

Skye passed the registration to Stevie. But as her friends looked over the paper, she turned to the mare. 'I don't know if the fact that your name's Smoking Barrel bodes well for me.' She grinned. 'But I like it.'

Chapter 3

Scottsdale, Arizona – March 4, 2025

Over the three months she'd travelled, Skye had started a list she'd titled 'A Girl's Guide to Not Getting Murdered'.

Rule Number One: *Never Overnight Alone*, she'd learned in the first week when she'd pulled into a vacant parking lot to sleep in the cab of her truck and had woken up to a man scratching on her windows. He'd had a too-wide grin and eyes that told her his exact intention. Her only saving grace had been that she'd locked herself and Smokey in before falling asleep.

She'd managed to crawl through to the front seat and start the truck before things had escalated. But she'd driven the rest of the night, struggling to see in the dark through her tears, too afraid to pull over again.

Rule Number Two: *Don't Get Naked on Publicly Owned Land*, she'd also learned the hard way, when she'd stopped overnight in Lake Eufaula State Park, Oklahoma. She'd taken one look at the pristine lake water and promptly stripped her clothes, desperate to wash the travel grime off her skin. If she'd been paying attention, she would have noticed the trail running right alongside her swimming spot. Instead, she'd given a group of college-aged hikers a full-on show. Despite their raucous whistles and Skye's theatre-worthy twirl, she'd gotten a stern talking-to by a dour-faced park ranger.

As the weeks passed and she moseyed west, driven to get to Hunt Ranch only by her dwindling finances, she added rules.

Some were simple. Rule Seven: *Never Say No to Travelling in Convoy.* Rule Twelve: *Accept Hospitality from Strangers – But Only When There's at Least One Woman.* Rule Twenty: *Stick to Small Towns.*

Some rules were more obvious. Rule Eight: *Don't Go to Bars Alone at Night.*

But her best discovery, which promptly became Rule Three, was: *Find the Rodeos First* – not just because there were like-minded people travelling and competing in events that she found fascinating, but because nobody blinked an eye when a single woman pulled up in her ancient truck, towing a horse in a trailer.

Instead, they smiled at her and asked her if she was competing, and when she told them that she was just learning the ropes, they took her in. They explained the rules of the eight pro rodeo events, which fell into two categories: Rough Stock and Timed Events. They passed on their cell phone numbers and told her where they'd be going next, in case she wanted to meet up again. They asked her what route she was taking and then shared safe places, private farms and barns that rented horse stalls by the night.

They gave her the first safe community she'd ever known outside of Andrea and Stevie.

It was Rule Three that ensured she travelled safely while she made her way across the country, hopping from rodeo to rodeo.

It was Rule Three that, for the next week at least, led her to Arizona and the annual Rodeo Scottsdale, just an eight-hour drive from her final destination: Hunt Ranch, Santa Barbara County, California.

Sheridan, one of the barrel racers she'd met on the road, had given her the name of a local dairy-farming family who took in stray rodeo folks for a small nightly fee. After two weeks of camping out with Smokey, Skye was more than happy to pay for the convenience of a hot shower and a clean bed.

She rolled over the cattle grid and onto the farm on Tuesday evening, two days before the rodeo.

Around her, Arizona spread for miles and miles, flat irrigated pastures running into flat red dirt running into flat paved roads. The brush was coarse and thorny. The only trees in sight were those up ahead, planted around the pretty farmhouse like a protective regiment.

Skye pulled up and climbed out of the truck. The temperature in March was already hovering in the high seventies in the day before dropping into the low fifties at night. But just then, it was crisp, the faint smell of cow riding below the breeze.

Skye raised her hands above her head in a long stretch, twisting her torso to either side. Unable to resist, she bent over, stretching out her hamstrings and calves. A long moan of relief and the words 'Holy crap' left her lips as her cramped muscles breathed after hours of driving.

The sound of a throat clearing had her popping upright.

She spun around, one hand to her racing heart.

A man stood a good six feet away, one hip cocked, his lean rangy build emphasized by old blue jeans and a fitted black T-shirt. He was probably in his early thirties, though it was hard to tell beneath the cowboy hat, stained with sweat. His work boots were as cracked and scarred as the Arizona dirt. When he stepped closer and held out one hand in greeting, she noticed his green eyes. They were laughing at her; of that, she was sure. But there was no menace in them.

'Sorry, didn't mean to scare you.'

Skye relaxed slightly. 'It's okay. Didn't hear you come up behind me. I'm Skye. You must be Mr Jones?' She returned the shake because it was the normal thing to do, but when his big, rough hand dwarfed hers, she broke contact almost instantly, keeping the greeting brief but polite.

'In a sense.' His grin was quick and devastating. 'Jesse James Jones. TJ. My father'd be the Mr Jones you're looking for.' He shucked a thumb over his shoulder, indicating a huge, white structure. 'He's doing the evening milking right now, but I can help you offload and show you your stall, give you the tour.'

'Ah, sure.' Skye cast one quick glance at the barn. 'Thanks.'

They walked around the trailer together. 'My dad said you were a friend of Sheridan's? In town for the Rodeo?'

'Ah, yeah. Sheri and I met in Oklahoma a few months back. We've stayed in touch, and she was kind enough to mention your place.'

'You a barrel racer then?' he asked. His eyes flickered over her. 'I haven't seen you around before.'

'Not quite,' Skye replied honestly. 'I only just got back into riding a few months ago, so I'm a way from anything close to barrel racing. I'd like to, though. Smokey – my horse – is still green. I've been trying to ride her every night, but she was a little sick when I bought her. And it's slow work when you're on the road.' Slower work still, she thought, when all your knowledge came from YouTube videos, and all your practice had to be done on the trail or the rare open field. 'But she's fast and athletic. She's going to need a job soon.'

They lowered the ramp together. Smokey, well used to life on the road, merely turned her head to look at them. She'd started shedding her winter woollies already, so her silvery coat gleamed.

TJ whistled low. 'Hey, pretty girl.'

Skye couldn't say why, but those words, issued in TJ's deep voice, wove a thread of heat through her. A fierce blush flooded her cheeks. She might have been more embarrassed had Smokey not seemed affected too. But the horse pricked her ears and blew a flirty snort in TJ's direction.

TJ shot Skye a wink. 'She likes me.'

'Go figure.' Skye climbed into the trailer, mock-chastised her horse with, 'You'd do well to remember who feeds you,' as she untied the lead rope and backed Smokey out.

TJ grinned but didn't say anything.

He led the way, chatting politely the entire time. 'That big white structure is the milking parlour. There's a barn attached to it for cows that are calving or need vet care. The others are pastured and then called in for feeding and milking.'

'What happens to them – the calves?'

'Most places put them in calf hutches for the first eight weeks.' He pointed to where a line of what looked like little white dog kennels sat, clearly unused. 'But my mom couldn't stand them being put straight into a hutch after coming into the world. She built a separate barn and pasture for them. She calls it "The Nursery". And you don't have to worry,' he added, when he caught her forlorn look. 'Those calves are better looked after than me and my sister ever were.'

Skye scrunched her nose. 'That obvious?'

He tipped his head slightly. 'You're all city beneath those blue jeans.'

'You *cannot* tell that just by looking at me,' Skye insisted. In her blue jeans, boots, a faded Wrangler tee, and a ball cap, she looked like any Western horse girl she'd ever met.

'Maybe not. But those hands . . .' He picked up her hand gently by the wrist, turned it over to show Skye her own palm. The calluses were there, but still new and raw. 'Those are city girl hands trying to adapt to rough living for the first time.'

It was the oddest thing, to be touched gently by a man, especially by a stranger. Skye felt it resonate all through her body, from her toes, which curled in her boots, to the base of her neck, where the fine hair pulled upright in gooseflesh.

Disconcerted, Skye tugged her hand back. 'You got me,' she said. 'I'm a city girl.'

TJ had watched her pull up in her clapped-out Ford, the trailer behind her barely roadworthy, and he'd stopped what he was doing to go and see to his parents' guest. Only, when he'd rounded her truck, he'd been greeted by a perfect ass, bent in his direction, and not even that, not even a woman in tight denim, could have prepared him for the moment when Skye had turned and looked at him with those knockout baby blues.

Still, despite the slap of lust through his well-honed system, he'd sensed that instant wariness in her. She'd hidden it well, but he'd felt it in the way she couldn't hold his gaze for long and could barely stand to touch his hand. She reminded him of a Mustang, corralled for the first time. Wildness and fear, contained. Barely.

He'd picked up her hand to make his point about her being a city girl, but right before she curled her fingers into a fist and politely tugged herself free, he'd seen her crooked ring and middle fingers, which could only have come from broken bones that hadn't been set and splinted right.

'You got me,' she said, blatantly ending the interaction. 'I'm a city girl.'

TJ should have let it lie, so he had no idea why he asked, 'What's a city girl like you doing in a near-dead F150, towing a cow horse across country? Doesn't seem too smart.'

Skye tucked her hand into her pocket, almost as if she knew that he was tempted to touch her again. 'I promise you, the city is far more dangerous than most of the back roads you've travelled.'

Her reply was a clear deflection, and although he didn't push, he wondered about that as he slid open the barn door and stepped inside. 'We have six of our own horses here . . .' He trailed off when he noticed that Skye hadn't followed him in. Instead, she stood just outside the barn with her horse, looking in *at him*, poorly veiled suspicion on her face.

When TJ backtracked to where she stood, her eyes followed his every movement. Warning signals fired.

'You okay?'

'Yeah.' Her voice was tight. 'I, ah – I might put her away in a bit. Let her walk around a little first.'

She didn't even take one step inside the barn, and though he had never had a woman fear him before, TJ somehow knew that was what was holding her back.

He stepped completely out of the barn. 'Why don't you go take a look? I put you in the last stall on the right. I'll go fetch your hay net and feed out the trailer.' He didn't wait for her to reply, merely turned on his heel and walked back in the direction they'd come from, giving her space to explore the barn alone.

At the trailer, his dad was already lifting the hay net out. 'Thanks for seeing to her, TJ.'

TJ took the net, but he didn't move back towards the barn with it. When his dad looked at him, his eyebrows raised, TJ explained, 'She's scared of me. I'm gonna wait until she comes back out.'

'What did you do?'

'Nothing. I haven't even hit on her. Yet.' Because he would, even if it was just to get a genuine smile out of her.

His dad wheezed on a rusty laugh. 'One of those girls is gonna bite you on the ass eventually, and I cannot wait to see which one.'

'Counting on it,' TJ shot back.

His dad shook his head, but his eyes tracked to the barn. 'Sheri said she's good people.'

'Yeah. But Sheri also gave an escaped convict a ride through Texas once,' TJ reminded him. 'Only one way to find out what her story is.' Because he'd be damned if some pretty pixie with restless hands and witch's eyes brought trouble to his parents.

'Don't pry, TJ.'

TJ cocked one hip as he settled in to argue. 'I'm not gonna *pry*. I'm gonna ask outright. I leave on Monday. I can't go if she's brought trouble.'

'You worry too much. I'm sixty-two and fit as a fiddle. I can hold my own.'

'I'd prefer not to test that theory, old man.'

His dad flipped him the bird, said, 'Go ride a cow!' – their family way of saying, *Fuck off.*

TJ just grinned. But because he hadn't torn his eyes from the barn, he saw when Skye came back out without her horse. He picked up the hay net in one hand, the bag of horse feed in the other. 'I'll take her feed in. If you want to show her to Mom, maybe *she'll* get it out of her.'

'Yeah,' his dad ceded. 'Your mom could make a clam sing.'

Skye stopped in her tracks when she saw TJ approaching. She looked like someone about to face the firing squad, and when she said, 'Ah, I realize I may have made things weird back there,' TJ put the hay net and horse feed down on the dirt by his feet.

He nodded slowly. 'I won't hurt you.' He thought it imperative that he start with that. 'You don't have to worry about that. I might flirt with you. Because you're beautiful. I might even try to kiss you eventually,' he said, and laughed when her blue eyes widened. 'Because I like kissing.'

Her cheeks flamed, and TJ saw her brain working overtime right before she frowned and said, 'Does this actually work for you?'

'You'd be surprised.' He was a professional bull rider with over four million in earnings; the girls didn't exactly play hard to get anymore.

'Isn't it important that you also – I don't know – maybe *like* the person you're kissing?' she asked.

'Actually, sometimes a little hate makes things hot as hell.'

She frowned, as if hot hate sex had never occurred to her. 'Oh.'

TJ took the second her guard was down to ask, 'Who are you afraid of, Skye?'

Those blue eyes flashed, but she didn't back down. And she didn't lie. She tensed her small body as if readying to give as good as she got. 'Why does it matter?'

He tucked his hands into his pockets, showing her that he was harmless. 'Will he follow you here?'

'No.'

'So, my parents don't have to worry?'

Realization dawned. 'No,' she insisted with a quick shake of her head. 'I would never . . .' Her eyes filled. She dropped her gaze. 'I would never endanger anyone,' she rasped.

TJ bit off a curse. 'Okay.' He took a step closer, noticed that while her head popped up, she didn't take that mirrored step back. But those lines of tension running all through her body remained. 'I'm going to give you a hug now. Because I'm not in the habit of making strange women cry.'

She froze up like an ironing board.

TJ gently pulled her into a hug. He wrapped both arms around her, like he still did with his sister, Julia, or his mom when they cried. He exhaled deeply out of habit, something he'd learned from a lifetime of working with spooked horses, and smiled when she released her breath in one big whoosh.

Her hands gripped the sides of his shirt awkwardly, as if she knew she was supposed to do something with them but wasn't exactly sure what. She relaxed, rested her forehead against him, and said, 'Hey, TJ?'

'Yeah?'

'I'm not gonna sleep with you just because you're being nice.'

A surprised laugh stuttered out of him. 'I wouldn't expect you to.'

Skye took that first step back. But when she smiled up at him, her blue eyes dancing with humour, his heart skipped a goddamn beat before picking up an adrenaline-fuelled pace that only bull riding had ever given him.

TJ felt it only fair to warn her: 'You're gonna sleep with me because you want to.'

She took another step back, as if she wasn't quite sure of his sanity. But instead of fear or anxiety, now he only saw surprise – and, if he guessed correctly, curiosity. 'Do you always proposition women you've known for five minutes?'

'Nope.' He picked up the hay and the feed, started back towards the barn, only pausing to toss, 'Barely ever actually,' over his shoulder.

She tried to hide it, but he caught her smile the second before she rolled her eyes and turned towards the trailer.

TJ kept on walking. But he couldn't help but mutter, 'Called it.' Because he'd known she'd have a killer smile.

Chapter 4

'You'll have to excuse TJ,' the older man said as Skye approached her trailer. 'I'd say the bull riding has made him irrationally confident. But the truth is that it's probably given him some brain damage too.'

'Mr Jones?' She wasn't sure why she asked it as a question. It was obvious that this man was TJ's father. They had the same rangy build, the same laughing green eyes and devilish sense of humour.

'Please, call me Ryan.' He reached out a hand, and this time, Skye returned the shake with no fear.

'He's a bull rider?'

'Yup.' The pride in his voice was obvious. 'Maybe you've heard of him. Jesse James Jones, or Triple J, as they call him at the rodeos.'

Skye shook her head. 'I've mostly been following the barrel races and hopping to smaller rodeos where I can overnight my horse.'

'That's one way to travel.'

'It's the best way to travel,' Skye corrected.

'That how you met Sheridan?'

'Yeah. I was camping outside my horse trailer in Oklahoma, and she was staying in her live-in. Next thing I know, she's asking me if I want to bunk with her instead and we're splitting a five-dollar bottle of gas station wine.'

'Sounds like Sheri.' Ryan turned and raised the ramp on her trailer, locked it. 'Why don't you grab your things? I'll show you inside, introduce you to my wife, Janey. She'll get you set up.'

Skye reached inside the cab of her truck and removed her duffle bag, her blanket and pillow, and her dirty laundry, in the hope that she could use the Joneses' washing machine.

Before she could take a step, Ryan took her bag from her. He led the way, chatting as easily as TJ had done. 'We have five hundred acres here. There's a covered arena behind the horse barn, so if you want to ride while you're staying, feel free. The entire spread is fenced, so you can't get lost.' He gave her a wheezing laugh. 'Honestly, my land's so flat you probably couldn't get lost if you tried. You can see the house and the trees from quite a distance, but if you're nervous, I'm sure TJ wouldn't mind taking you around.'

'I don't want to waste his time,' Skye said quickly, because the notion of being alone with TJ was anxiety-inducing. Not because she was afraid of him, per se, but because it had taken only one interaction for her to know that she didn't have the experience to handle him. 'I'm still learning, so I go slow.' She slanted Ryan a look. 'And something tells me slow is not exactly TJ's speed.'

'Maybe not. But the boy could still learn.' He frowned. 'Probably.'

'It's doubtful, Mr Jones,' Skye said mock-gravely.

He grinned. 'Something tells me you'd do just fine.'

Skye didn't reply as they approached the farmhouse – a pretty white southwestern-style home with stone walls and native desert landscaping contained within a ring of trees. The roof extended over the tiled front porch that led to the front door, and a wicker furniture set sat beneath a lazily swirling ceiling fan.

Ryan opened the front door to a mass of wriggling fur and excited yips. Skye got a glimpse of three distinct dogs before one of them took her down. She landed on her butt, her hands covering her face to no avail. The slobbery kisses had laughter bubbling from deep in her soul.

'Down!' Ryan shouted.

The dogs didn't even hear him, only continued to pounce on Skye.

'Janey! Your beasts are mauling our guest!'

A female voice shouted through, 'Bandit! Southpaw! Brisket!'

Skye's laughter morphed into a cough as one of the dogs licked her full on the mouth. Eyes closed against the onslaught, she felt more than saw when someone grabbed her by the elbows and hauled her back to her feet. Her giggle died when she opened her eyes to see TJ scowling down at her.

He held her at arms' length as he turned on the dogs and commanded, 'Sit,' in a voice that had all three bottoms plonking to the floor. His eyes scanned Skye for injuries. 'You okay?'

'Peachy.' She raised her hands to her short hair, smoothing it down where it was spiked with dog slobber and subtly dislodging his casual hold on her. 'Nothing a shower won't fix.'

Skye looked down at the three dogs, all of whom looked sufficiently chastised. She might have been more confused by their names had she not been looking at a cattle dog with a black bandana-shaped patch around his neck, an ancient pittie who was missing his right front leg, and a fat corgi who definitely needed to cut back on the brisket.

She went down the line, giving them each a rough head rub. 'I don't even have to ask who's who.'

'My mom collects strays. But she's too soft-hearted to train them once she has them, so instead of finding them homes, she foster fails on the regular.'

'I heard that!' a voice called from somewhere close.

'You were meant to!' TJ shouted back.

A delighted laugh preceded TJ's mother. She was tiny and waiflike, with black hair that framed her face and dark-brown eyes. She wore jeans and ratty house shoes with a dishtowel strung over her shoulder. 'I'm sorry about my ill-behaved dogs. I promise they're friendly – just a little *too* friendly.'

'It's no problem,' Skye assured her. 'I was never allowed pets growing up, so every time I see a dog, I have to stop and say hi.' Her hand found the cattle dog's head. 'They don't bother me.'

'That's good. It'd be a long weekend for you if they did.' Mrs Jones extended her hand. 'Janey.'

'Skye.'

Janey looked to her husband. 'Ryan, if you could put Skye's bag in the guest room by TJ's? I'll show her the rest of the house.'

Ryan nodded and left, taking Skye's things with him.

'TJ, I believe our guest might like a drink.'

Two pairs of eyes focused on Skye, flustering her. 'Um, whatever y'all are having is great.'

'I'm riding this weekend, so I'm sticking to water. But Mom hoards red wine by the gallon?'

'You're supposed to store it,' Janey said, defending herself. 'It ages better.'

'I don't think that includes the bottles you get from the Quik Mart, Ma.'

Janey flicked at TJ's legs with her dishtowel while Skye looked on, unsure of what to do or say but, 'Wine is perfect. Thanks.'

The moment TJ walked off, Janey took Skye's hand in her own. 'You must be so tired, honey.'

Before she could think to give a polite reply, the words 'I really am' slipped from Skye's lips.

Travelling alone as a woman was an endless lesson in vigilance, and while Skye prided herself on the fact that she had adapted well and quickly, she felt fatigue fighting to take over, now that she was finally somewhere completely safe. It settled deep in her muscles, dragging her down.

'Well, if you want to have a shower now, I'll wrap up dinner and then you can pass out as early as you need to.' Janey led her into the kitchen. 'The fridge is stocked with snacks, so please help yourself.' She pointed to clearly marked jars on the counter that were labelled *Coffee*, *Tea*, and *Sugar*. 'Coffee mugs are in the cupboard above the espresso machine. I'm an early riser, so I can show you how to load the portafilter in the morning.'

On the other side of the kitchen was a family lounge. The furniture was walnut-coloured leather but well loved and patinaed with age, the rug beneath it worn and faded.

The dining room had an eight-seater table, perfect for company.

Skye's room upstairs was white with blue accents: blue bedding, blue abstract art on the wall, and blue towels on the foot of the bed. Fresh flowers were in a little vase on her nightstand. Skye raised her fingers to the petals of a tiny pink wildflower. What type of woman collected wildflowers for guests she didn't even know?

Her own mom had never taken her side against her father's abuse, so it was the strangest thing to feel that this tiny stranger would have stood up for her in the same situation.

But maybe it was easier to stand up for someone else when your own world wasn't in constant turmoil. Maybe people who had the time and energy and courage to help did so because their own lives weren't a constant struggle for survival.

Skye's eyes burned as her fatigue and emotions warred. She wasn't an idiot. She'd done her research. She'd spoken to Margo, the therapist at the women's shelter. She knew that there was deep trauma guiding her mother's actions – or, rather, lack thereof. But knowing the psychiatry didn't make it any easier to always be the little girl who suffered because of her mother's inability to break free. And it didn't make the shame she carried for leaving Caroline lighter to bear.

'Unfortunately, you'll have to share a bathroom with TJ. But I swear he's housebroken—' Janey's laugh died as she saw Skye's glassy eyes for the first time. 'Oh, baby.'

Mortified, Skye swiped at her eyes, managed, 'I'm sorry. I think I'm just more tired than I thought.'

'Of course you are, honey. Rodeo life's rough.'

The endearment, the completely natural way this woman said things like *honey* and *baby*, filled Skye with so much warmth that all she could do was try to deflect. 'I'm not competing. I'm just travelling with them.'

'Smart girl.' Janey sat on the bed beside her, but she didn't ask for details, only said, 'I admire you all so much. Travelling alone for most of the year. Looking after yourselves. I'm too scared to even stay overnight at a hotel without Ryan.' She laughed self-deprecatingly.

Warning bells rang in Skye's head. How many times had she heard her mother say something similar, typically something regurgitated from her father: *You're not competent enough to travel alone, Caroline*, or *I think it'd be best if you told your friends you aren't available* or, when people started to wonder why Caroline was never available, *Do you think it's wise to continue your friendship with someone clearly so ill-suited?*

Skye searched Janey's face for that glazed look of the marionette. It was always there in the persecuted; sometimes, it only hid behind a well-rehearsed smile. Instead, all she saw in Mrs Jones's eyes was understanding and compassion.

Still, Skye was compelled to ask. 'Do you like travelling with him then?'

Janey must have seen through her question, because she took Skye's hand in her own. 'Oh, baby, more than anything in the world.' She laughed lightly. 'I can't sleep when he's not snoring next to me – which is saying something, because when he is snoring next to me, I'm typically plotting ways to kill him.'

Skye heard the almost girlish love in Janey's tone and relaxed. Abused women didn't talk about their men with that reverence, only with an odd type of obedience that they mistook for love. Embarrassed that she'd let her defences slip so quickly, Skye redirected. 'How did you know he was the one?'

Janey pursed her lips. 'I wish I could say it was something

definite. But it was more a *feeling*, I guess – a certainty that he'd always do everything he could to love and protect me. And then, over time, with every kind word and loving gesture and laugh *and fight*, that feeling was realized.' At Skye's long look, Janey clarified, 'A couple has to fight. My mom used to say it was so that women could get the things they carried off their chests and so that men could be reminded of their many flaws.'

Skye nodded cautiously. Her parents had never actually *fought*. Fighting implied a mutual attack. Instead, her father had laid down the law, and if her mother had ever questioned it, irrespective of how quietly, she had been punished. And not always physically – that had come later when Skye had started to stand up to him and her father had started hurting her mother in retaliation. Holden had a way of tormenting Caroline psychologically that was far more brutal than any slap. And every cruel word, cold shoulder and sigh of disappointment was delivered with a sort of remorse – as if, in his own mind, he was merely a loving husband, trying to survive an incompetent spouse.

'You seeing anyone special?' Janey asked.

Skye shook her head. 'I don't like men very much.'

Oh, she'd learned to listen patiently whenever a man spoke to her, to act normal, but the moment he moved physically into her space, she started to feel uncomfortable. Her confident façade wavered. Panic hovered. It made her so anxious that, whenever she went out with Stevie and Andrea, while her friends flirted and teased, Skye told any man who showed more than a passing interest that she had a boyfriend.

'Maybe you just haven't met the right man yet?' Janey suggested.

'Maybe,' Skye ceded.

'Or woman?'

Skye mirrored Janey's grin. 'I wish. My life would be a hell of a lot easier if I was attracted to women.' Realizing she'd told this particular woman far too much already, Skye pushed to her feet. 'I'll be down as soon as I've had a quick shower.'

'Take a long one. There's no rush.' Janey stood and raised one hand to Skye's cheek. 'You're gonna be fine.'

Lost for words, Skye just nodded.

TJ was halfway up the stairs, Skye's wine in his hand, when his mom came down. She took one look at him and shook her head. 'Not this time, TJ.'

'I have no idea what you're talking about,' he said innocently. 'I'm just bringing our guest the wine *you* requested I get for her.'

She took the wine from his hand and disappeared upstairs with it.

TJ didn't dare take another step, but he waited for his mom to come back down because more had to be said.

When Janey reappeared, she took one look at him and sighed.

'I would never hurt anyone,' he said. 'Least of all someone with all that pent-up anxiety.'

'I know. And you've obviously sensed that in her. But I don't think many men can understand what it is for a woman to be reduced to a prey animal, and so I am telling you: *give her space.*'

'I was just trying to get a smile out of her.' TJ raised a hand dramatically to his heart, asked, 'You seen her smile yet?'

His mother loved him enough to laugh. 'Not yet. But I imagine a smile on an already beautiful woman only makes her more so.'

Sensing that the worst of the danger was over, TJ walked down the rest of the stairs with her. 'It's bad?'

'She wouldn't give me the specifics. But any woman who's travelling alone, following rodeos to stay safe, must be running from something far more terrifying.'

TJ tried to imagine the type of man who could hurt a woman, let alone one like Skye, who was so small, almost fragile. But he couldn't. It said something about the community he was raised in that such men might have been the stuff of fairy tales and poorly scripted movies.

'I'll give her space,' he promised. And not because his mother had told him to, but because he really wasn't sure how to be anyone other than himself. And he was Jesse James Jones.

A man had to have a wild side and a perverted sense of humour if his chosen profession was sitting atop an animal that weighed several thousand pounds and wanted to kill him. TJ's wild side was a mile long, and his sense of humour was wicked, inappropriate, and almost always flirtatious. But maybe, that wasn't what this particular woman needed. Or wanted. And for all his faults, he was man enough to know that was important.

So, he'd give her space.

And if he stole a few glances at that heart-shaped ass while nobody was looking – well, he was only a man. And, by his own admission, a flawed one at that.

Chapter 5

Something was different.

Skye couldn't say why. All she knew was that instead of those laughing eyes and hugely aggressive sense of humour, TJ seemed to have been replaced by a man with all the manners she'd have originally expected from a stranger.

He'd taken his cowboy hat off for dinner, revealing dark-brown hair trimmed short. He made polite conversation with her from across the table, and although he listened intently whenever she spoke, he focused more on the food in front of him than her, and when he did make eye contact, it was quick and polite and impersonal.

She knew something had been said by the way Janey acted as if nothing was off, but Ryan looked at TJ as if his son had sprouted another head at the dinner table.

Skye hated that she'd been so obvious, hated that she'd panicked with TJ at the barn and then gotten teary when Janey had shown her to the guest room. She told herself that she was just tired, but the truth was, there was something about the Jones family that just made a person feel safe and welcome. It was them as much as it was her. They were the family she'd always dreamed existed once she'd realized her own was a living nightmare.

Still, she refused to be the type of woman everyone tiptoed around. Her own mother had taught her how quickly those habits could become a lifestyle. So, when TJ pushed back from the table with, 'If you'll excuse me, I'm going to see to the horses,' Skye got up too.

'I'll help.'

'You really don't have to,' he hurried to say. 'I'll see to Smokey.'

'No, *I'll* see to Smokey.' She looked to Janey for permission out of habit. In Holden's house, dinner was to be on the table by seven and cleared, the dishes done, by eight. 'Could I help you clear up before I go?'

'No, honey. But thank you for offering.' Janey stood and started gathering dishes. 'You two go on.' She smiled sweetly, but Skye caught the pointed look she gave TJ, one that had him rolling his eyes the moment his mom turned her back.

When they were out of hearing from the farmhouse, Skye demanded, 'What did your mom tell you?'

TJ slanted her a sideways glance. 'I don't know what you're talking about.'

'Oh, come on. In the space of thirty minutes, you went from Cowboy Casanova to the perfect gentleman.'

His heavy footfall crunched over the dry red dirt.

Over dinner, the sun had gone down, giving way to blue dusk that cast an eerie glow. If she'd been on the road, Skye would have found a stopping place already, but here, with TJ, she was too irritated to be nervous.

'Look, you're reading too much into it.'

'I don't want to be treated differently just because you feel sorry for me,' she insisted, and because he was rapidly walking ahead, ignoring her, she grabbed him by the arm and yanked him.

TJ spun around. For just one second, his posture was charged with temper, his eyes dark and dangerous.

Skye instinctively took two hurried steps back.

TJ's demeanour changed instantly. His body softened, and

although she saw that it cost him, his eyes went carefully blank. 'My mom's a giant softie.' He grinned, trying, she knew, to distract her from her fear. 'She thinks you can't handle me.'

In her anger, Skye didn't even remember that she'd had the same thought. 'What's to handle?' she demanded. 'A middle-aged bull rider who thinks he's God's gift to women? Buddy, you're a dime a dozen.'

For one crystal second, all he did was stare at her. But just when she thought he'd say something, he surprised her by throwing back his head and laughing – loudly.

Skye crossed her arms and cocked one hip, refusing to be charmed by the deep, husky sound of TJ letting loose. He raised his fingers to the bridge of his nose and pinched as if it would help him regain himself.

Once he'd sobered some, she asked, 'You done?'

Those eyes, laughing again, found hers. 'I knew it.'

Skye just raised her eyebrows.

'You see, Mom thinks you're fragile. But me' – he grinned wickedly – 'I see you beneath that porcelain doll exterior. And you're more likely to bite a man's hand off than run from it.'

Skye hunched into her jacket. She desperately wished that were true. But it wasn't. Not even close. And it hurt to hear him so confidently mislabelling her.

She'd run. And she'd left her mom behind with nobody to defend her against Holden. And that . . . that about killed her. The guilt rose. That carefully controlled grief consumed her so suddenly that she couldn't catch it, couldn't stamp it back down. So, instead, she channelled it. She took all that pain and shame and used it to summon a wicked smile.

'Damn straight,' she replied. And before she stepped past him, she let her teeth flash dangerously. She leaned in, whispered, 'So, you'd best be careful where you put your hands, TJ.'

The warning, issued in a low, feral tone, had the opposite effect than Skye had intended. TJ's body roared to life, flooding with heat. The words *Fuck me* flitted through his mind. And those hands she'd just warned him to keep to himself itched with the urge to touch her, if only to show her how much she'd like what they could do.

With any other woman, he would have settled in for the chase. But that same warning signal flashed, reminding him that Skye was running from something. And that changed the rules of the game.

He needed time to think about that.

TJ stepped into the barn ahead of her, giving her the choice of where she wanted to go.

She moved as far away from him as possible, using Smokey as an excuse to go to the other side of the barn, but it didn't bother him. TJ considered it progress, considering she hadn't been able to go inside with him only a few hours earlier.

'Do you have social media?' she asked, drastically changing the subject.

'Sure. It's a good source of revenue if you have a following. Why?'

Skye pulled a hoof pick out of her tack bag and disappeared into Smokey's stall. She raised her voice to be heard. 'I've been thinking of starting one. I have a personal Instagram, but I don't post to it anymore—' She stopped talking abruptly, but when she carried on, her voice was more cautious. 'But if I started a travelling one, I could use a pseudonym, for privacy, kinda build a community on there. Maybe eventually make a little money on the side.'

He didn't ask any questions, just rolled with her new topic of conversation. 'It's not a bad idea if you have the time to make content. I'm shit at it, so I pay a content creator to do all my videos.'

'I'd have to do it myself. I'd called it "A Girl's Guide to Solo Travel".'

'"Wild Skye",' he stated.

'What?'

'"Wild Skye". Short, to the point.'

'Hmm. I'll think about it.'

'You're welcome.'

Skye snorted. 'Your arrogance knows no bounds.'

TJ just grinned as he ran a curry comb over his gelding, Kai's, coat. He'd already groomed all the horses, but just then, he couldn't think of anywhere else he'd rather be than standing in his family barn with a pretty girl, surrounded by the familiar smell of horse.

'How many followers do you have?' she asked.

'Last I checked, maybe half a mil or so.'

'What?' she squeaked.

TJ grinned. 'Most people don't think I'm a *dime a dozen*.'

Her light giggle reached for him, called to him, and wanting to be closer, TJ let himself out of Kai's stall. He slid the door closed, then sat on the concrete floor and leaned his back against the warm wood.

He could see Skye through the slatted top of Smokey's stall, and obviously unaware that he was watching, she wrapped her arms around her horse's neck and rested her cheek against the warm horseflesh. She closed her eyes and smiled, and even though it was supposed to be a private moment, TJ couldn't tear his gaze away.

When she moved to let herself out of the stall, he finally shifted and pretended to be preoccupied with dusting his mud-caked boots.

Skye hesitated, but he just picked up the conversation, saying, 'If you post while you travel, make sure to leave a lag time.'

'Lag time?' She walked over to where he sat.

TJ's heart pumped thickly as she closed that distance by choice for the first time. He barely breathed as Skye sat down beside him, their shoulders a mere foot apart. When he replied, his voice was husky. 'Backlog content, so that you only post about a location once you've moved on. There're some crazies online. I had one girl stalk me to six rodeos in a row before I wised up.'

'Really?'

'Yeah. It was actually kinda terrifying. She knew my parents' names and that they owned a dairy farm. I hadn't realized before that, to the wrong person, every little snippet, every post or story, is a goldmine of information.'

'I know how to be careful.'

'I bet.'

'But thanks. I'll leave a lag time.'

Not wanting the moment to end, TJ asked, 'Do you know where you're going after Scottsdale?' He saw the indecision weigh in her eyes at the question, and added, 'I'm heading to Little Rock for a PBR ride next week, New Mexico after that.'

'PBR?'

'Professional Bull Riders – it's the organization we all compete under outside of the rodeo. Different league than the PRCA rodeos. There're no other rodeo events, just bull riding. More flash. More money. More women.'

Skye just rolled her eyes and leaned back against the stall. 'You compete in both – the PBR and PRCA?'

'I do. But I typically have to prioritize the PBR events at some point in the season.'

She seemed to relax more, the more information he gave her. 'I've been travelling for over three months now,' she said finally. 'I started with the intention of maybe taking three or four weeks to get to California. But once I was on the road, I just couldn't stop. There's so much to see.'

'So, California's the destination?'

She turned those big, wary eyes on him. 'Yeah. Probably soon. My finances are dwindling, so I don't really have a choice. I'm hoping to find a job.'

'What type of job?'

'There's a place I went to with my mom about six years ago – Hunt Ranch.'

'I know it.'

'*Wait, really?*' In her shock, Skye didn't seem to realize that she had reached out and gripped his arm.

But TJ sure as shit did. Her tight grip seared through his shirt. But he didn't dare move, too afraid that if he did, she would break that contact. 'Yeah,' he replied. 'My dad and I actually stayed with the Hunts a few times before it became a resort. Maverick and his best friend, Benji, were team ropers at a lot of the youth rodeos I went to. Our folks knew each other, so they'd host us in California, and we'd host them here in Arizona. We kind of fell out of touch when I switched to bull riding, and I think the ranch kept Mav too busy to go pro once his folks died. Benji would never do it without him; they were joined at the hip.' At Skye's blank look, he explained, 'The rodeo world gets pretty small.'

'Do you think they'd hire me as a wrangler?' Before he could reply, she started defending herself. 'I know I'm still learning, but I'm a hard worker and a fast learner. I'd give it everything I've got—'

'Skye—'

'I wouldn't let them down—'

'I believe it.' That shut her up. 'I'm sure they'd give you a shot. Maybe not with guests horseback riding at first, but on the ground, sure.' Although he didn't say it to her, he'd find Mav's number and pave the way.

Skye settled. She let go of his arm slowly. But as the conversation moved on, TJ had to ponder the snippets she'd given him.

He knew the nightly fee at Hunt Ranch, so knew that if Skye had gone there with her mom, she came from money. Which begged the question: what was a city girl with money doing on the road, driving a dilapidated truck and travelling with the rodeo to stay safe? If she was running from someone – and it was clear that she was – why hadn't her family stepped in to help?

Chapter 6

Skye laughed and readjusted her stance as the calf she was bottle-feeding threatened to push her off her feet with each aggressive nuzzle at the teat. 'They're strong,' she said in surprise. 'And so darn cute.'

'Oh yeah. Greedy too.' In the next nursing pen, Janey was feeding two calves at a time. Despite her petite stature, she held a bottle in each hand.

The rest of the calves bleated and crowded around the gate, eager for their turn. The barn, snug with fresh hay they'd replaced that morning, smelled good despite the underlying scent of cow and manure.

Janey dropped the bottles she'd been using in a nearby pail and let the calves she'd fed back out. She herded the next two in. 'It took me a while to get used to being a farmer's wife. But even after all this time, I figure I can know and appreciate where my food comes from and still be a bleeding heart, so long as the work gets done.'

Skye guided the next calf into her own feeding pen before picking up another full bottle. As the calf latched and tugged, she looked over the nursery. There were still a good twenty calves to feed. 'You do this twice a day?'

'For the most part. Some require three feeds a day, especially when they're newborn.'

'How long does that usually take you?'

'I'm a veteran. Maybe ninety minutes in the morning and then again at night. See those bottle-holders on the fence there?' She pointed to some simple wire brackets that were linked over a wooden two-by-four on the top of the pen's fence. 'If I'm doing this alone, I have another three calves feeding themselves in there.'

'And when you go on vacation?'

Janey laughed. 'Oh, baby. I'm a farmer's wife. Vacations are harder to come by than you'd think, and with TJ competing across the country, most of our time off is spent at rodeos within driving distance.' She leaned one hip against the fence. 'But we have a manager who knows how to run things if we want to take a few days every now and then.'

Mention of TJ had Skye's thoughts shifting in his direction. He might have been flirtatious and cocky, but he was *fun* in a way that she'd never really been exposed to before. She wondered if she could have been like that in another life. If she'd had parents like Ryan and Janey, could she have been someone who smiled and joked and flirted so easily? Or maybe it wasn't his parents who'd made him so quick to laugh at life but the absolutely insane career he'd chosen? Surely, when you looked death in the eye on a weekly basis, you learned to appreciate life more?

'Is it scary? Watching him bull ride?'

'Every eight seconds is the worst eight seconds of my life,' Janey said without pause. 'And that's if he doesn't get thrown and end up on the ground. Watching him on the ground, as the bullfighters and barrelman try to distract the bull . . . There're no words for that type of fear. It's one only a mother can understand.'

'But you still go and watch?'

'Well, sure. He's my kid, and for better or worse, bull riding is what makes him happy. I'm very proud of how hard he's worked to get to where he is, even if I don't really understand why the hell he'd want to do it.'

'For the girls,' Skye informed her, making Janey laugh appreciatively.

Skye wondered if she had ever made her mother proud. If she had, her mom hadn't had the energy to tell her. The things her mother had taught her had been so much more important. Things like: *Don't make noise in the house if your father's home. If you hear raised voices, don't go look; lock yourself in your bedroom. Don't talk back. Better yet, don't talk at all.*

'He's very lucky to have you,' she said eventually.

'At this stage, I figure it's God's way of levelling the playing field.'

Skye frowned. 'How do you mean?'

'Well, I got everything I ever wanted. Seems only fair one of those things gives me endless grief.'

Skye smiled. She tugged the teat from the calf's mouth and let the animal out.

She'd just moved on to the next pen when TJ himself walked in.

Today, he wore a different pair of faded blue jeans, a long-sleeved Western shirt, and the same ancient cowboy hat and boots. His green eyes settled on hers, and he smiled. 'Hi, ladies.'

He shouldn't have made her pulse jump and skitter – but he did. Frustrated by her own reaction, Skye didn't return his greeting, only said, 'Your mom was just telling me you cause her endless grief.'

TJ gasped in mock-insult. 'I am the light of her life.'

Still holding both bottles, Janey looked over her shoulder at him. 'What do you need, light of my life? You done fixing the south fence already?'

'No, ma'am. I was about to head out but thought I'd see if Skye wanted to tag along.' He came to the pen she was in, leaned both forearms on the top. Those eyes met hers, challenged her. 'Figured we could take the horses, see where you're at and what you might need to improve on for that wrangler job.'

Although the notion of spending time with TJ filled her with nerves, Skye knew she'd be a fool to turn down the offer. But she looked to Janey for permission. 'Is that okay?'

Janey frowned. 'Baby, you're a guest. You aren't here to work.' She waved her off. 'Go on.'

Skye looked guiltily at the calves that still needed to be fed.

'Lord have mercy.' Clearly sensing her hesitance, TJ let himself into the pen with her. 'I'll help you wrap up here first if that'll wipe that guilty look off your face.'

Without waiting for her reply, TJ hip-checked her out of the way and reached into a pail for two full bottles. Like Janey, he placed one in each hand. Unlike Janey, who crooned and used a baby voice with the calves, TJ said, 'Rib-eye, T-bone, come here,' and randomly coaxed two calves into the feeding pen by tapping a bottle on the fence and then closing the gate behind them.

Skye refused to laugh. But it took effort.

Janey just shook her head. 'If I'd known you'd be so helpful as soon as a pretty girl showed up, I would have hired one ages ago.'

He'd watched them from his lean against the barn door for a whole five minutes, enjoying the sight of them talking and laughing while they worked. His mom was a bleeding heart, true. But it was also clear that she'd developed a quick and deep fondness for Skye.

TJ supposed it would be hard for anyone not to fall for those big, blue eyes, especially when thrown in with Skye's mercurial personality, which was half painfully cautious and half tentatively wild.

Now, he hustled down the feeding line with his mom and Skye, and the moment the final calf slurped up the last of the milk from her bottle, TJ dumped the empties in the pail and, grabbing four of the bucket handles, carried the bottles to the adjacent washroom to be cleaned, sanitized, and refilled for the evening feed.

'Ready?' he asked Skye when he came back out.

Again, she looked to his mom, who just smiled and said, 'Go on, honey.'

As he led her from the nursery to the horse barn, TJ tucked his hands in his pockets, half because he wanted to make Skye feel comfortable and half because he was tempted to find an excuse to touch her again. But he wouldn't.

Outside, the midday sun was high. The temperature hovered around a perfect seventy-five. The red dirt beneath his boots complemented the cloudless blue sky.

As if she'd read his mind, Skye said, 'I never really thought of Arizona as beautiful.' She crinkled her nose. 'Actually, I don't think I've ever really thought about Arizona at all. But there's something about that dry red dirt and big blue sky that just makes the world feel so much bigger . . .'

'A lot of folks aren't naturally drawn to the desert. But we're growing. Sometimes it feels like people are moving here in droves every day.'

'Dallas is the same.'

'So, city girl from Dallas.'

She didn't seem alarmed at her slip, just replied, 'Yup.'

'I figured.'

When she raised her eyebrows in silent question, he explained, 'You dropped a "y'all" last night, but your accent isn't Deep South.' Leaning forward slightly, he mock-whispered, 'And you have Texas plates.'

She gave him one of those quick, self-conscious smiles, putting him at three total.

Inside the barn, they each disappeared into their own stalls to groom and tack their horses, and Skye soon came out to where he was waiting, leading Smokey.

Her saddle was an ancient, off-brand trail saddle, the leather cracked and worn. It sat oddly on Smokey's back, almost as if it was balancing instead of conforming to the horse's form. He knew immediately that the tree – the frame beneath the leather – had semi-Quarter Horse bars instead of full. More than that, the seat had to be sixteen inches, a good two inches too big for Skye.

She caught his perusal. 'I know.' Her cheeks pinkened. 'It's old and it doesn't fit great. But it's what I have for the time being.'

Aware that he was in sensitive territory, TJ didn't lecture her. He didn't tell her that the saddle would eventually hurt her horse's back or cause saddle sores from the contact. He passed her his reins. 'Hold Kai for me for one sec. I have something that might work.'

'I don't want charity.'

'We'll trade for it,' TJ replied, and without giving her a chance to argue, he backed Smokey into the nearby cross-ties and secured her.

He disappeared into the tack room, selected a saddle that would, at least, fit a hell of a lot better than hers. It was a trophy saddle from his roping days with the Arizona High School Rodeo Association. His name was laser-engraved on the fenders with the year and event he'd won. Despite its age, he'd kept the leather supple with regular maintenance.

TJ lifted it with one hand and carried it out. He'd always figured he'd pass it down one day anyway.

Skye held Kai, but her eyes tracked his every move. 'TJ, what are we going to trade?'

'I'll think of something.'

'Yeah. That's what worries me.'

He might have laughed if he hadn't heard the new dread in her voice. Instead, anger, quick and sharp, sliced through him. He took a deep breath and met Skye's wary eyes over Smokey's back. 'Do I look like the kind of man who'd need to trade sexual favours for horse tack I haven't used in fifteen years?'

Skye's spine snapped straight. But she didn't back down. 'No, you don't. But I won't be indebted to you either. To anyone.'

TJ wasn't sure how to respond. He didn't have experience handling the very specific things Skye seemed to be running from. So, instead, he chose humour. 'Well, shit. I was kinda hoping you'd say yes.'

She frowned. But the moment she realized he'd been teasing her, a laugh, sudden and bright, spilled from her. It lit up her already beautiful face. TJ's breath caught. His grip on the cinch tightened, making Smokey snap her head back in warning.

'Sorry, girl,' he crooned and gave her stomach a pat.

On Smokey's other side, Skye sighed. 'It's so hard to be serious when you're always trying to make me laugh.'

TJ shrugged. 'You've got a great laugh.' But he dipped his head down and focused on cinching the saddle so that Skye couldn't see his face. He felt a little shaken. Typically, he was confident and smooth, but interacting with this particular girl felt like riding a bull. Uncertain. Thrilling. Terrifying. He was as excited as he was wary of which direction she'd go in next.

God only knew – both what she'd do next and why he was so goddamn excited to find out.

When he was done with the saddle, he left Smokey standing in the cross-ties and went to take his horse from Skye. 'Try that one out for size. If you like it, you can keep it.'

Skye ran her hands reverently over the leather. When she slowly traced his name in the fender with her index finger, a small smile playing at the corners of her mouth, TJ felt it like a touch to his own skin.

'I'd feel better if I could pay you for it.'

'It's over fifteen years old.'

'It's a Billy Cook saddle with your name on it,' she argued, and flicked the branded strap holder that declared *Billy Cook Genuine, Sulphur, OK*. 'If you're as famous as you tell me you are, you could sell this for something.'

'I said I'd trade, so I'll trade.'

She didn't just accept it. She leaned against the saddle, said,

‘Okay. Let’s hear it.’

‘When you win your first trophy saddle in a barrel race, you give this to someone who needs it more.’

‘That hardly benefits you. And who said I was going to start barrel racing?’

‘We’ll call it a universal trade. A pass-it-on.’ TJ made a play at nonchalance. ‘I could use the good karma.’ And because he knew that barrel racing would be impossible for her wild side to resist, he added, ‘And we both know you’re going to race. It’s just a matter of when.’

She unclasped Smokey from the cross-ties and led her through to where he stood with Kai. And right before she exited the barn, she looked over her shoulder at him, said, ‘You know, for this saddle, I might have traded sexual favours.’

TJ knew she was returning his teasing, but that didn’t stop the flood of lust through his system. ‘Let’s renegotiate!’ he called after her.

Skye just laughed, easier this time.

Chapter 7

They mounted their horses and made their way to the south fence.

Smokey held her head high and pulled at the bit, eager to go. Although her heart raced, Skye kept a death grip on the reins, holding the horse in line with TJ and Kai. Beneath her, TJ's roping saddle was an entirely new experience. The seat was reinforced, the thick horn wrapped. Although the stirrups were far too big, she figured those would be easy and cheap enough to change out.

His trade had taken her by surprise, but it was a reminder not to take TJ at face value. It was obvious, even to someone with her limited experience of men, that he wasn't like Holden.

'You've got a good seat,' he said as they walked through the scratchy brush, their horses' hooves crunching over dry soil. 'But it's very' – he affected a British accent – 'English dressage.' He mimicked her erect posture and stiff hands, making her laugh.

Where Kai was relaxed and plodding with it, Smokey, impatient and excited, walked almost in a diagonal, pulling at the bit with every step.

'Show me what to do.'

'Start by taking a deep breath and relaxing your body.' As Skye did what he instructed, TJ continued, 'The Western riding disciplines predominantly originated from actual ranch work.

Roping cows to drag them to the fire for branding, reining to move them during cattle drives. Think all day in the saddle, one hand controlling your horse, one hand free to do the work or open and close gates. Relax,' he said again. 'Give Smokey her head and let her neck find its natural position.'

'She's so fast,' Skye said, but she did as he instructed.

Smokey immediately took the relaxed bit as a cue to go. She broke into a rapid trot.

'Bring that left rein in tight and pull her into a circle until she stops. Once she stops, straighten her out and then back her up.'

Again, Skye did as she was told, but it wasn't easy. Smokey fought her the entire way. When she backed up and stopped, TJ and Kai came abreast of them.

'Every time she breaks into a jog or a lope without your cue, you do that. Turn a tight circle, stop, back her up, and then release the pressure and let her sit and think about it. She tries to step forward without your cue again, you back her up immediately. Repeat. She'll learn pretty quick that she doesn't go anywhere without your say-so.'

It took five circles and backups before Smokey stood still instead of trying to move forward immediately. And the mare wasn't happy. She arched her neck and looked back at Skye in the saddle, as if to say *Since when are you in charge?*

'Good. Now push her forward with a small hip roll. She's responsive, so you probably won't even need to give her a squeeze with your legs.'

Skye shifted her hips, rolling forward slightly. Smokey walked off immediately, slower this time, clearly wary of being pulled in another circle.

'You feel her body relaxing beneath you?'

'I do actually.'

'Good.'

As they moved forward, picking their way through the coarse Arizona vegetation, Skye noticed TJ's spurs. 'Does Kai need those?'

she wondered out loud.

'Spurs are a precision tool. When used correctly, they require the slightest pressure in the right place on a well-trained horse. But we don't have enough time to teach you that, and until you've both mastered moving off leg pressure, stay away from them. Too many people wear them because they want to look cool instead of doing things right, and it's unnecessary.'

'This coming from the guy who rides bulls that have their testicles strapped?'

TJ shook his head. 'That's not true.'

'Really?'

'No. The bulls are bred from specific bucking lines. And the flank strap – the rope that goes around the bull – is tied around the *flank*, just in front of the hips. It is irritating, but not painful. I can promise you, no male with his nuts in a bind is taking one step, let alone bucking.'

Skye hadn't known. 'I'm sorry. I didn't mean to offend you.' She laughed lightly. 'I seem to be doing that a lot.'

'You didn't offend me,' he assured her easily. 'Besides, somebody's gotta educate the city girl.'

Skye snorted. 'Rude.'

She watched as he effortlessly side-passed Kai around a thorny bush with the smallest shift of his leg, and although she didn't comment, she found the seamless way he rode undeniably appealing. He was confident but easy in the saddle – so much so that she found herself watching him intently, trying to learn by absorbing everything he did.

TJ picked up on it. 'See something you like?'

Skye flushed – but only because she had. Undoubtedly. Still, knowing his ego did not need a boost, she simply said, 'I wish I could ride like you.'

'You will. Give it time.'

When Skye used the bit to move Smokey around a bush, TJ saw it.

'Be gentle on her mouth,' he instructed softly.

'I'm trying, but she's so pushy.'

'You've got it. I can see you know what you're doing with your legs. But every time she gets stubborn, you panic and overcompensate with your hands. Relax. Breathe. You know more than you think you do.'

Concerned, Skye said, 'There's so much I don't know.'

'One summer at Hunt Ranch and you'll be a veteran in the saddle.'

'*If* they hire me.'

'True,' TJ replied philosophically.

Skye's heart dropped. God, what would she do if she couldn't find a job?

'Hey.'

She glanced up at TJ.

He must have been watching her face because he said, 'That was a joke. They'll hire you. You're good in the saddle and pick up instruction first time. They might start you on labour jobs, but you'll get to wrangling quick enough.'

Skye wished she had his confidence.

When they came to what Skye assumed was the south fence, she pushed all that worry to the back of her mind.

She could see where the single strand of barbed wire had snapped, the two pieces dangling forlornly, leaving a huge gap in the middle of the four-strand barrier.

TJ dismounted and looped Kai's reins over the fence post. Kai didn't move an inch, only cocked one hoof and dozed where TJ had left him.

'For now, let's add mending a fence to your resume.'

'Ah, I don't think Smokey will stand tied. If anything, she'll pull that fence out the ground.'

'She'll be fine.' TJ rammed one of the metal posts with both hands. 'We set the posts in concrete. Here.' He walked to her and took her reins. As soon as Skye had dismounted, he led Smokey to the fence and tied some fancy knot that Skye knew she'd never be able to replicate.

The moment he released her, Smokey started nibbling on the knot. TJ patted her neck. 'Good luck getting out of that one, pretty girl.'

His tone curled through Skye's womb. Lust, alarming in its intensity, gathered in an uncomfortable knot in her stomach, and surprised by it, Skye could only duck her head and pretend to dust off her jeans as TJ set out his tools and crouched by the fence. She might have been inexperienced, but she was still a flesh-and-blood woman living in the technological age. Between the internet, romance novels, and the vibrator Stevie had gifted her last Christmas, she had all the tools she'd ever needed for hot and heavy orgasms.

Or at least, she'd assumed she had.

And still, Skye just understood that TJ would know his way around a woman's body.

'Skye?'

'Hmm?'

'You okay there?' He looked up at her, a slight frown marring his features.

Mortified by the direction of her thoughts, she cleared her throat and crouched next to him by the fence. 'Yes. Show me what to do.'

'Here.' TJ tugged his gloves off and passed them to her. 'Don't want those city girl hands taking a barb.'

Skye didn't argue, only tugged the gloves on. They were far too big but comfortingly warm. Thrown by the odd intimacy of his remnant body heat, Skye curled her hands inside the gloves as she watched him work.

TJ quickly and competently unthreaded the two lines of wire and slipped off the sharp barb. He dropped it onto the scrap of leather he was using as a work surface. 'You do the next one.'

He moved aside, watched Skye closely as she mimicked his

previous movements and easily slid the next barb off the broken wire. 'Good.' He reached for the wire stretcher. He attached both ends of the broken fence line to it and then ratcheted the stretcher until the wire was pulled tight. 'Now, we're just going to bend these ends into hooks, about six inches in width. And do the same on the other side and to the replacement wire.'

Skye watched, mesmerized, as his big hands worked, quickly looping and coiling the ends of the broken fence with the repair wire. By the time he was done, the new piece of wire stretched through where the previous gap had been.

TJ cut the loose ends and removed the stretcher. 'Easy-peasy?'

'I'm actually kinda impressed by how quickly you did that,' she admitted. 'I honest to God thought we were gonna be out here for hours.'

Like her, TJ was on his haunches, the blue denim pulled tight over his muscular thighs, his forearms resting on his knees. He angled his head up, meeting her eyes. 'And you still came out?'

'I want to learn.' She smiled when he just stared at her, as if he couldn't quite figure her out. 'I was never allowed to do anything growing up – clubs, sports, *anything* my father hadn't previously approved or that might be considered beneath his standard. I wasn't even allowed to socialize with other kids from school who he considered beneath us.'

'He sounds like an asshole.'

'Yeah.' Skye indicated the scraps of wire and tools lying on the leather. 'This is legitimately romantic to me. Being able to choose what I do from the moment I wake up to the moment I go to bed is something I'll never take for granted.'

TJ didn't give her that pitying look people often did, even Andrea and Stevie. He raised one eyebrow comically and asked, 'Are you saying it turns you on?'

Skye just gave him a playful shove, knocking him off-balance in his crouch so that he toppled over and onto his ass.

'Whoops. Sorry,' she said, her tone mocking.

TJ shook his head dramatically. 'You know what this means?' he asked gravely. But his eyes, glinting with playfulness, gave him away. A skitter of excitement danced up Skye's spine, and even though she waited for that fear to kick in alongside it, it never came.

She pushed to a stand and took three quick steps back before he'd even gotten to his feet, but by the time she had turned, he was chasing after her, his manic laugh pulling a high-pitched squeal from a part of her soul she hadn't known had existed.

Skye looked over her shoulder and saw him only a step behind her. She dodged at the last minute, dancing out the way as his arms closed on air.

'I thought you were an athlete, TJ,' she taunted.

He wheezed dramatically and bent over to place both hands on his knees. 'You have youth on your side.'

Skye knew it was a ploy, and half-tempted to be caught, she took one step closer. 'You okay, old man?'

'Just winded.' TJ eyed her from beneath his cowboy hat. His body was still. Too still. But not relaxed; his muscles were tense and ready.

Skye held both hands up. 'Truce?'

Before he could reply, before he could reach out and grab her as they both knew he would, the sound of stomping hooves distracted them. They turned in sync to look at Smokey, right as the horse yanked her head back and pulled at the knot she'd nibbled loose.

The reins slipped from the knot. TJ's, 'Well, I'll be damned,' morphed into a quick curse as Smokey freed herself the rest of the way and, turning her butt in their direction, gave one gleeful kick before galloping away, the reins dragging dangerously on the ground in front of her.

Skye watched her horse rapidly disappear back towards the farmhouse. 'What was it you said? Something about, "Good luck getting out of that one, pretty girl"?'

'Shit.' TJ pulled out his phone and called his dad. Skye got the gist of what he said from his side of the conversation. 'Hey, Dad. Skye's horse got loose and is headed back to the barn . . . Yup . . . No, she's fine. We were on the ground . . . Damn mare undid a bowline knot . . . Okay . . . Ah, hold on, let me ask her.' He looked to Skye, asked, 'You okay to ride double with me on the way back?'

Skye hesitated.

TJ obviously saw it because he added, 'My dad will come get you in the truck if you'd prefer?'

'No.' She didn't want to make a big deal of it. And she certainly didn't want to make work for Ryan. 'I can ride double.'

TJ went back to his call. 'We're good. We're headed back now . . . Okay. Bye.' He hung up the phone, said, 'My dad will grab Smokey and put her in her stall.'

TJ rerolled the leather scrap with the tools and the wire and then secured it to his saddle before unlooping Kai's reins from the post and climbing on.

Skye went to him, looked up at him on the horse. He was so handsome, so competent. But that didn't stop the instant anxiety that flooded her chest, leaving no space for her lungs to draw in air, so that when she asked, 'What now?' it came out tight and rasped.

TJ could see the new fear in her and immediately tried to calm it. 'Don't be nervous. Just take a deep breath. You got this.'

'I've never ridden double before,' she said breathily.

'We'll go slow,' he promised. 'I'm going to take my foot out the stirrup,' he said, and did just that. 'And then you're going to mount just like you always would – except, instead of swinging into the saddle, you're going to swing onto Kai and tuck yourself behind the saddle. After that, all you have to do is hold on, either to me or to the cantle – the back of the seat.'

'Okay.'

Because she still looked worried, TJ reached forward and tapped her chin up until she met his eyes again. 'Do you trust me?'

Her eyes glassed over, but she whispered, 'I think so.'

TJ felt the impact of those three little words like nothing he'd felt before. They *hurt*, like a knife to the gut when he'd been hoping for a smile. The fact that she was unsure of doing something as simple as sitting on the back of a horse behind him was eye-opening, especially when he'd felt her barriers lower only five minutes before.

Without a word, he dismounted.

Skye's instinctual step back was all the affirmation he needed.

'What are you doing?' she asked.

'Hop on. I'll walk.'

Her relief was obvious. Her entire body relaxed. The panic in her eyes calmed. But instead of doing as he said, she looked in the direction of the farmhouse. 'How about we both walk? It can't be more than two miles.' She frowned. 'Can it?'

'It's about one and a half,' he confirmed.

'Think you can manage that?'

TJ grinned, because he knew she was trying to deflect from her previous panic. Pleased with the compromise, he grabbed Kai's reins and started walking. 'Only one way to find out.'

Skye fell into step beside him.

They were quiet for the first five minutes, the only sound the crunch of their boots on the ground. But when Skye spoke, she surprised him by saying, 'Thank you.'

'I told you I wouldn't hurt you, Skye.' But knowing that humour was easier for her, he affected an exaggerated sigh. 'And, despite my rugged charm and devilish good looks, I am a man of my word.'

Skye slanted him a look over her shoulder. 'I'm beginning to think that might be true.'

‘What? That I have rugged charm and devilish good looks?’

Skye used both her hands to shove him playfully. And when TJ stumbled dramatically, and Kai let out a condescending sigh, Skye’s laughter peeled out. ‘You’re unbelievable.’

He righted himself. ‘Okay, okay. We’re being serious now.’

She picked a stick up off the ground. As they walked, she broke it into tiny pieces, her movements quick, frenetic. ‘I don’t know many men.’

TJ fell quiet as he listened. He barely even breathed, too afraid that if he made a sound, he’d spook her away from telling him the truth.

‘In fact, I purposefully avoid them. And even when I think a man might be good, it doesn’t quite squash the anxiety response sometimes. And once it’s there’ – she tapped her hand over her heart and took a shaky breath – ‘it’s hard to come back down. The panic kicks in. TJ . . .’ She laughed sadly. ‘You might be the tenth guy I’ve had a full conversation with. Ever. I’ve never even been on a date. The only time I tried to have sex, I picked someone I knew was incapable of physically harming a fly, and he had to call my best friend to pick me up from his dorm room because I had a panic attack. And we didn’t even do anything.’

TJ didn’t know what to say in response to that deeply intimate secret. He’d lost his virginity in the cab of his truck at sixteen to an eighteen-year-old city girl who’d come to the rodeo with her friends. And even though he was far from the Casanova Skye accused him of being, he hadn’t exactly been discerning since. He loved women. He loved their soft skin and their pretty perfumes and their mysterious ways. And while he’d always assumed he’d meet the right one and know it instantly, so far, it hadn’t happened. But he sure as shit had fun while he was waiting for her to show up.

‘I’m not telling you this to make things awkward,’ Skye said, her cheeks pink with embarrassment. ‘I’m just trying to explain . . . *me*, I guess. I do trust you,’ she said, her words firmer now. ‘But that doesn’t necessarily mean I’ll always be at ease with you.

Both can be true.'

'I think I'm beginning to understand that,' he replied. Because he was. But there was also another part of him that rebelled at the idea of her being so hurt, so afraid. And the fact that she was afraid *of him* just about killed him. 'How about I be your practice dummy?'

'My what?'

'Well, anytime you want to try something new, I'm the guy you trust to show you.'

'What's the "but"?' she asked.

'You have to ask me *directly* for what you want. I am a flirt. And I have a real thirst for you, Skye.' He watched her eyes widen at that. 'But I'm not going to take one step towards you unless you've asked for it. I think it would be safer for both of us that way, with one exception.'

'What's the exception?'

'Could I still take you on a date?'

Her brow pinched. She looked up at him, almost as if she wasn't sure she'd heard him right. 'What?'

'It's a crime that you've never been taken on a real date.' TJ stopped walking. He faced her, letting her see the absolute honesty in his eyes when he said, 'I promise, I won't so much as touch you unless you ask. But we need to rectify that.'

Skye gnawed on her bottom lip. 'I don't know what to say to you.'

He shrugged. 'Say yes.'

'What would we do on this date?'

'I'm not telling you where we're going. The surprise is half the fun. But we'll get off the farm, have fun.' And because he sounded desperate, he teased, adding, 'Maybe you'll even ask me to give you a kiss goodnight by the end of it.'

She didn't baulk or even roll her eyes at that, only looked at him with those huge baby blues.

TJ wanted to be the one to unlock all those firsts for her, and not because he wanted her – or, not *only* because he wanted her. But because he'd meant what he'd said: it was a crime that she hadn't experienced all those scary intimacies of growing up.

She straightened her spine as his challenge settled between them. Her eyes flashed, and while she might not have noticed, TJ saw that wildness rise up and consume her anxiety. 'Okay,' she finally said. 'I'd like to get that out the way anyway. It may as well be with you.'

He snorted. 'Hey, Skye?'

'Yeah?'

'Wanna bet you actually enjoy it?'

Chapter 8

TJ did not waste time, Skye thought, as he left her at the front of the house after they'd unsaddled and brushed down both horses, saying only, 'Wear jeans and boots. I'll pick you up at six.'

She watched him walk away with a half-smile on her face, but the moment she stepped inside, very real anxiety settled in her stomach. She didn't know anything about dating, about men in general. And TJ was so experienced, so confident.

Instead of making herself sick over it, Skye went up to her room. Bandit, who had met her at the front door, followed closely on her heels. She showered and then headed back to her room to change, while the dog dozed on the rug on the floor.

Deciding that there was no better time to do it, Skye spread out on her bed and started a new Instagram account.

After twenty minutes of searching for a username that wasn't taken, she settled on *recklessskye*. She uploaded that first picture Stevie had taken of her and Smokey, and then, because they were on her mind, followed Andrea and Stevie first.

They both followed her back within five minutes. Stevie, who ran a fashion lifestyle account with over two hundred thousand followers, gave her a shoutout in her stories, so that Skye's follower count hit two-fifty before she'd even posted.

She sent Stevie a text:

Thank you! Now I just have to figure out what to post every day! LOL . . .

Just think of it as your own reality TV show. You're doing this super cool thing! Document everything!

Skye gave the message a thumbs-up, but because her date with TJ was still hovering on the forefront of her mind, she replied with:

Have a date tonight, btw.

Stevie didn't reply. She FaceTimed. Immediately.

Skye answered the call with, 'That was quick.'

'This is momentous! Who? What? Where? Tell me everything?' Before Skye could get a word in, Stevie added, 'Actually, hold that thought. Let me add Andrea.'

Skye waited patiently while Stevie added Andrea to the call, knowing that she'd rather tell them both at once anyway – and then take whatever advice they gave her and find the middle ground.

Andrea answered with, 'Guys, I'm at work. Can I call you back tonight?'

'Skye has a date!' Stevie blurted.

Andrea's eyes widened. 'Give me one minute.' She stood up from her cubicle and tucked the phone against her shirtfront, blocking her camera while she walked, and when she came back on the screen, she was in the restroom. 'Oh my God, you have a date?' she squealed.

Skye tried for nonchalance. 'Jeez, if I'd known y'all would get so excited, I'd have done this ages ago.'

But the girls saw straight through her.

'It's okay to be scared,' Andrea said gently.

Stevie propped her phone on her kitchen counter and sat down on a barstool. 'Are you kidding? Given what you've been through, it'd be weird if you weren't.'

'I'm not scared of him – physically. He's . . .' How did she even begin to describe TJ? 'He's super arrogant, but in a kinda self-aware, playful way.' Skye thought back to the way TJ had wordlessly dismounted and walked back with her, instead of making her ride double. 'I think he's a good guy.'

Stevie clasped her hands together and did an old-school cartoony victory pump.

Andrea frowned, clearly worried. 'I'm concerned. What's his name? Let me verify him.'

'*Verify* him?'

'I'll pay for a background search.'

Skye rested her chin in her hand. 'No, you're not paying for a background search. But I love you for caring.'

'What's his name?' Stevie asked. 'We're at least allowed a vibe check, right?'

'Jesse James Jones.'

Stevie's mouth fell open. 'You're going on a date with *Triple J*?'

Andrea leaned back on the restroom sink. 'Wait, Stevie, you know this guy?'

'Oh my God, you don't even . . . Girl.' Stevie fanned exaggeratedly as her face. 'Hold up. I'm sending you his Instagram.'

Stevie's camera blacked out while she used her phone, but in less than ten seconds, a post came through to a new group Instagram DM. The photo was one of TJ on a huge, black bull mid-buck, his left hand in the air, black Stetson shadowing his eyes. His wicked smile was the only part of his face that wasn't in shadow.

'Holy cow. Literally,' Andrea said.

Skye clicked through to his profile. Sure enough, he had over half a million followers. His aesthetic was all dark and dangerous. Professional pictures, all action shots, the shadows amplified, the highlights dimmed. Even what he wore – black chaps hiding his jeans, black shirt, black boots, black Stetson – was pure sex appeal.

Seeing it for the first time lodged a fist in Skye's throat. 'I'm so out of my depth. Oh, God.' She groaned and covered her eyes with one hand.

'No. No, no. This is good. Right, Dre?'

Andrea looked less sure. 'You said he's a good guy?'

'I think so . . .' Skye thought about how to explain. 'At the very least, he makes me *feel* safe. When I'm with him, I want him,' Skye added, and even though she was talking to her two best friends, she blushed furiously. 'That's new for me.'

'Does he know about Holden?' Andrea asked.

'No. He definitely suspects *something*, but I don't want him to get that look or start treating me differently. I just want this feeling to last.' She rubbed a hand over her heart. As the truth of that washed over her, Skye exhaled a deep breath. 'I think he's going to be my first. And I know I've said that before, but this time, it feels *right*.'

Andrea just stared at her over the screen.

Skye knew why her friend was sceptical. The last time she'd said those words, Andrea had had to come and pick her up when she'd changed her mind.

But TJ was different. Skye knew that, even if she couldn't explain why.

Needing to defend herself – or perhaps convince herself – Skye hurriedly added, 'I mean, why wouldn't I? He's single, he's interested, he's experienced, and if I asked him to stop, I believe that he would. It's like the universe dropped him in my lap at just the right time.'

Stevie nodded slowly. For the first time since hearing about the date, she seemed cautious. 'While I trust that you know yourself, please go slow. If this guy is genuinely a good guy, he won't pressure you. Just remember that one thing, okay? It's important.'

'Okay.' Skye shifted, met Andrea's eyes. 'Dre? Just say it. I can hear it.'

'Are you doing this because you want to or because you have something to prove?'

Skye didn't get defensive. She knew that both of her friends loved her and that, sometimes, loving people meant asking the difficult questions. 'Both.' Her answer was firm. 'I do have something to prove. To myself. Because I'm ready. But I also want him.'

Stevie didn't give her humiliation space to grow. She said, 'Amen. Because, again, have you seen this guy, Andrea?'

Andrea sighed, but when Skye just smiled at her, she shook her head. 'Okay.'

'Say it,' Stevie whisper-chanted. '*Say it. Say it. Say it.*'

Andrea rolled her eyes. 'He's *smoking hot*, okay? I have eyes. It's not his looks that I'm worried about,' she stated. 'Call us tomorrow?'

'I promise.'

'Love you!' Stevie blew them a kiss and ended the call.

Alone again, Skye flopped back onto the bed as the immensity of what she'd decided to do rose within her. She couldn't say why, but it was different this time. She'd meant what she'd told her friends: she wanted TJ. And that was new and exciting – and yes, a little terrifying.

When TJ pulled his truck up to the front of the house at six, Smokey and Kai in the trailer behind him, Skye was sitting out on the front porch with his parents. His mom and dad shared a two-person wicker chair. Skye sat on the single tiled step leading up to the house, her legs stretched out in front of her, her hand on Bandit's head.

It was a shock to see them there together, so comfortable, Skye simply slotting in.

‘Ready to go?’ he asked as he got out.

Skye nodded and turned to his parents. ‘See you later?’

They all heard that it was phrased as a question, like a plea for consent. TJ had noticed that she did that often.

‘Go, baby. Have fun,’ his mom told her.

Skye came to where he stood by the truck. Bandit followed. She was dressed in boot-cut Wrangler jeans and a skintight black top that he suspected might be one of those bodysuits women wore – and TJ loved. Her ancient riding boots were on her feet, and her ruthlessly stylish pixie cut was free of her signature ball cap.

‘You look gorgeous,’ he said, trying to say the words casually so that she didn’t baulk.

Skye smiled tightly. ‘Thanks.’

He leaned into the truck and took out the tiny potted cactus he’d stopped and picked up from the garden nursery in town.

Skye’s eyes instantly brightened, losing that wariness his compliment had settled there. She laughed. ‘Aren’t you supposed to get me flowers?’

‘Nah. Too predictable. Besides, flowers die. This way’ – he passed her the pot – ‘you’re going to be thinking about this date – and me – for a long time to come. Possibly years. It’s native to Arizona, so even if you throw it out your window, it’ll just thrive.’

She rolled her eyes. But when she took the cactus from him, she couldn’t quite bite back her smile. ‘Thank you. It’s ridiculous. I love it.’ She turned, said, ‘I’m just gonna go put it in my room quick.’

She hurried inside, leaving him to walk back to his parents while he waited.

‘Where are you guys going?’ The question was asked casually enough, but TJ heard the concern in his mom’s tone.

‘We’re going to start at Tia’s. I booked Skye a barrel lesson. Given that we’ll have the horses, I’ll probably pop out and grab some burgers while she wraps up her ride, and then we'll head back here.'

'Sounds like a good night,' his dad observed.

TJ relaxed slightly when his mom smiled at him and added, 'It sure does.'

Skye hurried back out, her boots clicking on the tiles. 'Okay, I'm ready now.'

This time, when Bandit followed them to the truck, TJ said, 'Bandit. Stay.'

The dog stopped immediately. He plopped his butt on the ground and watched as TJ walked Skye to her door. When he closed her inside his truck, Bandit whined.

'That dog's gonna go with her when she leaves,' he warned his mom.

'I know it.' She winked at him. 'Foster fail, my ass.'

TJ grinned as he walked to the driver's side. 'We both know you'll have rescued another one in under three days – one that *I'll* have to train.'

She scoffed.

His dad laughed.

TJ waved and climbed into the truck. He started the engine, felt a small trickle of alarm when Kip Moore's 'Hey Pretty Girl' filtered through the Country radio. He loved the song, but he didn't want her to think he'd put it on as some ploy for intimacy.

But Skye just sighed, and said, 'I love this song.' She reached for the volume, cranked it up and, to his absolute delight, started singing along in a voice as smooth as honey.

TJ didn't speak. Hell, he barely breathed as he listened to her sing.

Chapter 9

When they drove ten minutes down the road and turned onto another farm, Skye looked round at TJ. 'What is this place?'

'A friend of mine, Tia Baker, is a barrel racer who's competing on the rodeo circuit at the moment.'

'The WPRA?' Skye asked.

'Yup. I booked you a lesson with her,' TJ said distractedly as he looked in his side mirror to check that the trailer was clear of the gate.

Skye stared at him while he navigated the truck and trailer through the ornate gate. A very real panic clawed its way through her chest and up her throat. It must have shown on her face, because the moment TJ saw her expression, he frowned. 'What's wrong?'

'I don't want to seem ungrateful . . .'

'Okay—'

'I'm not ready,' she blurted. 'It'll be a complete waste of your friend's time. And embarrassing for me.' She gripped the inside handle of the door as if she could physically stop the truck from rolling down the long drive. 'Oh, God.'

'Skye—'

'What are we gonna do?'

The truck stopped abruptly. 'Skye,' TJ said gently but firmly, 'look at me.'

It took a few seconds for the words to register through her anxiety, but when they did, she forced her gaze to his.

'What's going on here?'

'I'm not good enough to do this yet,' she explained.

'I hate to break it to you,' he said, leaning close and lowering his voice as if to tell her a secret, 'but that's kinda implied. It's a *lesson*. By definition, she's supposed to teach you.'

Skye wasn't sure how to explain to TJ, who was obviously so perfect at everything, that she . . . well, wasn't. She had to work really hard at most things she did, and she always fell short. Just thinking about trying to run the barrel pattern had Holden's voice echoing in her head, his routine *You're simply going to have to do better, Skye* sounding over and over in that disappointed tone, as if she'd disgraced him past redemption.

It hadn't mattered what it was – school exams, piano recitals, luncheons – Holden would judge her performance and find her lacking. As a child, she'd worked harder. She'd thought that if she could only be better, he would be proud of her.

So, she'd studied until she'd fallen asleep with her books on her bed, prompting Holden to call her a slob. She'd practised piano until her fingers had cramped, and after her recital, when she'd known she'd delivered a technically flawless performance, and she'd walked off the stage, her chest full of hope and *pride*, he'd said her performance had lacked passion. She'd opted to be silent at social gatherings, because it was easier to not do anything wrong when you didn't do anything at all, only to have Holden criticize her for being unable to hold a conversation.

She couldn't say any of that to TJ, so settled on, 'What if I do it wrong?'

'Oh, you're one hundred per cent going to do it wrong,' he said confidently. 'Probably hundreds of times. And if you don't, Smokey sure as hell will.'

Skye buried her head in her hands. 'Oh my God, you're right. We can't do this.'

'Hey.' When Skye didn't move, TJ softened his voice, urged, 'Give me those blue eyes.'

She lifted her head again, barely.

'I told her you're a beginner. If she even brings the barrels out, it'll be to walk the pattern or for her to demonstrate something. Okay?'

Skye managed a shaky nod.

'Why are you freaking out now? You were fine on our ride earlier . . .'

'That was different. You were fixing a fence. All I had to do was ride out there with you and watch. There were no expectations.'

'There are no expectations from anybody now either.' He tipped his head. 'Except you apparently.'

'Making me humiliate myself on our first date isn't exactly what I had in mind,' she whispered.

'Me neither. In fact, why don't you ask me: TJ, why did you organize a barrel lesson for our first date?'

'No. Because you're going to say something ridiculous to try and make me laugh, and I don't want to laugh right now.'

'Come on, Skye . . . Ask me. You know you want to.'

She sighed, but she made it long-suffering. 'TJ, why did you organize a barrel lesson for our first date?'

'Because I promised I wouldn't touch you unless you asked, and watching you ride is the next best thing.'

'What?'

TJ shrugged. 'You're sexy as hell on horseback. And if I can't touch, I sure as hell am gonna look.'

She knew that he was trying to distract her, but goddamn him, it was working, because now all she could think about was the fact that TJ thought she was sexy. And it mattered.

'Did that help?'

'No. I think you made it worse.'

'Why?'

'Because now I not only have to get it right but try to look sexy while doing it.'

There was a perfect beat of silence before TJ threw his head back and laughed. The sound filled the truck, wrapping Skye in warmth and diffusing the worst of her anxiety.

Even though she didn't want to smile, she couldn't quite stop it either. 'You're ridiculous,' she accused, raising her voice to be heard over the sound of his laughter.

TJ swiped at his eyes and gave one last deep chuckle before giving Skye his attention again. Only, the moment he did, he saw that while he had distracted her, that anxiety still rode just beneath her smile.

He hadn't expected it. If he were honest with himself, and he always was, he'd thought he was being so smooth, signing her up for her first barrel lesson. So, having her on the verge of a panic attack wasn't something he'd prepared for. 'Nobody's going to be there except you, me and Tia.' He didn't drive the truck forward; instead, he added, 'I really think you should try, but if you're set against it, I won't be offended. We can haul the horses home, maybe go for another ride around the farm?'

'It's not that I don't want to try,' she insisted. 'I'm just afraid of getting it wrong, of wasting her time.'

'Tia's being paid. So, even *when* you get it wrong, she's been compensated for her time.' He thought about how he could get through to her, but nothing came. He'd never met anyone with such a deep and irrational need to be perfect at something new. 'What's the worst that could happen?'

She shook her head.

'Tell me. I want to know.'

'I'll ruin *my* first ever date because *you'll* see that I'm nothing. A disappointment.'

He hadn't expected a reply, let alone one so specific – or heart-breaking. 'I knew you were special before we even met.' When she just stared at him blankly, he leaned forward and, resting his arms on the steering wheel, looked out the windshield. 'Sheri called, said she had a friend who was working her way west with a horse and trailer. She said she was worried about you because you didn't have much experience and might need some help. And I thought: *now, what kind of woman travels across the country alone, towing a horse, when she has no experience?* And you know what I concluded?'

'She must be batshit crazy?' Skye drawled.

'It takes a little crazy to do what you're doing,' he ceded. 'But no. I thought: *she must be something; I can't wait to meet her.*'

Skye groaned and let her head fall back on the headrest.

'You can be scared, Skye. You're allowed to be scared. But if you expect to be perfect all the time, you are going to routinely disappoint yourself. Nobody else. *Yourself.*'

She seemed to mull over that for a moment. 'Do you promise you won't judge me?'

'Promise. I won't even watch if you don't want me to.'

'Okay.' She nodded once, but he noticed that she didn't release her death grip on the door. 'Let's do it.'

'Yeah?'

'Yeah.'

TJ shifted the truck back into drive and continued towards the big, covered arena up ahead.

In the passenger seat, Skye was quiet, her body tense. He almost hated pushing her, but he knew, absolutely, that she would have fun once she let herself relax a little. And he wanted that for her. He wanted to be the one to give her this particular first.

By the time they pulled to a stop in front of the arena, Tia had come out of the barn to wait for them. She was a small woman in her early forties, only an inch or two taller than Skye. Beneath her Stetson, she wore her long black hair in a braid that fell down her back. Twenty-five years of Marlboros had lent her voice smoke, so that it sounded warm and husky when she said, 'I saw you come in. Was starting to worry you'd changed your mind.'

TJ walked around the truck to where Skye had gotten out. 'We were just having a little pep talk. Skye's nervous.'

Skye glared at him as if he'd shared a state secret.

But Tia just laughed. 'I almost peed myself the first time I ran a barrel. But you don't have to worry; we won't be doing anything fast today.' She moved towards the back of the trailer unprompted. 'Let's get your horse unloaded and tacked up.'

'I brought Kai too. I'm gonna tie him while you ladies get started, maybe pop out and pick up some burgers if you and George are interested?'

'Thanks, TJ, but we have the kids coming over later.'

TJ turned to Skye. 'Burger preference?'

'However it comes is fine. Thanks.'

He stayed for long enough to help Skye tack up. But it was only when Tia had left to get her own mare ready that he asked, 'You gonna be okay if I head out?'

Skye exhaled a long breath. 'Yeah. She's nice.'

'All right. If you really don't want me to watch, I'll head back in an hour or so.'

She leaned against Smokey's shoulder, as if she were drawing strength from that bond. 'I don't mind if you watch.'

'I'll come straight back then.'

Before he could take a step away, Skye walked into his chest. She wrapped her arms around his waist and gave him a huge squeeze. 'Thank you for this. I'm sorry for freaking out.'

The smell of her hair flooded his senses. The soft press of her small body short-circuited his brain, so that it took him a good three seconds to respond, to raise his arms and link them behind her. By the time he had, she was already stepping back, forcing him to let her go.

The gesture had thrown him. There was something intensely erotic about chasing a woman who didn't quite yet understand the power she had. She was just as likely to seduce him deliberately as she was accidentally – but he figured he'd enjoy it either way.

'Try to have fun,' he said.

TJ left them there to get started, unhitched his trailer, and then headed out to pick up the food.

By the time he got back, thirty minutes later, darkness was settling. Under the covered, lit arena, the girls were both mounted on their horses. Tia, on her palomino mare, sat in the saddle at a standstill while she instructed Skye. 'Good. Now push her back into that circle pattern and use your hands and your inside leg to keep her shape. Every time she surges and tries to break into a lope, you're going to halt her completely and back her up. You're the boss here, and Smokey needs to understand that.'

TJ climbed onto the piped arena fence and sat on the top rung to watch Skye do as she was told, her face pinched in concentration. She only had to back Smokey up once before the mare kept her pace at an even jog, instead of breaking into a faster gait.

Their form was good. If they hadn't been a little too tight, Skye could have passed as someone who'd been riding her entire life. Her movements were small and precise, her control pristine.

'Good. Now make your circle smaller.'

Skye adjusted her body, seamlessly turning Smokey into a tighter circle, and the moment she got it right, Tia called, 'Now do it all again – this time, in the other direction!'

As Skye turned in the opposite direction and began working her circle again, Tia rode to where TJ was perched. He knew by the look they shared that she'd seen what he had.

Tia sat back in her saddle, said, 'She could do it.'

He'd known it the first time he'd seen Skye ride – or, maybe, the first time he'd seen that flare of wild snarling behind the fear in her eyes. 'I know it.'

'She'd need to learn how to get out of her own head though.'

'Yup.'

'Poor girl's sweating more than her horse.'

'I think she's had a rough time of it, and she's afraid of screwing up,' TJ explained. 'She wants to be perfect.'

'Yeah, but it might slow her down later. There's no such thing as a perfect run, a perfect ride. You know that.'

'I'm hoping that working with horses will cure her of the notion soon enough.'

Tia laughed. She shifted her horse with a subtle leg cue, but before she rode off to wrap up the lesson, TJ quietly called her back. 'Hey, Tia? Could you tell her – that she could do it? If I say it, she'll think it's a line. But it's important for her to hear it.'

'Sure, TJ.'

He watched in silence for another fifteen minutes, and it was only when Tia said, 'Good, Skye. That was perfect. Let's stop her there,' that he climbed down into the arena.

As he walked across the freshly graded sand, he heard the end of Tia's, 'If you keep at it, I'll be running against you soon enough.'

He watched Skye's face as first surprise and then pleasure bloomed.

Skye saw him approaching and turned to give him those big blue eyes, but when he raised a hand to stroke down Smokey's face and asked, 'So?', her smile inched free. And it was bright, if a little embarrassed.

'It was good,' she said. 'Overwhelming. There's so much we don't know still. If I could just be better at—'

'How about we focus on the fact that it was good for now?' he asked. 'Take a deep breath and just fucking enjoy it.'

He'd meant it metaphorically, but she inhaled deeply, slumped in her saddle, and said, 'You're right. I'm ruining the moment.'

This time, when she smiled, he realized that he'd lost count of them.

'You hungry?'

Skye placed a hand low on her stomach. 'I don't know. I was so nervous; I think I still feel a little sick actually.'

'Well, why don't we untack Smokey while you think about it? We can take the food home.' He waited for her to nod before turning to Tia. 'Thank you – especially given the short notice.'

'Anytime, TJ. Good luck this weekend. We'll be cheering you on!' she shouted as she walked away, her horse's tail swishing.

Chapter 10

Back at the farm, they unloaded and fed the horses. When they were done, they sat on the tailgate of TJ's truck beneath the dim glow of the barn's single outdoor light and ate sweaty hamburgers.

Skye had never been happier. 'Tia's amazing,' she gushed. 'I'm going to have to YouTube some of her races. Maybe even go and watch a few if she's ever in California.'

'I'm sure she'd like that. She travels with George now that Beau, their son, can handle the farm, but it still gets lonely on the road. Sometimes, even when you're surrounded by people, it can feel like you're the only person in the world.'

Skye pushed the takeout bags into a small pile so that she could lie back in the bed of the truck, her legs dangling. 'How did you get into it – bull riding?'

TJ's eyes flickered down her body, igniting that hot, slow burn deep within her. But he didn't so much as move an inch in her direction. Instead, he mimicked her position: he lay down and folded his hands over his stomach as he looked up at the night sky. 'I grew up a rodeo kid, so I used to watch the bull riders all the time. I thought they were the coolest guys on the planet.'

'And you wanted to be like them when you grew up?'

'Maybe in a detached kinda way. But it wasn't until I started chasing girls that I began to seriously consider making the switch from team roping to bull riding.'

Skye laughed, remembering that she'd teasingly told Janey just that. 'I totally called it.'

TJ's grin flashed in the dark night. 'I was a teenage boy. There was nothing I wouldn't have done to look cool to the girls.'

Skye just shook her head condescendingly.

'Anyway, I was about sixteen, and I figured, I'm gonna try it. Just once. See if I have the balls for it.'

Skye looked up at the blanket of stars as he talked, too rapt by his deep voice to ask all the questions she wanted to. Like, *What was it like to be a regular sixteen-year-old?*

'So, I look around, and I realize: hey, you idiot, you literally live on a farm packed full of cows.'

Skye levered onto her elbows at that. 'Please tell me you did not ride a dairy cow?'

He inhaled through his teeth. 'I wish I could. The funny thing was, we even had a couple of bulls. I was just too shit-scared to try it out on one of them the first time.'

She could picture him, sixteen years old, sitting on a poor dairy cow. 'What happened?'

'I just hopped on one in the pasture. This cow turned and looked at me over her shoulder as if to say, *Well, this is new*, and then just went back to her cud. She didn't even take one step.'

Skye's laugh bubbled out. 'Poor cow.'

'Oh, don't worry. It was humiliating for me too. I hadn't realized my dad was at the fence, watching me. So, when I get off, he walks over, and he looks at me like he's really worried I'm not the sharpest tool in the shed.'

Skye's chest squeezed tight. She knew what it was like to disappoint a parent and then live with the consequences. 'What did he do?'

'He said, "Ah, TJ. What the hell you doing?" And then he explained why dairy cows aren't for riding. He built me a practice barrel and got me in with a family friend who used to ride bulls. Jack taught me all the theory a man could know about the sport. And not wanting to die taught me the rest. Real quick.'

His words hollowed her out, leaving her sad and confused.

'You okay?'

Skye hated that he could so easily sense that turmoil in her, but desperate to be understood, she lay back and took a deep, bolstering breath. And she tried to explain. 'The only thing worse than being slapped by my father was living with my fear when he would be nice. Because then it was a constant mind game. Just waiting . . . Now, I can see the pattern, but as a child . . .'

TJ was quiet for a moment, as if he needed a few seconds to come to terms with her confession. But when he spoke, he only said, 'You just wanted to be loved.'

'I did. I would have done anything for him. Even at the end, even after all that therapy, when he'd be nice, I'd find myself trying to please him again. It's like you're so trained, so conditioned, that it just clicks in and takes over. Until he snaps again. I was made to believe that I was unworthy, that I was stupid, and on the rare occasion I dared to question his judgement of me, then I was ungrateful and undeserving of the life he had provided. The first time I truly fought back, he had me put in an in-patient mental healthcare facility. For almost a year.'

TJ's head snapped up at that. 'Your mom didn't try to stop him?'

No. She couldn't say the word aloud, couldn't let him judge her mother for that. And TJ would, if only by default, having Janey as a yard stick. 'She loves me. But she's so trapped, so afraid, that she's never been able to stand up for herself, let alone for me.' Tears fell slowly, trickling down her temples and dampening her hairline.

Skye hated appearing weak. It went against every defence mechanism she had learned over the years to share these details with TJ now, but she made the conscious decision to do it for one reason: she'd meant what she'd told Andrea and Stevie. She wanted TJ to be her first, but experience had taught her to prepare for the worst, and this way, if she had a panic attack, he'd at least understand why she was the way she was.

And TJ did. He asked, 'Can I touch you?' and when she nodded, he surprised her by linking his fingers through hers. 'So, that's why you don't date?'

Skye nodded. 'I'm good at reading eyes, but only with people who aren't guarded.'

'Guarded?'

She was quiet for a moment. 'When people are presenting themselves without pretence, their eyes don't lie. They either say, I'm open and friendly or a grouch or a flirt,' she added, and shot him a pointed look. 'My problem is that my father taught me that people who want to lie can mimic those same expressions. They can make themselves appear harmless, affable, or even charming. My father is highly esteemed at work. He donates generously to charity.' She smiled at that. 'Women find him charming. Sometimes, at home, he was funny or sweet, even kind. But when you've been abused by someone, even once, those funny, sweet, kind gestures are not comforting. They're terrifying. Because you're waiting, wondering what you're going to do wrong to have that mood changing, wondering how he'll punish you when it does. Because it *always* does. And when it does, you're left wondering why you always fuck up, why you're always to blame.'

'You are not to blame.' Temper licked at TJ's tone. 'And while I might never be able to empathize, I can promise you, Skye, that I am not that man. I would never hurt you or anyone else deliberately.'

'I know that.' He shot her a doubtful look, prompting Skye to insist, 'I do.' She let go of his hand. For some reason, she needed distance for the words she was going to say next. 'The only reason I'm telling you all this is because I'm going to have sex with you. And before we do that, I need you to understand why it won't be easy for me to trust you during . . .' Her cheeks blazed. Skye could only thank the dark night and dim barn light, which hid the worst of it.

TJ expelled a long, pained exhale. He sat up and bent over as if his stomach hurt, hung his head. 'Give me a second,' he said tightly. 'This is a first for me.'

Skye frowned. 'What is?'

He angled his head to look at her, his eyes black with something she could only label as hunger. 'Being told I'm going to have sex with someone. Usually, there's a lot of foreplay, some teasing . . .'

'I'm not good at that,' she informed him with a quick shake of her head. 'I don't . . .' *know how.*

'Skye . . .' TJ trailed off. He sighed, clearly thinking about what to say.

It hit her like a slap. He was rejecting her. 'Interesting. I would never have guessed you'd say no.'

'I'm not saying no, necessarily. Because I am a flesh-and-blood man, and I've wanted you since the first moment I saw you. But you can't just say shit like that and then expect me to forget it. I am saying,' he added cautiously, 'that we have a lot of ground to cover before we get there.'

'Like what?'

'Flirting, touching, kissing. Because you *want* to. Not because you think it's an item on the list.'

Skye thought all of that build-up would just be awkward, given her inexperience. 'I'd rather we just did it.'

TJ made a strangled sound. His jaw tensed. He took a deep breath in through his nose, muttered, 'You can do this; you ride bulls for a living.'

Before she could say anything else, he leaned over and cleared up the takeout trash, putting it back in the to-go bag it had come in.

He was leaving. Shame suffused her, but beneath that dragging weight of shame, there was relief. She sat up and reached over to grab her phone from the tailgate.

But TJ threw her completely off-balance by taking her hand in his, raising it to his lips and kissing her palm. He linked his fingers with hers again and shimmied closer so that their thighs were bumping.

His hand was rough and callused but so warm. Strong. It wrapped around hers completely, like a shell.

The immensity of it made her shiver.

TJ felt it. 'Is this okay?' He gave her hand a squeeze.

'Yes. Just new,' she whispered.

'I know. Which is why I won't just take you, even though I want to.' He ran his thumb over the back of her hand, sending a lick of sensation up her entire arm. 'Do you understand?'

'Yes.'

'Those little gestures of interest are important, Skye. They're how we . . . *bond*, I guess. And they make it better – when you have sex. The delayed gratification—'

'Okay.' She was so flustered and hot, so on edge that she couldn't physically stand to have his attention this focused on her. 'We'll do it your way.'

TJ was going straight to hell. Here he was, sitting with Skye after she'd just told him she'd been routinely and systematically abused by her own father, and still, half of his brain was reeling over the fact that she wanted to have sex with him. All he could feel was the soft curve of her thigh and her small hand clasped in his.

The part of his brain that could function knew that there was no excuse on God's green earth for what her father had done to her, *his own child*. In TJ's mind, it was simple evidence of insanity. Of wrong. Of evil.

It was a revelation, even to him, that new knowledge, issued in a few short sentences, could so drastically impact someone with thirty-three years of living under his belt. Maybe it was just because it was the first time he'd interacted with someone who'd lived through that. Maybe it was because he cared about Skye.

It hit differently when it was personal.

'My dad had a rough childhood,' Skye began to explain. As if she needed to excuse him. As if anything could. 'His dad was a veteran with untreated PTSD. According to my mom, it was really messed up—'

'Yeah. I don't give a fuck.' He stroked the back of her hand with his thumb. But because he'd heard the bite in his own voice and felt her hand tense in his, he forced himself to soften. 'There's no excuse for that, Skye. None. Plenty of people have rough childhoods without turning into monsters. And it sounds like that fucker,' he said hotly, 'had the resources to educate himself and to get professional help before he started taking it out on his family.'

Skye averted her gaze.

But TJ didn't let her get away with the avoidance. 'Hey . . . Look at me.'

When she didn't – or maybe *couldn't* – TJ used their joined hands to gently bump her chin up. But the moment their eyes met, hers welling, he was helpless to do anything but break his hold on her hand and raise both of his to her face. He used his thumbs to swipe her cheeks. 'You can use that knowledge to understand why he was the way he was, why he was so damaged and weak, and why it was never about you. But you don't make excuses for him. You hear me?'

She nodded silently.

'What does he want from you?' TJ asked. 'I mean, I'm assuming that's why you're running?'

'There's some money involved,' Skye replied cautiously. 'My grandma made me trustee of her estate upon my twenty-fifth birthday. So, in just over two years' time, I'm going to take control of my father's primary source of income. And I'm going to cut him off. He'll lose over half of what he needs to keep up his lifestyle.

And that – his appearance – is *everything* to him.'

TJ heard the vehemence in her tone. And even though he didn't want to pry, he had to ask, 'What will he do – when you cut him off?'

'I don't know. I'll revise the trust as soon as I'm in control, so that he gets nothing upon my death. I want to believe that murder is too risky,' she said. 'And Holden's smart. He's a criminal defence attorney. He has two years under State law to contest the will. Which he will. If that doesn't work – *which it won't* – he might try to have me declared legally incompetent. He's done it before. And he'll use that – my mental health history. But it'll still be difficult to prove, considering I'm reasonably sane and given how much he has to gain.'

'Fuck.'

Skye just laughed at that.

'What are you gonna do?'

'Wait.' She sighed. 'I have time.'

'Yeah, no. You should have someone look over everything. Get legal advice. I mean, there has to be measures in place for this kind of thing, right?'

'I've spoken to Mr Simcock, my grandmother's lawyer. We've done what we can pre-emptively. Until Holden actually makes a move, our hands are tied.'

'Skye—'

'I don't want to talk about it tonight. Please, TJ . . .' She shifted closer, her movements a little unsure.

But TJ knew what she was asking. Even as he looked at her face, trying to confirm it, her eyes changed from two wells of fear and grief to black pits of need. 'You have to say the words. Tell me what you want.'

Skye did not hesitate. 'I want you to kiss me.'

The words punched through him. All his worry and fear for her took a back seat as his body took over his mind.

He said, 'Fucking finally.'

He crushed his mouth to hers, stole into her with none of his usual charm or skill, only a desperate and unfamiliar urgency.

He groaned as her taste flooded him. She was so sinfully sweet. Temptation embodied. Bewitched, he took without thought, sliding his tongue against hers in a desperate plea for more.

It was only when he heard her quick inhale and felt her stuttering, uncertain response that he stopped. He pulled away, took a huge gulp of air, and cursed himself. 'I'm sorry.'

'It's okay—'

'No. It's not.' He'd lost himself.

TJ might have hated himself for it more if he hadn't been so shocked. He'd never, not once, not even at sixteen in the cab of his truck, lost control with a woman. It was a point of pride for him. But he didn't think he'd ever, even at sixteen, wanted a woman with this unhinged thirst.

He turned to Skye to apologize again, saw her huge eyes, filled with stunned disbelief, watched as she raised her fingers and tentatively touched them to her bruised lips. 'Don't be sorry. That was nice.'

TJ went from half-mast to raging hard instantly. He bit off a groan and took five long seconds to get control of his body. 'It was nice. But it wasn't what I wanted to show you.' He reached for her, stopped when he saw how she tensed up. 'I want to hold you,' he explained. 'I want to show you that I can be gentle.'

She nodded cautiously.

He lifted her small body easily, settled her sideways on his lap, her legs dangling over one side of his, her weight pressing down on his erection.

She shifted, trying to reposition herself over the intrusion and forcing TJ to grab her hips and hold her still. He let his forehead drop to hers. 'You need to stop squirming.'

'Oh.' The single, breathy word danced over his cheek, making him smile.

He gently tapped her right leg, said, 'Here,' and patted where he wanted it on his other side on the tailgate.

Skye shifted, straddling him, her knees on the hard tailgate, her centre hovering over his, denim stretching over her slight curves. He took her hips again, and even though he pulled her closer, he stopped before they touched. 'Now you can choose how much contact you want.'

She placed her hands on his shoulders, and she lowered back down onto him.

'Let's try this again,' he said, and this time, he pressed his lips to hers in the faintest of touches, and when she didn't return the kiss right away, he gently, tenderly, rubbed his lips over hers, wordlessly showing her what he wanted and giving her the option to take that next step.

She sighed open for him. Her tongue danced with his in long, gentle strokes that slowly stirred his blood. Her hands rose to his head, brushing over his short hair before her arms wrapped around his neck. As if she needed to hold on to him. As if he were capable of going anywhere.

She sank down onto his lap, pressed herself firmly against him. TJ wasn't even sure she was aware of what she was doing until she broke the kiss to breathlessly murmur, 'More, TJ. I want more.'

He searched her face, trying to see if what she wanted was actually what she needed. But her face – eyes black with lust, lips swollen from his, cheeks pink with a sensual blush – told him what *he* wanted, not what *she* needed.

For the first time in his life, he didn't know what to do with a needy woman in his arms. Oh, he knew what he wanted to do. That was easy. But if his parents had taught him anything, it was that sex and doubt of any kind were never to be mixed.

So, he tried to take the high road. 'Slow, remember? We have time.' But even as he said it, his mind screamed, *Not enough!*

Skye must have had the same thought, because she argued. 'No, we actually don't. I leave on Sunday.'

He tried humour. 'How long do you think it takes exactly?'

Skye just scowled. 'Don't joke.'

He sent one quick prayer heavenwards, a simple, *God, give me strength.* And then he tried to be a good man, an honourable one, one last time. 'I'm trying to do the right thing, Skye. Not the easy thing,' he explained. 'Because it would be so easy to take you right here, right now.' He used both hands to pull her up and over his erection again. 'I want you. You know that. But I don't want you to have regrets.'

'I won't,' she insisted. Her voice took on a husky tone that shot straight to his balls. 'Please. I feel like I could just explode.'

'Sweet Jesus.' He could feel his defences crumbling. His fingers actually rose to toy with the button of her jeans. His eyes dropped to her waistband – and inadvertently caught the tailgate in his peripheries.

'Not here.' Close to losing his mind, he lifted her off his lap.

Skye threw her arms up, her wild side sneaking through. 'Where? When?' she demanded. 'If you don't want me, then just—'

Before she could finish the sentence, he stole the words. He pried her lips open and took her, letting his greed reign for a full three seconds. But the moment she recovered from her shock enough to respond, her arms rising to grip his shirt, her lips slanting to give him better access, he pulled back.

'Don't fuck around,' he warned her. 'You know I want you.'

She deflated. 'You're right. That was a stupid thing to say.'

'If you still want me tomorrow, I'll be here. Meet me at the front of the house at seven.' He pushed off the tailgate and grabbed the takeout trash with one hand. Before he left her there, he ended the conversation with, 'And wear a dress.'

Chapter 11

'Wear a dress,' Skye muttered to herself the next day as she rifled through her meagre supply of clothes in search of something remotely appropriate.

She'd spent the day helping Janey with the nursery and inwardly cursing TJ for walking away from her. Not because she disagreed with him necessarily. In fact, once she'd had time to calm down, she'd realized that it hadn't been easy for him to take that step back.

Still, she cursed him because it hadn't been easy for her either. She'd had to swallow every iota of her pride to put herself out there, and then he'd had to go and take the high ground, making all the anxiety and build-up pointless.

Now, all that sick dread was still there, collecting in her stomach like a swarm of angry bees. And to make matters infinitely worse, she didn't have a dress.

She'd refused to take anything from Holden's when she'd left. Instead, she'd restocked on essentials only, packing those things she'd thought she'd need on the road. Things that would last a long time. Jeans, shorts, workout gear. She'd even bought two oversized pairs of sweatpants, which was indicative of how low looking nice for a man had been on her list of priorities.

Once she'd bought Smokey, she'd slowly added horse gear to her supplies, picking up odd items at Tractor Supply and second-hand tack shops, so that while Smokey had a waterproof sheet and a thick blanket for the colder days, Skye didn't own a single stupid dress.

Frustrated by her thin wardrobe, she yanked out a pair of denim shorts and a cropped top, then bundled her clothes and her toiletry bag under her arm and walked down the hall to the bathroom. She locked the door, turned on the shower. As she waited for the water to heat, she studied her face in the mirror.

Although only three months had passed, she looked older than she had when she'd set out. She certainly didn't look twenty-two anymore. While her skin was youthful, her cheeks still slightly full, her eyes aged her. She'd seen too much, lived too hard to look so young.

'And yet, you're still a virgin,' she said with resigned embarrassment. But not for much longer, she promised. Not for a single day more.

She gripped the edge of the sink as her nerves rose, but instead of succumbing to them, Skye glared at her reflection. 'Enough. Just get it over with. You'll be fine.' And when that didn't help, she reminded herself, 'TJ won't hurt you.'

She closed her eyes and recalled the feeling of his big hands on her hips, his thighs beneath hers, his hard length pressing awkwardly into her leg. She remembered the incredible kiss they'd shared, and, oddly, she drew comfort from his insistence that she take the day to think about it – about *them.* Not because she'd been unsure, but because it was proof of what she already knew: he was a good man.

He wouldn't pressure her. He would stop if she asked. Knowing it, remembering it, calmed her. Twenty-four hours might not have weakened her resolve, but it had given her time to be sure.

It was only when she moved to strip her clothes that she saw TJ's clean jeans and button-down hanging on the back of the bathroom door, waiting for him to shower and get ready.

She walked over to where the clothes hung and raised her fingers to touch the white linen shirt. On impulse, she lifted the hanger from the hook on the door and held the shirt up to her shoulders, so that it fell to mid-thigh.

Her laugh was a little wild. But this time, when Skye spun around to look at her reflection, the shirt draped over her, a lick of confidence sliced through her nerves. 'He did say to wear a dress.'

Riding on the whim, she hurriedly showered and changed, sliding her bra and pants on first, followed by her denim shorts and, lastly, TJ's shirt.

Back in her bedroom, she took stock of her appearance. Although the shirt was long enough, it bagged everywhere else, making her look like a head and legs sticking out of a sack. The sleeves were so long that her hands weren't visible at all.

'I can work with this,' she said dubiously, and rolled the sleeves up past her elbows. She found her belt in her duffel bag and shortened it enough to fit tightly around her waist, cinching the baggy shirt to her figure. She pulled on her boots and sat down on her bed to do her makeup.

As a little girl, she'd loved the ritual of it, had loved watching her mother so expertly transform herself, using nothing but pots of cream, bottles of foundation, palettes of colour, and tubes of mascara and lipstick. But over the years, as Caroline had used her knowledge and skill to hide her haggard fatigue and unhappiness, the wonder of it had soured. And when she'd taught Skye to do the same, when wearing makeup had become synonymous with hiding her pain, the last of Skye's fascination for the art had turned to disdain.

These days, she barely ever bothered, and when she did, like tonight, it was solely because her vanity and Holden's voice in her head whispered, *You look so much better when you make an effort.*

She wondered what her mom was doing at that moment.

Maybe she was reading in her favourite chair while Holden locked himself in his office. Maybe she was standing in the kitchen, worrying over dinner. Holden never commented when he didn't enjoy something she'd cooked, merely left the table, leaving his food largely untouched.

More than anything else, she wondered if her mom was as lonely as she had been over the past three months. Because for a long time, before Andrea and Stevie, all they had had was each other.

And now her mom had nobody.

Despite her promise to sever contact, Skye picked her phone up off her nightstand.

She pulled up her mom's number and dialled before she could change her mind. She slowly raised the phone to her ear, counted four long, mournful rings before her mother's voice answered with, 'Hello?'

Skye was too afraid to speak, too afraid to break that connection. She gripped the phone tightly, as if she could somehow reach through it and wrap her mom in her arms.

For a long stretch of time, the only sound was of each of them breathing, and then, *so quietly*, her mom said, 'Skye?'

Skye swallowed down the sob that climbed so easily into her throat. 'Hi, Mom.'

'Oh, Skye. I've been hoping you'd call.' Caroline whispered, as if talking to her only child was a crime of the highest order. 'We were all so angry last time.' Skye closed her eyes, knowing what was coming before her mom said, 'But your dad is sorry. He misses you.'

Skye wanted to snap *Wake up, Mom!* But she didn't. She was too desperate to hear her mom's voice, too anxious that she might break that fragile connection if she started pushing.

Instead, she said, 'I bought a horse, Mom.' Those words conveyed all the things she didn't say: things like *I got out, I'm free, I'm living.*

There was a beat of stunned silence. 'Oh, Skye. That's amazing! I'm so very—'

The sound of a door opening cut Caroline off. Before Skye could even ask, her mother's false laugh trickled over the line. 'Mary, Holden just got home from work. I better go. But let's talk about the fundraiser tomorrow.'

Skye opened her mouth to say goodbye, but no words came.

'All right. Bye-bye.' Her mother hung up.

The silence echoed in Skye's ears as she slowly lowered the phone back down.

Grief took her by the throat and squeezed. Guilt laughed maniacally in her head. But the shame . . . The shame of what she had done nestled in the deepest pocket of her heart and made its home there.

She rocked gently back and forth in an attempt to self-soothe.

'Shit,' she mumbled when she realized that she was crying. She swiped angrily at her face, and when her fingers came back black with mascara smudges, Skye laughed bitterly. 'Great. Just fucking perfect.'

She pushed off the bed to go and fix her face. But as she quickly and efficiently cleaned up the black smudges around her eyes, all she felt was tired.

Nobody, including her therapist, had told her that leaving would be the easy part. They all said, *Get out*, *Leave*, and *Don't look back*, as if breaking the cycle was all there was to it. But none of them knew how difficult it was to start at zero, to build from a foundation that somebody else had slowly and systematically torn down, to build with no knowledge of how such a feat was done. Nobody knew how much effort it took to constantly pick yourself up when you lived with another person's voice in your head, calmly telling you how stupid and weak and worthless you were.

With each upward stroke of the mascara brush, her anger grew. And it wasn't anger at Holden. It was anger at herself, at her own inability to cut his voice out of her head. Anger over the fact that she had left her mom behind, with nobody to look out for her, nobody to love her.

With that anger came a wild need to do something reckless, to prove to herself that she could do whatever the hell she wanted, be whomever she wanted to be, her father be damned.

TJ didn't see that wildness in her when she first stepped out onto the porch. He was too distracted by her stunning face and lean legs, left bare between where her white shirt ended and her black boots began. *His shirt*, he belatedly realized, and welcomed that flood of greedy approval. 'I was looking for that.'

'I didn't have a dress,' she informed him, and walked past him with a sassy smirk.

TJ followed, aware that he was acting like a dog, drooling at the end of a leash. He waited until she reached the passenger door of his truck, then reached for her hand. Because he figured kissing was fair game now, he walked her backwards into the cold metal door and lowered his mouth to hers in a gentle kiss.

Skye didn't tense or seem scared. Instead, she rose up on her toes, gripped his shirt with both hands and took the kiss further. Her mouth was hot and desperate on his. Her body, pressed close, vibrated with need and something that felt eerily like anger.

His hands shifted to cradle her face.

It was then that he saw that blue wildfire burning. And it was as hot as it was dangerous.

'What's wrong?'

'Nothing.'

'Try again.'

'TJ—'

'I can see it in you, Skye.'

'See what—'

'The wild,' he replied immediately. But he didn't let her go.

He couldn't. Instead, his thumbs brushed over her cheekbones, as if he could sweep away all that feral anger. 'You forget, I hang out with men who ride bulls for a living. *I'm* the well-adjusted one of my friend group.'

'What if I don't want to talk about it?' she asked and tipped her chin up.

'Then I won't take you out.' He couldn't say why he knew that was important, only that she was looking to make mistakes. And he wouldn't be one of them.

'Are you fucking kidding me?'

'No.' When she tried to slap his hands away, he only took her chin in one hand.

Skye yanked her head back and snapped her teeth at his hand. TJ didn't laugh; he was too angry, too aroused. 'You wanna fight with me, baby?'

'No. I want to go out. And if you won't take me, I'll just go alone.'

'The hell you will,' he told her, and crushed his mouth to hers to make his point. He took her deep, fast. But the moment she relaxed, the moment she softened, he pulled back. 'Don't do that. Don't shut me out. Christ, Skye, this *matters*.'

He hadn't meant to say it. He hadn't even known how true the words were before he'd let them out into the world. Even if what they had was casual, a week-long love affair, it was important that someone tell her that simple truth. *This matters.* You *matter.*

TJ pulled away on a curse, but Skye stopped him. She roped her hands around his head and yanked him right back. Her mouth was hot and hard on his, her need painfully clear.

She coiled one leg around his and plastered her body against him.

TJ's brain blanked.

He took a quick step back, breaking contact before his greed took control.

They stared at each other for one crystal moment, both their chests heaving, both their clothes rumpled.

'Get in the truck.'

He didn't move to help her, knowing that if he touched her again, he'd risk disappointing himself and probably hurting her. She didn't need sex just then. She needed so much more.

They drove in silence for twenty minutes.

TJ didn't say where they were going.

But Skye didn't ask. She sat in the passenger seat, her arms crossed defensively over her chest, her eyes glued to the desert landscape outside, her mouth set in a stupidly sexy pout.

When they reached the outskirts of town, with nothing but desert for at least a mile in each direction, he pulled off the highway onto an old mining road and stopped the truck.

Skye frowned. 'What are we doing here?'

TJ turned the engine off. 'We're talking.' At her blank look, he grinned. 'The way I figure it, you would have gone out looking for trouble anyway.' He indicated the desert through the windshield. 'This way, you're kinda stranded until you tell me what's wrong and what the fuck happened to put that look in your eyes.'

'You're kidnapping me?'

He thought about that, settled on being amiable instead of angry. 'Yeah. I guess I am.'

He held his breath as her hand reached for the door. For one moment, he actually thought she'd get out and walk, but she settled at the last moment, and TJ noticed her rounded shoulders and the way she shifted so that she could hug both arms around her stomach.

'I called my mom.'

He almost hated making her talk when she turned those eyes on him. All that wild rage had been replaced by a deep, deep sadness.

Unable to leave her sitting there, looking so alone, TJ got out of the truck. He walked around the back and let the tailgate down on the way to her door. He unclipped her seatbelt. The moment it slid loose, he lifted her out and wordlessly carried her to the tailgate as he tried to ignore the smell of her hair and the feel of her soft curves flush against his body.

He put her down gently, climbed up behind her and pulled her back into his chest. Because he had noticed that she always stood with her arms wrapped around herself protectively, he gave her what she needed and roped his around her instead. He kissed her temple, just once, and said, 'Tell me.'

She surprised them both with the strangled sob that left her lips. But she caught it. She fought it for a full minute, her small body shuddering with effort.

TJ didn't say anything. He didn't move. Just waited quietly.

Once she'd fought her way back to calm, Skye whispered, 'It was only for a minute. Because my father came home. But I told her I bought a horse. And she was happy for me. But all I could think about once she hung up was that I'm here, free, and going on a date with this really nice guy while she's stuck there with *him*.' She spat the last word with something that far surpassed bitterness. TJ might have called it hatred if it had been so simple.

'Did you try to get her to leave?' he asked gently.

'Yes, but—'

'Did you stand up to your dad?'

'That's not the point—'

'Is it your responsibility to endanger yourself for someone who refuses to accept your help?'

She didn't answer his question, only said, 'You don't know what it's like.'

And then the tears came.

TJ held her as she curled against him and lost herself to her grief. As he crooned senseless endearments – 'I've got you' and 'Let it go, baby' – it occurred to him that if any other woman had broken down in his arms after just two days, he would have run for the hills. He certainly wouldn't have held her tighter, as he did with Skye.

It didn't scare him that she was different. Mostly because he chose not to think too deeply about it. It was too much, too soon. It was too big.

She cried for a long time, and when the last of it had left her, she slumped against him, exhausted, her face red and splotchy, her eyes painfully blue against the black mascara smeared everywhere.

'I bet I look real pretty,' she said, her voice raspy and congested.

'You are absolutely the most beautiful racoon on the planet.'

As he'd hoped, she smiled. But it was still so tired. So heavy. As if just that small gesture was a weight to lift.

'I'm sorry.'

'Don't be,' he insisted.

'Some date, huh?'

He kissed her lips softly. 'We're working backwards.'

'Hmm?'

'Well, typically, it goes: dinner, dancing, hotel, and then the date ends with you leaving in my shirt the next morning so that I can nap and get room service.'

She elbowed him in the ribs at that.

TJ bit her neck gently in retaliation before adding, 'But this time, we're starting with you in my shirt. So, dinner and dancing next?'

She shook her head.

'Do you need to go home?'

She sighed and let her head fall against his collarbone. And she said, 'Hotel.'

Chapter 12

Skye couldn't say why she'd expected TJ to book a mid-range hotel, probably by the hour. Only that she had. So, she was surprised when he pulled his truck into the crescent-shaped drive of the Savant Hotel.

The Savant line was five-star rated, and the Scottsdale location was no exception. The hotel had been built in the southwestern style, using terracotta-coloured adobe, stucco, and natural stone. The landscaping was comprised entirely of vegetation native to Arizona, yet somehow, the prickly cacti, alien-looking succulents, and desert scrub had been artfully arranged to still look beautiful.

Everything was pristine, and Skye, feeling self-conscious, tried to rub off the last of her mascara smudges in the rear-view mirror before climbing out of the truck.

TJ passed the keys to an immaculately dressed valet with a name tag identifying him as *Mike,* who asked, 'Checking in, sir?'

'Yes. Last name's Jones.'

TJ linked his hand with Skye's, so he could lead her into the hotel.

He checked them in quickly, and in less than five minutes, they were waiting for the elevator in the lobby, their linked hands heating, forging a connection that was as new as it was exhilarating.

The elevator pinged. Skye looked up right as the doors slid open to reveal another cowboy. And though Skye preferred TJ's rugged good looks, the man she was looking at now was undeniably beautiful. Almost too beautiful. He was dressed all in black. Unlike TJ, whose hair was cut military-style and short, this cowboy's thick black hair fell in waves to his shoulders beneath his black hat. His eyes were dark brown in the dim light; they focused on her face, flickered appreciatively down her body. His smile was devilish, but the cocky tilt of it told her that he undoubtedly thought himself God's gift to women.

Beside her, TJ tensed. She felt it in the air around them, in the quick jerk his hand gave in hers. He greeted the other man coolly. 'Savage.'

'TJ.' The cowboy grinned, but he didn't look at TJ, just kept those wicked eyes on Skye. He tipped his hat, said, 'Ma'am,' as he made a show of exiting the elevator, sweeping off his hat, and extending his other arm to hold the door open for her.

Skye walked forward, despite the prickle of unease that whispered over her skin. It wasn't that she thought the other man dangerous, necessarily, just that the odd energy between the two seemed volatile. Like a pair of wolves circling. As if one of them might pounce on the other at any moment – with her in the middle.

TJ made a predatory sound from deep in his throat, but he followed her inside. As Skye turned, she caught the cheeky wink the other cowboy sent her but didn't have time to roll her eyes as the doors slid closed again.

'Who was that?'

'Matthew Savage. He's the world champ bronc rider at the moment.'

'You don't like him?'

'I didn't mind him until today.'

'What? *Why?*'

'He was looking at you,' he said instantly. TJ shook his head. 'Not cool.'

Skye craned her head back to look at him. 'Are you *jealous*? Because he *looked* at me?'

'Hell, yeah, I am.' He brought his face close to hers, nipped her bottom lip playfully. 'And don't pretend you didn't look back.'

Skye couldn't even deny it. 'He is objectively beautiful, but I like my men a little less . . . polished.'

TJ pretended to take an arrow to the heart. He stumbled around as if he was mortally wounded, making her laugh.

'Oh my God, stop,' she begged when he pretended to slide down the side of the elevator. 'You're being ridiculous—'

The doors pinged open on a random floor.

A couple dressed in elegant cocktail attire hesitated when they saw TJ half-sliding down the ornate glass siding.

On the other side of the elevator, Skye had to bite her tongue to keep from laughing.

TJ cleared his throat and stood up. He dusted off his spotless shirt, said, 'Sorry about that. I tripped.'

Skye snorted, and then immediately raised a hand to cover her mouth.

The couple stepped inside. The man pressed the button for the rooftop, where the bar was located, and then pointedly stood between his wife and TJ.

The elevator continued on its way, the heavy, awkward silence prevailing.

Don't laugh.

Don't laugh.

Don't laugh.

Opposite her, TJ focused on her face, but Skye refused to meet his eyes, knowing that he was trying to get her to cave.

When they exited at their floor, he tipped his hat, said, 'Have a good night.'

The second the doors closed, they both descended into giggles.

The moment was light and fun in a way that Skye had rarely experienced. Even with Andrea and Stevie, so many of Skye's interactions had been governed by heaviness, by their need to check in and deal with the latest abuse. On the rare occasions when they had done something silly and foolish, it had been to pointedly escape whatever else Skye had been dealing with. But in these five seconds with TJ, it was just her *being*. Experiencing. Living.

'You and Matthew actually have something in common,' TJ observed.

Skye frowned. 'Oh?'

'Hunt Ranch. He worked there back when it was still a ranch. That's actually how he got his start in bronc riding. The owners, James and Ava Hunt, sponsored him in the beginning. By the time they passed in a car accident and their son, Maverick, converted the cattle operation to a resort, Matthew was well on his way.'

'Really? You've known him that long?' Skye was surprised. The two men hadn't seemed friendly. Or even familiar, really.

'Nobody *knows* Matthew Savage,' TJ commented. 'He keeps to himself – and whichever woman he's pursuing that day.'

The moment they came to their room, all thought of Matthew Savage vanished. TJ didn't open the door. He passed Skye the keycard, leaned against the nearby wall, and watched her from beneath inky lashes.

She understood that he was letting her take that next step – and she didn't hesitate. She pressed the keycard to the pad, opened the door with one clammy hand, and stepped inside.

The room was gorgeous. And it wasn't a room, she realized as she walked through a genuine foyer, but a suite: a home away from home, with a full lounge area, a kitchen, and a bedroom behind sliding ornate doors.

Skye wasn't sure how she felt about it. 'Do you usually fork out several thousand dollars a night for a quick hook-up?'

TJ's green eyes darkened. 'Not typically,' he replied, his tone carefully controlled. 'But it's not a *quick hook-up* either.'

While she stood frozen in the middle of the foyer, he walked to a beautiful display table that held an ice bucket and an ornate flower arrangement. He pulled a bottle of champagne out of the silver bucket, his movements quick and impatient.

Skye noted the rigid lines of his body, and tried to explain, to soothe. 'I don't want you to treat me differently.'

'Tough shit.' He very carefully put the chilled bottle on the table and turned to face her. 'You are different. You *matter*,' he reminded her. 'Jesus, Skye, just the fact that you've never done this before has me in a full fucking sweat.' He took off his hat and wiped his hairline with his sleeve, as if he needed to prove his point. 'I'm terrified I'm going to scare you or do something wrong, or worse – hurt you. Fuck.' He hung his head. 'I couldn't stand it if I hurt you.'

The nerves in her stomach twisted tighter at that. But there was one thing she was absolutely sure of: 'You don't scare me, Jesse Jones.'

It took all the courage she possessed to take those last few steps towards him, to close that distance and leave girlhood behind. But Skye did it because she absolutely knew, wherever their paths took them, there'd be no one quite like him again.

She rose up, placed her lips on his. The kiss was deep and slow, a gentle exploration of each other. But the soft pressure of his lips and tongue did nothing to calm the fire within her. Skye was consumed with it, *by* it. It rose within her like some destructive, inextinguishable flame that licked at the most intimate parts of her, igniting sensation everywhere.

She reached for his belt buckle, but TJ caught her hands in his. 'Slow down.'

When she just frowned, he reached down and swept her off

her feet. He carried her through to the bedroom, with its giant bed, and gently tossed her onto the middle of the mattress.

He reached for her boots, tugging first one and then the other off.

Burning with need, desperate with it, Skye moved to help him. She undid her belt, grabbed the hem of the shirt she wore and lifted it off, yanked her shorts down her hips and then sent them flying across the room with a single kick of her legs.

Her underwear was nothing special, only a pair of boyshort pants and a matching racer-back sports bra. The black cotton set might have lacked sex appeal, but the pants fit her small hips snugly and the bra moulded her boobs.

TJ didn't seem to care that she wasn't in seductive lace or prettily designed lingerie. He stood at the foot of the bed, staring at her, his eyes dark. 'You're beautiful – you know that?'

Skye smiled shyly as that news first washed over her. She watched as he untucked his shirt and pulled it over his head, before tossing it on the floor, swallowed thickly as she took in his long, lean body. TJ was all corded muscle and tanned skin.

When he turned and sat on the edge of the bed to take off his boots, Skye saw the huge bull skull tattoo on his back. It was black and white. And beautiful. The bull's horns spread over each shoulder blade, the forehead extending down his spine to where the lower jawbone ended a few inches above his waistband. The bull's horns served as the balance beam for a scale: a weight tray dangled off either horn, down the sides of his back. In one tray, the word *Live* had been inked into his skin. In the other, *Die.* Skye noticed that the *Live* side was favoured, hovering slightly lower, heavier.

TJ yanked off his boots, and even though Skye held her breath in anticipation, he didn't take off his jeans. Just climbed onto the bed and came to where she lay.

He levered onto his elbow so that he could look down at her. Skye's nerves pulled that knot in her stomach tight, but oddly, there was very little panic now. It was as if the anticipation had displaced all that fear of the unknown.

TJ kissed her. Just once. Deeply. As if he wanted to go slow so that he didn't scare her.

But Skye simply gave him a shove and sent him sprawling onto his back. She climbed onto him, straddling him low so that their centres pressed together through the layers of their remaining clothes.

TJ's hands found her hips and squeezed. 'I don't know what to do with you, wild girl.'

She saw that it cost him his pride to admit that he was out of his depth. But the fact that he could be vulnerable only made her feel safe. And in that safety, she found the courage to say, 'Just treat me like you would any other woman.'

TJ groaned, but he levered into a seated position. 'You'll talk to me,' he said. 'Tell me what you want as we go?'

'Yes,' she promised.

He reached for the back of her sports bra, stopped, asked, 'Please, for the love of God, can I take this off now?'

Skye nodded. She raised her arms as he lifted, helping him, but the moment her bra came off, she lowered them back down, covering herself. Her breasts were small and insignificant, and just then, it was almost painful to contemplate all the things her body lacked compared to the women TJ must have been with.

He didn't force her protective shield away. Instead, he raised his hands, one to each breast, and he whispered, 'I've got you.' And the moment Skye dropped her arms, he used those big, warm hands to cover her nakedness.

He took her mouth as those clever hands worked, squeezing and kneading until her core throbbed with pressure. His tongue teased hers.

'TJ, please . . .'

His body trembled beneath her, as if all that trapped need was escaping through his skin, and when he said, 'Please, baby, let me look at you?', his voice was stretched painfully tight.

Skye nodded. How could she not? The honest need in his eyes coupled with that word, *baby*, undid her. She would have given him anything.

TJ dropped his hands. His gaze followed. Skye waited, thinking she'd see that flash of disappointment. But instead, he groaned in approval, and he said, 'Fuck me.' He raised one hand, covered her entire breast with it. 'Perfect fit.'

Leaning forward, he tugged her into his mouth, used his tongue to circle her peaked nipple.

A shock of pleasure slapped through her as the new sensation radiated from that tiny point of contact and through her body to pool between her thighs. Skye was helpless but to grab hold of him and let her head fall back as she succumbed to it. A long, guttural moan left her lips, and with TJ's hot, wet mouth on her, she wasn't embarrassed. She was too steeped in pleasure, too lost in the new adventure he was taking her on.

'Does that feel good?' he rasped, his voice heavy with his own battle for control.

'Yes.'

He dropped his head to her other breast, tortured her in the same way, balancing out the shockwaves that ricochetted through her.

Swamped by unspeakable pleasure, her core filled to aching, Skye unconsciously ground over him as if she could relieve that building pressure with just that. She almost did. The orgasm built quickly, rising in one uncontrollable wave, but the moment it hovered, the moment she braced for it, relaxing her body to welcome it, TJ stopped.

'Jesus Christ. Holy shit,' he panted, his eyes wide and wild. 'Not yet. Too soon.'

She whimpered and thrust her hips over him again.

TJ's eyes dropped. 'Fuck, I can feel you soaking my leg through my jeans.'

'Please, TJ.'

'Please what?'

'Make me come.'

'Tell me you want me to taste your pussy,' he demanded roughly.

Skye was too needy to be embarrassed. 'I want you to taste my pussy.'

The world spun as TJ flipped her over in one fluid move, so that she was on her back and he was levered over her. Skye froze in anticipation of that panic kicking in.

TJ felt her tense.

He didn't stop, only gentled, trailing his fingers down her chest, between her breasts to her navel.

And for Skye, the panic never came. She expelled a relieved breath, one that immediately caught again as TJ's wandering fingers dipped below the waistband of her underwear to stroke the sensitive skin beneath.

He watched her face as his fingers closed around the fabric. He waited for her to nod before he tugged her pants over her hips and down her legs, leaving her completely naked to a man's gaze for the first time.

TJ shifted, briefly pushing to his knees so that he could reposition himself between her legs. But as he did, Skye saw his bulging jeans, his erection pressing up against the taut fabric.

Skye hadn't known how being desired could make a woman feel so strong. And in control. Power surged through her.

But then TJ blew a breath over her inner thigh. Anticipation filled her. Skye's breath caught. She waited as he used his tongue to slowly lick his way up her thigh, towards her centre.

Helpless to resist, she watched the top of his head shift between her spread legs.

Her breathing became laboured.

She collapsed back against the mattress, too embarrassed to watch, too aroused to hold herself up. 'TJ . . .'

'Say my name.'

'Jesse.'

A rumble of pleasure left his lips as he licked through her.

Equal parts shock and arousal slapped through Skye. The sensation of his wet tongue lapping at her was impossibly odd and unspeakably sexy at the same time.

'Fuck, you taste so good.' TJ used both his hands to spread her legs wider. He groaned. 'And you're so pretty.'

Holy shit, Skye thought as he lowered his face back down and kept on going. And this time, he wasn't gentle. He consumed her, his lips and tongue working over her flesh with skilful tugs, pulls, flicks, and twists.

Skye squirmed in his hands as she tried to fight the building pressure, but when it became too immense to contain, she reached for him and, holding the back of his head, pressed her hips forward.

TJ's rough groan of approval tore through her. 'You wanna come, baby?'

'Yes,' she panted.

He shifted to her clit, tortured her with flickering strokes there as he pressed a single finger into her tight heat and curled it upwards.

Skye exploded.

Chapter 13

TJ didn't stop as Skye shuddered and moaned while the orgasm ripped through her. Her taste was too ripe, the way her body bucked and twitched against his mouth too addictive for him to cut the moment short. Instead, he closed his eyes and buried his face in her, savouring her as her legs closed around his head.

It was only when she went lax, her legs slackening their grip, that he slowed. He kissed his way up her body, moving from her navel to her breasts to her lips while his hands stroked over her, touching her everywhere that he could.

He was crazed. Frenzied, and desperate with it. A few days wouldn't be enough. He'd never be able to have enough.

He took her lips in a deep kiss, his tongue sliding over hers as he spread her with his fingers, stroked through that hot, wet heat until she pulled back, her panted breaths striking his cheek, her hips shifting in small thrusts as she climbed back up.

He wanted to push her over a second time, wanted to watch her shatter under the weight of the pleasure he gave her. 'Again,' he demanded.

Her arms roped around his neck. She pulled him close, whispered, 'I want you to be inside of me this time.'

TJ groaned. He pulled back, hurriedly stripped his jeans

and briefs, and rolled a condom onto his aching dick. It was only when he moved to the bed again that he saw Skye, her anxious blue eyes fastened on his erection, her lip caught between her teeth, that he realized: he'd forgotten. It shamed him, but for just a moment there, he'd forgotten how inexperienced she was.

He purposefully slowed his movements, lay beside her on the bed and pulled her close, so that they were nose to nose. 'Don't be scared.'

'I'm not scared,' she declared.

But TJ only kissed her cheek, murmured, 'I'll go slow. Talk to me; tell me how you feel.'

'Actually, I'd prefer if we went fast the first time. Just get it over with, you know.'

'You sure?'

'Yes.' She said the word firmly, leaving no doubt in his mind that it was what she actually wanted.

But, terrified that he might hurt her, he asked, 'Do you have a vibrator?'

'Not on me,' she replied.

'No. Uh, I just want to know what you *have* had inside you . . .'

Skye buried her face against his chest, clearly humiliated by the conversation.

'Skye?'

'It's not that type of vibrator,' she said, her voice muffled against his skin. 'It's a clit stimulator. But I use my fingers . . .' He felt her skin burning with a blush against his chest. 'Inside.'

'Hey, look at me,' he urged quietly.

Skye tore her face away from his chest, but TJ saw that it cost her by the pretty blush flushing her cheeks.

'Why are you hiding?'

'I don't want to talk about my inexperience right now.'

He thought he might understand that. But he tried to eradicate that embarrassment with a truth of his own. 'Do you know what it does to me – knowing that I'm the only one who's been here?' He kissed her deeply as he ran his hand down her bare skin. 'And here.' Raising his fingers, he stroked through her, his movements languid. 'Here,' he said and slipped a single finger inside her as he'd done earlier.

Skye was tight, but she was so wet that, even as her body cinched around him, he moved inside of her easily.

Her breath hitched.

'Talk to me.'

'I can't think when you do that,' she argued, and instead of pulling back, she pressed her hips forward – and she whispered, 'More.'

TJ slid a second finger inside of her and gently pushed them deep. He watched as they sank to the knuckles, murmured, 'Look at your pretty pussy taking me,' through the haze of lust narrowing his vision.

Skye squirmed against the new pressure – or maybe, the pleasure. 'More,' she demanded again, and when she raised her head and looked him straight in the eye, he slipped his fingers out of her and into his mouth, sucked them deep, cleaning her off of him.

Skye visibly trembled. The words 'Holy crap' fell from her lips.

The words, the surrender in her tone, snapped something in him. TJ couldn't wait any longer. He grabbed a pillow from the top of the bed, tapped her thigh. 'Lift for me.'

When she did, he slipped the pillow under her, raising her hips. He knelt between her open legs, and even though it was physically painful to tear his gaze away from her pink, wet pussy, he did. He met those blue eyes, so big and concerned, stroked her thighs as he said, 'Talk to me, okay?'

Skye nodded. She tugged her bottom lip between her teeth and bit down, clearly anxious. But her eyes dropped to watch.

TJ gripped her hips, one in each hand, and slowly guided his aching dick into her. He inched inside of her slowly, but because she had said she wanted fast, as soon as he was comfortably positioned, he plunged.

He took her in one thrust, burying himself balls-deep in her silky grip.

Skye gasped.

TJ stopped. He didn't dare move, only instructed, 'Relax. Breathe.'

Skye took a comically big breath. She squirmed, so that TJ had to grip her hips tighter and close his eyes as he tried to hold on.

Slowly, she relaxed. He felt her body give. Her hips in his hands dropped. Her small body's tight grip on his cock eased. She exhaled again. 'I'm fine.'

He looked down to where they were joined, felt a surge of possessiveness overcome him. Her trust in him shattered him, and wanting to give her more, he found her clit with his thumb and slowly stroked whisper-light circles over her, building that fire back to blazing.

When she started panting in time with the rising waves, when her body pulsed around him in preparation, he began to move, slowly at first, just the tiniest of thrusts.

Skye's nipples were peaked, her body arched. TJ thought she might have been the most beautiful woman he'd ever seen, and in the back of his mind, he worried how quickly they had gotten here.

Even then, he held his urge to fuck her senseless in check, too afraid he might hurt her if he really unleashed. The restraint was so painful to exercise that sweat gathered on his brow.

But then Skye opened her eyes and saw his face, and she said, 'More.'

He pulled out, gently slid back into her.

Her eyes darkened. 'Stop holding back, TJ.'

TJ cursed. But he said, 'Yes, ma'am.' And withdrew to the tip before slamming back into her.

Skye reached both arms behind her and splayed her hands on

the headboard, bracing herself. 'Yes,' she whispered. 'Like that.'

'You want it rough, wild girl?'

'So bad.'

'Fuck.' He lost it. The animal within him, the one he'd caged for fear of scaring her, broke free to join hers.

He took her roughly. The sound of their flesh meeting slapped through the room.

Skye writhed in his hands. Her body tightened around him and had his vision blackening around the edges. 'TJ . . .'

'I'm right there with you. Let go.'

She came on a long moan, her body shuddering around him, her back arched, her tits pressed forward prettily.

TJ didn't hold on.

He couldn't.

The moment her body calmed, he pressed into her, sinking deep, and followed her over the edge, before collapsing onto the bed facedown next to her.

As the rush from her orgasm faded, Skye became self-conscious. TJ had given her everything – kindness, intimacy, and *two* orgasms – and she hadn't done anything, hadn't done much except lie there and be taken. Knowing that had her promising, 'I'll be better at it next time.'

On the bed next to her, TJ turned his head. His green eyes studied her face in confusion, almost as if he was trying to figure out something particularly complex. 'I'm not going to get mad,' he said quietly, almost to himself, 'but I am going to ask what you mean by that?'

'I didn't do anything. I didn't—'

'It doesn't work like that. It's not a one-for-one system. It's . . .' He sighed and pushed off the bed.

For a moment, Skye thought she'd angered him. She even

opened her mouth to apologize. But TJ stripped the condom and walked into the bathroom to dispose of it. When he came back, he climbed onto the bed completely naked and with no self-consciousness. He pulled the covers back, grunted exaggeratedly as he lifted her hips to roll the comforter out from beneath her.

Skye smiled, but then he fluffed her pillows and dragged her up the bed to prop her against them. He lifted the comforter over her boobs, tucked it around her sides, and instead of getting in next to her, lay in her lap over the covers, his head resting on her thighs, his lean, muscular body splayed out for her.

The intimacy of his every gesture clogged her throat. Skye raised one unsteady hand to his head, ran her fingers lightly over his short hair, so that it prickled her skin.

TJ grunted and pressed his head more firmly into her hand.

They stayed like that for minutes, not talking, just basking. Being.

'It's not an exchange,' he said finally. 'It's a give and take, sure, but not act for act. Nothing you could do to me could be sexier than the way you ride my mouth when you're close to coming. I'd rather that than a hand job or a blow job any day.' He sighed. 'I'm not explaining this well. But I want you to know: I've been with dozens of women. Experienced women. Beautiful women—'

'Okay,' she drawled.

TJ's smile curved against her thigh over the blankets. 'This was different for me.'

Skye was both immensely pleased and embarrassed at the same time. 'You don't have to give me words—'

'I do. Absolutely,' he argued. And then he said those two that terrified her so much. 'It matters.'

'TJ, I can't—'

'I'm not asking you for anything,' he assured her, soothing. 'But I am telling you because words are important. I don't want you to think the first guy you slept with did it because you were available and willing.' He flipped over, rested his back against the headboard, and when she didn't move, he reached for her, tugged her into his arms. '*You* matter,' he said, and he kissed her on the top of the head.

Skye nestled in, snuggling deeper into the blankets, deeper into his arms. She was too afraid to give him any more of herself, too afraid to give him all the words sitting on her tongue, unspoken. Words like, *I need you*, *Thank you*, and *I don't think there will ever be anyone quite like you.*

The part of her that had been so routinely torn down couldn't bear to trust another, a man, so soon. She second-guessed all those new feelings, told herself she was just infatuated – and worse, grateful. She was terrified that if she said those things to him, he would freeze up and try to let her down easy.

So, she didn't.

But she did relax against him, content to laze with *her lover*. The thought made her smile, and when TJ caught it, he asked, 'What?'

Skye said, 'I have a lover.' And she said it proudly.

'Damn right you do.' He tugged the covers off her breasts, sucked one hard nipple into his mouth, so that she sighed and raised her hands to hold his head close.

TJ pulled back almost as soon as her body responded.

'Hey!' Skye pouted.

'Brakes on, pretty girl.'

'Why?'

'I still have to take you on a date.' He looked at the clock on the side of the bed. 'We missed our dinner reservation, but we could still hit up a bar. I'm not drinking for tomorrow, but I can look after you while you do.'

She shook her head.

'No?' he asked. 'We could—'

'I want to stay here.' As true as the words were, she also knew that, had she not been there, he would have been home preparing, resting for his ride.

'You sure?'

'Yes. We can order room service, watch a movie, and actually get some sleep.'

'You want to stay overnight – with me?' he asked.

'Oh . . .' Skye flushed. 'Is that not what you had in mind?'

'I'd hoped. But you realize, if we don't go home, my parents are going to know . . .'

She wondered if that embarrassed him, asked, 'Does that bother you?'

'Not at all. You?'

She thought about it, and although she worried that Janey wouldn't be happy about her new association with TJ, she had to admit, 'A little. I don't want to hurt your mom. But I also really want to stay.'

'Hurt her?'

'She warned you away from me.'

'Um, no. Or yes, I guess. But she most certainly was looking out for *you*, not me.'

Unsure of what to say to that, Skye just said, 'Okay. Let's stay.'

His green eyes lit with a sincere smile. 'That's settled then. I'll let them know we won't be home. In the meantime . . .' He got up and walked through to the lounge, came back with the room service menu. 'Why don't you order? Then we can have a shower while we wait?'

Skye moved to grab the menu, winced as her body, tender and sore, rebelled at just that small shift.

TJ saw it. 'How bad?'

Six, she thought. But said, 'A four maybe,' because she didn't want to waste the time she had left with him.

'Little liar.' He took her mouth in a quick kiss. 'I'll run a bath instead.'

He walked away, and Skye couldn't help but watch him, his

muscular ass and thighs rippling as he strutted away, the muscles in his broad back flexing easily beneath his golden skin.

'Could you order me a burger?' He turned, caught her looking. 'You like what you see?' he asked with an arrogant smirk.

Skye couldn't even deny it. 'You know I do.'

TJ's grin was wicked, his green eyes devilish. 'Same goes, pretty girl.' He took a step towards her, stopped, shook his head. 'No. Bath first,' he said to himself. And when Skye laughed, he pointed at her, accused, 'You're trouble,' before walking away.

Seconds later, she heard the water run as he filled the tub. Skye perused the menu. She chose linguini for herself and then called room service and ordered.

By the time she'd hung up, TJ was back, a single flute of champagne in hand. He passed it to her and, the moment she took it, he reached forward and scooped her out of the bed and into his arms. Skye yelped and tried to balance the flute to stop from spilling on the lush carpet beneath them.

'I have legs, you know,' she drawled, but only because she hated to admit how much she liked being carried by him. It was new and sweet and exciting. It was an intimacy she would never have allowed another man, if only because it left her completely vulnerable.

TJ just grinned. 'You have great legs. But I like the way we fit.' He carried her into the bathroom, set her on her feet by the tub, and gently unfurled her fingers from the glass of champagne so she could climb into the hot water.

Skye sighed as the heat seeped into her sore muscles. Her heart skipped a beat when TJ didn't leave her but slid in behind her. He passed her the champagne again, stretched his long legs on either side of her and pulled her back into his chest. He tormented her, his fingers trailing drops of water down her arm and then her chest to her breast. He circled her nipples, first one and then the other, with his middle finger.

Skye relaxed back against him. 'What's your usual routine the night before a ride?'

'Rest. If there's a gym near where I'm staying, I'll go in, maybe stretch and foam roll, sauna if there is one. Otherwise, I try to stretch in the hotel room.'

'You stay in hotels?'

'Yeah. Not ones as nice as this usually. But I'm too old to rough it.' When she snorted, he bit her shoulder gently. 'I've got over a decade on you, and most of it rife with bull-riding accidents.'

'Your right hip?' she asked because she'd seen him favouring it.

'My right hip. Both shoulders. Right wrist. Back. Neck. Knees. Right ankle and foot. My body has some miles on it.' He wrapped both arms around her. 'Thank God my credit card does too.'

'Do you get nervous – when you ride?'

'Sure. Every time. But as soon as I'm in the chute and sitting on that bull, nothing else exists. Just me and him. There's a lifetime in those eight seconds. Every time. When the buzzer sounds, it's like everything restarts.' His laugh echoed through his chest and into her back. 'And then I have to dismount without dying, which is sometimes scarier than riding the bull in the first place.'

'I've watched the bull riding at a few smaller rodeos.' She knew the basic rules too, but, just then, with TJ's big body wrapped around her, she couldn't help but tease. 'You just hold on for eight seconds, right?'

TJ bit her neck gently. 'Rude.'

Skye craned her head back to laugh up at him. 'I'm just kidding. I know there's a lot more to it.'

'There is. And it's not just riding. It's travelling – which is exhausting. Being away from home, not being able to work a regular job, having to sleep in a strange bed most nights of the year – although that gets easier over time. It's tough,' he ceded. 'And that's if you're one of the rare people who can make enough money a year doing it. And if you don't have anyone waiting for you at home.'

Skye heard the cautiousness in his tone. 'Don't worry, Casanova. I know what we're doing here.'

He frowned. 'You see, when you say it like that, I really don't think you do.'

'What's that supposed to mean?'

'I'm not going to stop you from going – because I understand why you need to. But,' he said cautiously, 'maybe we could meet up when we can both get time off?' Leaning forward, he kissed her gently. 'You should think about that.'

Skye was so shocked, so panicked, that she didn't – *couldn't* – reply. She might have been inexperienced, but she understood how dating worked. In theory. You went out. If you liked each other, you kept seeing one another, and then you either called it off when things fizzled out or took things further when they didn't.

She just hadn't expected that TJ would want to date her – or even, she could admit to herself, want to stay in touch once they parted ways after the weekend.

Life had taught her several hard truths, including that it was best not to rely on anyone but yourself. You could never truly know what happened behind closed doors or inside another person's mind. And men, in general, were not to be trusted.

'Why does that scare you so much?' he asked gently.

'I don't know. You could be with anyone,' she pointed out. 'But I also think it's because I don't know what I'm doing. And not just with you. With *my life*.' She chuckled, but it sounded a little panicked even to her own ears. 'TJ, I have five thousand dollars to my name. No home. No job. And a twelve-hundred-pound animal I have to look after. I'm . . . fucking terrified,' she admitted, perhaps for the first time. And in admitting it, decided, 'I have to build a life I'm proud of, and I can't do that chasing a guy who things may or may not work out with. I have to do it *for me*.'

'I know,' he said simply. 'But, maybe, we can still meet up when our schedules allow – for me?'

Chapter 14

At three o'clock the next day, TJ hiked his gear bag over his shoulder and stepped out of the farmhouse. It was a good day. He'd spent the night with a beautiful woman, one who made his heart pound and his blood swim. The weather was clear and bright. He felt well rested and ready. Overall, the universe seemed to be on his side.

His dad sat on the porch, a Coke in one hand, a tattered Stephen King novel in the other, his reading glasses falling down his nose. He looked up when the front door slammed shut. 'You heading out?'

TJ internally sighed. But he put his bag on the floor.

Despite his father's nonchalance, a farmer sitting on the porch mid-afternoon meant one thing: his dad had meant to be there. And judging by the pointedly roundabout way he stalled, he wanted to bring up something specific. 'Yeah. Mom said she'd bring Skye over later.' His eyes dropped pointedly to the soda 'You sneak that?'

'Don't tell her.'

His dad's refusal to admit that his mother knew everything he did was one of life's great mysteries. 'What was it you wanted to say, Dad?'

He sighed heavily. 'That obvious?'

'It's three p.m.,' TJ pointed out. 'We both know you have a zillion things to do.'

'I'm gonna get to the point then.'

'Please.'

'Your mother's worried.'

TJ knew, instantly and without doubt, what his mother was worried about. But, by God, he'd make his father say it. 'About?'

His dad sighed. 'You and Skye.'

'Why the interest in my sex life now?' TJ demanded hotly, irritated. 'Jesus Christ, I'm thirty-three years old.'

'It's not you she's worried about.' His dad nodded to the chair closest to TJ. 'Sit down.'

As frustrated as he was, TJ sat. His father was one of two people in the world he respected absolutely, second only to his mom. But he'd have his say too. 'Why is everyone treating Skye like she's made of glass? She doesn't deserve that. She's fucking fierce.'

'Do you remember that stray dog we picked up off the side of the road when you were about ten?'

TJ settled in for the story, knowing that there would be no escaping it. 'Of course.' The dog – a mutt of indiscriminate lineage – had been abandoned on the side of the road, probably left to die when his owner realized he'd taken the beatings and routine starving too far to escape a vet's notice.

'The poor thing was bone thin, covered with mange, and had open wounds over most of her body,' his dad said patiently. 'And despite how weak she was, how tired, she fought us the entire way to the vet, snapping and snarling and trying to take a bite out of us every time we tried to get close.'

'I remember. When we brought her home, Mom cried.'

What he didn't say, what they both remembered, was that his mom had then spent the better part of two months loving that dog, showing her that not all humans were bad. Janey had called her Ladybug, but it hadn't mattered how much she had loved her – the dog had been too wary of TJ and his sister to keep permanently. Eventually, they'd rehomed her to some friends of theirs who didn't have kids.

'Sometimes,' his dad said patiently, 'being *fucking fierce* is not resilience or strength of will. Sometimes, it is uncontainable fear leaving the body.'

'I understand that,' TJ argued. 'I do. But both can be true. I know Skye's afraid. Because unlike you and Mom, *I've* talked to her about it. She doesn't want or need to be babied because bad things have happened to her. She wants – *needs* – to be treated like someone who has fought her way out and survived. Like someone who is strong and in control and capable. Because she is.'

His dad used his own words against him. 'Both can be true.'

'I would never hurt her.' It had to be said. Because their concern chaffed.

'I can see that. And in my defence, I told your mom this girl was different.' Ryan put the paperback down on the table. 'But she worries; it's her nature.'

TJ kicked out his feet and linked both hands behind his hat, defeated. Agreeing with his dad's observation felt like too much, too soon. So, he gave an easy truth: 'I feel like I knew everything about women just a few days ago,' he said, and ignored his dad's amused snort. 'But now, suddenly, the rules have changed, and I don't know a damn thing. But for the first time, I *want* to. I want to know everything about Skye. And, worse, I want her to know everything about me. Which is ridiculous,' he added and glared up at the ceiling fan. 'I've known her three days.'

'I knew I was going to marry your mom the first time I saw her.'

'So, you've said,' TJ drawled. But only because talk of marriage made him sweat.

'Well, I don't want to nag. But I promised your mom I'd say something, so this is it: be careful with that girl.'

'I will.'

'Okay then.' Ryan tipped his head, dismissing him. 'See you on the dirt.'

'Yeah.'

'Give 'em hell.'

'I always do,' TJ replied as he stood.

But as he walked away, his dad called him back. 'Hey, TJ!'

TJ braced, half expecting another lecture. 'Yeah?'

'I'm really proud of you.'

TJ relaxed. He waved one last time before walking to his truck.

But as he drove, he mulled over what his father had said – and he second-guessed himself.

Skye was fierce. And she absolutely deserved to be treated as such. But his dad hadn't been wrong either. Those telltale signs of fear were still there. Even just the way she watched everyone, as if she needed to be able to defend herself or bolt at any minute, reminded him of what she'd been through. But how was she supposed to heal if nobody let her get used to those little everyday things?

It bothered him. So much so that, when he pulled into the WestWorld venue and navigated his truck to the parking lot, he was lost in his thoughts. Distracted.

It was only when he got out and heaved his gear bag over his shoulder that he remembered where he was and, more importantly, why he was there.

It took effort, but TJ pushed Skye to the back of his mind. Distraction was a dangerous game in bull riding.

Even as he tried to calm his mind, those familiar nerves kicked in. But TJ didn't let them take over. He slipped his AirPods out of his pocket, put them into his ears. He turned on noise cancelling, to avoid outside distraction, and hit play on his Post Malone playlist as he walked towards the Equidome.

He had a few hours to relax and prepare. He'd visit the sports medicine folks in their mobile unit and have his bad hip massaged and his shoulders taped, maybe shit talk with the others in the back while he coated his bull rope with his personal rosin, glycerine, and oil mix.

And then he'd leave it all on the dirt.

TJ was walking through the barn that had doubled as last year's locker room when he saw a group of guys up ahead. They were unloading their gear bags and, even though he had his earbuds in, he didn't have to hear them to know they were talking shit.

'Boys,' he said as he dropped his bag on the floor and popped out a single earbud.

'Triple J!' A fellow bull rider, Dale Smith, whooped. At twenty, Dale had years of riding still ahead of him. He was a good rider, a little cocky. But TJ figured they all were; they had to be. 'Ready to get your ass handed to ya, old man?'

'Why? Is Da Silva here?' TJ mocked.

The others sniggered.

One of the rodeo clowns, Chad Jameson, was sitting on a rickety chair and looking in a small mirror while he slathered his face in white paint. 'Da Silva broke his hip in Milwaukee last week. He's out.'

TJ's head snapped up. 'Shit, really?'

'Oh, yeah.'

'Which bull?'

'The brindle motherfucker with one horn.'

'Freight Train,' one of the pickup men supplied. 'Da Silva was in the well. Lost his balance, but his hand got stuck in the bull rope. Bull's hind legs caught him, dragged him under. Son of a bitch is lucky he only broke a hip. I for sure thought that arm was gonna come off.'

'Fuck.'

They all nodded.

'You know Da Silva, though. He fucking belly-crawled away while the guys distracted the bull. Stood up, limped off the dirt on one leg.' Chad mimicked dragging his leg behind him, making the others laugh, despite the morbid topic of conversation.

Ride through the pain was a sacred rule of bull riding. Guys rode injured all the time. TJ himself had ridden with a broken collarbone, fractured ribs; once he'd had to cut his boot open to get a swollen foot in before a ride. He'd taped the boot shut again, but the ride had been excruciating, and when he'd dismounted, the jump to the ground had made the injury worse. It had taken two surgeries to fix the damage, and the nerves in the bottom of his foot still burned.

Unlike Dale, after more than a decade of bull riding, at the age of thirty-three, TJ understood that his days on the pro circuit were numbered, if only because his body wouldn't keep up for much longer.

Still, he'd give 'em hell while he could.

He listened to the conversation with one ear as he tied off his bull rope and rosined it. So, he heard when a loud wolf whistle pierced the conversation, followed by a familiar voice. 'TJ, that pretty little thing from the hotel gonna be here tonight?'

He didn't even look up at Matthew Savage, just said, 'Yup.'

'Think she'll wanna try out the broncs for a change of pace?'

TJ's blood heated. He felt the flush of it sear his veins. But knowing that Matthew was just giving him shit, he forced himself to remain calm. 'Probably not. She's not a buckle bunny.'

Dale, having overheard the conversation, asked, 'So, what? You got a girl now?' He looked almost disappointed, as only a twenty-year-old could, as if his personal hero had let him down.

TJ couldn't blame him. While some of the guys had girlfriends and even wives, most of them were single – and they all took full advantage of their unattached status. TJ included. 'Nah. She's passing through. But I'm gonna try to fly out and visit her when I can. This one's a keeper, man.'

'She hot?' Dale asked.

'Fucking beautiful,' TJ replied.

But Dale, having obviously lost trust in TJ's sanity, looked to Matthew for confirmation.

'Oh, dude. Cadillac,' Matthew affirmed.

TJ looked up at Matthew, met laughing brown eyes. 'Watch yourself, Savage.'

Matthew grinned. 'You worried she might choose me?'

'No.' TJ lowered his voice, so that only Matthew could hear him. 'Look, she's been through shit, man. Don't box her in. If you want to shoot your shot, be my guest. She can handle herself. But be nice. And don't corner her.'

Matthew's eyes darkened – but not, TJ was surprised to see, with anger at being warned off, only concern. 'I didn't mean anything by it.' He caught himself, shot TJ one last wink and said, 'She is smoking hot, though.'

TJ couldn't even be mad. He just sighed and ended the conversation with, 'Agreed.'

Skye arrived with TJ's parents an hour before his ride and joined the throngs of people moving en masse in and out of the Equidome.

Over the past few months, she'd mostly followed smaller barrel races, events where the stands were spotted with family members and riders waiting their turn to race and everyone was dressed in work-washed denim and scarred boots. The fanciest people at those races had been the racers themselves, some of whom chose sparkly shirts in bright colours or hats that matched their horses' polo wraps and boots. The few rodeos she had been to had been in small towns where everyone knew everyone and came straight from work. Still, she had been expecting the dress code for a ticketed event to be closer to what she'd seen of the NFR on social media, so it was a shock for her to see more people dressed like her, in their faded denim and plaid shirts, than girls dressed to the nines.

For every girl dressed in a tiny skirt, dress, or jumpsuit, there were three cowgirls. The only commonality between all of them was the cowgirl boots on their feet, which seemed to come in every style and colour.

'I was expecting it to be flashier,' she said to Janey.

Janey, dressed in jeans and a long-sleeved shirt tucked in at the waistband, explained, 'The stadium rodeos are different. The NFR and the American are more of a fashion show than a rodeo these days, but I can't begrudge that too much considering how much popularity – and funding – they've brought to the sport. But this one, we call, "The West's Most Western Rodeo". A lot of these folks are local.'

Skye's Wrangler jeans and T-shirt, both of which she'd picked up at Tractor Supply ages ago, were faded from wear. Her Ariat boots were scuffed from everyday use. She fit right in.

'I didn't know that.'

'We tend to like it that way. But everyone's welcome so long as they're respectful of what it is we do here.' Janey leaned close. She nodded subtly towards a girl dressed in a microscopic skirt and tall, white cowgirl boots. The girl was beautiful – and the group of cowboys subtly nudging one another to point her out clearly thought so too.

'Those are really nice boots,' Skye commented. But as she watched the girl saunter off, she had the vague and disconcerting thought that she was probably closer to what TJ was used to – women who looked like *that*. Women who knew what the fuck they were doing.

Janey just laughed and gave Skye's hand a quick squeeze. 'Come on. Our seats are right up front.'

They picked their way through the blue plastic seats until they found theirs, which were right up against the rail. When Janey and Skye sat down, Ryan kept standing. 'I'm gonna go see TJ before he rides.'

Janey smiled at him, and although she couldn't decode the message that passed between them, Skye knew they communicated something. Ryan reached for Janey's hand, kissed the back of it.

Before he left, she said, 'Pick up some beers on your way back.'

'Yup.'

The moment he disappeared into the crowd, Janey leaned back in her chair. 'He worries as much as I do. Sometimes, seeing TJ before a ride, seeing how relaxed and confident he is, helps.'

'I can't imagine,' Skye said. And it was true. She'd only just met TJ, and knowing what he was about to do had a fist of anxiety lodged in her stomach. She couldn't begin to conceptualize what it must be like to watch your child, someone you'd raised and nurtured, cling to the back of a bucking bull.

As they waited for the bull riding, which was the last event, Skye and Janey watched the rodeo. They talked easily, as if they'd known each other for years, and when Ryan came back, three beers triangulated in his hands, he passed them one each and then slotted into the conversation without pause. 'TJ drew Cuddles.'

Janey sighed. 'He's a devil of a bull.'

'I'm sorry, did you say *Cuddles*?'

Ryan grinned. 'Yeah. Most of the time, the bulls are given the tough names. Things like Man Hater, Ridin' Salty, and Buck Nasty.' He listed off a few names that even Skye had heard of. 'But the Morris Family like to have a laugh, so theirs are always named things like Cuddles and Fluffy.'

'Remember that white Brahman-Hereford cross?' Janey asked.

'Marshmallow,' Ryan supplied.

Skye watched in fascination as the rodeo progressed like a well-oiled machine. They'd missed the bronc riding and steer wrestling but got to watch the team ropers, tie-down ropers, and barrel racers. After every five barrel races, the dirt was dragged by three men on tractors, working together seamlessly. There were no pauses, no breaks in the schedule, just one event after another.

Skye slowly relaxed. She got into the spirit of things and clapped and cheered for the athletes. But just when she'd calmed enough to start enjoying herself, the announcer's voice boomed, 'All right folks, next up we have the bull riding. For those of you who aren't familiar with the sport, it's pretty simple: hold on for eight seconds, until the buzzer sounds! And if you're from Scottsdale, we have our very own Jesse James Jones competing tonight. You heard me: Triple J himself, Scottsdale's four-million-dollar bull rider and PBR World Finals qualifier, is here. And he is ready to give y'all a show!'

The crowd roared.

Janey raised two fingers to her mouth and released a shrill whistle that had Skye jumping in her seat.

On her other side, Ryan silently leaned forward and rested both elbows on his thighs as he watched the arena like a hawk.

Skye watched in fascination as the first rider, a kid called Dale Smith, lowered himself down onto a bull called Lucky Strike. Their seats were close enough to the sand that she could make out the rider as he set up, the bull thrashing beneath him in the chute.

There was a moment of stillness, where both rider and bull paused.

The rider nodded.

The chute opened. And Lucky Strike did not hesitate. He came out forelegs first, head down, his powerful hindquarters up.

Dale held on as the bull bucked, each kick out seemingly more frenzied than the last, each twist and spin rag-dolling him.

The buzzer sounded.

Skye released her breath in one whoosh of air as Dale freed himself and then fell to the ground and landed on his knees. It took a second for the bull to realize the rider was off his back, but the moment he did, he turned – looking, Skye thought, like he wanted revenge.

'See, now the bullfighters step in to distract the bull,' Janey said, right as a bullfighter in clown makeup slapped Lucky Strike on the rump, calling the bull's attention back to him and away from Dale as he hurriedly got to his feet and ran for the piped corral fence.

'I don't know who's crazier,' Skye commented as the bullfighters formed a circle around the bull and took turns dodging its horns while they pushed him back towards the pen's gate.

'Baby, let me tell you something: you gotta have a few screws loose to get to this level in any rodeo sport.'

Skye did not disagree. And as she watched the first three bull riders, two of whom didn't make the required eight seconds, she thought that maybe they had more than just a few screws loose.

And then it was TJ's turn.

Crazy or not, he was undeniably sexy in his black leather chaps, vest, and hat.

She held her breath as he lowered down onto Cuddles's back. On one side of her, Ryan was eerily silent. On the other, Janey unconsciously reached out to take Skye's hand in a death grip, her whispered 'Here we go' full of dread.

'Mother' by Danzig started blaring over the speakers.

Skye squeezed Janey's hand back, but she couldn't speak. Couldn't look away as TJ leaned forward, laced his free arm on the side of the chute, and then nodded.

Cuddles came out of the chute like a bullet, bucking and spinning as if the devil were on his heels – or maybe on his back. He jumped mid-kick, so that all four feet were off the ground.

Ryan inhaled sharply through his teeth.

TJ rode, his body moving fluidly despite the turbulent ride, his free arm following in the wake of his body's movements.

'Come on, TJ,' Ryan murmured.

Everything passed in slow motion; every tick of the clock was an eternity. Skye's lungs burned as her trapped breath heated and expanded. She vaguely thought she might throw up.

At one point, with only two seconds left on the clock, TJ slipped forward. For a single blip in time, it looked as if he was going to fall.

It took everything within Skye not to cover her eyes like a child watching a horror movie she wasn't supposed to. *Please, God.*

But TJ righted himself at the last moment.

The buzzer sounded.

Skye's heart started beating again.

TJ released his hand from the bull rope and dropped onto his feet as the crowd went wild.

'A beautiful ride from Triple J and Cuddles,' the announcer stated. 'And it looks like the judges agree! That's a 90.50 score for Jesse James Jones, which puts him in the lead for tonight's rides!'

Skye and Janey expelled relieved breaths at the same time and then looked at each other and grinned.

When Skye turned back to the arena, TJ wasn't pumping the crowd or walking back towards the gate. He was standing in the dirt, his grin wide and cheeky – and he was looking right at her.

Chapter 15

By the time TJ got home, it was nearing midnight. He dumped his bag by the front door, kicked off his dirty boots and went looking for Skye.

Instead, he found his parents at the kitchen table, a glass of wine in front of each of them, playing Go Fish. He wasn't surprised; they always waited up for him after a rodeo when he was home or waited up for his call when he was on the road.

His dad groaned as he pushed to his feet. He pulled TJ in for a rough hug, said, 'Good ride today.'

'I almost kissed the bull there for a second.'

'Almost. But you caught yourself.' With one last pat on the shoulder, Ryan moved past him for the stairs and his bed.

When they were alone, his mom looked up at him, her eyes full of concern. 'How do you feel?'

Everything hurt. His bad hip ached, sending a slow burn of sciatica down his right glute and quad. His shoulder muscles were tired and aching. He had a serious case of whiplash. So, all in all, he'd come away lucky. 'Like a million bucks,' he replied honestly. Because in bull riding, it could always be worse – and often was.

'Make sure you head in early tomorrow to see the sports med team.'

'Guaranteed.'

'All right.' She patted his cheek, said, 'We're gonna get some sleep. Skye went out to the barn a while back. Think she was a little shaken up.'

'Why?' he asked immediately. 'What happened?'

She tilted her head, very near condescendingly. 'She watched you ride a bull.'

'She's watched bull riding before,' he argued.

Janey just shook her head and muttered, 'Men,' as she walked past him.

TJ didn't wait. He put his boots and jacket back on and hurried out to the barn to find her.

Skye didn't hear him come in, but he saw her immediately. She was standing next to Smokey as she brushed the horse, her short blonde hair gleaming in the dim barn light. She was singing, the lyrics of Luke Combs's 'She got the Best of Me', sweet and smooth.

TJ didn't dare move, just stood there and watched her as that feeling overcame him, the one he'd tried to explain to his dad earlier, that one that left him drowning in the immensity of him and Skye, *together*.

It was only when she sensed him and spun around, her eyes wide with fear, that he walked forward, both palms up. 'Sorry, didn't mean to scare you.'

She visibly relaxed, her stiff shoulders dropping, her smile blooming. To his utter surprise – and delight – she murmured, 'TJ,' and then let herself out of the stall and ran to him.

She jumped into his arms.

He caught her. Of course, he caught her. She wrapped her legs around his waist and squeezed. And because that feeling was flowing over, he laughed and spun her around.

'Now that's a welcome home,' he said the moment they came to a stop.

Skye sighed. She buried her face against his neck, hiding her embarrassment from him. 'You were amazing. Insane,' she added, and *finally* gave him those big blue eyes. 'But amazing. When you tipped forward, I for sure thought you were going to fall, and then . . .' She puffed air out of her cheeks, shook her head. 'You were amazing,' she repeated. 'Truly.'

Unable to resist, TJ rubbed his lips gently over hers, and when she sighed open, welcoming him, he slipped inside.

Her taste, her smell, her feel, the way she gushed about his ride . . . Everything about her overwhelmed him. He wanted to bury himself in her, almost as much as he wanted to just keep holding her. Undone by the immensity of feeling, by the newness of it, he pulled back. 'I'm really glad you were there to watch me today, Skye. It was . . .' He thought about how to describe it, but when nothing sufficient came, settled on, 'New. It was new,' he repeated. 'But it meant a lot.'

She braced. He felt her entire body go brittle in his arms. He tried not to internalize it, tried to soothe her with, 'Stop worrying so much.'

'I'm trying not to,' she said and unhooked her legs to drop back down to the floor. She paced away, clearly frustrated. 'I just . . . I don't know what to do. You're the first, TJ.' She spun around to face him. 'And I'm trying to make sense of it, trying to find where my infatuation with you ends and all those other feelings begin.'

'That makes two of us,' he said simply.

'Really?'

'What, you think just because I have more experience than you, I'm incapable of being out of my depth?'

'Yes,' she replied matter-of-factly.

TJ nearly laughed. If she knew how out of his depth he really was with her, she'd probably laugh too. Or run fast in the other direction.

Skye caught the glint of it that he didn't manage to hide in time. 'It's not funny.'

'It's a little funny,' he corrected.

'How?'

'Well, here I am thinking: *I've never felt this way about a beautiful woman before. She must be special.* And there you are thinking: *I've never felt this way about a hunky man before. I must be out of my mind,*' he teased.

'Doesn't it worry you?'

TJ sobered. 'Well, sure,' he admitted. 'But if we meet up when we can, we'll have time to figure it out.'

Because she had taken to pacing again, he walked to her, took her by the hand and spun her so that she tripped into his arms. 'Is that not what you want?'

'It is,' she insisted. 'That's why I'm worried.'

TJ settled. Just hearing that they both wanted more was enough to calm him. 'At some point, you're going to have to start trusting people. Start with me. Trust *me*, Skye. I won't let you down.'

'What if it doesn't work out?' she asked.

TJ didn't say *What if it does?* He was tempted, but Skye was too used to experiencing the worst of people to believe it. 'If at any point it's not working, we'll be honest with one another. It'll suck. And then we'll move on.' He sighed dramatically. 'I'll retire and marry an uber-rich Victoria's Secret model for her impressive . . . portfolio. You'll end up falling in love with a balding plumber from one of the I states. But you'll probably be happier than me in the long run. That's how it works.'

'Stop trying to make me laugh,' she demanded. But she'd lost that worry already. TJ could see it in the way her mouth tipped up and her eyes shifted from a deep, stormy blue-back to that familiar sea-ice that could sink an unsuspecting man.

His hands slid down her body to grip her ass. He nipped playfully at her bottom lip, said, 'How about I make you moan instead?'

He'd been playing, so he almost tripped and took them both down when she looked over her shoulder at the stalls and asked, '*Here?*'

It wasn't the single word that took him by surprise; it was

the sexy, breathy tone she'd said it in, as if the thought of them having sex in the barn turned her on.

'Would you like that?' he asked quietly.

She tugged at her lip in that telltale anxious habit. But she didn't reply, only blushed prettily and dropped her gaze, suddenly shy.

'Hey.' He tipped her chin. 'Talk to me.'

She didn't. Or, maybe, couldn't.

In that moment, TJ was glaringly aware of the fact that the closer they got, the more vulnerable and shy she seemed. As if, the more she trusted him, the more that wildness in her softened, but in it softening, her defences fell and all those fears of hers started coming to the surface. It was the reminder he needed to go slow, to let her experience all those firsts in safety rather than the rush of greed that would have been so much easier.

So, he didn't take her in the barn, although he desperately wanted to. He turned and gave her his back. 'Hop on; I'll give you a ride to the house.'

Skye affected superiority. 'Really?'

TJ slanted her a grin over his shoulder. 'Come on, you know you want to.'

She rolled her eyes, but after another three seconds, she gave in. She jumped on his back and laughed when he hooked his arms beneath her thighs. She roped her arms around his neck, and when he stepped back into the dark night and started for the farmhouse, she brought her lips to his ear and she set his heart to racing when she said, 'You're dangerously close to becoming my favourite person in the world, Jesse Jones.'

They locked themselves in the bathroom by mutual agreement and for one reason only: it was the room furthest away from where TJ's parents slept, and the running water would lend them soundproofing.

'You're the first girl I've ever had sex with in my parents' house,' TJ told her as he stripped his long-sleeved black shirt with his sponsors' logos printed on the sleeves.

'Don't talk about it; you're going to freak me out,' Skye insisted as she yanked off her boots. It didn't matter that his parents knew they were sleeping together; it was still weird. If Skye had had foresight on her side, she would have realized that and stuck with the barn. But now that they were here, she was too desperate for him, too greedy for all the things he could do to her.

Dressed in only his jeans, his feet bare, TJ reached into the shower and turned the water on. As they waited for it to heat, he leaned against the sink and tugged her between his knees using her belt loops.

Skye went willingly, but her acquiescence didn't eradicate all her nerves. They were there, dancing in her stomach, and needing something to distract herself with, she ran her hands over his head, smiled when he groaned and murmured, 'I love that you do that.'

'I like the way it feels against my hands.'

'I like the way *you* feel against my hands,' he countered, making her roll her eyes playfully.

TJ grabbed the hem of her shirt, but he waited for her to nod before lifting it up and over her head. He threw it on the floor next to his, and right before he brushed those big, callused palms down her sides, Skye had the thought that their laundry co-mingling on the bathroom floor was very domestic – intimately so.

But then TJ leaned forward and placed a single kiss on her forehead, and all coherent thought fled. Her body took over. Her heart quickened in her chest, heating her blood so that her skin flushed. Pressure collected between her thighs, and wanting to hurry, chasing the first rise, Skye lifted her sports bra up and off.

There was no self-consciousness now, just the desperate need to be satiated.

And TJ did not disappoint.

His hands covered her breasts, moulding and massaging as a

rough groan left his lips. 'Fuck, I can't get enough of you.'

Skye trembled.

Because she believed him.

And for the first time, she gave him the words in her own heart in return. 'You make me feel really beautiful, TJ.'

It was a first for her, a feeling that could only be fully realized in absolute safety and trust.

Knowing it brought tears to her eyes.

'What's this?' TJ asked when the first one slipped over her lashes. He reached up, used his thumbs to brush them from her cheeks.

Although she hated that Holden was there, in her head in what should have been a selfishly intimate moment, she couldn't deflect. 'He stole so much from me.'

TJ ran one hand down her back. 'Tell me.'

Because she wanted him to understand her, she tried. 'You learn to be careful, to defend yourself – emotionally, because physically, you don't stand a chance. You become cautious, hypervigilant. It becomes second nature. So, instead of just making friends or having fun or talking to a cute guy in a bar or having casual sex, there's this whole other set of emotions you have to work through before you even open yourself up to the possibility that you'll be fine. And usually, by the time you've worked through all that fear, the moment's passed, leaving you behind. You miss out on so many normal things. It's not living. It's surviving.'

'Not anymore,' he said, and she understood that it was a promise. 'He won't ever touch you again.'

She didn't argue with TJ. She was too afraid that she'd like whatever promise he made next too much. Instead, she reached for the button on her jeans and popped it open before sliding her zipper down.

TJ's hands found her waist. His eyes dropped, watching her like a hawk, darkening with every inch of skin she exposed. 'Don't you want to talk about it?' he managed.

Skye actually laughed. 'No. Not anymore. Not tonight.' When she had the jeans down to her knees, she used his shoulders to steady herself and stepped out of them.

'I love your body,' TJ said reverently. 'Every part of you fits perfectly in my hands.' As if he needed to prove it, he reached behind her and gripped her ass. He tugged her forward, bent his head, and trailed whisper-light kisses down her neck.

Skye's body pulled inwards as the pleasure from just that touch bordered on unbearable. She *throbbed*. 'Please touch me.'

TJ's smile curved against her skin. But he brushed his fingers up her inner thigh, asked, 'Here?'

Too needy to play along, too impatient to tease him in return, Skye grabbed his hand in hers and guided him to her aching centre.

TJ shifted her underwear aside, cursed when he stroked through her and felt how soaked she was.

He stood suddenly, his movements frantic. But when Skye took a step back, he hesitated. He slowly reached out one hand, waited for her to take it, and when she did, he turned her so that her back was plastered to his chest, his hard erection beneath his jeans, pressing into her spine.

One of his hands held her hip; the other snaked around her torso and under the waistband of her underwear to find her again. His middle and index finger slid through her repeatedly, slowly stoking that fire within her.

Needing relief from the heat of it, Skye moved her hips, grinding against the pressure as TJ held her and tormented her at the same time.

He bit her shoulder playfully, pulled back to murmur, 'That's it, baby. Ride my hand.'

She whimpered as his words pushed her higher. She could feel the orgasm as it rose, welling past any containable threshold. She gripped the back of his neck, needing to anchor herself to something, to TJ.

He shifted those clever fingers to her clit and circled her, but twice was all it took to have the wave breaking.

Her back arched off his chest, a noiseless cry of release left her lips.

'Fuck,' TJ rasped. He pulled his fingers out of her, held her wilting body with one arm as he fished in his pockets. 'Condom.' He turned to face the bathroom mirror, taking her with him, repeated, 'Condom,' frantically as he opened the vanity and pulled out boxes of band-aids, bottles of ear and eye drops, and wrapped bars of soap. 'Fuck. Wait here.'

Skye giggled hysterically at that, and when TJ focused on her face for long enough to actually register that she was naked and rumpled, and quite incapable of going anywhere, he grinned. 'I'll be right back.'

He waited for her to nod before he let himself out of the bathroom, being careful not to make a single sound even as he let a gush of cold air in – and not even a full minute later, he came back, a wrapped condom proudly caught in his fingertips.

Skye ran one hand through her messy hair as he quickly stripped his jeans and briefs, squeezed her thighs tight when his penis sprung free.

When he ripped the foil open and took the condom out, she whispered, 'Can I try?'

The words fell into the bathroom between them. Skye wasn't even sure where they'd come from, only that she felt that urge to touch him, to drive him as wild as he did her.

Still, a fiery blush flooded her face when TJ's eyes snapped to hers. 'If you don't want me to—'

'You don't have to ask to touch me, Skye. Ever.' He passed her the condom, and when she just stared at it in her hand, he laughed and gave her a quick kiss. 'You don't have to be shy now. We've done everything else, and I promise, there is no way you could touch me that could be wrong.'

Skye reached for him cautiously. She ran her hand down his

hard length once, familiarizing herself with the feeling of hot, soft skin sliding over iron.

TJ groaned. He placed both hands on the wall above her head, bracing himself as she did it again, firmer this time, and when he whispered, 'Fuck,' a surge of power shot through her.

His reaction to her fumbling efforts made her bold. Skye put the condom on and slid it down his length with painstaking care. It was only when TJ grunted and said, 'If you don't hurry up, we're not going to need it,' that she unravelled it to the end.

'How's that?' She looked up when she asked the question, met those familiar green eyes, eyes that were open and honest and filled with too much.

Her breath caught at the intensity of it.

TJ exhaled. He hung his head for a moment as if he needed to regain himself. His hands on the wall were spread, his biceps and shoulders flexed.

'TJ—'

'Perfect,' he said. 'You're perfect. Stop overthinking.'

Skye welcomed the opportunity to leave that huge emotion unacknowledged. Instead, she stripped her underwear and took a step forward, pressing herself against him.

TJ leaned down and took her mouth in a deep kiss, one that made her sigh and close her eyes as that emotion welled. When he broke it, he trailed his lips down her neck. His hands, roughly textured but so sweet and gentle, touched her everywhere, lightly exploring, and when he dropped his fingers to her, finding her hot and wet and ready, he trembled. She felt it pass from him and into her, and she marvelled at it. She craved it.

'Tell me what you want,' he demanded roughly.

'I don't care, so long as you're inside of me in the next—'

She gasped as he picked her up, let her head fall back as he slipped inside of her, pushing past the remnant discomfort from the day before to bury himself inside her.

All she could do was whisper, 'Yes.'

He pressed her back against the wall, used one hand to protect her spine from the cold tiles as he took her, each thrust pinning her harder, pushing her higher against the wall.

Skye basked in the odd tug of war between discomfort and pleasure. Because there was no fear, only trust. No anxiety, only need.

She wrapped her arms around his neck, held him tighter as her body climbed, and right before she let go, she crushed her mouth to his, so that the sound of their moans were swallowed, savoured, by one another.

Chapter 16

Skye woke up late the next morning, sprawled over TJ's chest as his hands traced light patterns over her naked back. His heart thumped against her ear as consistently as a metronome, lulling her enough that she sighed and snuggled in, murmured, 'That feels so good.'

TJ dropped his hands to her butt and squeezed. 'Good morning.'

Skye yawned and slowly levered up to look at his face. TJ in the morning was a whole other animal, his smile soft, his green eyes happy but quieter somehow.

Waking up with him was something she didn't think she'd ever get used to. It felt like one of those half-awake dreams where you knew you were dreaming, lost to another world, but chose not to pull yourself out of it.

The house around them was quiet. TJ's bedroom, furnished with dark wood and navy blues, was dark and cool. A ray of bright sunlight lasered through the gap in the drapes, slicing the King bed in two and illuminating a collection of rodeo buckles neatly displayed on the far wall.

Skye squinted at the window. 'What time is it?'

He stretched out one arm to tap his phone screen. 'Close to nine.'

'Nine?' Skye scrambled into a seated position. She scanned the room for her clothes – or really, anything she could put on to make a quick dash to her own room.

But before she could move to dress, TJ reared up, wrapped both arms around her, and pulled her back down. 'Relax.'

'I have to feed Smokey!'

'I took care of it already,' he replied.

'No. She's got a sensitive stomach. She's on—'

'Gut X and ImmuBiome. I know. I gave her both.'

'You did?'

'Yup. You were sleeping like the dead.' He rolled onto his side, pulling her into little spoon. 'I didn't want to wake you up.' He kissed his way up her neck.

She couldn't concentrate when he did that, but managed to say, 'I would have taken care of it.'

'I wanted to end up back here,' he said easily, 'and I wasn't sure you'd get back into bed once you were up.' He playfully pressed his hips into her from behind, making her laugh.

Skye rolled over, so that they were nose to nose. 'I'm usually up and on the road by six if it's a driving day. Even if it's not, the sunrise rides are the best.'

He frowned at that.

'What?'

'I don't like the idea of you driving alone.'

Warning bells sounded in her head. She froze. But when she spoke, she very clearly said, 'I'll do whatever I want, TJ.'

He pulled back slightly to better see her eyes, searched her face, his own mapped with confusion. 'What's happening right now?'

'I don't like when men do that – make suggestions that are really orders. Holden—'

'Don't do that. Do not compare me to that fucker.'

The bite of temper in his tone didn't help her current frame of mind. It put her back up. 'That's what he does. He issues demands as sweet suggestions. *Don't you think you'd feel better if you put some effort into your appearance? Don't you think your friend Stephanie is a little inappropriate? Don't you think—'*

'I'm not going to apologize for caring about you,' TJ shot back. He climbed out of the bed, ran both hands frantically over his head, his bull skull tattoo shifting dangerously as his back flexed. He spun around to face her, his lean body gloriously naked. 'Jesus, I can be concerned without being controlling. I can worry about you without enforcing my will on you. Skye, if we're going to date, I'm going to be honest with you. And I expect that you'll be honest with me in return. You need to think long and hard about that. Because sometimes it won't be easy to hear.' He exhaled a big breath, shook his head. 'Fuck.'

She'd hurt his feelings. It was humbling to know that she could have that kind of power over a man. And, still, it was imperative he understand that she would never acquiesce to somebody else's whims again. 'I'm sorry. I didn't mean to compare you. TJ.' She waited for him to look at her. 'You are nothing – *nothing* – like my father. The fact that I'd even get angry at you or talk back is . . .' She blew out a puff of air as she searched for the right words. But when nothing came to adequately describe the relief, she settled on a tepid, 'It's really nice.' She remembered what he'd said about her watching his ride, and added, 'It's new for me. I've never known a man well enough to be honest with him and certainly not to fight with him. But' – she regulated her tone – 'I will always make my own decisions.'

He deflated. 'I won't ever hurt you.' He let his head fall back. 'Maybe that's not true, because two people in any type of relationship are bound to hurt one another eventually. But I'll never be like him. I'll never trap you or hold you back. But I will worry, Skye. Because I care. And because you're a five-two woman on the road alone.'

'Okay,' she said simply.

'Yeah?'

'Yeah.' She smiled, trying to ease the tension. 'I mean, I did have to watch you ride a bull yesterday, so I figure I know the feeling.' Wanting to close that distance between them, she moved over the bed and went to where he stood. She wrapped her arms around him, rested her cheek on his bare skin, and said, 'Thanks for caring.'

He sighed and roped his arms around her. 'Are you going to come watch me ride today?'

'Of course.'

He briefly let her go to grab his black hat off the corner post of his bed. He plopped it on her head, said, 'Do me a favour? Wear the hat?'

Skye rolled her eyes playfully.

But when she retook her seat between Janey and Ryan at three p.m. that afternoon and settled in to watch the show, TJ's black hat was firmly on her head.

The crowd was thicker today, almost every seat in the house taken. People chatted and cheered between performances, got up and down to get refreshments and take bathroom breaks, but the action on the sanded arena never rested.

Events flowed, one into another. Skye was eager, anxious even, for TJ's ride to come – or, maybe, to go. And, still, when the announcer's voice boomed, 'All right, folks, next up we have the *bull riding*!' the crowd roared and Skye's stomach dipped.

'Also known as the toughest sport on the dirt, the objective of bull riding is simple: stay on. Ride well. Don't die.' While the crowd laughed, Skye huddled over in her seat, unconsciously trying to weigh down those anxious flutters in her stomach. 'And for any of you who missed his ride yesterday, we have Scottsdale's very own Jesse James Jones competing this weekend. That's right, folks – Triple J himself is here at the Equidome!'

'Remember the Name' by Fort Minor blared out the speakers.

One row behind Skye, a woman on her cell phone said, 'Hurry, babe. They're starting!'

They watched four rides, and while two riders made the full

eight seconds, it seemed to be a night for the bulls. The huge animals, fuelled by the flank strap and the loud crowd, came out fierce and had no mercy on the humans holding onto their backs for dear life. Once they'd performed, the bulls trotted off with their heads held high, shoulders perked, as if they'd communicated before the rodeo and come to an understanding that tonight was theirs for the taking.

'I always thought it a little cruel,' Skye observed offhandedly. 'But now, after watching this weekend, I gotta say: the bulls look like they know their job, maybe even like it.'

'Oh yeah. The bulls are athletes,' Ryan said. 'They're listed as such on the PBR's website, alongside the riders. And they're treated like stars. A healthy, strong bull performs better and pulls in more rodeo money. As their earnings increase, so too does the value of their bloodline – and their semen. It's an entirely separate revenue stream for bull breeders.'

'Honey, I'm sure Skye doesn't need to hear all this.'

'Oh, it's okay,' Skye insisted. 'I find it fascinating.'

'Well, in that case, what Ryan is conveniently leaving out is that a big portion of the bucking genes are passed down from the female line. They call those cows *stud dames*,' Janey explained. 'Their offspring are so valuable that some farmers do yearly embryo transfers – kinda like modified IVF. Embryos are extracted from the stud dame and placed in other cows to carry to term.'

'I had no idea,' Skye marvelled.

'Most people don't.'

Janey's eyes snapped to the arena when the announcer said, 'Next up we have Triple J, riding Dancing Devil! TJ is a four-million-dollar bull rider and four-time PBR World Finals qualifier from right here in Scottsdale, Arizona!'

The entire crowd roared their approval.

'For those of you who haven't seen TJ ride, you're in for a wild time. Let's go!'

Skye barely heard. She was so focused on TJ, her eyes lasered in on him as he lowered himself down onto the bull, set himself up, and then pushed the bull from side to side with his legs, before gripping the side of the chute.

His eyes were obscured by the black hat he wore, but Skye saw his lips moving. The men around him laughed at whatever he'd said.

'Only TJ would tell a joke right before he's about to ride,' she mumbled.

Next to her, Janey released a surprised chuckle. But she sobered almost instantly, whispered, 'Come on, baby.'

Everything slowed.

TJ nodded.

The chute opened.

The bull charged out with a vengeance, bucking and twisting his powerful body. But TJ stayed on, his every move perfectly countering the bull's.

Please, God, Skye prayed as the clock counted up.

Though she barely heard it, George Thorogood's 'Bad to the Bone' boomed through the Equidome. People were on their feet, shouting and cheering as the clock hit five seconds.

When the clock hit seven, Skye found herself on her feet too, shouting and cheering alongside everyone else. And when the buzzer sounded, she jumped up and down like a teenage girl, and then turned and hugged Janey, who was just as riled up.

Ryan, still seated, clapped loudly. But his eyes didn't leave the arena until TJ dismounted.

TJ landed on his feet, took his hat off his head and pumped it in the air, his shouted 'Come on!' travelling to where they sat.

Skye laughed when he turned – looking, she knew, for her. Their eyes met. They both smiled. He took one step towards her – and then everything went wrong.

Dancing Devil caught sight of TJ walking away. The bull tossed his big head, his horn catching the nearest bull fighter and sending the man somersaulting over his neck and shoulders to land on the dirt behind him.

The bull charged.

Skye opened her mouth to warn TJ, to call out, but nothing came.

He saw the look on her face and turned, but not in time.

The bull mowed him down.

TJ's body vanished beneath the mass of black hide and dust.

Chapter 17

All they were told for the first four hours was: *He's being assessed. We'll let you know when we know more.*

They sat in the waiting room outside the ICU, Janey and Ryan huddled together, alternately holding hands and dozing against one another as the evening passed. Their cell phones rang with alarming frequency, as concerned friends who'd either watched the accident or heard about it called to offer comfort and support, and though they'd both tried to take the first few, after a while, they had stopped answering altogether.

At one point, Ryan took his phone back out. 'We should call Jules,' he mumbled, but he just stared at the phone in his hand while Janey battled a sob.

'Would you like me to do it?' Skye asked. It wasn't just a kindness; it was selfish too. She needed something to do, needed something to distract herself from the recurring image of TJ smiling at her right before the bull hit him.

Ryan didn't even nod, just passed her his unlocked phone, Julia's contact pulled up on the screen.

Skye took the phone with her around the corner, but the moment she was alone, the shaking started. The image of TJ being carried off on a stretcher, his face covered in blood, his eyes closed, flashed through her mind relentlessly. If TJ had left the arena quicker, if she hadn't distracted him, if she hadn't been there at all . . .

From as early an age as she could remember, Skye had learned one particular skill very well: how to lie and pretend that everything was fine when it really was not. She engaged that skill now. She straightened her spine, forced that stillness she'd learned from her own mother.

And then she dialled the number Ryan had pulled up.

Skye didn't even know where Julia lived or what she did for a living or if she'd be awake at midnight, but she dialled anyway, held her breath as the phone rang, half hoping TJ's sister wouldn't pick up at all.

But she did.

'Dad.' Julia laughed. 'Perfect timing. Luke just woke me up for his midnight feed.' When Skye didn't – couldn't – speak right away, Julia said, 'Dad? Did you butt dial me again?'

'Julia?'

'Ah, yes. Who's this?'

Skye heard the frown in Julia's voice, and unsure of where she fit or where she belonged, she just said, 'I'm a friend of TJ's – Skye.'

There was a single beat of dread-filled silence. But when she spoke again, Julia didn't ask what had happened, only, 'How bad?'

'They haven't told us anything yet. But he's been back there almost four hours now.'

'Four hours! Where are my parents? Why haven't they called me?'

'They're here. Ah, I think they're in shock. Everyone's been calling and wanting to know how to help, but I think they just don't know what to do.' When the panic threatened to take over, Skye closed her eyes and very clearly said, 'You need to come. It's bad, and I can't . . .' *do this.* 'I don't know what to do. And your mom and dad aren't capable of making any decisions for him right now.'

'I'm packing as we speak. I'm in Tucson, so I can be there in under two hours.' Julia briefly moved the phone away, but Skye heard her distinctly say, 'Sly, get up!'

And a man's grumbled, 'What's going on?'

'TJ's been in a bull-riding accident. Here, take Luke.' Over the line, a baby started crying. 'I'm packing. Get changed. Grab the keys.'

'He okay?'

'No.'

Julia didn't say more. She came back on the line, asked, 'Which hospital?'

'Scottsdale Osborn.'

'See you soon,' Julia said. 'Tell my parents I'm on the way.'

Skye hung up.

She leaned heavily against the nearby wall, completely drained. Feeling fear for someone other than herself wasn't new. She'd always felt it for her mother and had tried to intervene between her parents, to refocus her father's wrath on her instead. But this was different. There was absolutely nothing she could do to protect TJ's body. There was nothing she could say to his parents to make them feel any relief. And even though she had no idea how to handle it, TJ being hurt had smothered her denial and made one thing abundantly clear: she was, somehow, already in love with him.

And that was not a comfort.

Skye already would have given him anything, and that worried her. She'd been trapped by a man who'd had that power over her once, a man who'd made her desperate to please him, desperate to be loved by him, and even though she'd sworn she'd never let it happen again, there was a terrible fear growing within her that it was already too late.

TJ did not have to be anything like Holden for that to be true. Overwhelmed by the intensity of her feelings, Skye began to panic.

Still, she forced the queasy feeling down.

She remembered what he'd said: *Trust me, Skye. I won't let you down.* And although it took immense courage, she allowed herself to believe it. Slowly, her urge to run was quelled. Her panic calmed.

TJ needed her.

So, she'd stay.

In the waiting room, she passed Ryan's phone back to him. 'Julia's on her way.'

He looked at it blankly for a moment before his eyes cleared. 'I'm sorry. I shouldn't have let you do that.'

'Don't apologize.' Skye sat down in the seat next to his. 'I'm happy to help. Can I get you anything? Coffee? A snack?' When Ryan shook his head, Skye looked past him to Janey. 'Janey?'

'Oh, no. Thanks, baby.' She tried to smile, but didn't quite manage it, only sighed and fell back into that catatonic stare, her eyes on the hallway – waiting, Skye knew, for someone to tell her if her son was alive.

Chapter 18

Skye did not have to wonder if the woman approaching was Julia. She had TJ's dark hair and green eyes but Janey's angular features and delicate, pointed chin. She barrelled down the hall in her pyjamas, a baby who couldn't have been more than four months old on her hip, the long ears on her bunny slippers flopping up and down with each frantic step she took. A handsome man who could only be Sly walked at her side, carrying a diaper bag. He was tall, maybe six-three, and despite the time of day, he was dressed impeccably in tan chinos and a black shirt.

Skye gently rubbed Ryan's shoulder, said, 'Julia's here.'

He came to, blinked several times. But the moment he looked up and saw his daughter running towards him, tears started falling down his cheeks. He uncrossed his arms and stood, pulled Julia and Luke into a huge hug before reaching behind them to shake Sly's hand. Not once did Ryan seem embarrassed by the tears streaming down his face. Even when he swiped them away, Skye knew it was only because of the need to clear his eyes.

Janey followed, hugging her family and murmuring that they had no updates in that hushed hospital voice. Unsure of herself, Skye remained seated.

She had never been hugged by her father. And she'd certainly never seen him cry.

With nothing to distract her, she saw the doctor approaching, his white lab coat trailing behind him like a cape as he hurried along.

Skye's heart slammed into her chest and stayed stuck there.

She stood on unsteady legs, and when the doctor stopped in front of their group, all she could say was, 'TJ?'

'Are you family?'

Skye wasn't sure how to answer.

It was Janey who stepped forward with, 'She is.' She held out one hand. 'I'm TJ's mother.'

'Mrs Jones.' The doctor returned the shake. He nodded to the others, and then began, 'TJ's stable.' The audible sigh of relief was cut short by, 'But his condition is critical. He's suffered a major head trauma and a spinal cord injury. We're prepping him for spinal surgery right now, after which we'll be keeping him in a medically induced coma for a few days until the swelling on his brain goes down.'

Skye's nose started to burn from the telltale flush of tears, but she turned inwards, repeated, *He's stable, he's stable, he's stable*, over and over in her head.

'What is the surgery for?' Ryan asked.

'At this stage, our main goal is to prevent spinal shock and inflammation. If we don't decompress the pressure on his nerves, the inflammation can cause secondary damage that's oftentimes more detrimental than the injury itself. We'll go in, remove any bone fragments, continue to assess the damage.' The doctor used a tone that came from years of delivering bad news to grieving families.

'What does that mean exactly?' Julia demanded.

'The bull hit him low, so the most damage occurred at T12 and L1, the last thoracic vertebrae and the first lumbar vertebrae.' He turned and tapped his lower back, showing them the approximate area of impact. 'The damage is bad,' he warned. 'But TJ is breathing on his own, which is extremely positive news. With technological advances—'

'How bad?' Ryan demanded.

'In simple terms,' Julia added.

'He'll need more diagnostic imaging and several more surgeries, but with stem cell therapy, focused physical therapy, and a lot of determination, I have every confidence that TJ will walk again.'

Janey's sniffle as she started crying again punctuated the heavy silence that followed.

'Walk . . .?' Ryan repeated quietly.

The doctor nodded. He lowered his voice, patiently explained, 'Obviously, TJ's bull riding days are over. It's going to be a long and difficult road to recovery for him as it is. I'm sorry to have to be the one to deliver this news. All I can promise right now is that he is in good hands.'

'Can we see him?' Julia asked.

The doctor shook his head. 'He's being prepped for surgery as we speak. Even if he wasn't, his system is at extreme risk from all variables right now. It'll be hours before he's even out of surgery and in recovery, maybe another twenty-four, possibly longer, until you can see him. I suggest you go home and get some rest. There's nothing you can do here for the next few days, and once he wakes up, TJ's going to need you all to be well rested and ready.'

'Thank you.' Ryan shook the surgeon's hand. But the moment the doctor turned and left, he asked, 'What the hell do we do? That boy hasn't sat still for more than five minutes his entire life.'

The entire family looked to Janey. TJ's mom took a deep breath and blew her nose on the crumpled tissue she'd been holding for the better part of the night. When she was done, she tucked it into the pocket of her jeans. Skye watched as she straightened her spine, looked each of them in the eye in turn, and said, 'Today, we thank God he's alive. Everything else, we take a day at a time.'

Chapter 19

When they pulled TJ from his medically induced coma three days later, he woke up with a head full of cotton and a throat so dry he could barely breathe.

For hours, he came in and out of sleep, too confused to stay under, too exhausted and weak to stay awake for long.

When he finally opened his eyes fully, they were scratchy and irritated. The first thought he had was: *Skye.* But the first face he saw, blurred and out-of-focus, was his mother's.

'Don't try to speak,' she said immediately. 'Just relax. Take it easy.'

His dad and a doctor in a white lab coat came into focus. TJ wanted to ask *What happened?* and even though he opened his mouth, no words came out.

'I said: *don't* try to speak.' His mom laughed. But to his absolute confusion, her laughter turned to sobs almost immediately. She slapped one hand over her mouth, mumbled, 'I'm sorry. I'm sorry.' When his dad reached for her, she shooed him away, 'No, no. I'm fine. Just happy.' She refocused on TJ's face, said, 'Baby, you've had my heart in a chokehold.'

TJ tried to look around, but the moment he turned his head,

fresh claws of pain tore down his spine and right leg, pulling all his muscles tight.

'Try to relax.' Perhaps sensing his panic, the doctor stepped forward. 'TJ, I'm Dr Kleiner, the neurosurgeon here at Scottsdale Osborn.'

Neurosurgeon?

TJ's mind roiled.

Agitated, he shifted.

'Relax, son.' His dad placed one heavy hand on TJ's shoulder, comforting him, grounding him, keeping him still.

Dr Kleiner checked TJ's eyes with a small flashlight, asked, 'TJ, could you blink for me?'

TJ blinked.

'Good. Could you very carefully nod and shake your head?'

Although the pain had his vision blackening, TJ did.

'Very good. TJ, do you remember what happened? How you ended up here? If you can try to speak again, that's great. If not, just nod or shake your head.'

TJ thought back. He remembered looking up after dismounting and seeing Skye . . . After that, everything was dark, the sound muffled. But the memory of the pain – that was real and raw and heavy and had him guessing, 'Bull?' even though the short, single word left his mouth sounding more like, *mull.*

'That's right. You were hit from the side.' The doctor regulated his tone, 'You've suffered some head trauma and a spinal cord injury.'

'*Motherfucker.*' He wasn't aware he'd mumbled it aloud until his parents and the doctor started laughing.

'I wholeheartedly agree.' Dr Kleiner smiled kindly. 'But you came out of surgery well. Typically, we'd want you up and trying to move within twenty-four hours after spine surgery, but due to the swelling on your brain, we kept you under for a few days.'

'How long?' His voice, weak and dry, was clearer then.

His mom fetched him a cup of water with a straw. She held it up to his mouth, said, 'Today's day three.'

TJ jerked in surprise at that. The straw popped out of his mouth, spraying water down his chin. To his absolute mortification, his mom hurried to clean him up.

'Don't,' he managed.

She stopped, caught the crushed tissue in her fist. 'Julia and Sly went home, but they're driving back right now.'

'TJ, the fact that you're talking already is extremely promising,' Dr Kleiner assured him. 'Your vitals are good, considering.' He stood. 'I'm going to ask you a few questions now, okay?'

TJ nodded.

The doctor moved the sheets aside, exposing TJ's legs. 'Any skin tingling, burning, or numbness?'

'Right hip and leg.' He rasped the words, but they were clearer, stronger.

'What's the sensation?'

'Burning. Tingling.'

'What's your pain right now, on a scale of one to ten?'

TJ felt like a rod had been jammed down his spine, but it wasn't necessarily painful. He was a bull rider. Painful was walking off the dirt with a bone sticking out of his arm and no medical-grade painkillers. 'Three.'

'We'll call it a five, given your chosen profession. But that's still good. You're on a lot of pain meds to help with that. If it gets any worse' – he pointed to a call button – 'this button will call a nurse.' He touched TJ's right thigh. 'Can you feel this?'

TJ nodded.

'How about this?' He touched his opposite foot.

'Yes.'

'All right. Can you wiggle the toes on your left foot?'

TJ did.

'Can you shift your right knee?'

TJ did.

There was a beat of silence. 'TJ, shift your right knee for me?'

'I did . . .?' At the blank looks, he started to panic. He craned his head forward to see, focused on his right knee and moved it again. It didn't budge. He stretched further, sending rivulets of spear-like jabs down his back, and focusing all his attention on just that knee joint, he forced his muscles to contract.

This time, he saw his knee twitch. It didn't shift. But the muscles fired ever so slightly.

'Good. That's amazing.' The doctor covered him with the sheet again. 'The damage is there, especially in your lower, right extremities. However, you're in much better shape than I was expecting. Your spine has been stabilized, so over the next few days, we're going to run a lot more tests, get the full extent of your fine motor skills documented. We're going to get you sitting up and then started on physical therapy. We want you moving as much as possible. We'll make any decisions about further surgeries once we know more.' He pulled TJ's chart out of the slot on the wall, jotted something down, and then walked back over. 'I know this is a lot to take in, TJ. But I'm absolutely thrilled by the fact that you can breathe without assistance, talk and move all your limbs to some degree. Most people that survive the extent of trauma you did aren't so lucky. But I'm hopeful that we'll get you walking again.'

Walking? Hopeful? Panic, a completely new emotion to him, reared. Still, his manners had him weakly nodding. 'Thanks, Doc.'

TJ waited for him to leave before turning to face his parents again. His mom was teary but smiling. His dad looked pale and tired. Old.

'Sorry.' He was too tired to add, *For scaring the life out of you.*

But his parents understood. 'We're just so happy you're okay. We'll get you through this, baby.' His mom gently took his hand.

TJ closed his eyes, exhausted from just ten minutes of interacting. But in the back of his mind, he was aware that something was missing. As he started drifting, he asked, 'Where's Skye?'

'She's out in the waiting room. She wanted to give us a chance to speak with your doctor in privacy.'

Some of TJ's panic settled. His mom had told him he'd been out for days, past when Skye was supposed to have hit the road. But she'd stayed.

For one glorious second, the knowledge warmed him. His heart swelled. He turned to his mom, hoping to ask her to go get Skye, but a sudden slice of pain down his entire right side had his vision wavering.

He gritted his teeth, refusing to cry out as tension ratcheted down his body, pulling the muscles in his back and chest impossibly tight. Everything spasmed, making his arms and legs twitch uncontrollably.

By the time it had passed, TJ was gulping air. Sweat coated his brow.

He looked up at his parents, an adult suddenly cast back into dependency. His mom was pale, her dark eyes huge. His dad had tears streaming down his face.

The fresh pain and the unexpected spasms added to that panic already consuming him.TJ had always assumed his life would be over in eight seconds; but he never could have guessed that all it would take was one. Because that's how long it took him to realize that he was in much worse condition than he'd assumed.

He might – *hopefully* – walk again.

But what would his life look like until then? Fuck, what would his life look like after that?

He couldn't know.

'Do you want me to get Skye?' his mom asked.

Skye. He closed his eyes, momentarily resisting. But when he said, 'Yes,' his voice was cold. Flat.

'I'll get her.' Ryan left the room.

Perhaps sensing what he needed to say, his mom smiled sadly. 'There's a right way to do this, TJ. Don't let your anger over what happened hurt that girl any more. Be kind. She already won't know how to handle this. But she's trying. She's been so strong.'

He laughed, but even the bitterness left his lips quietly. Weakly.

'For just a moment there – a day – I had everything.'

A soft knock on the door had his mom pushing to a stand. 'I'll give you space.'

'Mom?' TJ said weakly, stopping Janey in her tracks.

'Yeah, baby?'

'Make sure she takes Bandit when she leaves; if she's going to be on the road . . .'

He didn't finish the thought, but he didn't need to. His mom left, holding the door for Skye on her way out.

TJ's heart shattered as Skye walked into the room, her pixie cut messy, her porcelain skin pale, her blue eyes dark with worry and shadowed from sleeplessness. When tears streaked down her face, his inclination was to soften, to soothe.

'TJ.' She came to the bed, gripped his hand in both of hers. Just that touch had him closing his eyes and basking in the feel of her one last time.

But he didn't squeeze her hand back. He was too afraid that if he did, she might take it as encouragement and stroke her hand over his head or kiss him. And if she did either of those things, he'd lose his courage. He'd ask her to stay – or, at least, to come back and visit.

And that wouldn't have been fair.

'I'm so glad you're awake,' she whispered.

'Why haven't you left yet?' he asked.

Her eyes widened slightly at his casually surprised tone. 'I . . . I wanted to wait until you were up and moving,' she replied, her own voice so unsure.

That word – *moving* – made him smile sardonically. 'Thanks for staying, Skye. But—'

'Don't thank me. I . . .' She took a deep breath. 'TJ . . .'

Terrified that he knew what was coming, he didn't say anything.

'I . . . I almost left.'

His heart ached, not because she'd nearly left, but because he wished she had. She had doubts; he'd sensed them in her when he'd mentioned meeting up in the future. And now, he wished she had run and saved him from having to cut his own heart out.

Skye reached up and ran one hand over his hair. But all the gesture did was hurt. 'I managed to convince myself that what I feel for you was just infatuation.' She bravely raised her eyes to his. 'But the crazy thing is: it's not. Or, at least, I don't think it is.'

That just about broke his fucking heart. What he wouldn't give to go back, to pay attention once he'd dismounted that stupid bull.

TJ steeled himself. 'Skye . . .' he began. But the words wouldn't come.

It didn't matter; she heard the caution in his tone. She blinked once. Realization slowly spread across her features. Then hurt. Then, to his absolute horror, shame. 'Oh.'

The single word was a knife to his gut. 'Let me explain.'

'You don't have to,' she hurried to say. She let go of his hand, casting him into a world that was suddenly so uncertain, so colourless.

She took a large step back from the bed, her face red with embarrassment.

TJ couldn't leave her thinking he didn't care. Time was irrelevant when you met the right person; he knew that now. 'Things changed. Skye.' He tried to regulate his tone, but the words still came out so angry. 'I might not *walk* again.'

She nodded bravely, even as her eyes filled. 'You will.' She swiped her tears away, cleared her throat.

'I want you to—'

'You don't have to explain,' she said frantically, cutting him off. 'I know how casual sex works, TJ. I just got caught up, I guess.' She wrapped her arms around herself, protecting herself *from him.* And she smiled; it was shaky, but it was so fucking brave.

When his throat clogged with the goodbye, TJ momentarily closed his eyes. Once he'd regained himself, he managed to look at her again, and oddly, that helped. Because this beautiful woman had her entire life ahead of her, and he wouldn't hold her back with him. 'You need to keep living your life. You just started.'

'I'll stay,' she insisted. 'I'll help.'

'No.'

'TJ . . .'

'I don't want you here!' The words were true. He couldn't bear for her to stay behind, to let her dreams go, only to watch him fumble back to a life that was suddenly so uncertain.

She was quiet for a moment. She searched his face with those big, beautiful eyes. But TJ saw the exact moment she realized he was telling the truth. Those eyes dimmed, losing their light. Her shoulders rounded. But she didn't get mad. She just smiled sadly, whispered, 'Okay.'

TJ's heart broke.

When Skye turned her back on him and started for the door, panic filled him.

And when the last sound he heard before she walked out of his hospital room was a strangled sob, he lost his resolve.

He didn't like hurting her.

He just wanted to spare her.

TJ tried to go after her.

Because he could move his left leg, he swung it over and off the bed. But his right didn't follow. His unevenly distributed body weight took him down to the floor, so that he landed in a heap. He cursed violently as the IV was ripped from his arm, as those new injuries sent rivulets of pain down his entire body.

He didn't dare move.

For minutes, he lay there, prostrate, his heart as broken as his back, blood pouring from where the IV had torn his vein. He waited for somebody to come as he gulped in air and tried to breathe through the pain.

It was his dad who found him. 'TJ!' He crouched on the floor, placed one hand on TJ's face.

'Help me up.'

'No. Fuck. Let me get a nurse.'

'Dad,' TJ insisted. 'Help me up.'

'Son of a bitch,' Ryan cursed. But he crouched lower, asked, 'Can you put your arm around my neck?'

It took effort, but TJ managed.

'On three.'

He nodded.

'One. Two. Three.' With one huge heave, his dad lifted him high enough that TJ was able to get his left leg under him. He cried out as he put pressure on the limb, swayed as the pain almost took him under.

A nurse walked in. She dropped the tray of pain meds she'd been carrying, said, 'What on earth is going on in here?' as she ran around the bed to help.

'I fell,' TJ replied dryly. When that grief rose heavily in his chest, when he thought about Skye, he added, 'Hard.'

They painstakingly rearranged him on the bed. The moment he was horizontal, the nurse said, 'I'm going to fetch the doctor and more morphine.' She picked up her tray and the needles off the floor and hurried from the room.

'What the fuck, TJ?' his dad roared.

'Skye . . .'

His dad sobered at that. 'What?'

'I just wanted to tell her something . . .' TJ let his head fall back on the pillow and closed his eyes. He laughed. 'I broke my back and got bit on the ass in the space of a few days.'

His dad sighed tiredly. 'I'm sorry.'

'It was the right thing to do.'

'Yes.' No kind, comforting words. Just the truth. 'That's girl's too young, too green to make a decision like this after a weekend-long love affair.'

TJ had known that, but hearing someone else say it was a relief. 'Can you get Maverick Hunt's number for me?' TJ asked.

'I have it on my phone.' His dad pulled out his cell and brought up the number.

Because TJ was too tired to even raise his hand to take the phone, he said, 'Dial him. Put it on speaker.'

Maverick answered on the second ring. Despite the fact that Mav had to be pushing forty, he still answered the phone with, 'Mr Jones?'

'Mav. It's TJ, calling from my dad's cell. Long time, man.'

'Son of a bitch. I heard about your accident. You okay?'

TJ actually laughed. His physical injuries were nothing compared to that new ache in his chest. 'I'm alive. Barely. Look, Mav, this isn't a social call. There's something I was hoping to ask you. A favour for an old friend.'

'Anything. You know that.'

'There's a girl headed your way. She'll be on the road alone, pulling a Quarter Horse mare in a rig that's barely roadworthy.'

'Okay . . .'

'She's going to be looking for work as a wrangler.'

'She any good?'

'She's green. But if you give her a chance, she won't disappoint you. Her name's Skye.'

'I'll keep an eye out.'

'Thanks, Mav.' TJ hated to break Skye's trust, but he also knew he had no other choice. He was a man who couldn't even walk, let alone protect her. But Mav . . . Mav could. And, TJ knew, he would. 'Ah . . . She's had some trouble recently. Her old man is an abusive prick, and she's trying to stay off his radar. If I knew I'd walk again, I'd be there. But—'

'Don't worry, TJ. Focus on getting better. If she shows up, we'll take care of her,' Mav assured him.

And it was that simple.

PART TWO:
RODEO

Chapter 20

Hunt Ranch, Santa Barbara County, California – January 7, 2027 (Nearly Two Years Later)

Skye slouched comfortably in her barrel saddle, an antique Billy Cook she'd picked up for cheap on Facebook Marketplace and redyed herself using a YouTube tutorial.

She'd kept her blonde hair short, so that one of the owners of Hunt Ranch, Sierra, had taken to calling her 'Tink' and inadvertently given her a nickname for the other wranglers to tease her with. But that was really the only thing that remained the same. Her body, still small and lean, had toughened after almost two years of working outside with horses. Her hands, once as white as alabaster and as soft as petals, were tanned and carried the calluses and scars of hard work done well.

But more than those physical changes, almost two years of working at Hunt Ranch had made *her* different. Her smile came easily. She laughed often. And even though she still looked over her shoulder sometimes, she'd long ago accepted that the habit was a small price to pay for freedom.

She looked out over the ranch and saw Bandit sitting on the ground, his tongue lolling from the hike, his eyes half-mast as he bathed in a stream of sunlight. Beneath her, Smokey was relaxed, maybe even bored, too used to being ridden for hours a day to put much energy into it – unless they were running the barrel pattern. The moment Smokey saw the blue practice barrels set up in the arena, the horse disappeared, and a dragon emerged.

When Skye hauled the mare to rodeos and barrel races, Smokey, still used to travelling after so many months on the road, was calm and at ease in the trailer. The horse could stand tied for hours, one hip cocked as she dozed. But the second they stepped into the arena, preparing to run, that dragon would take over. Smokey would prance and pull on the bit as they moved down the alley. The mare would rock forward, shifting from side to side with impatience as Skye held her back, and the moment Skye let her go, there was no stopping them.

Smokey might have been born to run, but from the moment she'd left Dallas, Skye had learned how to run too. Barrel racing wasn't just fun for them; it was instinctual. And over their time at Hunt Ranch, under Sierra and her husband, Benji's, tutelage, the duo had left their remaining fears behind. They'd become good. Very good.

Skye had spent the previous year filling her WPRA permit whenever she had a weekend free and could haul Smokey to nearby races. And although she'd set out with the intention of earning the thousand dollars required to get her WPRA pro card, they had raked in over twenty grand over the course of last season. She'd won – and given away – her first trophy saddle, and even though she'd considered giving away TJ's instead, Skye couldn't bear to part with it – and had stoically chosen not to ponder why. Just as she didn't like to dwell on why she'd not only kept the cactus TJ had given her on that first date – but also named it Bob.

But now, it was time to move on, to embrace the next chapter. Maybe it was her twenty-fifth birthday, in just a few months' time, that had made her uneasy and solidified her decision to leave Hunt Ranch for life on the road, hopping from one barrel race to another, but Skye didn't overthink it.

It didn't matter that she hadn't seen Holden in over two years; he had subtly let her know that he was watching her. The first time had been over six months prior, when Skye had answered a call from her mom – only to be greeted by Holden. He hadn't made any threats. He'd said all the right things: 'I'm sorry', 'You know how much I love you', and 'Please forgive me?'

Skye had seen through the crocodile tears. Still, that particular betrayal had hit her twice as hard, because only her mom could have told Holden she had Skye's number.

The second time, three months prior, Skye had received a gift. The custom barrel saddle had arrived wrapped and packed in a crate. Skye had unpacked it as she might have a box full of snakes – with dread in her stomach and bile in her throat. But she'd taken one look at the beautiful leatherwork and the name *Skye Marchant* engraved into the fender, and she'd snapped. Under the horrified gazes of the rest of the wranglers, she'd carried the saddle outside, doused it in lighter fluid, and set it on fire.

Once she'd realized that Holden knew where she was, the decision to join the rodeo circuit had been an easy one. Holden would come. She knew that absolutely. But, by God, she'd make it difficult for him to find her.

Next to her, Sierra sat on her big grey gelding, Ty. Like Skye, Sierra wore Wrangler jeans and riding boots. Unlike Skye, Sierra also had a light layer of pristine makeup on. Her one forearm rested on the horn of her saddle, her hand loosely holding the reins. 'What are we gonna do without you?' she asked.

For Skye, it was hard to think about leaving. Hunt Ranch – the Hunts, the staff, the animals, the *lifestyle* – had become the first true home she'd ever known. 'You'll find someone to replace me.'

'The work, sure. But not *you.*'

Skye smiled, but only because the alternative was bursting into tears. 'I never said thank you. For taking me in. For giving me a chance.'

'I didn't,' Sierra reminded her. 'That was all Benji and Mav.'

'Maybe the initial job,' Skye ceded, because when she'd first arrived at Hunt Ranch, Sierra had been recovering from the tragic loss of her baby and had never come down to the barn voluntarily – until Skye had asked for help. 'But you started Smokey and me on the barrel pattern. You gave me a purpose.'

'Oh, God, don't thank me for that,' Sierra insisted. 'I'm so excited to see how you do this year. Maybe by December, we'll be visiting you in Vegas.'

Skye laughed lightly, even as her stomach churned with nerves and excitement. 'That would be incredible. But I'm planning for the NFR closer to year five.'

'We'll see.' Sierra sat up in her saddle, used one hand to lift the reins while her legs did the rest. 'Should we go see if Benji survived the twins?'

Skye looked out over Hunt Ranch one last time. In January, the weather was still crisp and damp. In the valley below, the resort spread over irrigated fields and pastures. The luxury cabins, resort buildings, and animal corrals were dotted below. Horses grazed, just little blobs of colour.

With one last sigh, Skye turned Smokey and picked up the conversation as they walked. 'Thanks for letting me use the ranch's address to register.'

'Of course. You have a place here, Skye. I shouldn't have to tell you that. Although God knows why you'd want to register in California, given that Texas has almost twice the number of circuit rodeos to choose from *and* no income tax.'

'It said *home address* on the form,' Skye explained. 'Texas hasn't been home in a while.' Her next barrel race in just six days would be in Odessa, but that would be the first time Skye had been back to her home state in over two years. 'Besides,' she added, 'I probably won't make enough the first year to even be taxed.'

Sierra rolled her eyes. 'Stop saying shit like that.'

'I'm just regulating my expectations.'

'No – you're lowering them. You have just as good a chance as anybody. Start acting like it.'

'God, you're sassy,' Skye muttered.

Sierra laughed.

But because talk of leaving made Skye nervous, she redirected the conversation. 'How does it feel – being back in the saddle?'

Sierra had stopped riding almost a year prior when she'd fallen pregnant with the twins, Willow and Wren. Today was her first day back since she'd given birth, and she'd asked Skye to go on one last ride with her before she and Smokey hit the road early the next morning.

'Amazing.' Sierra navigated Ty down a slope. 'I never thought I'd be this happy again. After Ava . . .'

'I can't imagine,' Skye said softly. She had experienced loss, but she'd never lost a child like Sierra and Benji had.

Sierra smiled sadly. 'Everyone has something – something that broke their heart, something they're running from, something they're afraid of. It's the burden of being human.'

Skye shifted uncomfortably in her saddle. Although she'd rather not say anything, it was important that everyone at Hunt Ranch knew not to share her travel schedule. So, she braced herself, said, 'So, that's actually something I've been meaning to talk to you about.'

Sierra arched one eyebrow, but she didn't say anything.

'In the next few months,' Skye continued, 'someone is going to come looking for me. He'll call or show up. Please, Sierra, don't let anyone share my schedule with him – with *anyone*.'

Sierra surprised her by saying, 'This wouldn't be Jesse James Jones we're talking about?'

'No.' Skye didn't so much as blink, though that old, dull ache flared. 'TJ wouldn't come looking for me.'

'You know he called Mav – before you arrived? Recommended you for the job.'

Skye's head whipped up at that. Her heart lurched, so that beneath her, Smokey snorted loudly and tossed her head from side to side, looking for the danger.

Skye reached forward and ran her palm through Smokey's mane, calming the horse, but her heart continued to tap impatiently. 'What?'

Sierra grinned. 'One day, you're gonna tell me the full story, Skye.'

'There's no story.' She ducked beneath an overhanging branch. 'I stayed with his family during the Rodeo Scottsdale event where he got hurt.' Skye flushed with embarrassment as she remembered how childish, ignorant, and infatuated she'd been. Now, she could look back and see that it was just a few days of fun, but back then, it had felt like so much more – like everything.

'That must have been awful,' Sierra commented quietly.

'Yes,' Skye assured her. 'It was.' Her past infatuation with TJ aside, that was true. His accident had been horrific.

'Well, apparently he's working the rodeos again.'

When Skye's spine snapped straight at that, Sierra grinned. 'No story there, my ass.'

'He's not bull riding—'

'No. He's working as a pickup man at PRCA events.'

Skye wondered how that was possible. The pickup men were mounted riders who rode in the arena during the Rough Stock events. They helped the bronc and bareback riders dismount the bucking horses or, if necessary, helped the bullfighters corral the bull and get it back into the pen.

It was an athletic and demanding job, one that required versatility and a range of skills unparalleled even by most of the rodeo competitors – one that couldn't have been easy with a spinal cord injury.

The PRCA and WPRA worked together to incorporate women's rodeo events – the barrel racing and breakaway roping – into the rodeos. So, if TJ really was working them, there was a near-certain chance that Skye would run into him during her barrel racing season. Probably more than once too.

Unwilling to ponder that, Skye simply said, 'My father, Holden Marchant, may come looking for me.'

'Is he dangerous?'

'Not in the way you're implying, and not to anyone but me.'

Sierra didn't get the chance to push for more as they came to the big Hunt Ranch and Resort barn, which was busy with wranglers hard at work and guests preparing for their trail rides.

They both wordlessly dismounted and led their horses inside.

Benji was waiting for Sierra in the barn, the two-month-old twins fast asleep in a ring sling baby carrier strapped to his chest.

Skye might as well not have been there for the way the couple focused on each other, but she was as used to it as she was unoffended by it. 'Here, I'll take Ty.' She reached out and grabbed Ty's reins.

Sierra looked down at the reins as if she'd forgotten she was even holding her horse. 'Are you sure?'

'Yup. Go on, boss.'

Skye smiled at Benji as she walked by with both horses.

Maybe it was the mention of TJ or seeing the connection between Sierra and Benji spark the moment their eyes met, but that old resentment she still carried for TJ flared. She hated herself for it more than she could ever hate him. It was her problem – and her problem alone – that she still felt so bitter over the whole thing.

There had been other men. In fact, after TJ, Skye had made a point of collecting all those firsts – first horrible date, first awkward one-night stand, first regrettable drunk sexcapade.

She had nursed her wounded pride by proving to herself that she could be casual, that she could be with any man without giving him a piece of herself. So, while there had been some nice guys thrown into the mix, Skye had purposefully avoided anything remotely serious.

She'd been hurt by the only two men she'd ever had in her life, and although her father's abuse had damaged her in many ways, TJ's abandonment had hurt more. Because she'd had a choice. She had willingly let him in. She had given him her trust and the power to cause her pain.

Never again.

Benji walked into the tack room. 'Do you mind coming over to the ranch house when you're done?' he asked. 'Mav and Nina want to say bye in person.'

Skye cocked one hip. 'You do realize I've known about the farewell party for, like, a month, right?'

Benji took his ball cap off. He ran his hand through his shaggy blond hair. 'Who told you?'

'Nobody. Sierra randomly asked me what my favourite food and cocktail were. And I walked in on the guys having an epic battle with wrapping paper and tape in the wrangler's cabin last night. There was literally a balloon floating in the rafters that said, *Good Luck on your New Adventure!*'

'Oh. Well, shit.'

Skye laughed. 'I'll still act surprised?'

'Appreciate it.' Benji turned on his heel. 'See you there.'

Skye took her time untacking Smokey and breathing in the smell of home one last time. She'd be on the road for most of the year, competing in over eighty rodeos and barrel races.

Travelling alone.

With only one horse to compete on.

'What could possibly go wrong?' she asked Smokey, and when the horse blew a puff of air out of her nose as if to say, 'Well, we'll certainly find out', Skye grinned.

She gave Smokey one last pat and stepped out of the stall.

Bandit was lying outside waiting for her. 'Bandit, come,' was all she had to say to have the dog popping to his feet and heeling at her side.

As she drove the mile to the ranch house, Skye rolled down

her windows and let the fresh air flood the cab of her truck. She looked out, smiled when she saw Farrah, the ranch's tiny Shetland pony that lived to wreak havoc, zipping around the pasture, giving an occasional buck of pure evil glee as her blonde mane danced in the wind.

Skye pulled up to the ranch house, turned off the truck, and took a moment to prepare herself for the surprise. In the passenger seat, Bandit whined, prompting her to reply, 'Yeah, yeah.'

She climbed out with a small groan for her tired muscles, walked across the front yard to the house.

Sierra opened the door before Skye could even ring the doorbell. 'Come on in. Mav and Nina are in the kitchen.'

Skye barely refrained from rolling her eyes, but she walked through to the kitchen, gave an appropriate gasp when everyone jumped out and shouted, 'Surprise!'

'You didn't think we'd let you leave without a proper send-off?' Sierra asked.

'This is awesome.' Skye raised her voice. 'Thank you, everyone!'

Maverick and Nina Hunt stepped forward first. To the rest of the world, Mav and Nina were Hollywood's most iconic love story. The cowboy proprietor and revered movie star who'd fallen in love when Nina had escaped to Hunt Ranch to recover from an assault in her LA home. But to Skye and the rest of the staff at Hunt Ranch, they were just Mav and Nina. When they weren't travelling for Nina's filming schedule, they were working the ranch and resort, getting their hands dirty like everyone else.

'We're going to miss you around here, Skye,' Mav said and handed her a sealed envelope. 'Your last paycheque. I've also included a list of all the rodeo folks I know, their locations, and cell numbers, in case you run into any trouble on the road.'

Because her throat burned with tears, Skye barely managed, 'Thank you.'

Nina wrapped her in a hug. 'Be careful. We can't wait to see what you accomplish, Skye.'

Nina stepped back, just as Poppy, Mav's six-year-old daughter, wrapped her arms around Skye's hips. 'I'll miss riding with you,' Poppy whispered.

Skye crouched down to the little girl's level. 'I'll come visit lots, so we can go riding together. Okay?'

''Kay. Maybe next time you come, Daisy will be big enough to ride too,' Poppy said. 'Or she can ride double with Daddy or Neens.'

'We'll see,' Skye promised, though she doubted the five-month-old would be quite there by the time she returned for the holidays.

As Nina and Mav filtered back into the crowd, Skye saw two familiar faces behind the body of cowboys. She had a single second to blink before Stevie and Andrea's combined 'Surprise!' rang through the room.

'What? You guys . . .'

Sierra, her arms now cradling one of the twins, laughed as Stevie and Andrea ran to Skye and pulled her into a group hug. 'And you thought you couldn't be surprised.'

Skye tucked her face between the girls. Her heart couldn't take much more. 'It's so good to see you,' she managed.

'You didn't think we'd miss this?' Stevie asked.

'We love you,' Andrea whispered. 'But we also got a free night at the resort.'

'*And* Sierra texted us your schedule,' Stevie added, 'so we're driving with you to Texas. We'll watch your races in Odessa and then fly out of Midland and head back to Dallas while you turn around to make your race in Colorado.'

'You're coming with me?' Skye asked in disbelief. 'For an entire week?' She stepped back, swiped her damp cheeks. 'This is the best surprise ever. It's been so long.'

It didn't matter that they texted each other every day and kept abreast of what was going on in each of their lives; texting wasn't the same as talking to your friends face to face or being able to touch them, to *hug* them.

Stevie, dressed in a tiny dress and thigh-high Western fashion boots, let her gaze track over Skye. 'You look *good.* Like, really good. And that's saying something given what you're wearing.' She sniffed at Skye exaggeratedly. 'Eau de Cheval?'

Skye laughed, unoffended. Her jeans were faded; her boots were scuffed. And although she didn't expect her friends to understand it, she wouldn't have changed a thing. 'It's this place,' she explained. 'It's . . . *home.*'

'It shows,' Andrea affirmed.

'Skye!' Sierra called her from across the room.

Skye walked to where Sierra stood with Mav, Stevie and Andrea trailing behind her. 'Everything okay?'

'We have a parting gift for you,' Sierra explained.

'You didn't have to—'

'It's something important,' Sierra said, cutting her off. 'Everyone chipped in.' She handed Skye a key with a ribbon tied through the hole at the top, then took her by the shoulders and, turning her around, propelled her back towards the front door.

Everyone followed.

Skye stepped out onto the porch and then simply froze. Because there, hitched to a Hunt Ranch Jeep parked on the front lawn, was a Sundowner living quarters horse trailer.

Skye shook her head in denial. 'You did not.'

Sierra shrugged as if the gift was something small and inconsequential. 'If you're gonna be on the road over forty weeks on the year, you need somewhere to sleep that isn't the cab of your truck.'

'I can't accept this,' Skye said instantly and tried to pass the key back to Sierra. Even second-hand, the trailer had to have cost them upwards of twenty grand.

'It's a '97 model we picked up at auction and fixed up,' Sierra argued. 'The heat doesn't work, one window doesn't open at all, and despite our best efforts to remove it, there's something that looks like a bloodstain in the middle of the carpet.' She held her hands palms up, refusing to take the key back. 'It's your starter home until you can afford something nicer.'

'But—'

Andrea took Skye's hand and gave it a squeeze, sealing the key between their palms. 'A lot of people chipped in to make this possible for you,' she said quietly.

'It's too much,' Skye insisted.

Sierra heard that. 'We all wanted to do it. If we hadn't, we wouldn't have.'

'I like her,' Stevie said simply, making everyone laugh. 'But, please, can we go look inside the damn thing now? I've only seen pictures.'

Skye looked down at the key in her hand and then back up at the trailer. Slowly, on shaky legs, she walked down the front porch steps and across the lawn, Stevie and Andrea close behind.

Perhaps sensing that she was close to tears, the others stayed back, giving her space.

Skye lowered the tailgate for the horse compartment first. Inside, to the left, there was a small tack room with a three-tier saddle rack and six bridle hooks. Someone had already neatly loaded her tack. Past it, three horse stalls separated by rubber-lined dividers stood side by side. The floors were lined with thick rubber padding; the overhead cargo light was working, and on.

Skye stepped into the trailer and opened the interior door.

The living quarters were small but cosy. There was a three-person couch set beneath a lofted queen bed. A microwave was recessed in a cupboard above a sink, with a mini fridge below. Two small closets held the toilet and shower. Storage cupboards and drawers were cleverly tucked away in every available space – above and beneath the sofa, along the side walls, and next to the microwave. A small TV had been mounted above the foot of the bed.

The trailer was almost thirty years old, and the age showed – in the faded linoleum on the walls and the tread-worn carpet, suspicious stain and all. But Skye was still immensely overwhelmed by the generous gift.

She'd pay them back as soon as she could, of course.

Skye plopped down on the sofa, while Stevie opened and closed cupboards. 'This is seriously lit.' She tapped the WiFi router that sat on the counter.

'They've stocked it with everything you could possibly need,' Andrea added and sat down next to Skye.

Skye let her head fall back on the sofa. 'Yeah,' she rasped.

Andrea took Skye's hand between both of hers. 'What's wrong?'

Skye wasn't sure how to explain except to say, 'I don't like being indebted to people. And a gift this extravagant . . .'

'They're not your father, Skye,' Andrea commented gently. 'They're friends. Their gifts don't come with the expectation of loyalty or forgiveness or silence.'

'Yeah. Fuck Holden,' Stevie added and raised her hand to Andrea's for a high-five.

Skye cracked her knuckles. 'He got me the Porsche for my seventeenth birthday.' The 911 had been parked in the front driveway with an ostentatious red bow stuck to the hood, one that had screamed, *Look what we can afford for our teenage daughter* to all the neighbours. 'I remember going outside and seeing it there and just feeling . . . *nothing.* No joy, no surprise. But I acted like it was the most exciting thing that had ever happened to me.'

Andrea didn't comment, just asked, 'Have you come up with a plan yet?'

'Keep moving. Don't look back. If Holden shows up, run. As soon as my birthday passes and I have control of the estate, cut him off, make sure that he gets nothing if anything happens to me.' Skye picked at a loose thread on the sofa. 'This is going to sound terrible, but I'm hoping he'll leave my mom when I cut her allowance. It was the one thing my grandma couldn't bring herself to do. But it's enabling her to stay with him.'

'You can't outrun him forever, Skye,' Andrea pointed out.

'I know.'

Her friends exchanged a worried glance.

'I'll deal with him when I have to,' Skye insisted. 'Until then, I just want to keep moving. Keep living. Keep racing.'

She knew they didn't necessarily agree. But neither one of them argued.

They exited the way they'd come in. Except this time, Stevie saw TJ's saddle hanging in the tack compartment. She flicked one fender with a long coffin-cut nail. 'You kept this?'

Skye tipped her shoulders self-consciously. 'I couldn't get rid of it.'

'*Why?*' Andrea asked.

'I dunno. I thought about it. But despite everything that happened, TJ gave that saddle to me in a moment of kindness.' Skye ran one hand over the well-worn seat. 'And destroying something I love just because he gave it to me seemed childish. When I see him again, he won't know how much he hurt me.'

Stevie held up one hand. 'What do you mean *when* you see him again?'

'Apparently, he's working rodeo events,' Skye explained, her tone carefully moderated. 'Which means I'll run into him eventually. Probably soon. I'm not sure if he's travelling, but my schedule takes me to Arizona quite a few times, because the Turquoise Circuit hosts a lot of co-approved rodeos with the California Circuit.'

'Well, fuck.' Stevie crossed her arms sassily. 'Dibs on the shovel.'

While Stevie resorted to dark humour, Andrea defaulted to worry. She caught Skye by the elbow, stopping her in her tracks when she tried to walk past. 'Are you going to be okay?'

'Yes.'

'Skye—'

'It's fine.' At Andrea's doubtful look, Skye added, 'I was naive and inexperienced. I read too much into it. But things are different now. *I'm* different now.'

'He hurt you.'

'Yes.' There was no point in denying it. Even if she hadn't told the girls everything, Andrea knew her too well. 'But never again,' she promised.

And she meant it.

On the farm later that same evening, TJ lay on his bed and stared up at the ceiling. He'd pushed his body too hard that day, so that now he barely moved, barely breathed, as pain sliced down either side of his back and a river of sciatica coursed through his right hip and leg.

His mom popped her head in, but TJ didn't even turn his head to look at her.

'Dinner's ready.'

'Not hungry,' he replied. Because only the thought of trying to make it downstairs hurt.

'TJ—'

When his phone started ringing, TJ used it as an excuse. 'You guys eat without me. I gotta get this.'

Janey offered him a small smile, but TJ noticed the hurt and the fear swimming just beneath it. He didn't – *couldn't* – acknowledge it, only frowned down at his phone and once he felt his mom move away, answered with, 'Mav?'

'TJ.' There was a smile in Mav's voice. 'Son of a bitch, it's good to hear your voice. We weren't sure how you were doing until we saw that you were riding pickup in Tucson.'

'Yeah, it's been a long road,' TJ replied cautiously. He'd worked a few rodeos, hoping that he'd get to participate in one last season. But just those few pickup gigs had been enough to remind him that he was well and truly done. Instead of enjoying himself, he'd had to fight through every second of pain. Instead of staying behind to bask in the fact that he was back at the rodeo, he'd had to run home or risk passing out in front of people who had once seen him take on goddamn bulls.

'Recovery's obviously going well?'

TJ wasn't sure how to reply to that, so he just made a noncommittal sound of agreement. But unable to resist, he asked, 'How's

Skye doing?' and held his breath as he waited for even the tiniest snippet from Mav.

'It's funny you should ask, TJ.'

TJ grimaced as he levered into a seated position on his bed. 'Oh?'

'Well, I was actually hoping you could return that favour . . .'

Chapter 21

The next morning, despite Stevie's protests, the girls hit the road just as the dark night shifted to the blue of pre-dawn.

They drove the full eight hours to Phoenix, stopping only for gas, restroom breaks, and a long lunch so that Smokey could stretch her legs and Skye could call Tia and ask if she could board Smokey at her place for a few nights.

Scottsdale was only a twenty-minute drive from Phoenix, and although Skye knew that she could have called Ryan or Janey and they would have welcomed her and her friends, she couldn't do it. It didn't matter that she and TJ were going to bump into each other eventually; she wasn't ready.

It was two-thirty in the afternoon by the time they passed the Phoenix city limit, three by the time Skye pulled up to the hammered metal gate outside's Tia's place.

She idled outside for a long moment. She had expected the memories; a woman couldn't escape those sensory reminders – the feel of wire in her hands, a faintly familiar scent clinging to a stranger in a crowd, hotel room sheets wrapped around a body. But here, now, looking at that gate, they were stronger than she'd expected.

'Skye?' Stevie touched her arm. 'You okay?'

'Yeah.' Skye shook her head as if she could clear it of the memories.

She leaned out the window and pressed the intercom. When the gate opened immediately, she drove slowly through and down the long drive towards the covered arena, where two people on horseback worked through a set of barrel drills.

Skye got out and walked over. As she got closer, she recognized Tia on her palomino. The other horse – a red roan Quarter Horse – was ridden by a man who might have been Skye's age or slightly older. He was a tall blond with quiet brown eyes that focused on her face.

Tia dismounted and passed her reins to the man with a few quiet words. He nodded and turned his horse towards the arena gate, leading Tia's horse behind his own.

'Skye!' Tia ducked between two of the arena's piped fence poles.

Two years hadn't changed her at all. She still had the same long, braided hair, dark eyes, and smoker's husky voice. She pulled Skye into a quick, friendly hug, said, 'Boy was I glad to hear from you.' She set Skye back. 'I knew you'd do it. The day you left, I told George: just you watch – that girl's gonna be leaving me in the dust before too long.'

Skye tipped her head, unwilling to agree with the compliment. 'We'll see how it goes. You competing this year?'

'No. Our breeding and training programme really took off last year.'

'Which makes travelling hard,' Skye commented.

'It does. But I'd be lying if I said that was the only reason.' Tia slipped her thumbs into the pockets of her jeans. 'I was *tired.* Always away from home, always sleeping on the road. If I thought I'd have a chance at the NFR, I might have kept at it for a few more years, but there's a point where the sight of all those young girls with more fire than you, more energy than you, and all those years ahead of them, just makes an old girl like me feel past her expiration date.' She released a raspy chuckle. 'Clearly,

I am no Lisa Lockhart.'

'There's only one Lisa Lockhart,' Skye replied. 'These are my friends, Stevie and Andrea. They're travelling with me to Odessa before flying back to Dallas.'

Tia greeted them warmly before walking around to the back of the trailer. 'Let's get Smokey offloaded and park your rig.'

At Skye's side, Stevie asked, 'Who's Lisa Lockhart?'

'Barrel Racing legend,' Skye explained. 'She's in her early sixties and still qualifies for the NFR like every year. I think she's legitimately competed in it twenty times.'

'That's wild.'

'Tell me about it.'

'Could you imagine if you got to compete against her one of these days?'

The thought made Skye want to hurl. And still, the strangest thing was that it wasn't outside the realm of possibility anymore. She'd be competing in Rodeo Rapid City, South Dakota in only a month. The rodeo was in the Badlands Circuit, and that was Lockhart's home circuit. Her only comfort was that barrel racing included a rider, her horse, and the clock, so even when she ran against the best in the industry, only their times would go up against each other.

'I probably won't even be at the rodeos at the same time.' *Praise Jesus*, Skye added internally. 'I'm choosing to run in the slack when I can.'

'The slack?'

'Yeah. Ah, so, basically, at events with a lot of contestants, we're split into "performance" and "slack". The overspill will run outside of the main ticketed rodeo show times. The slack.'

'You don't want to run during the performance?'

'Not really. Smokey still gets a little spooked by big crowds,' Skye explained. 'So, running in the slack is actually easier for her. No crowds.' Although she didn't say it, Skye preferred it too. There was no pressure when there was no crowd. There was no expectation of entertainment. No televised event her father might be able to use to track her whereabouts.

Tia unbolted the trailer and lowered the ramp. 'You better work on desensitizing her, because once you start making the big rodeos – the American, the NCFR, Rodeo Houston – there is no slack anymore.'

'Yeah,' Skye agreed, though the chance of her making any of those rodeos this year was slim to none.

They offloaded Smokey and, after letting her walk around, settled her into her stall with food and water. It was only once they had hooked up the trailer to the water and sewer that Tia said, 'Well, I'll let you relax and get settled in. You're welcome to come by the house for dinner if you'd like? We're having a few people over for a barbecue.'

'Thanks, Tia. I think we're going to wash the travel grime off and then head into town for a few drinks. We'll stop for food when the mood strikes.'

'Stop by anyway, so I can give you a gate remote in case we're sleeping by the time you get back. You're welcome to leave your dog with ours while you go out too.'

'Thank you. Oh, and do you mind if I use the arena tomorrow morning?'

'Not at all. If you text me when you're tacking up, I'll come watch.' She winked at Skye. 'Maybe this time, you can give me some pointers.'

'I doubt it.'

Tia grinned. With one last wave, she headed towards the farmhouse.

In the trailer, while Stevie showered and Andrea emptied her huge bag in search of something to wear, Skye opened the YouTube app on her TV and pressed play on a throwback playlist. She turned the volume all the way up, so that 'Fireflies' by Owl City pumped through the confined interior of the trailer.

'I love this song!' Stevie shouted from inside the shower.

Andrea walked over to the mini fridge. 'And *look* what some kind soul stocked in the fridge.' She pulled out a bottle of champagne. With a few expert moves, she twisted the cork off.

Skye opened the cupboard over the sink, took stock of the meagre supplies. 'I have exactly two glasses – and they're water glasses.'

Andrea tipped the champagne bottle back and took a huge sip – then immediately started coughing as the bubbles fizzed down her throat. 'Holy shit,' she rasped. 'It's been a while.' She passed the bottle to Skye at the same time that Stevie stepped out of the shower wrapped in a towel.

Stevie snatched the bottle out of Skye's hand and took a sailor's swig before passing it back.

Skye looked down at the bottle. 'Fuck it.' She raised it up, said, 'To the best friends a girl could ask for,' and then followed suit.

The bubbles raced down her throat, tightening her chest. But as the sensation faded, Skye's body relaxed. Her muscles calmed. So, she had an insanely stressful year of racing ahead of her and a father who might or might not pose a very serious threat to her safety? She'd deal with those the only way she knew how: one day at a time. But tonight . . . Tonight was for the girls.

As 'Fireflies' transitioned to 'I Gotta Feeling' by the Black Eyed Peas, as Stevie and Andrea started dancing and singing, Stevie still in her towel, Andrea stripping her shirt as she danced, Skye accepted that for each thing that was out of her control, there was another that was not. Despite everything, she had found two world-class friends, work and an extended family that she loved, two animals she'd literally take a bullet for. And those things, however irrevocably small to another, were everything to her.

They were things she could be proud of.

They were things she would fight for.

Chapter 22

Because they were drinking, they Ubered into Phoenix.

They started with dinner at an upscale restaurant before making their way from bar to bar. By only nine p.m., they were well and truly hammered, but after a long walk down Jefferson Street, all three of them felt sufficiently revitalized for one last round.

The January air nipped along Skye's skin as they meandered towards the bar Andrea wanted to go to, a small honky-tonk a half mile away called Dave's. In the microscopic black dress Stevie had insisted Skye wear, about as much was left to the imagination as was protected from the elements. Skye huddled deeper into her denim and shearling jacket, thankful that at least her upper body was practically dressed.

At her side, Stevie wore baggy black jeans, a cropped sweater top, and platform sneakers. Andrea, after much debate, had settled on an outfit that Skye always thought of as her uniform: a short skirt with black winter tights underneath, a white blouse with a sweater vest over it, and Doc Martens on her feet.

They might have been an odd-looking trio, different in style and looks and personality, but they drew plenty of attention. Never more so than when they stepped into Dave's.

The door closed behind them.

The loud chatter died suddenly, leaving Whitesnake's 'Here I Go Again' the only sound in the room. It seemed as if every eye focused on them.

After a beat of silence, Stevie asked, 'Anyone wanna buy a girl a drink?'

A few hands shot up.

A low whistle sounded from the bar.

Skye looked up to find the cowboy she'd seen at Tia's. He sat at the end of the bar, his blond hair free of his hat, his long legs clad in denim. He waved them over.

As everyone went back to their drinks, Skye led the way to where the cowboy sat. 'You were at Tia's earlier.'

When he smiled, twin dimples winked. 'Beau Baker, Tia's son.'

Skye made introductions. 'Skye, Stevie, Andrea.'

Beau greeted the girls in turn and then stood to hunt up an extra barstool. The moment he was out of earshot, Stevie whispered, 'Dibs.'

Skye snorted.

Andrea didn't say anything, just linked her hands in front of her like a schoolgirl about to be chastised.

'So, what'll it be?' Beau asked once he'd set the barstool down and the girls had taken their seats. He leaned over the bar so that all three of them heard him clearly. 'Word to the wise: stick to the basics. Last time I ordered a house cocktail here, I was sick for a week.'

Before they could even place an order, Stevie said, 'Four shots of tequila, please!' and did a drumroll on the bar top.

Skye's mouth watered at the thought of forcing the shot down.

Her stomach roiled.

Andrea groaned aloud. 'I can't.'

Beau looked down the bar at them, his grin wide. 'I take it you ladies have had a bit of a head start?'

'I think we're on hour five,' Andrea commented.

'You guys are fine,' Stevie insisted. 'You just need to add a glass of water for every cocktail.'

'I'm pretty sure that's not how it works,' Skye commented. 'And I am not fine.' Somewhere between leaving the cold air outside and entering the overheated bar, she'd started to feel the weight of her decisions. 'I haven't had this much to drink *ever*. My stomach feels pickled.'

The bartender placed the shots on the bar in front of them.

'Put them on my tab, Tommy,' Beau instructed. 'We'll close out.'

Skye couldn't speak over the lump of bile fighting its way up her throat. She gingerly pushed the tequila shot towards Beau. 'Please. I insist.'

'I'm driving you all home,' he argued. He passed both shots down to the couple sitting next to him with a simple, 'On us.'

'Boo.' Stevie threw back her shot, and when Andrea made no move to down hers, Stevie shot hers too. 'What happened to going dancing?' She slammed the shot glass on the bar.

Saliva pooled in Skye's mouth. She stood up, accidentally tipping over the barstool in her rush. It clattered to the floor. Everyone turned to look at her. But Skye didn't care. Unsure of where the restroom was but one hundred per cent certain she was going to throw up, she started running for the exit.

She flung open the door, took a greedy gulp of air.

Her vision swam.

A self-pitying sob pushed up her throat. 'Oh, God. Please no.'

It was going to happen.

She was going to be sick on a public sidewalk.

She braced for it just as a familiar voice, one that she'd tried to cut out of her memory, cut through her panic. 'Skye?'

Skye looked up into TJ's green eyes, eyes that were wide with shock. She sobbed, '*Fucking perfect.*' And, leaning over, threw up on his boots.

TJ's heart was racing like a Thoroughbred's on the track. For a second there, he'd almost managed to convince himself that she was a figment of his imagination. How many times had he imagined running into her? How many times had he *wished* for it? *Feared* it?

Before he could recover from the shock of seeing those fucking blue eyes again, so panicked, she stumbled down the sidewalk, using one arm to try and hold herself up on the nearby wall as the next wave of sick came.

Without a thought to his boots, he followed her. 'Hey,' he said quietly, 'relax. Stop running.'

'Please leave me alone,' she begged. But she stopped moving, plopped onto her butt right there on the dirty sidewalk and, burying her head in her hands, burst into tears.

TJ reached for her, but right as his fingertips grazed her hand, right as his heart jackhammered at that first contact after *so long*, Skye jerked out of his grasp. She leaned away.

Someone shouted, 'Skye!' from the bar's entrance.

TJ managed to make out two girls before they descended on him like a pack of wolves. The black-haired one's eyes widened when she saw him. But she didn't say anything, just swayed tipsily.

The other silently inserted her body between Skye and him, forcing TJ to stand and move away.

'TJ?'

TJ glanced up to see Beau Baker. 'Hey, man. Sorry I'm late. One of the bulls got out.'

'No worries. I was just about to text you.' Beau looked down at Skye, and TJ could have sworn the other man's eyes softened. 'Raincheck?' Beau asked. 'I gotta get these girls home.'

'She's staying with you?' TJ asked, and although he was surprised, he shouldn't have been. He'd always known Skye would never willingly look up his family again.

'Yeah.' Beau looked back and forth between TJ and Skye. 'Ah, Skye's a friend of my mom's. Barrel racer.'

'We'll Uber,' the brunette said, changing the topic. But she clearly knew who TJ was. She glared at him, as if he were a threat. As if he were dangerous – to *Skye.*

'Yeah, we're to'lly fine,' the girl with black hair slurred.

Beau put both hands on his hips. 'Yeah, no. A, we're going to the same place. B, I'm not letting you get into a car with a stranger in your current state.'

'C,' Skye whispered and, ignoring TJ completely, raised her eyes to Beau, 'I would rather throw up in your truck than an Uber?'

'Atta girl.' Beau crouched down in front of Skye, extended both hands palms-up. 'Need some help?'

'Yeah,' she managed, but the words were shaky. And she didn't so much as look at TJ.

'All right. I'm gonna lift you, okay?'

''Kay.'

When Beau reached under Skye's bare legs and around her back, TJ closed his hands into tight fists.

'Ah, raincheck? Tomorrow?' Beau asked TJ distractedly. 'Same time?'

Unsure of what to say, TJ just nodded and stepped aside.

He watched Beau walk down the street, Skye in his arms, her head resting on his shoulder. Her friends stuck to either side of him, forming a defensive wall.

As the shock of the meeting began to fade, as the stunning blow of seeing Skye again sank in, the pain came back in full force. TJ's spine spasmed from when he'd crouched on the floor. The muscles in his right side flickered and twitched. A torrent of angry fire spread from his right hip down to his knee, but below that point, all his nerves were numb.

He closed his eyes and took a deep breath as he fought the tremors. His entire body was a constant and painful symphony – one he would never be rid of.

The entire encounter with Skye might have spanned three minutes. But it was enough to remember:

Every second he'd spent with her.

The weight of the bull coming down on him.

After . . .

But as he watched another man – a *friend* – carry her in a way he'd never be able to, as the pain had sweat coating his brow, he remembered why he had hurt Skye, and why he would ride through the pain for one last season.

TJ looked towards the doors of Dave's. Although the promise of oblivion beckoned, called to him even, for the first time in a while, he didn't give in to it. He turned on his heel and walked the short distance back to his parked truck, his right leg hitching in a pronounced limp. If he was going to try and speak to Skye in the morning, he wanted to be clearheaded. Calm.

He drove home without detouring, and when he walked into the kitchen, his mom looked up from where she was making a cup of tea. She frowned. 'That was quick. Beau cancel?'

'Ah, no. He had to drive some guests of Tia's home,' TJ said. He opened the fridge, foraging for something to eat. But because he was still hovering in some state of disbelief, he closed the door almost immediately, asked, 'Did you know Skye was staying with the Bakers?'

The spoon his mom was stirring her tea with clattered on the counter, answering his question before she said, 'What?'

'Yeah. I just saw her.'

'No. I mean, you told me she's racing this year, of course. But, no, I didn't know she was in town.'

'Her and two friends. They must be passing through.'

'Oh.' For just a moment, his mom seemed sad or maybe disappointed. But she caught herself. 'How did she look? Happy?'

TJ almost smiled. He didn't think anyone could focus on being happy while actively throwing up. But he answered honestly. 'She looked the same.'

And he thought: *Beautiful. Perfect. So fucking far out of my reach.*

Chapter 23

Skye woke up in the trailer the next morning with a throat that was desert-dry, eyes that were swollen and achy, and a pounding headache, the likes of which she'd never experienced before.

Next to her, Andrea's socked feet twitched while she slept. On the sofa below, either Stevie or Bandit snored softly.

Skye sat up slowly and raised one hand to her head. She let her forehead sink into her palm as everything came flooding back.

She'd run into TJ.

And she'd vomited on his boots.

Skye groaned as the memory had a wash of saliva flooding her mouth. Of all the ways she'd imagined them meeting again, *that* had certainly not made the list. Goddamnit, it was supposed to have happened at a rodeo, a big event where she could saunter past him, give him a casual smile and a nonchalant, 'Oh, hi, TJ.'

Instead, she'd been sick as a dog. She'd thrown up on him. And worst of all, she'd *cried*. And while he might not have known that some of the tears were over him, over the shock of seeing him again so unexpectedly, *they had been*. 'Idiot,' she muttered to herself.

'Stop shouting,' Andrea mumbled. She lifted her head from her pillow at the foot of Skyes's bed to glare at her.

Skye nearly laughed. Although she'd managed to change into her pyjamas, Andrea hadn't gotten to removing her makeup. Her mascara was ringed around her eyes. A smudge of lipstick had somehow stuck to her cheek even though her lips were long clear of it.

'You look terrifying.'

Andrea sniffled. 'At least I managed to change.'

Skye lifted the covers. Sure enough, she was still in the tiny black dress, which had hiked to her waist while she'd slept. 'Whelp. That's embarrassing.' She wiggled her toes. 'Who put my socks on.'

'You were wearing them already, but Stevie took your boots off.' Andrea rolled over to peek at Stevie on the sofa.

Skye followed suit.

Stevie's face was clear of all makeup. Her sleep headband was neatly holding her hair back. Her Eeyore pyjamas looked cosy and clean. Bandit was curled up at her side.

'I don't know how she does it,' Andrea commented.

Without opening her eyes, Stevie replied, 'I told you: you gotta go one for one – water to booze ratio.'

'That's literally not how intoxication works,' Andrea stated. 'Time is the only thing that can reduce drunkenness.'

'It's not about *reducing drunkenness*,' Stevie mimicked Andrea's pert tone. 'It's about staying hydrated so that you don't feel like ass the next day.'

Skye and Andrea exchanged a laughing glance. 'We do look awful,' Skye admitted.

'And I do feel like ass,' Andrea seconded. 'You?'

'Oh, yeah.'

'Told you,' Stevie mumbled and, turning on her side, spooned Bandit as she dozed off again.

Skye climbed out of bed. She winced as her stomach sloshed with every step. 'I need a shower, some Advil, and an unholy amount of refined carbohydrates.'

'I would offer to go, but I can't drive your truck.' Andrea moved up to the head of the bed so that she could flick on the TV.

Skye waved her off. 'I'll go.'

She showered and changed, and even though Bandit didn't seem particularly inclined to move from Stevie's side, she called him so that she could let him out and feed him. Only, the moment she opened the trailer door, Skye stopped dead in her tracks.

Because there, leaning against the piped arena fencing, a box of to-go coffee and a bag of bagels in his hands, was TJ, the man she'd tried so hard to forget.

How Skye got through the next few minutes, she'd never know, but she managed to summon a tone of indifference as she finally said, 'Look, we had a fling ages ago. It ended. We both moved on. There's nothing to talk about. And there's certainly nothing to rehash.'

'Glad we agree on that,' he replied casually.

Skye ground her jaw as her anger bloomed. 'Yup.'

'I half expected you to be pining after me all this time.'

Fury burst through her instantly. She tipped her head back to glare at him. 'Do not fucking push me.'

TJ's eyes glinted with a dark and twisted triumph. Leaning close, he whispered, 'There you are, Wild Skye.'

She bit off a curse, turned her eyes away from him, and crossed her arms defensively. 'What do you want?' she repeated.

TJ was quiet for a moment. 'There're things I need to say to you, Skye. Things I need to tie up.'

'I'm not a loose end that you get to put a pretty ribbon on, TJ.'

Frustratingly, he just said, 'I know.' He handed her the box of coffee and the bagels.

Skye stared at the offering as if it were some malicious bargain, a deal with the devil.

'Don't be stubborn.'

'I'm only taking this because I genuinely have battery acid in my stomach,' she informed him. But she took the bag of bagels, gripped the coffee by the handle.

'Come to dinner tonight.'

'No.' The refusal was instant. As much as the invite surprised her, not even coffee and bagels softened her that much.

'My mom knows you're in town. She wants to see you.'

Skye shook her head, frustrated that he'd go there. Because she genuinely adored his parents. 'How are they?'

'Good.' He tipped his head. 'But you could come see that for yourself.'

Skye was curious – and hated herself for it. 'We're heading out actually.' It wasn't a lie. The moment she'd seen TJ again, she'd made up her mind to move on. And even though she would have loved to have seen Janey and Ryan, she couldn't spend more time than necessary with TJ. It hurt too much.

'They'll be sorry to hear that.' He tapped the arena fence. 'I guess I'll just be off then.'

'Be seeing you,' she replied nonchalantly.

And although he replied with a cryptic, 'Yup,' Skye was too focused on his severe limp as he walked away to think much on the words.

TJ's right leg hitched with every step, and when he came to his truck, he had to use the interior grip to haul himself into the vehicle.

She watched as he drove away, scowled when he gave a friendly honk off his horn before heading down the drive.

Skye turned back for the trailer, the bagels and coffee in hand. She saw Stevie and Andrea, their faces glued to the window, and couldn't help but sigh when they ducked down. By the time she opened the door, Stevie was sitting on the sofa, brushing her hair. Andrea was lying in bed again, her eyes glued to the TV.

'Coffee and bagels.' Skye dumped both on the counter by the sink.

'Wow, that was fast,' Andrea commented.

'Is there a place nearby?' Stevie asked casually.

Skye leaned back against the sink. 'You guys know you can just ask, right?'

Stevie went first. 'Are you okay?'

'Yes,' Skye answered honestly. 'I'm glad it's over.'

'What did he want?'

Skye frowned, but she answered Andrea's question. 'I have no idea. He said he had some things to say to me – and then never actually said them.'

'That's it?' Stevie flopped back against the sofa. 'Huh. I was kinda expecting him to grovel.'

'He had that look about him – last night,' Andrea affirmed. 'He looked at you like you were the last drop of water out the well.'

'Don't.' The single word had both her friends' eyes snapping to her, but Skye just shrugged and pushed off the sink. 'It was a fling. Just a few days.'

'Skye.' Andrea shimmied closer over the mattress. 'You don't have to pretend with us.'

Skye exhaled a stuttered breath. 'I was so young, so inexperienced. And I saw something, felt something, that wasn't there. Rehashing it now just embarrasses me. I'm going to exercise Smokey while you guys eat, and then we'll head out if that's okay with you? Coming back here was a mistake.'

Stevie smiled. 'Sure. We're just along for the ride.'

When TJ got home, both his parents were waiting on the porch for him. They weren't even pretending to be busy, just sitting, waiting.

His mom stood when he got out of his truck and walked across the front yard.

'Well? What did she say?'

'She's heading out, Mom. But she sends her best.'

His mom deflated. 'Oh.'

'I saw Bandit though,' he added, trying to take the edge off her disappointment. 'He looks great. Skye has him trained better than any police dog.'

Janey smiled at that. 'He was hers from the moment she walked in the door.' She reached up one hand, placed her palm on his face. 'Are you okay, baby?'

TJ kept his face carefully free of bitterness. 'I'm fine.' The truth was that he hadn't been okay for a long time, not since that last ride. His life was simply one constant and draining battle with pain. Still, he'd learned early on that there was no point in dragging his family down with him, especially given that there was nothing any of them could do about it.

'I'm fine,' he repeated. It was his signature response, one of those quick replies that cut off any attempts to dig deeper.

His mom smiled sadly. 'You hungry? I could whip you up some eggs or a sandwich—'

'No. I'm gonna do the fence check, try and figure out where Tank slipped through last night.' TJ included his dad in the conversation when he added, 'Are you going to be okay without me?' It was an open-ended question, and when his mom's eyes filled, TJ added, 'Working the rodeo again is going to take me away for most of the year.'

His mom stared at his face as if unsure of how to broach the subject without making him angry. But eventually, she reminded him, 'Doctor Wu told you to stop, TJ. You're exacerbating—'

'I did stop, Mom,' TJ snapped, unable to contain his anger. 'Or have you forgotten that first year? I didn't ride. I didn't run. I didn't so much as sneeze without perfect posture, and it didn't make one fucking inch of difference.'

'Watch your mouth,' his dad warned.

His mom was unconcerned by his language. But she didn't let him off the hook either. 'Is this because of Skye?'

TJ didn't lie. 'In part. I need to close that circle.'

'Why?'

TJ knew what she was asking: *Why are you wrapping up your*

life? Why are you talking like you have a deadline? What are you planning? But he didn't answer the loaded question the way she wanted him to. He only told her a different truth. 'Mav called. Apparently, Skye's had some trouble. He asked me to keep an eye on her.' He could see that his mom wasn't buying it, and unwilling to tell her any of Skye's secrets, he added, 'I hurt someone I cared about. And I'm not going to be at peace until I make things right.'

She nodded at that. 'Okay.'

His dad sighed audibly. 'When do you leave?'

'Tomorrow.'

'TJ—'

'You better see to that fence,' his dad said.

'Yeah. I'll be back to help with the evening milking.'

In the barn, TJ slowly and painstakingly tacked up Kai. Instead of swinging into the saddle with ease, he walked the horse to a big, concrete mounting block his dad had built for him. He climbed the steps carefully, slid into the saddle with absolute control.

It hurt.

But then again, everything hurt. All the time.

He pushed Kai into a walk with a subtle roll on his hips, braced and then breathed through the pain as the horse started forward.

They picked their way over the land together, TJ's mind on another time and place. Another TJ. It was odd to think about how different his life would be if those two seconds hadn't happened. Instead, here he was, a broken man with no future at all.

The thought didn't make him sad. He'd come to see death as nothing more than an end to suffering, an absence of pain. There was peace in that.

Chapter 24

Odessa, Texas – January 12, 2027

The girls spent four perfect days in the town of Silver City, New Mexico, en route to Odessa. They hauled the trailer into the Gila National Forest, a wilderness area spanning over three million acres.

In the early morning, while Andrea and Stevie slept, Skye rode Smokey on the allocated horseback riding trails, Bandit trotting at their side. She didn't push her horse, only gave the mare the movement she needed and the rest she deserved leading up to the Sandhills Stock and Show Rodeo in Odessa.

Once her friends were up and about, the girls spent the days hiking the numerous trails and swimming in the lakes – following Rule Number Two, of course, and wearing their bathing suits. They saw the Dragonfly Trail Petroglyphs and spent one night lying on their backs under a billion stars at a Gila Cliff Dwellings' dark sky gathering. They hiked to the Kneeling Nun National Monument and, in an odd hour free and with nothing better to do, decided to go and look at where Billy the Kid's mother was buried.

It was only when they were driving into Odessa at the end of their trip that Andrea said, 'God, Skye. You're so *free.*'

Skye didn't point out the difference between roughing it for a few days versus making it a lifestyle, one where you constantly worried about your finances and your safety. She didn't say that, sometimes, being alone on the road was scary and exhausting and *so lonely* and that, often, she doubted her own sanity. She just said, 'It definitely has its perks.'

She shifted down to first gear as she carefully navigated her trailer through the gates at the Ector County Coliseum.

'I envy you,' Andrea added. 'Both of you. Tech marketing sucks.'

'Your problem, Andrea,' Stevie added, 'is that you're too much of a rule follower.'

Andrea scoffed. 'I am not.'

Stevie got out when Skye parked outside Barn B, but before she slammed the door shut, she said, 'Skye, back me up here.'

Andrea was eerily quiet.

'There's nothing wrong with following the rules,' Skye offered cautiously, as she turned the engine off.

'What about when the rules stop you from living a full life?' Andrea asked quietly.

'You want my honest opinion?'

'Always.'

'Rewrite them,' Skye said with a shrug. 'I did. And if I can do it with nothing but a truck to sleep in, God knows you can too.'

Skye looked out the windshield when Stevie slapped the hood and shouted, 'What are you guys doing? Let's freaking go!'

Andrea sighed. 'She's exhausting.'

'Yeah. But I wish I had her energy.'

Outside, Stevie grabbed Bandit's front paws and started dancing with the dog, right there in the parking lot.

Skye and Andrea climbed out of the truck together. 'I'm going to get Smokey settled into the barn if y'all want to walk around. The show animals should be here already if you want to look. Just remember: they're not pets. And don't get into any trouble.'

'Trouble? Me?' Stevie asked innocently and batted her lashes.

'Oh, boy.' Andrea took Stevie by the hand like a mother with an overactive child. 'Come on. Skye, text us when you're done and we'll go get dinner?'

'Yeah.'

Skye waited until they'd disappeared from sight before taking a huge breath. She leaned against the hood of her truck, crossed her arms over her chest, and stared towards where the huge steel ribs of the Coliseum building rose.

That anxiety that always churned in her stomach before a race was there, and it was so much stronger than usual. This wasn't just a random race she had time to fit into her work schedule. This was her career now. The stakes were so much higher. Still, she told herself, *No big deal. You're running in the slack. Nobody's gonna be watching. It's just you, Smokey, and the clock.*

TJ saw her the second she walked in, Smokey's lead rope in one hand, Bandit trotting at her other side, a familiar black cowboy hat on her head. He also saw the second she looked up and spotted him. Her face fell, and although he couldn't blame her, he also couldn't help but feel her dread as it lashed through him.

Once, he'd counted her smiles. Now, he knew he'd probably never see one directed at him again, and as much as it hurt, he couldn't move on until he'd made things right, until he'd made sure she was safe from her father for good.

Just as she'd done outside her trailer at Tia's, she walked up to him, her eyes twin blue flames, asked, 'The fuck, TJ?'

Because Kai had his big head over the stall door, TJ ran one hand down the horse's soft face. He stoically tried to ignore the impatient tap of his heart in his chest. 'I'm not here to bother you, Skye. I'm working.'

'You're *working*?'

'Yup. Got a few pickup jobs lined up this season.' He didn't say that he'd pulled in every favour he could to get signed up at rodeos that coincided with the schedule Mav had sent him.

Skye looked down at the tag on the stall next to his, scowled when she realized that their horses would be stalled next to one another. 'You better say whatever it is you want to say to me, because I'm not going to spend the entire season dodging you.'

TJ nodded slowly. He didn't really have a plan outside of apologizing, explaining why he'd done what he'd done, and making sure she was safe from her father before he left. 'I'm sorry – that's the first thing.'

Skye exhaled a frustrated breath. 'I told you – it's history. We had a fling—'

'Bullshit.'

'What the hell is that supposed to mean?' she demanded.

'Fling, my ass.'

Skye paled. She fisted both hands around Smokey's lead rope. 'It was a few days.'

'Time is inconsequential in reference to what happened between us. You know that; otherwise, you wouldn't be so angry.'

Skye's blue eyes were huge in her face. Worse, they were sad. 'Why are you doing this?' she whispered.

'Because I need you to understand why I did what I did. I need you to know that I did it for you.'

'You used me.'

'No.' It crushed him that she thought that, even though he'd always known anger would be best for her. 'I let you go because I couldn't fucking walk. And, worse, I wasn't entirely sure that I ever would.' When that anger and resentment over what had happened threated to drag him down, TJ took a deep breath. He very calmly added, 'I wouldn't tie you to me. Not after such a short time. Not when you had your whole life to get started on.'

She looked away, focusing on something over his left shoulder. 'Why now?' she asked. 'I know for a fact that you worked the rodeos at least part of last year. So, if it was that important to you to see me, why did you wait so long? Why now?'

Why now? It was such a simple question, but there was no simple answer. 'I want closure – for both of us. And I want to make sure you're safe.' He leaned against the stall, taking weight off his back. 'Only a few months to go before your birthday.'

TJ saw the fear slip into her eyes a second before she stifled it. She didn't address that, only said, 'I don't need closure, TJ.' She led Smokey into the stall, took the mare's halter off before stepping out and sliding the door shut behind her horse. 'I haven't thought about you in ages.'

She walked away without another word or a backwards glance, but TJ couldn't help but shout, 'Nice hat!' to her back.

Skye flipped him the bird over her shoulder. And she didn't look back.

There was a grin working around the corners of his mouth for the first time in almost two years. His eyes, which had been flat and dull for a long time, sparked. A flicker of light ignited in his dark heart.

He got back to grooming Kai as Skye walked back and forth, hauling her tack and feed in.

Although she solidly ignored him, TJ didn't mind. It was enough to be close to her, to hear her moving about and mumbling words of love to her horse.

For just ten minutes, TJ was at peace.

But the calm made him lax. With his mind on Skye, and not on his posture, he bent over to pick Kai's hoof. In his distraction, he didn't go slow, didn't keep his mind and body focused on every inch of movement to minimize the pain. His back protested at the casual movement. A sharp spasm gripped him by the spine, momentarily rendering him useless as the muscles in his back and chest twitched in protest.

Aware of Skye standing so close, TJ bit down on his tongue, refusing to make a sound.

But, unable to remain upright through the spasms, he lowered down to his knees and made a show of looking closely at Kai's leg.

Kai, always in tune to TJ's erratic heartbeat, moved his hindquarters away from where TJ knelt, effectively blowing his cover. The horse swung his big head in TJ's direction and blew a questioning breath against his face.

TJ reached out one hand and gripped a chunk of Kai's mane, and when he whispered, 'Back,' the horse took three steps back, dragging TJ to his feet.

The moment he was upright, TJ leaned against Kai's side. He tried to keep his panted breaths quiet, tried to wipe the sweat on his brow before it became noticeable. He fisted his hands and waited for the spasm to pass, but his head pounded with every twitch of his back. Bile clogged his throat.

When he finally looked up, Skye was standing in Smokey's stall. Through the vertical bars separating their horses, TJ saw the wide-eyed fear and – worse – pity on her face.

And he couldn't bear it.

He clenched his jaw against fresh movement, slid open the stall door, closed it behind him, and left the barn. And even though it took all the strength he had left, he kept his fucking spine straight as he walked away.

Chapter 25

Even though Skye had told Stevie and Andrea numerous times that she'd be riding in the slack and that there would be zero pomp and circumstance, the girls hadn't listened. They'd dressed as if they were going to the American Rodeo, both of them in shorts and cowgirl boots despite the chilly weather.

And they'd made a banner.

Skye could see the monstrosity of glitter from where she sat on Smokey, waiting in the holding area with her drag. And although she'd rolled her eyes and told them they were embarrassing her, it made her grin to see her name up in the empty stands.

With the rodeo performance only starting that evening, the people in the thin crowd were mostly other racers and their relatives. The blue arena seats were largely empty, so Skye saw TJ the moment he sat down.

Dressed in dark blue jeans and a black button-down, his black hat obscuring his eyes, he looked like the devil's own messenger, sent to tempt women away from their straight and narrow paths.

She hadn't seen him since the day before, when she'd turned around to snap at him – and instead of standing and grooming his horse, he'd been on his knees on the floor of his stall, his eyes closed, his jaw tensed, his arms visibly twitching.

Skye hadn't known what to do. It shamed her now, to admit that. If she'd been clearheaded, she would have dropped her curry comb and gone to help him. Instead, she'd been too afraid. Afraid of hurting him, of embarrassing him. But more than that – and something she was struggling to forgive herself for – she'd been afraid of touching him. Of being close to him. Of breaking that no contact barrier.

Instead of pondering it, Skye blocked the thought. When the announcer said, 'Next up, number seventy-four, Georgia Laraby and Who Can Catch Me out of Stephenville, Texas,' she snapped to attention.

She was next.

Number seventy-five.

She tried to focus as Georgia and Who Can Catch Me pranced down the alley. As the duo broke into a gallop and headed to the right for the first barrel, Skye purposefully shifted her gaze away.

She moved Smokey to the mouth of the holding area, waited seventeen seconds for Georgia and her horse to come racing past them and out the gate at the end of their race, before stepping Smokey into the alley.

And then everything changed. The narrow alley tunnelled her vision to the third and final barrel up ahead. Skye took a deep breath to try and calm her racing pulse. Smokey, perhaps hearing Skye's screaming heartbeat or simply knowing her job, started pulling on the bit and stomping her hooves.

Skye held the horse back as the announcer's voice boomed. 'Number seventy-five: Rookie Skye Marchant and Smoking Barrel from Santa Barbara, California. Let's go, girls!'

The chorus of 'How You Like Me Now?' blared through the speakers.

Skye blocked everything out.

Beneath her, Smokey rocked forward impatiently.

Skye took one last deep breath.

She focused on the feel of her horse beneath her.

Everything slowed.

There was one moment of perfect stillness – and then Skye gave Smokey her head.

The moment the pressure on the bit released, Smokey shot down the alley.

The last thing Skye heard was the announcer's, 'Whoo-hoo! Look at them go!'

Skye took the left barrel first, getting Smokey's weaker side out of the way. They took the barrel in three strides and surged towards the second with a mighty lurch that pushed Skye deep into her saddle. She switched leads effortlessly, rounded the second in a hiccupping stride that threw them slightly off course for the third and final barrel.

Skye corrected instantly, but she internally berated herself for losing that half-second of time. They turned the third and sailed down the straight and across the laser line.

Skye didn't look back at the clock. But she heard Stevie and Andrea screaming her name, and rising above their shouts, she caught the announcer's, 'That's a 14.99, folks, and the time to beat during today's go-round.'

Skye pulled back, halting Smokey's adrenaline-fuelled dash down the alley. She managed to bring her horse down to an abrupt halt right before they crashed into the gate.

'Easy,' Skye crooned, and reaching down, patted Smokey's neck as the assistant starter opened the gate and let them back out of the arena.

Aware that other riders were still being fed into the holding area and that Smokey's adrenaline hadn't quite drained, Skye dismounted quickly. She took Smokey by the bridle and led her away from all the activity.

And that was Round One done. Years of training, weeks on the road, thousands of dollars on gas and vet bills and performance feed for a race that lasted about fifteen to nineteen exhilarating seconds.

The thought made Skye grin.

So, it wasn't for everyone.

But goddamn, it was for her.

TJ stood at the side of the warm-up arena, out of Skye's line of sight, and watched as she prepped Smokey for their first go round. While the WPRA's dress code was relatively strict, requiring jeans with no fashionable holes or slashed knees, Western shirts and hats, Skye had put her own twist on the outfit by opting for black jeans, a black, long-sleeved shirt and a bright-pink hat. Both the shirt and the hat had the Hunt Ranch brand on them, making TJ think that Mav and Sierra must have partially sponsored her for the season.

Smokey wore tendon boots and a saddle pad in the same shock of pink. The colour contrasted with the horse's ash-grey coat perfectly, but together, the girls definitely caught a person's eye.

It wasn't just their gear either. It was *them* – the way they moved together. Skye rode fluidly, running through drills with perfect precision, her hands and legs cuing Smokey with the smallest of motions.

It made TJ happy to see them, to know that Skye had become the horsewoman she'd always wanted to be. Looking at them now, nobody would know that they'd only been riding consistently for two years.

When Skye's group was called to the holding area and the five girls in her drag started exiting the warm-up arena, TJ turned and made his way to the stands to watch.

He took a seat a few rows below Skye's two friends, who'd brought a ridiculous banner that had Skye's name in bright-pink glitter. Down below, the tractors left the arena after grading the ground for the next group of girls. The moment the arena was cleared, the event crew hurried to put the barrels back in place.

The music's volume lowered, and the announcer came back on with, 'Next up, number seventy, from Blackfoot, Idaho: Sarah Goddard and her horse, Mickey's Fortune.'

TJ shifted instinctively every thirty seconds or so as he tried to find a comfortable seated position on the hard plastic chair.

He watched as the four girls before Skye ran, held his breath as number seventy-four took the straight and bounded down the alley towards the exit gate.

He didn't even hear the announcer as he introduced Skye, just focused on the woman and the horse as they stepped into the alley. Smokey immediately started prancing, her excitement clear. Skye, looking calm and collected, held the mare back.

She took her moment – and then let go. The mare was off like a shot. She galloped down the alley, rounded the first barrel perfectly. The second wasn't as smooth, but TJ held his breath as they managed to straighten out for the third. They took the last barrel and popped out of the turn fluidly. There was no stopping them on the straight.

'Yes!' he yelled and pumped both fists in the air as they passed the starting line, and the clock froze on 14.99. '*Goddamn.*'

He'd always known she'd do it. But watching her, seeing just how good she was, filled him with a ridiculous sense of pride.

Before he could stand to leave, Skye's friends bracketed him in, taking a seat on either side of him.

The black-haired one cracked her knuckles as she greeted him with, 'Triple J.'

The other one merely looked forward at the arena and asked, 'What are you doing here?'

TJ didn't lie. He sighed. 'I'm watching Skye. Just like you.'

'We don't like you,' she said.

The comment didn't surprise him. But it did hurt. There had been a time when he'd had only friends. Now, people he didn't even know apparently hated him. The burn of that had him replying, 'You don't know me.'

'You broke our friend's heart,' the black-haired one said simply. 'That's enough to put you at the top of our shit list.'

TJ, oddly, understood that. And it didn't make him angry. It filled him with relief to know that she'd always have these girls in her corner. They were oddly terrifying considering neither of them could have been more than five-five. 'I'm glad she has you.'

They both seemed a little taken aback by that.

'What's your game here, TJ?' the brunette asked. 'Skye has too much going on right now to worry about you too.'

TJ nodded slowly. 'Her dad?'

'That's none of your business,' the black-haired one told him.

'Maybe not,' TJ said carefully. 'But who do you think is going to look out for her when you two go back to your lives?' When they both just stared at him, he pushed to his feet. 'Let me know once you figure it out.'

He started walking away. But he only got three steps before the brunette called, 'Wait!'

'What are you doing?' the other one hissed when TJ turned around, eyebrows raised.

'He's right, Stevie. And as much as I don't like him, he's all we have.' She turned her big brown eyes on him, said, 'Fuck,' with a dramatic sigh. 'Please.' She indicated the seat he'd vacated with a regal tip of her head. 'Sit.'

TJ complied. But only because he assumed they had more information than him. If he was going to keep his promise to Mav, if he did one last thing for Skye, he'd make sure she was permanently free from her father's abuse. Even if he had to kill the asshole, TJ figured he had nothing left to lose.

'I'm Andrea. This is Stevie.'

TJ nodded. 'Has he contacted her at all?'

'Not that we know of.' Andrea leaned back in her seat. 'He contested the will a few years ago, but it never went anywhere. Her grandma's attorney was able to shut it down without pulling Skye in. The only contact Skye's had with home is weekly calls to her mom. They have a schedule: Sunday at three, Central Time – because her mom leaves the house for Bible study and calls Skye from her car on the way.'

TJ wondered what kind of mother could sit through Bible study after willingly putting her child through such restricted contact. 'Do you think he'll come after her?'

'Not in the way you're implying. Holden's smart. He won't do what you expect. He'll play mind games from a distance, torment her, maybe use her mom as leverage and force her to change her mind about cutting him off.'

'She's scared,' Stevie added. 'But she won't admit it. She thinks she knows Holden – and she does. But we know her. And when Holden uses Caroline, Skye will end up giving him anything he wants.'

Andrea looked out over the arena. 'And if he does physically threaten her, he'll use somebody else, make sure it doesn't tie back to him.'

TJ spoke his thoughts aloud. 'Which makes it worse.'

Stevie nodded. 'Because it could be any stranger on any street corner at any time.'

'Look, if it were up to us, Skye would have gone to the cops a long time ago. But all we had was video documentation after the fact, and she insisted that it would just turn into a "he said/she said". The last time that happened, he ruined her life.'

TJ remembered that Skye had told him her father had had her institutionalized.

'We're planning to come back, alternate spending time with her around her birthday—'

'But,' Stevie said slowly, 'we know there's only so much we can do. And even we can't be with her every minute of every day.'

'I'll think of something,' TJ promised.

'Holden is a goddamn criminal defence attorney.' Andrea leaned forward and ran both hands over her face, clearly stressed. 'He'll know every trick in the book.'

'I can handle him,' TJ said coolly.

'What do you mean by that—'

'If something happens,' TJ cut Andrea off, 'something that may or may not be completely legal, do you want to be associated with it?'

'Do *you*?' Stevie demanded.

'There's nothing I wouldn't do for Skye,' TJ replied honestly.

'Why? She hates you.'

Stevie's observation was a knife to the heart. But TJ just shrugged. 'I did what I thought was best for Skye based on the information I had at the time. She can hate me, but I know, absolutely, that I did the right thing. And it wasn't easy. It was the hardest thing I've ever done.'

TJ tipped his hat and pushed to his feet slowly. 'Stay close to her. Once you fly out, I'll take over.'

'Skye will have a few things to say to that,' Andrea predicted.

TJ just sighed. 'Oh yeah. I bet.'

Chapter 26

Because Skye knew it would be fun for Andrea and Stevie, she willingly attended the rodeo performance that night, even though she knew TJ would be working it. And if there was, maybe, a tiny part of her that wanted him to see that she was unaffected by him, Skye didn't overthink it.

From the stands, now packed full of spectators, she watched as TJ and Kai skilfully navigated the arena. They stood on alert as each bronc and rider surged out of the chute, but the moment the rider was thrown or the buzzer sounded, signalling he'd made eight seconds, TJ and the other pickup man fluidly rode in.

They aligned themselves on either side of the bucking bronc. TJ grabbed the bronc rein and pulled the horse's nose inwards as the rider wrapped both arms around TJ's torso and, using TJ's bodyweight, hauled himself out of the saddle, over Kai, and down to the arena dirt.

Skye had been watching TJ's face, looking for signs of pain, but his eyes remained obscured by his hat, hiding any discomfort.

The second pickup man released the flank strap. The bronc calmed but kept running, forcing the men to stay abreast of him until they'd driven him back into the holding pen.

As soon as the horse was safely penned, they retook their

positions out of the way of the next bronc and rider.

Skye couldn't take her eyes off of TJ. Her mind was in tumult. Half of her wondered why he'd sign up to work when his back clearly couldn't handle it – his spasm the day before had told her that much. But the other half knew that it was because of her. He'd told her he wanted closure. And they were in Texas, for Christ's sake. Horsemen – *pickup men* – were a dime a dozen, so the fact that he'd wormed his way into the rodeo in Odessa could only mean he'd pulled strings to make it happen.

But more than her tumultuous mind, her body betrayed her – there were no two sides about it. Just watching him ride, so skilled, so sexy, had those little reminders of what he could do to her rising up and stirring a torrent of need.

As if he'd sensed her gaze burning into him, TJ glanced over his shoulder. He tipped his head back slightly, so that he could see her from under the brim of his hat. When their eyes met, Skye just raised her eyebrows condescendingly.

The gate opened, releasing the next bronc and rider. TJ refocused on the arena.

At her side, Stevie waved both hands in front of her as if clearing the air. 'Jesus, I can't breathe through all this sexual tension.'

Andrea snort-laughed.

Skye groaned. 'I'm being punished.'

Stevie leaned comically closer, whispered, 'He doesn't exactly look like a hardship to me.'

On her other side, Andrea looked down towards where TJ rode. 'Maybe you'd both be able to purge the demons. Get closure.'

Skye looked from one of her friends to the other. 'Okay, what's going on?'

'What do you mean?' Stevie asked innocently. And it was that – Stevie acting innocent – that gave them away.

'You two were ready to rip TJ's throat out outside of Dave's last week, and now you're encouraging me to jump his bones. Uh-uh. Spill.'

‘We’re not encouraging you to jump his bones,’ Andrea argued. ‘Just suggesting that, maybe, things might be different this time around.’

‘Okay,’ Skye ceded. ‘But why? Why the change of heart?’

Stevie tapped her lips with her index finger. ‘It’s not a change of heart, per se . . .’

‘More like, a necessary compromise,’ Andrea added.

Skye’s spine began to tingle. ‘Guys . . .’

‘We think you should let him help,’ Stevie blurted.

‘Help? Help with what?’

‘See, the fact that you’re genuinely confused is why we’re so concerned.’ Andrea met Skye’s eyes. ‘Your dad—’

‘Father,’ Skye corrected.

‘Your *father*. You’re acting like nothing’s wrong.’

Skye almost laughed at that. If only her friends knew how that fear kept her awake at night, how it had her watching over her shoulder in broad daylight and second-guessing every time a stranger so much as glanced her way. ‘I’m doing the only thing I can,’ Skye said slowly. ‘I’m staying aware. I’m moving locations as often as possible. He won’t do anything drastic before my birthday; he needs me. *I’m* the one with the control.’

‘But wouldn’t it make you feel better to have one other person looking out for you?’ Andrea said. ‘Because we’re supposed to leave tomorrow, and we’re shit-scared of getting on that plane and leaving you behind. And, worse, we can’t even take you with us because that would be dropping you right in Holden’s lap.’

Stevie took Skye’s hand in hers. ‘We’re worried, Skye. Like, really worried. And despite everything that happened between you two, TJ wants to help – he told us so. To us, that’s a hell of a lot better than nothing.’

Skye tried to smile but couldn’t quite manage it. Although she knew her friends were coming from a place of concern, she didn’t think they truly understood how deeply TJ had hurt her. ‘I’ll think about it.’

That seemed to appease her friends, who turned back to watch the rodeo.

But as Skye's gaze gravitated back towards TJ, as her blood began to swim again, that fear grew. And just beneath it, swimming below the uncertainty and doubt and anxiety, was a wild and dangerous need. And it wasn't just lust. It was the need to prove to him – and to herself – that she was over him. It was the need to be done with that chapter of her life. It was the need to move on, to finally let him go.

Throughout the night, TJ was as aware of Skye as she was of him. He could feel her eyes searing into him and tightening the pressure on his already too-tight spine. The one time he'd chanced a glance at her and met her eyes, he'd felt that slow roll of need through his long-neglected system.

Still, because once he'd been distracted and lived to regret it, he kept his mind on his work. He powered through the events, somehow keeping conscious through the physical effort it took to manage the pain. Although it had his mind fighting flashes of black and his throat clogging with trapped air that felt like dirt, he managed to smile and raise a hand for the crowd when the announcer showed the replay of his accident, saying, 'Here with us tonight, we have Triple J, who is back in the saddle after dancing with the devil two years ago. Goes to show, you can't stop a cowboy unless you kill him.'

He sat on Kai, ignoring the sweat that coated his body when the bull riding started. He'd stopped watching it at home because it hurt too much to remember – the thrill, the fame, the pain, the defeat. But here, where he couldn't avoid it, he settled in. And when the memories from that weekend rose in angry flashes, he distracted himself by forcing his mind to memories of Skye instead.

It was only when the last bull rider had taken his turn and

the spectators had already started filtering out for the night that TJ rode Kai back to the barn.

It was nearing eleven. Although the night was dark, the coliseum lighting cast a blanket of light over the grounds. While the spectators filtered across the parking lot to their cars, chatting about a fun night of entertainment, behind the scenes, athletes, stock contractors, and barn hands still worked.

Stalls were being cleaned; animals were being fed, watered and checked over for the next day of events.

As TJ approached Barn B, the country music station filtered out to him, the mournful notes of Kip Moore's 'Pretty Horses' hitting a little too close to home.

TJ blocked the song out and prepared to dismount Kai – something he didn't dare do in the arena in case anyone saw. He took three long, deep breaths, leaned forward and took his right foot out of the stirrup. *One, two, three,* he counted, and then, holding his breath, swung his right leg up and over the saddle. He didn't so much dismount as fall to the ground.

He landed with a bone-smashing jolt.

As the pain sliced up and down his back and all through his right side, he simply leaned against Kai and took a moment to balance himself. His eyes watered from the pain. Sweat coated his brow from the effort.

'You okay?'

Skye's voice, so cool, coming from just behind him, had him gritting his teeth and pushing upright, despite the pain. 'Yup,' he replied. But he didn't dare look at her, didn't dare let her see how just that – standing upright – reduced him.

She walked by him without another word.

TJ took Kai by the reins and followed, his limp more noticeable despite his best efforts to hide it. Up ahead, he watched as Skye walked, her blue jeans snug over perfect curves, her shoulders hunched in her denim jacket, her blonde hair hidden under the hat he'd once given her.

He couldn't tear his gaze away, so he saw the moment she looked into Smokey's stall and froze, her hand pausing over the sliding bolt as she prepared to open the stall.

She didn't move for one long moment – and then she was saying, 'No, no, no,' and rushing into her horse's stall, her hands fumbling in her panic.

'Skye?'

TJ tried to pick up his pace, even though every step had his vision narrowing. When he came to Smokey's stall and looked in, his heart dropped.

Smokey stood inside the stall, her head hung low. A long, shallow gash ran down the length of her side. The shavings beneath her hooves were red with droplets of blood – blood that Skye knelt in as she tried to assess the wound.

She looked up at him, her face white, her big eyes dark with shock, and she whispered, 'What do I do?'

TJ snapped to. Rage like he had never known before flared out of his shock. He hurriedly put Kai in his stall, leaving his horse fully saddled in his rush. When he stepped back out, he saw one of the barn hands walking with a clipboard up ahead.

TJ shouted, 'Hey!' and when the girl turned, he said, 'Call the cops; a horse has been injured over here.'

'*What?*' The girl ran over.

Around them, people started filtering out of stalls and hurrying over.

As TJ stepped into Smokey's stall, everyone crowded around. 'I've got to call the event manager,' the barn hand said, her voice shaky with panic.

'Cops first,' TJ instructed. 'Whoever did this might still be here.'

Smokey tossed her head, clearly overwhelmed by the crowd. 'Okay, pretty girl,' TJ crooned, momentarily forgetting his own pain to soothe the horse.

He ran one palm down her neck, felt some relief when that horsey warmth seeped into his hand. On the floor, big tears ran down Skye's pale face. Her hands, spread over Smokey's bloody side, trembled.

'Hey,' TJ said quietly, and when Skye looked up at him, he added, 'I need you to let go so that I can have a look.'

She bit back a sob, but she didn't move, only closed her eyes. TJ reached forward and, taking her hands in his, gently lowered them.

He kept them linked with his, Smokey's blood drying between their fingers, as he assessed the damage.

The cut was long and clean, one that could only have been made with a knife or a scalpel. But it wasn't deep. Its placement seemed deliberate. To scare, yes. But the way the cut ran the entire length of the horse's body, over where both cinches would attach, told him that whoever had done it meant to ensure that Smokey would be out of commission for a while.

'I need the on-call vet,' he said to the crowd behind him.

'I've called already,' someone said. 'He's on premises, seeing to a show bull in Barn A. He'll be here in five.'

'Are all the other animals okay?' TJ asked. He knew as surely as Skye did that they would be, but the question had the crowd dispersing to check their own horses.

He looked down at Skye. She must be still in shock, because she hadn't yanked her hands back yet. She tilted her head to meet his eyes and, in a voice that was so small and tired, whispered, 'He found me.'

Chapter 27

Of all the things Skye would never forgive her father for, this took first place. As she sat in a pile of wood shavings and blood – *Smokey's* blood – she promised that he would live to regret the day he'd had someone take a knife to her horse.

'Jesus Christ.'

Skye looked up as the vet, his medical box in one hand, slid the stall door open and stepped inside. 'What happened here?'

'We don't know,' Skye said.

'Ford.' TJ greeted the vet by name. 'Someone meant to do this. It's too clean to be accidental.'

Skye looked down and felt her heart lurch when she saw TJ's familiar hands, so strong and competent, folded over the backs of hers, Smokey's blood drying between them. Binding them.

Unable to think about why that contact was still so comforting after everything he'd put her through, Skye shook him loose. She curled her hands into fists as the vet knelt at her side and TJ slowly got to his feet and took a step out of the way.

'Ford Anderson.' The vet, a large, handsome man with a shock of red hair beneath his cowboy hat and kind green eyes, introduced himself. He raised his fingers to the wound on Smokey's side, carefully shifted the loose skin back and forth as he assessed the damage. 'I have to agree with your assessment. This was deliberate.'

Skye couldn't focus on that just then, only asked, 'Will she be okay?'

'Oh yeah.' Ford leaned back on his haunches and opened his medical box. 'It's not deep at all, just inconveniently placed. Only this part' – he showed her the first three inches on the cut – 'will need a stitch or two. The rest we'll clean, disinfect, and treat with antimicrobial. It doesn't even need a bandage so long as you keep everything nice and clean. Just wound powder.' He paused what he was doing to meet her gaze. 'I'm sure I don't have to tell you, but this will take her out. Probably for at least three weeks while the worst of it closes, maybe longer.'

'I don't care,' Skye replied. 'As long as she's okay.'

'You have any idea who'd do this to your horse?' Ford asked as he prepped a syringe of what Skye assumed was a painkiller.

'No.' The lie came instantly.

Behind her, TJ made a low sound of warning in the back of his throat.

Skye tilted her head back to glare at him. 'You don't have a say in this.'

'Think again,' he replied, his eyes flashing dangerously.

'While you two figure that out,' Ford interrupted, 'could you get me a bucket of clean warm water?'

TJ left to go and do Ford's bidding.

Skye followed. 'I don't know who the hell you think you are,' she spat at his back as he walked away.

TJ turned slowly. He faced her with his back straight and his eyes bleeding fury. 'If you refuse to take the necessary steps to start getting these assaults on file, then I will.'

'You don't get to make decisions for me,' Skye said, lowering her voice.

'Maybe.' He took one ominous step closer, sending her treacherous pulse into a full gallop. 'But that doesn't change the fact that I will do anything to make sure that fucker doesn't hurt you. When the cops get here, this is going on file.'

'I'll never forgive you.'

TJ laughed bitterly. 'Yeah, what else is new?'

He started to walk away again, and Skye's panic took over. As angry as she was with him, she couldn't let him talk to the cops. 'It won't work.'

The words stopped TJ in his tracks. He sighed, his shoulders drooping visibly. 'Skye—'

'No,' she cut him off. She closed the distance between them, glared up into familiar green eyes. 'This isn't a bad movie, TJ. Holden *is smart.* He'll have his whereabouts accounted for – he wouldn't do the dirty work himself. He'll act shocked and hurt and – worse – sad. He'll spin a story about my mental health, and *my medical history* will affirm it. To top it all off, he'll take his anger at me out on my mom.'

'We have to do *something*,' he insisted. 'Otherwise, it'll never end, Skye. You know that.'

'It will – as soon as I cut him off. He'll have no leverage and nothing to gain by harming me.'

'And until then?' TJ demanded hotly. 'You're just going to run? Constantly look over your shoulder and hope that the next time it isn't you he takes a knife to?' TJ leaned in close. 'Not good enough.'

Skye gritted her teeth. 'What else am I supposed to do?'

'Either you accept that I'm along for the ride this season, and let me travel with you, or I tell the police what's going on. It's your choice, Skye. But pretending the threat isn't real – *running* – is not the right way to handle this. Not anymore.'

Skye saw the trap – of course she did. Because it was expected, she muttered, 'Motherfucker.' But because she absolutely believed that he would talk to the cops, she said, 'Fine.'

TJ's eyes flashed with triumph.

Unwilling to let him have the last word, she added, 'But you realize my season is over, right? I'll have to turn out of tomorrow's run. You heard Ford: Smokey's out for at least three weeks. Even if I had another horse to run, the rodeo has started. It's too late to submit a horse change form.' The disappointment clawed through her, making her eyes burn.

TJ walked to her. His eyes bore into her face. 'So, we submit a horse change for Colorado.'

'Change between who?' Skye asked, throwing up her hands.

'Smokey for Kai.'

That took the wind out of her sails. 'What?'

'He's patterned. He's fast. He's in shape.' When she just stared at him, TJ shrugged. 'Tia's been training him.'

'You want me to run your horse?' she asked.

TJ put both his hands on his hips. 'Absolutely.'

'What about your pickup schedule?'

'They won't struggle to replace me,' he shot back, reiterating her earlier thoughts.

In a panic, Skye ran both her hands over her face. 'This is crazy.'

'Maybe. But you turning out here without the option of a horse change *while you're in first place* means you're going to lose your chance at at least six thousand dollars. That's going to hurt, and we both know you can't afford to skip races this early on if you want to get anywhere this year.' When Skye didn't reply, TJ added, 'You know I'm right. The girls at the top qualify for the big rodeos with huge cash prizes; they can ride in as few as thirty events and still make the NFR. You don't have that luxury. You have to make as many of the smaller rodeos as possible. Right now, Kai is your only hope of doing that.'

'Agh!' Skye closed her eyes as the frustration burst from her. But once she'd taken a deep breath, she held up one finger. '*If* Ford says Smokey can travel, we let her rest a day before heading west to Colorado.'

TJ nodded. 'Deal.'

As he walked away to go and get the water Ford had requested, Skye stared at his back. The entire situation was crazy. Reckless.

Stupid, even. So, she had no idea why, as she stood there with an injured horse and an insane travel schedule, a little flicker of relief spread through her.

The police took TJ and Skye's statements and, with little to no information to go on, departed with a vague promise to look into the animal abuse case.

The event manager, Sharon, wasn't so quick to let it go. She stood with TJ outside Smokey's stall as Ford gave Skye the wound care instructions. 'I'll send the police all the video footage they requested, but I'll go over it myself too.'

'If you find anything, you call me.' TJ took his phone out to give her his number and added, 'Not Skye. She has too much to worry about already,' in a low voice.

'Okay.' Sharon added his number to her phone. 'I've posted two of my hands to do security checks at random intervals tonight. But this seems to be a singular incident.'

Because he knew Skye, knew that she wouldn't leave Smokey's side again, TJ replied, 'We'll bunk here tonight.'

'If it was my horse, I would too.' Sharon ran one hand tiredly through her hair. 'Is there anything else I can do for you?'

'Could you send us the turnout form for visible injury? And could I leave my truck and trailer here for a day or two? My dad can fly down and pick them up, drive them back to Arizona.'

Sharon nodded. 'I'll get you an extended parking pass. Send the turnout form back to me when you're done, and I'll confirm the injury with the secretary myself. That way, you don't have to wait for her to come on over and check.'

'Appreciate it.'

Ford and Skye stepped out of the stall. Where the vet looked calm and collected; the panic and shock had left Skye. In its place was a stormy rage that TJ felt resonating in the depths of his own soul.

He turned to Ford. 'Can Smokey be hauled tomorrow?'

'Yes. Actually, keeping her still for a few days wouldn't be the worst thing for her,' Ford replied. 'Just make sure she stays hydrated while you're on the road. And call me if she stops eating or if her temperature rises above 103. I've given Skye Smokey's antibiotics. But even once she's feeling better, it'll take time for the skin to knit properly. Try to keep her relatively quiet so she doesn't reopen the wound. Remove the stitches after fourteen days.'

TJ held out his hand. 'Appreciate it, Ford.'

'Anytime.'

'Do we need to settle up?'

'Skye took care of it already.' He tipped his hat, said, 'Ladies,' to Sharon and Skye before walking off, his vet box in his hand.

Sharon said goodnight and left with the promise to send the turnout form within the hour.

Alone with Skye again, TJ turned to look in on Smokey. The mare was dozing on the drugs Ford had given her, her right back leg cocked, her neck hanging low.

Skye rested her forearms on the stall door next to him. 'This isn't something my father would typically do. He's usually more subtle. The only times he hit me, it was because I retaliated or picked a fight with him.'

'So, what does he gain by taking Smokey out?'

Skye shrugged. 'I stop racing. Go back to Hunt Ranch.'

'And then he knows exactly where you are at all times,' TJ finished.

Skye didn't argue, only whispered, 'He'll pay for this.'

TJ didn't argue. He'd see to it, so just said, 'Yes.' But because he desperately needed to take the pressure off his back, he took a step back, said, 'Why don't you go shower? Grab what you need for the night. Update your friends. I'll take first shift.'

She nodded once, coolly, and turned on her heel. But she stopped a few feet away, her back straight. She sighed loudly and without turning, said, 'Thank you. I appreciate the help.'

TJ tried not to smile at her tone, which was one hundred per cent martyr-going-to-slaughter. But he felt that glimmer of his old cheek peeking through and had to ask, 'How much did that hurt?'

'You'll never know,' she shot back.

The moment she was gone, TJ let himself into Smokey's stall. 'Hi, pretty girl,' he crooned. And when Smokey tossed her head in alarm, he didn't change his tone, didn't slow his movements, just said, 'You're okay. It's just me.'

He lowered down to the floor, taking it one inch at a time as he tried to control his descent. From his butt, he lowered to his elbows, and then flat onto his back. The rubber stall mat, covered in shavings, felt good on his spine. As he lay there, his body militantly straight, his arms lax at his sides, the weight on his spine slowly decompressed. The pain ebbed slightly, and although it would only last twenty minutes or so before he'd have to wake up and change positions, TJ had learned the hard way to take every minute of relief he could.

He closed his eyes and fell asleep instantly.

He dreamed he was on the back of a bull again, his heart pumping furiously, his ears ringing with the sound of the music, the pounding hooves, and the crowd shouting his name. Although he didn't see her, he knew Skye was there, sitting in the stands, wearing his hat. He could *feel* her. The sound of the buzzer made his heart stop. But he loosened his grip on the bull rope and dismounted fluidly. For one moment, he looked up, his heart light and free. But he saw Skye's eyes, filled with fear, right before that impact hit him.

He woke up silently, keeping his back still even as he came out of the nightmare. His eyes opened. His spine throbbed from being in one position for too long. Except, this time, instead of being prostrate on some shitty hotel mattress, he was on his back in Smokey's stall.

Skye was sitting against the stall door, her legs next to TJ's feet. She looked up from her phone when TJ shifted, watched him like a hawk as he painstakingly pushed up into the most painful position for him: a seated L.

TJ dusted the wood shavings from his hair. And because Skye was still staring at him, he made a show of sniffing his armpit. 'That bad?'

'Ha,' she replied dryly. But she put her phone down next to her.

They were both quiet for a moment.

TJ couldn't help but soak up the proximity to her after all this time. Since his accident, he'd told himself over and over that whatever he'd felt for Skye had been too new, too tentative to put her through his injury and his failed recovery and pain management. But here, now, he remembered why pushing her away had cut him so deeply. A plant in its first cautious stretch out of the soil was still a plant. Maybe its roots still had to grow and strengthen; maybe it was more vulnerable to those elements in that initial stage, but the potential was there – *it* was there. Despite his attempts to convince himself otherwise, he thought he'd always known that what he'd felt for Skye had been real. It had been full of potential.

As if she'd read his mind, she said, 'You know, TJ, I would have understood.'

He didn't ask her what she was talking about. 'I know.'

'So, why?' She shook her head lightly. But her eyes stayed dry. And angry.

'Because you would have stayed.'

'It was my decision to make.'

'No.'

'It was—'

'You didn't have the life experience to sign up for something like that!' TJ snapped. He took a deep breath to try and calm the anger and the self-pity. 'You were free for the first time in your life, and the last thing I was going to do was hold you back from that. Jesus, you were twenty-two fucking years old.' He shifted, readjusting for the pain. 'It took me six months, Skye. Six months to take steps without a goddamn walker. I couldn't even use the restroom by myself for five weeks.'

'You could have told me,' she insisted, her blue eyes glinting. 'I would have understood. Instead, you cut me off like I was just some random hook-up.'

'I thought the anger would help,' he explained, defeated. But there was another truth, one that he didn't know how to explain to someone who lived free of chronic pain, and that was that, since the day he'd been hit by the bull, coherent thought often eluded him. Instead, every thought, every tiny movement – be it breathing, turning, or sitting down – was governed by torrents of agony that surpassed his mind's ability to focus on anything else – even Skye. He wasn't sure what thoughts had occupied his stream of consciousness before the accident.

'Why now?'

It was a question she'd asked before, but TJ evaded again. 'It's time,' he said simply.

'What do you *mean* by that?'

TJ shook his head. 'It doesn't matter now. What does matter is that I make things right. The fact that I hurt you is the only regret I have, Skye. But the way I figure it, we have the season to see that I make up for it, to get rid of your father, maybe even cinch a few arena records along the way.'

He could see that she still wanted to push, to ask those questions sitting on her tongue. But she didn't. She just leaned back against the stall door and closed her eyes.

Chapter 28

Sometime during the night, Skye had lain down too. And she must have shifted in her sleep. That was the only reasonable explanation for why her back was tucked against TJ's side, the curves of her ass pressing into his aching hip.

TJ closed his eyes again and memorized the soft give of her body everywhere that they touched. Despite the bone-deep ache and the accompanying burn of sciatica down his right leg, he didn't dare move. He'd lie through an eternity of pain just to stay there like that with her.

He got ten minutes before Skye popped awake and scrambled into a seated position. Not wanting her to be embarrassed or – worse – angry, he calmly closed his eyes and pretended to sleep as she hurried to her feet. He felt the chill creep back in where only moments before he'd been filled with warmth.

Skye walked over to Smokey. She crooned to her horse as she checked her over, and only when that was done did she gently nudge his leg with the toe of her boot. 'TJ?'

He slowly opened his eyes, blinked a few times for effect. 'Morning.'

'I'm going to go and say goodbye to Stevie and Andrea. They should be getting ready to Uber to the airport.'

'Go. I'll see to the horses.'

She eyed him sceptically. 'Don't you need to shower or – I don't know – eat?'

'I'll get to it,' he replied tiredly. But he didn't make a move to sit up. He didn't want her to witness that first big movement in the morning, which was always excruciating.

'Do you need h—'

'I said, I'll get to it.'

Skye's spine straightened at his tone, which had come out cold and impatient. 'Fine,' she snapped back and spun on her heel.

He waited for her to leave before slowly rolling onto his side, then one elbow, then all fours, his face contorted with pain, his eyes stormy and hateful. Bitter. He took one deep breath as he swung his left leg underneath him, felt the beads of sweat grow as the movement stretched a spine that wasn't supposed to be stretched.

By the time he was on his feet, there was a thick brick of bile in his throat. His mouth watered. His empty stomach tossed about.

TJ fought the urge to throw up. He leaned against the stall's siding until the feeling receded, and as soon as it did, he steeled himself. And he got to work.

He fed and watered the horses, and by the time he got to mucking, Skye was back. This time, Bandit was on a leash at her side. Skye wordlessly grabbed her own shovel, and because he was in Smokey's stall, she started on Kai's.

For a long while, the silence stretched between them. But because he needed to get as much time with her as he could, TJ broke it first. 'Once he's digested a bit, you should run Kai. Get a feel for him.'

Skye leaned on the handle of her shovel. 'Where?'

There were typically rules and associated fines for practising in the arena, especially once it had been graded. But TJ knew he could work something out. 'There's no slack today. If we hurry, they might let us get a few turns in before they grade for the stock shows at noon.'

They opted to see if they could wrangle some arena time, and only a few hours later, with Smokey safely locked in the trailer, Skye took Kai through a few warm-up drills. She wasn't quite sure how TJ always managed to bend the rules but decided not to question it.

Beneath her, Kai was soft, his every movement smooth. He was big, maybe sixteen hands, with a gait that felt stretching compared to Smokey's. But he was responsive and calm, with none of Smokey's attitude.

In the corner of the arena, TJ didn't say anything, only watched, and when Skye had warmed up sufficiently and asked, 'Ready?' he walked to the starting line with Bandit, a stopwatch in hand.

'Take him right first,' TJ instructed as Skye handed him her phone to keep safe. He slipped it into his pocket. 'Give him space to turn the barrels; he's a lot bigger than Smokey. Push him hard on the straights. He has the leg for speed.'

Skye nodded. But she had her doubts. Kai was calm and quiet beneath her, with none of that typical fire she associated with barrel horses. The only reason she knew he was ready was by his ears, which were pricked forward, his head slightly raised.

She took a breath and pushed him into a lope behind the starting line. She completed one circle, and the moment she was straight, cued him into a gallop with only her legs and a single click.

Kai surged, pushing her back in her saddle so quickly and with so much force that Skye had to correct her balance as the horse approached the first barrel. She managed to right herself just in time, but Kai needed no guidance. He took the first and pushed for the second, his form perfect. By the time they turned the third barrel, Skye was grinning, and when they sailed past the finish line, she was outright cackling.

She pulled Kai to a stop in front of TJ, looked down into his grin, and in lieu of a better way to describe her shock, simply said, 'Hot damn.'

TJ showed her the stopwatch. '15.65.'

Reaching forward, she gave Kai's neck a pat. 'You said he's been training with Tia?'

'Yeah.' TJ shrugged. 'He's from barrel racing bloodlines. He's got the heart for it. And I figured, if he ever needed to be rehomed, it would be better to have as many disciplines started on him as possible.'

That same unease she'd had the day before filled Skye, ruining the moment. The way he talked scared her. 'Why do you do that – talk like that?'

TJ looked up at her for a long moment. Skye held her breath, certain he was about to tell her something vital. But instead, he smiled, said, 'The minimum requirement as a horse owner is making sure your horse is well-trained enough to be rehomed if something happens to you. You know that. And I know that better than anybody else.'

Skye nodded, knowing he wouldn't give her more. But far from satisfied with his answer, she added, 'We're not done talking about this, TJ,' before she turned Kai back to the start to run again.

They pushed him through the pattern three times before Skye dismounted. 'I think I've got his style down. At least enough to run him in Colorado. We'll keep learning as we go.'

At her side, Kai was sweaty and tired. But he popped his head over her shoulder and leaned his big neck on her, making her laugh. Skye reached up and ran her palm down his forehead. 'Charmer.'

TJ rolled his eyes. 'Kiss ass, more like.'

They exchanged a mutually mocking glance.

And then both paused.

It might have been the first easy, friendly gesture between them since they'd reconnected.

'Could we call a truce? Just through the season? It's gonna suck travelling together if you hate me,' TJ asked.

Skye frowned. 'I never hated you, TJ.' Odd that she might only just be realizing that now.

TJ opened his mouth to reply, but the sound of Skye's phone ringing in his pocket stole his words. 'Add that to the list of things we're not done talking about,' he said, before handing her the phone.

Skye took it, and froze when she saw *Unknown Caller* flashing on the screen.

TJ saw her face. 'Who is it?'

'I don't know,' Skye replied. But she answered the call and put it on speaker.

'Hello?'

There was no reply, only the calm and steady sound of someone breathing over the line.

Skye momentarily closed her eyes as her blood ran cold.

But then she remembered Smokey. She remembered the warm, sticky blood on her fingers and the fact that, even then, her horse was locked in her trailer because Skye was too afraid to leave her alone in the stall she'd paid for. Her cold blood warmed, then blazed.

'Just a reminder, Holden, that your rent's due April first. Going rate for that property in that location is – what? – fifteen grand a month?'

Bandit, hearing her unusual, angry tone, whined on the end of his leash. Skye reached out and soothed her dog.

The breath on the line hitched, not with shock. With rage.

Skye grinned when she heard it. And she let her wild out. 'Tell you what, *Dad*. I'll give you a deal, for old times' sake. Let's call it fourteen thousand, nine hundred, and ninety-nine per month.'

Holden – for it could only be him – didn't say anything.

He hung up.

Skye took a deep breath. 'Coward.'

TJ, his face red with rage, shook his head once. 'It's just beginning – and you know it.'

Skye didn't reply, only walked past him, leading Kai in one hand and Bandit in the other. 'I'll brush him down and put him in his stall. Why don't you go shower? No offence or anything, but two days of horse doesn't smell good on anyone.'

TJ caught her elbow in one hand, his grip gentle but uncompromising. 'From now until we figure out how to end this, you don't go anywhere alone.'

Her pride was the only thing that had her smirking. 'He's not going to be hiding around a corner, TJ.'

TJ didn't reply. He made a warning sound in the back of his throat and fell into step beside her.

Skye sighed, but there was a gentle ripple of sweet relief spreading over her wild anxiety too. She and TJ might have had a lot of unresolved issues between them, but it helped, to have someone along. 'You may as well move your shit into the trailer. That way, I don't have to follow you every time you need to source a shower or some food.'

'I want us to sit down and go over everything today. Before Colorado. I need all the facts.'

'Fine.'

'And we need to start thinking of a way to get your mom out.' When Skye stopped walking, TJ looked over his shoulder at her. 'What?'

She wasn't sure what to say.

Perhaps thinking she was gearing up to argue, TJ held up one hand. 'Look, this only ends one of two ways: either Holden wins, or you do. But if you don't start fighting back, he's going to creep up on you. But if we're proactive, if we get your mom out, get her help, then we can go to the police and settle all of this. She's the breaking point. We focus on that.'

Skye hated that he was right. Worse, she hated that she wasn't so sure whose side her mom would choose if forced.

She didn't say any of that to TJ, just, 'Okay, I can work with that.' She shrugged. 'It's better than my plan anyway.'

'What was your plan?' he asked.

'Well, I figured I'd donate all the money the moment I become trustee. That way, I could send Holden a picture of me passing off one of those jumbo cheques – you know, maybe a hundred million to the Dallas Women's Shelter, the other hundred to a horse rescue.'

TJ actually laughed. The sound, the rusty pleasure in it, filled the pit of her stomach, coating over some of the sick nausea that speaking to her father had left there.

'That would be objectively awesome.'

'Yeah.' Skye had seriously thought about it. There was only one problem. 'But the only person left to deal with all that rage would be my mom.'

Next to her, TJ's limp had her slowing her stride, despite how much taller he was.

'We get her out,' he reiterated. 'It's the only way this ends.'

Chapter 29

Denver, Colorado – January 15, 2027

On the ten-hour drive to Colorado, TJ made friendly conversation when the mood struck and brooded in silence when it didn't. Skye alternated between replying to his polite questions and pretending to doze when the space between them became too overwhelming to navigate.

They arrived at the Denver Coliseum and hauled the trailer to the contestant's parking area, where Skye signed her release of liability and picked up her number for the race. Although he wouldn't be allowed in the arena, TJ got a helper pass for access behind the scenes. Skye didn't object, knowing that any argument would have proved futile anyway.

'What did you draw?' he asked when Skye ambled back to the trailer, her number in her hand.

She held up the number, showing him the big, bold *5* printed on it. 'Eighty contestants and I have to run fifth,' she whined.

'At least you're not first?' TJ offered.

'Yeah, but they only drag the arena after every five, which means I'm going to be running an unfamiliar horse for the first time on churned-up dirt.'

'They hand rake after every run here,' TJ told her.

'Really?'

'Yup.'

Skye perked up at that, but she eyed TJ as they moved to the back of the trailer. 'How do you know so much about barrel racing anyway?'

TJ unbolted the right door, Skye the left. 'Rodeo kid, remember.'

He braced his entire body as he lowered the ramp down for the horses. Skye didn't step in or take over, knowing he wouldn't appreciate it, but it hurt to watch him sometimes. She itched to go to him. To help. To do *something*. Because, whatever their history, she still carried a deep and real sadness for what had happened.

'You know, TJ, I never apologized . . .'

TJ frowned as he stepped into the trailer. 'For what?'

Skye bit the corner of her lip when her eyes burned. She'd always thought the memories would fade; instead, she could remember that exact moment he'd raised his eyes up to the stands, looking for *her*. She could still see his cheeky grin. And then the moment the bull hit him.

TJ rummaged around in the tack compartment, then looked out at her, repeated, 'Skye, for what?'

'For distracting you that day.' The words were said quietly. And when TJ didn't reply, just stared at her, she started rambling. 'I've played it over in my head so many times. And every time, I think of some way things could have been *so different*.' Her eyes burned, but she refused to cry. She'd get this off her chest. Finally. 'Your life could have been so different.'

TJ stepped off the back of the trailer. He stood right in front of her, and even though there was a part of her that wished he'd reach out, just once, he didn't. He just said, 'Skye, look at me.'

She tipped her head back.

'Don't ever fucking apologize for that again.'

She'd expected him to argue, of course. But she hadn't expected the rage. The fury. 'If I hadn't been there—'

'If you hadn't been there, I would never have known what it felt like—' He bit off whatever else he wanted to say with a sharp twist of his head. But his green eyes stayed angry.

'I think about it all the time,' Skye whispered as her vision went glassy.

TJ laughed bitterly. 'Yeah, me too. But only because it was so *pointless.* So fucking stupid. If *I'd* just been paying attention, like *I* was trained to, like *I* was supposed to . . . But in that moment . . .' TJ's eyes glazed over. 'I was king of the fucking world – and cocky with it. Careless. I had triumphed over the bull. I had my girl in the stands, and she'd watched me do it.' He met her eyes again. 'I don't think anything will ever beat that single second in time. A lot of people will never know that feeling.' He shrugged. 'Maybe the bull was God's way of levelling my playing field.'

Twin tears fell from her eyes.

TJ raised his hands as if to swipe them.

Skye braced, not in trepidation. In *anticipation* – of that touch, that contact.

But TJ saw her rigid posture, and he misinterpreted it. He lowered his hands back down, said, 'Don't carry what's not yours, Skye. It pisses me off.'

Disappointed, Skye lashed out. 'Says the man who's inserted himself into every facet of my life when I didn't ask him to.'

TJ searched her face. 'Does it bother you that much that I care? That I want to make sure you get through this unscathed?'

She rolled her eyes, but TJ didn't let her get away with avoidance.

'No. Don't do that. Be honest with me,' he insisted. 'Would you rather do this alone?'

'No.'

'Well then.'

He stepped back into the tack compartment.

Skye couldn't help but ask, 'What would you have done if I'd said yes?'

'Said, "Tough shit," and stuck to you anyway,' he replied.

Skye scowled at his back.

'This weekend, you have two performance go-rounds. Back to back. The top three averages from each bracket advance to the semi-finals. There're three semi-final performances on Saturday. Only the top four from each semi-final performance move on to the finals on Sunday. Which means—'

'Which means I have to place in the top twelve to make the finals. I know.'

'You nervous?'

She was sick to the stomach, her anxiety swirling unchecked. But she leaned against the side of the trailer, said, 'Nope. Just another day in paradise.'

'Liar.' TJ poked his head back out. 'We have an hour before you have to warm up. Let's walk the horses for a bit, give Smokey some controlled movement, and check her dressing. There's no point in stalling her until after you run.'

'Yeah.' Skye stepped into the trailer. She belatedly saw TJ's roping saddle, hanging on the top saddle rack and kicked herself for not hiding it in the trailer's luggage compartment.

'You kept it?' TJ asked.

Skye tried to act nonchalant. 'It was a gift.'

'And the cactus?'

'I wasn't going to take my anger at you out on Bob.' Skye cocked one hip.

'Bob?' TJ queried.

'Bob. And I actually *needed* the saddle.'

'Where's the other one I sent you?'

A chill ran down Skye's spine. 'What?' she said very quietly.

TJ looked over his shoulder at her.

Skye raised both hands to her face as horror filled her. 'Please don't tell me you sent me a custom barrel saddle a few months ago? Black seat, tan basket-weaved leather, *Skye Marchant* engraved on the fender?'

TJ shrugged. 'I heard your name making the rounds, figured you might need a pro saddle.'

'Oh my God.'

TJ frowned. 'Jesus, what's wrong?'

'TJ . . . I thought it was from Holden. I burned it.'

'You *what*?'

Their eyes held for a long moment.

The silence stretched.

Then TJ started laughing, first in stuttered chuckles, and then in big, deep belly laughs.

Skye didn't find it funny at all. But her lips twitched as she watched him lose himself. For just a second, it felt like it had back when they'd first met. Light. Good. *Fun*.

But then she remembered the smell of that new leather burning and groaned. 'Why didn't you send a card or something?'

TJ swiped at his face, but he couldn't quite stop his grin. 'Well, Skye, given our history, I thought you might burn it.'

The reminder was all she needed to take a big step back, her dry, 'Ha. Ha,' falling awkwardly from her lips.

Unsure of what else to say, swamped with regret, Skye moved through the trailer, offloaded Smokey first and, once TJ had taken her lead rope, went back in for Kai.

When both horses were safely out, they started walking side by side, TJ leading Smokey, Skye leading Kai.

Around them, the coliseum grounds were swarming with people and animals. Contestants were signing in and offloading their horses. Event staff were running around, trying to get everyone organized, answering questions, and generally attempting to contain the chaos.

Next to her, TJ tipped his head to look down at her. 'You really set it on fire, didn't you?'

'Yup. I even had to use lighter fluid to get it to ignite.' Saying it didn't make her feel any better. 'Damn it, TJ. That saddle was beautiful. But all I could think was that only Holden would use something so gorgeous, so important to me, as a threat.'

'I'm sorry. I should have thought of that.' He nudged her shoulder. 'I'll order a new one.'

'No. If you give me the details, *I'll* order a new one. I don't want anything from you.' She said the words kindly. Because they were true. She didn't want to ever be beholden to him; he already had too much of her. Too much of her past, too many of her current thoughts. He took up space she didn't have to spare – or, maybe, didn't *want* to spare.

TJ didn't reply, but she knew by the cool tip of his head that she'd hurt him.

She wanted to apologize, or maybe explain, but she didn't know where to start.

So, she didn't.

TJ braided Kai's mane as Skye, dressed in her black jeans, black shirt, black boots, and bright-pink Hunt Ranch hat, wrapped Kai's legs in the matching polo wraps. If Skye and Smokey had looked eye-catching in the contrasting colours, Kai, with his black coat, added to the effect.

Although Skye was quiet and focused on her task, TJ could feel the anxiety rolling off her as her race time rapidly approached. When she stood and dusted imaginary dirt off her pristine jeans, he moved forward and flicked the brim of her hat up, calling her attention to him. 'Breathe,' he demanded. 'Get out of your head.'

She didn't argue, only took a deep, shaky breath. 'I hate running the perf.'

'Why?'

'Too much pressure to put on a show for the crowd instead of compete.'

'That's all in your head.'

'Gee, thanks, TJ,' Skye drawled sarcastically. 'That pep talk made me feel a whole lot better.'

'Think of it this way,' he said, trying for a different approach. 'How many people in the crowd do you think could legitimately do what you do as well as you do it?'

'Ten, maybe.'

'Ten out of ten thousand. So, 0.1 per cent of the people in the crowd might – *might* – be judging your ride. To the others, you're a badass bitch, however well you ride.'

'Lack of knowledge or skill never stopped anyone from judging,' she argued. 'If it did, we wouldn't have Sunday Night Football.'

'Hey. Look at me,' TJ demanded. 'You've got this.'

Skye nodded. 'I do.'

'So, let's fucking go.' He locked Smokey back in the trailer and walked across the parking lot to the warm-up arena, leading Kai, with Skye at his side.

The rodeo was well underway in the coliseum. The combined sound of the music, the announcer, and the crowd boomed chaotically from the covered building. While it didn't seem to bother the seasoned rodeo animals at all, there were a few that TJ could see were relatively new to the game. A dun mare trotting in the warm-up arena spooked and skittered sideways every time the noise from the stadium surged and took her by surprise. A grey Appendix gelding backed up quickly as his rider tried, unsuccessfully, to mount.

He stepped inside the arena, holding Kai as Skye swung into the saddle. 'I'm going to be close by. If you see anything – *anything* – that strikes you as odd, you dismount. Immediately, Skye. I'll get to you as quickly as I can. Otherwise, you warm up, you run, you meet me outside the arena afterwards. If I'm not there yet, wait for me. Stay where the people are.'

'Don't you think this is all a little extreme?' she asked.

'Better safe than sorry,' TJ said.

As he watched Skye and Kai warm up, he rested his forearms

through the arena fencing, taking some of the pressure off his back.

'Didn't figure you the type for serious.'

TJ angled his head to look over his shoulder at Matthew Savage. The bronc rider was dressed in his chaps and vest, both of which boasted the logos of his extensive sponsorships. TJ hated the burn of jealousy that settled in his throat. Once, he'd had the best sponsors across the board. All the big names had lined up to pay him. Now, he wore the black chaps he rode at home in. Still, he tipped his head, said, 'Savage.'

Matthew nodded to where Skye was circling Kai in a smooth lope. 'That's the girl from Scottsdale, right?'

'Yup.'

'You two serious?'

TJ sighed. 'What do you want?'

'Nothing. I was just looking for this girl I saw earlier. Event photographer.' He whistled low. 'Redhead. Curves that would tempt Jesus himself in far less than forty days.'

'Haven't seen her.'

Matthew nodded. But he didn't leave. He parked next to TJ, lifted one booted foot to the bottom rung of the arena, and watched Skye ride.

Hating the silence, but also genuinely curious, TJ asked, 'Which bronc did you draw?'

'Devil's Advocate.'

TJ knew the horse: an athletic Draft-Quarter Horse cross with impressive strength and a penchant for extreme twists. 'Good horse,' he commented.

'So, how you doing, man?' Matthew didn't look at him when he asked the casual question.

To most people, it was a simple query, one shoved into small talk when you didn't really care but had to make conversation. For TJ, it was a complex and painful topic. In the end, he just replied, 'Better than dead.'

'Heard you're working pickup tonight?'

'Nope. Skye's riding my horse, so I pulled out. Is that why you're wasting your time here?' TJ's frustration slipped into his tone. 'Afraid I'll let the bronc finish you off?'

'Nah.' Matthew grinned. 'You don't have the *spine* for cruelty.'

A surprised laugh left TJ's lips before he could bite it back. But he added a casual, 'Dickhead,' for good measure.

'Anyway, just thought I'd check in, pay my respects.' Matthew didn't look at him when he quietly added, 'You know, I was real glad you came back from Scottsdale, TJ. That was a bitch to watch.'

'Yup.'

Matthew tapped the piped arena fence once and stepped back. 'I'll just be off then.'

'Good luck this weekend,' TJ drawled without looking back.

'Thanks. Same to your girl.'

TJ didn't bother correcting him, and as Matthew walked away, undoubtedly in pursuit of his redhead, TJ refocused on Skye.

She was at a standstill, gently bending Kai's neck to either side.

She might not be his girl anymore, but he'd always be stuck on her.

He stayed close as she warmed up, and although he watched her, he also kept one eye peeled for anyone that seemed out of place.

Nothing unusual caught his attention, and although a few staff and helpers watched the girls warming up in the arena, none of them seemed particularly fixated on Skye.

When the first drag was called, numbers one through five began moving their horses out of the warm-up arena and towards the coliseum. The moment Skye and Kai stepped out, TJ moved beside them towards the holding area.

Skye looked down at him, her big blue eyes full of nerves. 'I might actually be sick,' she whispered as the girls in front of her filtered into the performance arena.

TJ caught Kai's reins. He crooked one finger at Skye, encouraging her to lean down. 'Best tip for avoiding performance anxiety?'

She nodded, listening intently.

TJ was damn tempted to kiss her. She was right there, her face so close to his. He almost – *almost* – risked her wrath just for one quick taste of her. It would give her that burst of anger she needed to distract her from her nerves. But instead, he flicked her ear at the last moment.

Skye reared back. Her hand rose to her ear – not, he knew, out of pain, but shock. 'What the fuck, TJ?'

'Distraction,' he said, and with one last wink, stepped back.

She muttered something undoubtedly foul beneath her breath. With barely a shift in the saddle, she moved Kai forward.

TJ waited until they were through to the secured event area, teeming with competitors and cowboys, before limping to his ticketed seat. He sat down right as the announcer's voice boomed, 'If you have a need for speed, you're in luck. Because next up, we have the barrel racers!'

'Tick Tick Boom' by Sage the Gemini blasted through the speakers.

The crowd cheered loudly.

TJ sat through the first four riders, none of whom ran in under sixteen seconds.

And then it was Skye's turn.

He leaned forward and linked his hands between his knees.

'Next up, we have rookies Skye Marchant and Sweet Lil Bullet from Santa Barbara, California. Tonight is Sweet Lil Bullet's first professional run!' the announcer said, introducing Kai by his AQHA registered name.

The music blared louder.

TJ held his breath as he saw Skye and Kai step out of the side chute and into the alley. Kai was calm but alert, his ears pricked forward, his eyes looking straight ahead.

Skye took her signature moment of stillness.

The crowd, confused by the delay, fell quiet.

And only then did they break.

They shot down the alley, Skye leaning forward as Kai's powerful legs churned the dirt. They rounded the first barrel easily at just over four seconds and shot to the next.

'Come on, baby,' TJ whispered as they pushed towards the third barrel.

They rounded the barrel a little too close. TJ held his breath as Skye's booted foot nicked the drum and sent it tilting. She managed to lean down and push it in the other direction just as Kai surged forward.

She didn't look back as they galloped down the straight. But TJ did. The barrel wobbled. For just one moment, it looked like it might tip in the opposite direction. It held for a second. And then slammed back into place.

'Yes!' he shouted. He pumped one fist in the air and turned just in time to see them cross the starting line again.

The clock froze on 14.76.

'Fuck yeah!' TJ laughed.

'That's gonna be the time to beat today,' the announcer said. 'That's just 0.28 from the Denver Coliseum's arena record.' As the event staff moved the barrels out of the way and the tractors drove on to drag the arena before the next group of riders, TJ started hurrying back to where he'd told Skye to wait for him. But he didn't miss the announcer's words: 'Looks like Skye Marchant and her horses, Smoking Barrel and Sweet Lil Bullet, are gonna be a trio to watch this season, folks.'

Chapter 30

Skye was standing outside the arena, holding Kai by the reins, by the time TJ got to her. A few barrel racers stopped to talk to her, and as he approached, TJ heard one of them say, 'Nice run. That was incredible.'

Skye beamed. 'Thanks. It was all Kai though.' She ran one palm down Kai's face and leaned into his big neck. 'He gives his all.'

'I can't believe it was his first performance,' one of the girls offered. 'My mare went full bronc on me during her first pro run. We hit the first barrel and skipped the other two entirely.'

Her friend laughed. 'It was objectively funny to watch.'

'But not to ride.'

All three of them grinned.

TJ, who had been hovering awkwardly to the side, wanted to congratulate Skye but didn't want to interrupt. Knowing people at rodeos, making friends, was a big part of the culture, and he wanted Skye to experience that. It could be lonely on the road, but running into people you knew always made it easier.

He was just about to take a few steps back when she saw him. Her smile was quick and lethal, brightening her blue eyes.

TJ counted, *One.*

'What did you think of your boy?' she asked.

'He did good.' TJ nodded at the girls, greeted them with, 'Ladies.' But his eyes gravitated back towards Skye almost instantly. 'You both did good.'

'We better get going,' one friend said to the other. She turned to Skye, explained, 'We're buddied for the fourth drag. We just got off to pee quick.'

They waved. The taller one said, 'See you around.'

Skye waited for them to walk off before turning back to TJ. 'Jesus, Kai turns like a spin top. Perfectly smooth, almost mechanically consistent.'

TJ cocked one hip, unconsciously trying to ease his aching back and tingling right leg. 'He knows his job. You can push him harder on the straight though. He's having fun, but he's not giving it his all.'

Skye tilted her head. 'He was as close to perfect as a horse gets, TJ. Wasn't it you who once told me that there's no such thing as a perfect run?'

TJ remembered, decided, 'Fair enough.' He reached for Kai's reins. 'Let me go untack him and brush him down.'

Skye only gripped them tighter. 'No. My ride, my responsibility.'

TJ wanted to argue, but only because he had a suspicious feeling that she was managing the amount of work he did. He'd noticed it earlier too, when she'd insisted he do the braiding instead of putting Kai's boots on.

Before he could think of a reasonable objection, she said, 'Come on – you can still keep me company,' and started walking back to the trailer.

Although he didn't show it, TJ was appeased. It was enough to be where she was.

They picked their way through the contestant's parking lot, filled with trucks and trailers. Horses were tied, some eating and relaxing for the night, others being prepped for their events. People gathered, some in small groups around portable heaters, others in camping chairs propped up near their animals.

The night air was cold and crisp. The Colorado sky was dark and star-studded. A faint breeze lifted, dragging Skye's scent towards him. Despite the pain, just then, TJ was at peace.

But then Skye whispered, 'TJ.'

His name fell like a stone in a glassy lake.

Her arm shot out, stopping him.

He lifted his eyes, took a few seconds in the dark to see what she did. Then the peaceful moment shattered. The tyres – two on the trailer and two on the truck – had been slashed, the rubber pooling slightly on the ground.

'Wait here,' TJ said.

'The hell I will. Smokey's in there.'

Skye stepped forward, but TJ caught her by the wrist and tugged her back. When she opened her mouth to protest, he said, 'Please.' And because he could see that she wasn't happy, he added, 'On the off-chance he's still there, I can't worry about you and Kai.'

She turned to look at Kai, and just like he'd known she would, she put the horse first. 'Fine. One minute, TJ.'

He approached quietly, making sure to keep his footsteps silent. He slowly rounded the back of the trailer and, seeing nothing, moved to the front of the truck. When he stepped on a stick that snapped beneath his boot, Bandit started barking madly from inside the trailer. But whoever had slashed the tyres was long gone.

TJ completed his circle. He waved Skye forward and then unlocked the live-in to let Bandit out, because he'd rather have the dog near Skye at all times. The dog yipped in excitement and wagged his tail, but TJ didn't miss the way Bandit hurried over to Skye and glued himself to her legs.

'Something's spooked him,' Skye said. Leaning down, she threaded the dog's ears gently through her fingers, soothing him.

TJ stepped into the trailer and approached the door to the horse compartment. He opened it slowly, just to be safe.

Smokey stood inside, her neck high, her ears pricked forward.

'Hi, pretty girl. It's just me.' He ran one hand down her sleek coat, but called out, 'She's fine!'

Skye lowered the ramp down.

They'd booked stalls in the barn for both horses for the weekend, but after Odessa and now this, it didn't seem safe anymore. 'We'll move tonight,' TJ said. 'Camp somewhere. Come back tomorrow.'

Skye left Kai tied outside and stepped into the trailer. She moved past TJ to go and check her horse over. 'I have sleeping bags. We'll camp out with them.'

'You need to sleep,' TJ argued.

'So do you,' Skye countered.

'Skye—'

'No.' She looked at him, her eyes burning blue with rage. 'This is personal. If you feel uncomfortable sleeping next to me, then you sleep in the trailer. I'll be outside with the horses.'

TJ couldn't even think of a good argument; if their situation had been reversed, he'd have done the same. 'How many spare tyres do you have?'

'Two for the truck. Only one for the trailer because they were new, damn it.'

'I'll text around, let people know what happened and see if we can borrow a spare for the trailer. We'll go into town tomorrow and pick up some spares.'

'I looked around before my stall was confirmed,' Skye said. 'Cherry Creek State Park is about an hour from here; they have RV hook-ups and allow horses. We'd have to drive there and back every day.'

'Doesn't matter.' TJ was done risking it. 'The safety of being in the middle of nowhere will be worth it.'

Skye sighed tiredly. 'Agreed.'

'While I hunt up some tyres for the trailer, why don't you offload Smokey? Let her walk a bit.' When Skye moved off, TJ caught her by the wrist. She raised her eyebrows at him, but he didn't let her sass bother him, just said, 'Stay in sight.'

He knew she was spooked by the fact that she didn't argue, just nodded, murmured, 'Okay.'

TJ waited for her to walk off with both horses and the dog before hauling out the spare truck tyres and the jack. He stared at the first slashed tyre with dread, knowing that his back would scream in protest with every movement. And even though he understood that he could ask any cowboy there for help, TJ couldn't bear the thought. So, he took a deep breath, braced himself, and then slowly lowered to the ground to loosen the bolts on the tyre.

Every twist of the lug wrench torqued his spine, and by the time TJ had loosened all of the bolts enough to jack the truck and replace the tyre, he was drenched with sweat from the effort of resisting the pain. His back, shoulders, and arms spasmed. A pounding headache started beating behind his eyes.

When Skye approached, her first words, 'Are you okay?', TJ snapped.

'I'm fucking fine. Stop asking me that.'

A cold silence slipped between them.

But TJ couldn't let it bother him. He just needed to finish the job.

He kept working through the spasms and the fire spreading down his right leg, and by the time he had changed both tyres on the truck and sourced another for the trailer and changed those, he could barely breathe through the pain.

The moment he pulled the jack from beneath the trailer, he sat back against the tyre and closed his eyes.

He couldn't think, couldn't focus on anything but the next agonizing breath.

When he heard Skye coming back, her booted feet crunching over the ground, he forced himself back to calm and opened his eyes.

She stared down at him, not with any fondness or affection, only pity.

'If you want to say anything about my back, please don't. I promise you, I'm aware.'

She didn't listen to him. 'Why don't you take pain meds?'

'I liked the numbness too much.'

'Why are you so stubborn about this?'

'Genetics.'

'Why don't you go back to physical therapy?'

'Because I'd rather be on the road with you.' The words slipped out in an unguarded moment of truth. But TJ felt no embarrassment just then; the pain was too intense for him to care about tiptoeing around her.

Skye didn't say anything for a long moment. And then she turned and walked back inside the trailer.

TJ thought she was ignoring him and his foul mood, but she came back out almost immediately, a bottle of wine in one hand, a sleeping bag in the other.

He watched her, his heart filled with equal parts dread and anticipation, as she unzipped the sleeping bag and spread it over his legs. She sat down next to him, close enough that she could slip under the blanket with him.

When she passed him the bottle of wine, TJ took a deep sip.

He sighed as Bandit came and curled up against his thigh.

For just one moment, the anger receded.

But the moment ended too soon.

'This isn't good enough for me,' Skye said as she took the bottle out of his hand and took a sip.

'Yeah, no shit. But until you find someone who can stick and has a working back, I'm your best bet.'

'I'm not talking about you. Or, not really, I guess.' She gave him those blue eyes, filled with concern. 'I'm talking about the way you ignore your body. It's not working, TJ.'

He wanted her to stop, needed her to just pretend that everything was fine.

But Skye didn't let it go. 'Something has to change.'

'I tried everything,' TJ replied quietly. And when Skye opened her mouth to argue, he said the only thing he knew that would stop her in her tracks: 'Do you think I would have broken my promise to you if I'd seen another way out? This is my life, Skye. This is what the rest of it will look like.'

Skye wasn't sure how to reply. She still held that anger over the way he'd ended things, but it was difficult to blame TJ now that she'd seen the gruelling pain he lived with on a daily basis. 'Did you ever think that if you hadn't cut me out, I could have helped you? Maybe even made the pain easier to live with?'

'Of course. I knew you'd stay, absolutely. That's why I did what I did. It wouldn't have been fair.'

Skye knew they'd hashed it out before, but still, she snapped, 'It was my choice to make.'

'You were too young to make it, Skye. Especially after just a few days.'

Oddly, Skye didn't think so. 'I think, after everything I survived before, being able to choose my place in the world would have been really nice actually.'

'You did choose your place,' TJ reminded her. 'And from what I've heard, you found a good one at Hunt Ranch.'

Skye rolled her eyes at him. 'I know you called Mav and got me the job there.'

'I knew him,' TJ replied simply. 'Why wouldn't I?'

'Well, I won't be mad about it because I genuinely love my life there.' Skye yawned, fighting the fatigue from the day – the long drive and the race and the vandalism. 'Do you mind watching the horses while I go shower quick? Once I'm done, we can head out for the night.'

TJ stroked one big palm over Bandit's head, and although she tried not to remember a time when that same hand had run over her skin, it was hard not to. A heavy weight settled between her thighs.

TJ stopped moving, letting his hand rest on the dog's head. 'Go for it,' he said, but his tone, tight and gravelly, had her swallowing.

She risked a glance at him, knew by the dark green of his irises that he'd read her thoughts, or maybe sensed her mood.

Skye didn't dare close that distance. She'd been snubbed by TJ before, and remembering it made her doubt herself, or maybe him. But she waited for three long, tension-filled seconds, hoping that he'd make a move.

He didn't.

He merely stared off over the fairgrounds.

Skye flushed with embarrassment. 'Thanks.'

She pushed to a stand and practically ran inside the trailer. But despite her mortification, despite the spark of anger beneath it, she couldn't quite dislodge the need. It had settled deeply inside her, like a thorn only she could reach to yank out.

Frustrated, desperate, and needy, she hurriedly stripped her clothes and stepped into the shower. She closed and latched the door behind her, turned on the water, and hoped that the frigid water would wash away the lust.

It didn't.

If anything, the jolt of cold sent her heart into overdrive and filled her with adrenaline.

With TJ on her mind and heat in her blood, Skye couldn't resist raising her fingers to her core. She stroked through, unsurprised by the hot, slick lust that drenched her and slipped down her upper thighs.

As she touched herself, she closed her eyes and imagined that it was TJ. And even as she quickened her pace to catch the rise, even as the pleasure bloomed through her, she remembered his lust-filled eyes and the way he'd purposefully turned them from her. And even as she bit back a moan and let the orgasm wash over her, she felt unsatiated. Empty. Angry.

Chapter 31

Skye came out of the trailer in a mood. Perhaps sensing her anger, Bandit rose from his place against TJ's thigh and slunk over to her, making his loyalty clear. Her dog's behaviour didn't make her feel good; it only angered her further.

She wanted to be cool and aloof, damn it. She wanted to be unfazed and detached when it came to TJ, not emotional and sensitive and – worse – *confused.* She deliberately cooled her tone when she said, 'You need to move if we're going to get going.'

TJ's eyes scanned her face. 'You okay?'

'Peachy.'

'Good. Because you're gonna have to pull that stick out your butt for long enough to help me get up.'

All of Skye's anger left her in one huge sweep. She approached slowly. She knew TJ, knew that he'd rather gnaw off his own hand than ask for her help with something as simple as standing up. 'It's bad?' she asked.

TJ nodded, and for the first time, Skye noticed the things she'd missed in her anger. TJ's face was pale, his hairline glistening with sweat.

'Sitting through the drive flared everything up, and then changing the tyres pushed me over.'

Skye swallowed thickly. She knelt at his side, asked, 'What do I do?'

'I just need help getting my feet under me. If you could get Kai . . .'

Skye hurried to Kai and untied the gelding's lead rope, then led him to where TJ sat, being careful not to get too close to his extended legs.

TJ groaned as he shifted. He bent his left leg and then used both hands to move his right into position. His skin was so pale that his green eyes looked black in comparison.

He clicked once, encouraging Kai to move closer, and the moment the horse did, TJ weakly raised his hands to grab either side of Kai's halter. He backed up immediately, pulling TJ to his feet with only a few steps.

The moment he was standing, TJ collapsed his weight against the truck and, leaning over awkwardly, threw up.

Unsure of what to do, Skye left him there while she locked Smokey and Kai back in the trailer and Bandit in the live-in.

The folks parked next to their trailer were sitting in camping chairs, waiting for their event or coming down from the night. They were watching TJ, their faces set in that look of pity that told Skye they knew exactly who he was and what had happened to him.

'Do you mind keeping an eye on my animals? I have to run him to the hospital, but I'll come right back.'

'Of course,' one of the men said. 'We're done for the night, so we'll be here shooting the breeze for a while. Go.'

Skye gave them her cell number in case they needed to reach her and then hurried back to TJ. 'Get in the truck.'

'We can't leave the horses,' he argued.

Skye's stomach filled with dread. She looked back, noticed that the group of men had moved their chairs to a spot between her trailer and theirs. 'Nobody will let anything happen to them.'

He sighed tiredly. 'I just need to sleep.'

'You can sleep in hospital, once they see to your back and give you some pain meds. TJ?' She waited for him to look at her, and though her heart wept for the blank expression in his eyes, she gave him an ultimatum. 'We go to the hospital, or I drop out of the season and ditch you and Kai back in Arizona on my way to Hunt Ranch. The choice is yours.'

'You know, you never used to be such a hard-ass,' he said bitterly.

'You never used to be such an idiot, but I guess we've both changed,' she snapped.

TJ wheezed out a tired laugh at that. But eventually he said, 'Fine,' and limped to the passenger door of the truck.

Skye searched for the nearest emergency room and sighed in relief when she saw that it was only a ten-minute drive.

As they left the coliseum behind, TJ didn't say anything. He didn't argue, didn't fight. Just stared out his window in silence, his face pale, his eyes blank.

Skye didn't try to talk to him. She was lost in her own guilt and regret.

It was becoming increasingly difficult to stay mad at him, but it was so much easier to be angry at a person than it was to be sad and scared for them. Being angry had agency; being sad and scared didn't. And yet, she knew it was already too late to turn back. Somewhere between Texas and Colorado, she'd unknowingly slipped back over that line from anger to forgiveness.

She pulled up to the ER's drop-off zone and hopped out, slamming her door behind her. The nurse standing just inside the doors, triaging every patient who walked in, must have seen her panic because she came outside. 'What's the nature of your injury?'

Terrified that they'd keep her away from him if they thought she wasn't family, Skye replied, 'My boyfriend has an old spinal cord injury and hurt himself working on my truck. He's struggling to stand. He threw up.'

TJ opened the door, so the nurse directed her next order to

him. 'Sir, please don't get out of the vehicle until I've fetched a wheelchair.'

'I can walk,' TJ argued.

'Don't you dare.'

Both the nurse and TJ looked at Skye as the demand left her lips. But while the nurse smiled and said, 'I have to agree,' TJ just scowled.

She passed Skye a form on a clipboard, said, 'Fill this out. I'll wheel him in as a priority, but given that he's coherent, it may be up to ten minutes until he's seen.'

'Thank you.' Skye waited until the nurse had hurried off to grab a wheelchair before turning back to TJ. 'I need your ID and your health insurance card.'

TJ passed her his wallet. 'This is bullshit.'

'Tough luck,' Skye snapped. 'You're obviously not making good decisions anymore, so from now on, as long as you want to tag along, you're going to start listening to me.'

Oddly, he didn't argue. He didn't say anything. And when Skye paused filling out the paperwork for long enough to look up at him, she was mortified to see that his eyes had glassed over. *Her* crying was bad enough, but *TJ* crying was intimate in a way that terrified her.

Unsure of what to do, she lowered the clipboard. 'TJ . . .'

'I can't think past the pain anymore,' he whispered, and raised his eyes to her.

The despair and hopelessness in him sent a streak of fear down her spine.

'I just want it to be over,' he said. 'And I know that's hard for you to hear, Skye, because you have the biggest fucking heart. But it's inevitable. I can't . . .'

His words were strangled by a choked sob.

Skye wanted to soothe. She wanted to hold him and promise that everything would be all right. But, somewhere, in the back of her mind, she knew TJ had probably been told that by everyone in his life with no measurable result. So, she steeled herself instead. She forced her tone towards matter of fact. 'We won't get anywhere unless you agree to start trying again.'

TJ just stared at her with that hangdog expression.

'Enough.' Skye put the clipboard on the dash and then leaned into the truck. She didn't threaten. She just said, 'Please.'

'Nothing I've done has worked,' he whispered. A tear trailed down his cheek, and TJ angrily swiped it away. 'I can't even *think*, Skye. Every part of me is in pain all the time.'

Afraid she'd start crying too, Skye leaned further in. She placed her lips on his, just a gentle brush. 'How about now?'

TJ's eyes were huge in his face. But he managed a breathy, 'I don't know. You'll have to do it again for me to be sure.'

Skye just smiled and stepped back. 'You're in there, TJ. We've just got to dig you out.'

The nurse came back out. 'This is Ralph,' she said, introducing the male nurse at her side. 'He's going to help you get out of the vehicle. Ma'am, if you'd like to come with us, the valet can park your truck.'

'Thank you.' Skye took her keys to the valet desk, then silently followed the nurses and TJ, in a wheelchair, as they entered the ER.

The lobby was quiet just then. A little girl with a cut on her cheek and blood on her shirt slept in her mother's arms, her face still red and puffy from crying. A teenage boy with a split lip sat sullenly in one of the badly upholstered chairs, his arms crossed protectively over his ribs in a posture Skye knew all too well. When the boy saw Skye and TJ, he lifted his hoodie up and angled his face away, hiding his bruises.

When they came to the exam cubicle, the nurse closed them inside. She pointed to the gown on the bed. 'Let me help you—'

'I've got it,' TJ said, his tone leaving no room for further argument.

'We'll manage,' Skye assured the nurse. 'Thank you.'

'I'll be back in a few minutes to take your vitals, and then the doctor will follow shortly.' She took the clipboard from Skye, scanned over the form. Her eyebrows rose as she read, and Skye could only imagine that she was at the *Physical and Behavioural Conditions* section, under which Skye had written *Spinal cord injury from bull-riding accident – March 2025.*

The moment the nurse was gone, TJ untucked his shirt. He looked at Skye over his shoulder. 'I'm fine.'

'Yeah, I'm not going anywhere until I hear what the doctor says with my own ears,' Skye countered.

'Suit yourself.' TJ raised his hands to his buttons. He didn't lift the shirt up and off as anyone else might have, just opened it up one button at a time and then painstakingly slipped it off his shoulders to reveal his back.

Skye had expected a scar, of course, but not the long, deep line that ran the entire length of his notched spine, cutting his bull skull tattoo unequally into two and rebalancing that scale, so that *Die* hovered slightly lower than *Live* now. Where he'd once been muscular and tanned, his back, still undeniably broad, was pale, his spine and ribcage defined through his skin.

Tears slipped uselessly over her lashes. A warbled sob left her lips.

TJ heard it. His spine went rigid. But he didn't turn around.

'TJ . . .'

He didn't even acknowledge her, so Skye closed that distance. She didn't say anything, just wrapped her arms around him and rested her face against his hot skin as her tears streamed unchecked. TJ froze at the touch, but Skye just whispered, 'I'm so sorry.'

'I thought we agreed you weren't going to apologize for that,' he said, but his tone was cautious and gentle, and he raised his forearm to cover both of hers against his chest. He sighed deeply, so that she felt his chest decompress as the air left his lungs.

'I wish I had been confident enough to ignore you, to stay anyway.'

'You couldn't have done anything for me, Skye. You still can't.'

She stepped back and swiped her eyes, said, 'We'll see.'

Unlike TJ, Skye had been born into a world of fear and helplessness. She had learned, year by year, abuse by abuse, that the only way out was to fight. It hadn't been easy. It had taken her years. But maybe that was something she could teach TJ.

'Are you really going to make me strip in front of you?' TJ asked.

'It's nothing I haven't seen before,' Skye commented. 'But if you want, I can turn my back.'

TJ just shook his head. 'Don't even bother; I need help taking off my boots.' He hobbled to the hospital bed and sat down gingerly.

Skye knelt on the floor. She grabbed his right boot by the heel and gently articulated his ankle so that she could yank the boot off. By the time she'd removed the second one, TJ was panting lightly.

First order of business, Skye thought. *Buy lace-up work boots.*

She pushed to a stand and lifted the gown off the bed, held it out so that he could thread his arms through the sleeves. Once it was on, she tied it and then stepped out of the room while he took off his jeans. Not because she was embarrassed or sensitive to how TJ's body had changed; she would have found him attractive irrespective. She left because it was too intimate to watch him undress completely.

And Skye didn't know what to do with that truth.

TJ sat on the bed and waited for the doctor to come. His back was pulled as tight as a violin string, his muscles spasming, his right leg burning in a river of nerve pain. But for the first time in a long while, it didn't steal all his attention. He was stuck on Skye, on the way she'd stood up to him and refused to listen when he'd insisted he was fine. The way she'd kissed him, the way she'd hugged him, her hot tears falling on his skin.

TJ had stopped grieving for himself a long time ago, maybe even on the day that Skye had left. It had been easy to stop caring when he'd looked at his life and seen nothing worth fighting for. His sister had Sly and Luke. Even his parents had the farm and each other. On days where he felt good enough to help, only a few hours of work were enough to set him back completely, so they'd gotten to the point where all he and his parents did was fight about what he could and couldn't do.

But here, now, with Skye, TJ felt a glimmer of *something*. It wasn't hope. It was peace. Or, maybe, relief.

Outside his curtain, he heard someone say, 'You must be TJ's girlfriend?'

TJ held his breath, and when Skye didn't correct the doctor, just said, 'Yes,' he slowly exhaled.

'I'm Dr Harris, the Chief of Orthopaedic Surgery here at Denver Medical. Apologies for the wait.' The doctor approached the curtain, said, 'Knock knock,' in lieu of any door.

'Yeah,' TJ replied.

The doctor and Skye stepped in, and Dr Harris introduced himself to TJ, then settled down on the wheeled stool in front of the bed. He read the form Skye had filled out. 'It says here that your spinal cord injury was the result of trauma from a bull in 2025?'

'Yes.'

'Could you give me as much detail as you can?' the doctor asked.

'The damage was mostly to T12 and L1. My SCI is classified as incomplete.'

'And the pain?'

'Permanent.'

'On a scale of one to ten, where does the pain level stay most often?'

'Eight.'

'How many hours of sleep do you get a night?'

'Three or four, in clusters of twenty to thirty minutes at a time.' And Christ, just saying it aloud had that fatigue creeping up on him and threatening to drag him under.

'What does your current rehab programme look like?' The doctor was taking notes as he worked, but when TJ didn't answer immediately, he looked up.

'I'm not doing rehab or physio anymore,' TJ said firmly.

The doctor lowered the clipboard. He levelled intense brown eyes on TJ. 'Are you on meds for the depression?'

'Yes.' That one hurt to admit in front of Skye.

'SNRI?'

TJ nodded. 'Duloxetine.'

'What does your everyday look like?'

'I'm travelling with the rodeo at the moment, so it's long days in the truck moving to the next location and then working with the horses until Skye races. Then we pack up and head to the next.' He shrugged. 'The season's just starting, so we're only at our second rodeo right now.'

The doctor nodded kindly, but his voice was firm when he said, 'TJ, you already know what I'm going to say. I don't even have to do an X-ray or get your medical records to know at least part of where you're going wrong.'

That panic gripped TJ by the throat, but still, he argued, 'It didn't work. I gave it a year the first time.'

'Considering the extent of your injury, a year isn't even scratching the surface. Rehabilitating an incomplete SCI isn't easy; it's a miracle of science. It takes time. But the technology is available – and it's only getting better. You have to commit to the process.' The doctor sat back. 'With your permission, I'd like to get the rest of your medical records sent here tomorrow. Tonight, we'll update your X-rays, confirm what we already know and then give you an epidural shot straight into the spine so that you can reach a level of comfort that allows you to start physical therapy again.' He tipped his head. 'Maybe you could even start sleeping.'

TJ opened his mouth to argue, but Skye stepped to his side. She placed one hand on his shoulder, asked the doctor, 'Could you give us a minute?'

'Of course.' Dr Harris stood. 'I'll be back in five to prep you for the X-rays.'

He left, closing the curtain behind him.

'I'm not doing it.' The words left TJ's mouth before Skye had even started her argument.

'Yes. You are.' She moved in front of him, crossed her arms over her chest. 'If I have to rope you and tie you down myself, I will. But you're going to get X-rayed. You're going to get that epidural. And you're going to restart a physical therapy programme that *I* will be overseeing.' She smiled, almost evilly. 'Enough of this horseshit. If you're not going to fight for yourself anymore, then fine. I'll fight for you.'

TJ hated that her vehemence filled him with a flicker of hope and – damn her – *need.* But more than the hope and the need, the fear was there. And it was a beast he could not contain. 'If it doesn't work, I'll have nothing left.'

'Rude.'

TJ's mouth actually twitched. 'I don't have you; I've just coerced you to where I want you.'

Skye leaned forward, and she whispered, 'Ditto, cowboy.'

For only a second, his eyes dropped to her lips. She was so close, so tempting. The things he'd do for one last taste of her were numerous and undefined.

But Skye took a sudden step back and ran both hands through her hair, her frustration clear. 'If it works, you'll be able to start living your life again. Doesn't that mean anything to you?'

TJ couldn't even believe in the possibility. 'Skye—'

But she just kept going. 'And you're going do *everything* your doctors recommend; otherwise, I'm dropping your butt back in Arizona.' She started counting off her fingers. 'No offloading, no grooming, no picking hooves, no heavy lifting.'

'This might be quicker if you list what I *can* do,' he drawled.

'No riding.'

TJ's head popped up, his refusal instant, but when he saw the stubborn gleam in her eyes, he knew he didn't have a bargaining chip.

Skye knew it too. 'We get your physical therapy plan from your doctor and we restart it. We follow it religiously. If the doctor says you have to hold your breath and hum the national anthem, then we do that. If he says take pain pills when you need to, then you take pain pills. If you're worried about how much you like them, I'll keep them for you to make sure you're only taking them when necessary.'

'You're demanding an awful lot considering I'm trying to help you.'

Skye smiled coolly. 'I could say the same thing about you. But that's my ultimatum, TJ. So' – she crossed her arms over her chest – 'what'll it be?'

Chapter 32

It was nearly midnight by the time Skye drove back up to the hospital entrance, after moving the horses and trailer out to Cherry Creek State Park. The tall building loomed, the bright lights inside boasting its perpetual wakefulness.

Skye moved through the lobby like a zombie, no thought behind the motions, just one foot in front of the other. She was just about to ask after TJ at the front desk when she saw Dr Harris walking down the hall.

He smiled at her. 'Good timing. We're just about to do his epidural.'

Skye followed him into the elevator. 'How were his X-rays?'

Dr Harris hesitated. 'I'll give you the debrief together,' he said. As they stepped into the hall, he continued cautiously, 'There is the matter of TJ's mental health that I'd like to discuss with you.'

The fatigue and worry and stress from the past few days was insurmountable just then. And, still, Skye said, 'Tell me.'

'Given TJ's current state, I'm legally and morally obligated to warn you as family: he's what I'd classify as at high risk of self-harm.'

Although it was excruciating to admit, Skye replied, 'I know.'

She'd heard the way TJ talked, like he was crossing items off a list. Preparing.

'For anyone else, I'd recommend therapy at the minimum and maybe even in-patient psychiatric care and pain management. But something tells me TJ would never agree to that.'

'He has to be active, to feel *useful*.' Skye sighed sadly. 'He used to ride bulls for a living, and now doing basic things sends him into spasms so bad that he can barely walk. He's lost,' she said, and she didn't think anyone had to have known TJ before his accident to see that.

The knowledge was just another reminder that TJ had been trying to protect her when he'd cut her off.

'I understand. But I think, with an extended period of focused rehabilitation and pain management, TJ's quality of life will drastically improve. The hard part – the part that's going to be unfair to *you* – is that you're the one who's going to have to keep him going. He doesn't want to try, but he said he's doing the epidural because you said he had to.' Dr Harris smiled. 'That kind of love is what's going to get him through this. Having just one person who refuses to give up on him is everything.'

That word – love – was too big for Skye to hold on to just then. She knew that it wasn't love guiding TJ's actions, only the ultimatum she'd given him. Still, her tears started again, and she groaned and swiped at her face. 'I'm sorry. It's been a long day.'

The doctor nodded kindly. 'I bet.'

The private room he led her to was spartan, just an X-ray table with its huge mobile arm in the centre, a chair in the corner, and various cabinets and medical items against the far wall. A viewing room sat off to the side, and TJ stood by the X-ray bed, scowling and holding his gown shut.

When he saw Skye's face, still red from crying, his scowl died. He came to her, asked, 'What's wrong?'

'Nothing,' she lied.

TJ studied her face, his brow notched with concern.

Dr Harris moved forward and spoke kindly but firmly. 'TJ, your SCI has resulted in systemic inflammation and a chronic secondary injury cascade. To be completely honest, I'm not sure how you've survived to this point without numerous epidurals and a horde of painkillers.'

TJ smiled darkly, but he looked directly at Skye when he replied, 'I have a high tolerance for suffering.'

'Well, I can see a clear path to things improving, but if you don't start taking the necessary steps, your situation *is* going to decline.'

TJ was eerily quiet.

So, Skye said, 'Tell us what we have to do.'

'We're going to start with the ESI – the epidural steroid injection. Once that starts helping with your pain management, we're going to get you back on a long-term physical therapy programme. You'll be on a full anti-inflammatory diet. I'm going to give you muscle relaxants and sleeping pills for the days when you need to pass out for a good ten hours. I'll consult with your surgeon, so that we can agree on a path forward, and so that he's fully updated when you go home. After the rodeo season, I think you should speak to your doctor about more advanced research possibilities and medical trials.'

'You ready?' Skye asked.

TJ just shrugged. 'Let's get this show on the road.'

Dr Harris moved around the table, pulling on a protective vest and goggles. 'If you could lie facedown on the X-ray table, TJ?' He turned back to Skye and pointed to a door in the corner. 'Skye, if you could wait in the viewing room?'

TJ passed her his phone. 'Could you hold on to this for me?'

Skye took it. She left to stand in the adjacent room and watched through the glass as the live X-ray was taken. When the doctor lifted a fat syringe off the nearby counter and pulled the cap off a huge needle, Skye's stomach turned over in one long slow roll.

In her pocket, TJ's phone continuously vibrated as notifications came through. Skye ignored it.

It was a quick but gruelling procedure, one that made her skin prickle with displeasure. As she watched, she couldn't help but wonder how many hours of sleep TJ had lost. How many antidepressants he had taken. And although she could still say that TJ had gone about it the wrong way, she finally understood that he'd shut her out for what he thought were the right reasons. For her.

It changed things. Had their situations been reversed, she knew now that she would have done the same thing. She would have tried to spare him.

Overwhelmed by the thought, Skye lost her patience when TJ's phone kept vibrating in her back pocket. She whipped it out, intending to turn it off, and paused when she saw that the notifications were all from social media accounts.

Curious, she pulled her own phone out. She looked TJ up for the first time in nearly two years.

Her heart beat dully in her chest when she saw his new Instagram aesthetic. Grief clawed through that empty ache.

Although his following had grown, hitting nearly a million people, his posts had changed. Still professionally produced, the videos were stitched together with a mix of actual footage that had been darkened to look like something out of a horror film, with punk graffiti spray-overs and heavy metal music. The content of his videos ranged from ones of him trying to walk in a harness and constantly collapsing to replayed footage of his accident, with dramatic pauses, music, and a skull and crossbones flashing across the screen as the bull took him down.

Bile filled her throat.

Her hands, holding the phone, shook – with rage and grief and confusion.

When the doctor waved her back in, Skye slipped both phones into her pocket. She took a deep breath and re-entered the room.

At the doctor's encouragement, TJ slowly sat up on the bed, holding his gown closed again.

Dr Harris removed his gloves. 'That's it. Now, the steroid's efficacy varies wildly. And it may take a few hours to a day or two to kick in fully. We'll be calling you in a few days to check in. Otherwise, once I get your medical records, I'll refer you to a physical therapist who'll send you an exercise and mobility plan you can do on the road.' He pulled the clipboard out from its slot on the wall and wrote some notes. 'I've prescribed you some pain meds. Be cautious with them. Use them only when absolutely necessary. Same for the muscle relaxants and sleeping pills. They're easy to abuse,' he said, and looked pointedly at Skye. 'However, if managed effectively, a few more hours of sleep can drastically change your outlook on life. There's a reason sleep deprivation is considered an effective means of torture.' He looked up. 'Do you have any questions?'

'No,' TJ replied.

Skye asked, 'How long will the steroid last?'

'It varies. Weeks to months. Some people find they only need one to get back into the flow of things. But given the extent of your injury, TJ, you may need to keep getting them every few months for a while. We can get your pain under control, but *healing* the injury is going to take time, patience, and trial and error.'

'Are there any other precautions we should be taking?' Skye asked.

'Any means to reduce inflammation will help. As I mentioned earlier: anti-inflammatory diet, no alcohol, no activities that would exacerbate his injury. There's a lot you can do day to day to help too. After the first forty-eight hours, hot compresses might alleviate some swelling and temporarily relieve pain. Orthopaedic massage therapy will help with sciatica. The hard part is going to be finding what works for you in addition to the demands of your mobile lifestyle.'

'We can stop travelling—'

'The hell we will,' TJ interjected for the first time.

Skye geared up to argue, but before she could say anything,

Dr Harris smoothly interjected. 'You'll find your balance. But you've just got to keep at it.' He passed Skye a packet that had been on the counter. 'This is everything you need to know about the next few days. Once the rodeo season is over, I'd strongly recommend enrolling in more extensive treatment options.' He held out one hand. 'Good luck.'

TJ returned the handshake, asked, 'Can we go now?'

The doctor looked down at his watch. 'Give it five more minutes in the lobby just to be sure you don't have any immediate side effects. Otherwise, you're good to go. No driving for twelve hours.'

'Thank you,' TJ managed.

'You're welcome. If there's one last thing I can stress to you, it's this: try to remember that the steroid doesn't heal the injury; it's only going to reduce inflammation and help with pain management. Healing is going to come down to how invested you are in rebuilding your life, one day – sometimes, one hour – at a time.'

The moment the doctor left the room, Skye moved closer. 'Let's get you dressed.'

TJ scowled at her. 'I'm not an infant,' he stated.

There was the slightest spread of relief soothing over his sciatica already, but oddly, that spreading numbness was as much a physical comfort as it was a mental torment.

TJ had accepted his fate. He had fought it for a long time, but slowly, the pain had worn him down and made him comfortable with, even ready for, the end. He'd lived with the knowledge that he'd leave for so long that he actually didn't know how to digest the possibility that, maybe, things could actually get better.

'Well, you might not be an infant, but you sure as shit are acting like a big baby.' She walked to the counter and grabbed his clothes, which the nurse had carried in earlier.

'For Christ's sake, I've got it!'

Skye jumped. For just one split second, he saw the fear streak through her eyes. She inhaled a quick, shaky breath.

Shame swamped him instantly. 'Skye—'

She dumped the clothes on the X-ray table. 'I'll wait outside,' she said coolly.

Rather than chase after her in the gaping hospital gown, TJ slowly changed, moving with habitual precision. But even though it still hurt to move, to bend and pull and yank, even though those twitching muscles felt filled with needles, TJ was very aware of the fact that he could articulate his right knee without having to use his hands to support it.

Out in the hall, Skye was leaning against the wall, waiting for him. When he closed the door behind him, she pushed up from her tilt. She didn't say anything, only watched him warily.

TJ went straight up to her, and even though he yearned to take her into his arms, he didn't. He said, 'I'm sorry. I don't mean to be ungrateful, Skye.' He tried to explain. 'When you're in chronic pain, other people's optimism – their *hope* – hurts too much.' Although he didn't say it, it was so much worse with her, because Skye made him *want* to try again. When she fought with him – or maybe, *for* him – it terrified him, because there was a TJ who would choose a life of pain over the option of never seeing her again.

Skye sighed, but she didn't move away. 'I always assumed I knew . . .'

Confused, TJ asked, 'What do you mean?'

'I thought I knew how much pain you must have been in, how hard it was for you. But after seeing those needles in you, I realized that knowing someone's in pain doesn't necessarily mean that you can conceptualize what it's like to live with it. I knew that you were hurt and scared and confused, but I don't think I truly appreciated until today how consuming that must have been.' She met his eyes. 'And I think you were right. I don't think I would have known how to handle it back then.'

'No. But I knew that you'd try.'

'Yeah,' she agreed. 'I would have.' She extended her hand, and when TJ just frowned down at it, she explained, 'We never actually shook on the truce.'

TJ returned the shake. 'Truce.'

By unspoken agreement, they started for the doors side by side. It was only when they were in the elevator together that Skye added, 'But don't think this means you're getting out of my ultimatum.'

TJ just growled.

Chapter 33

Despite the horrifically long day and late night, TJ, ever a farmer's son, woke up with the sun. Habit had him opening his eyes before so much as shifting his neck or his back.

Still groggy from sleep, it took him a full ten seconds to realize that he had complete feeling in his right leg, down to his foot, and that the sciatica was a flowing tingle instead of a steady stream of fire.

He was lying in a sleeping bag on the floor of Skye's trailer, because the hard surface had felt better on his back when they'd passed out here last night.

Now, he inhaled deeply, and when none of those agonizing tugs and pulls gripped him, he slowly rolled over onto one elbow, before pushing himself. The seated L was still painful, but it was nowhere near as bad as it had been yesterday.

TJ ran one hand tiredly through his shaggy hair, overwhelmed by the relief, by the lack of agony.

On the bed, Bandit gave a big yawn and rolled onto his back to stretch all four paws in the air, but despite the dog's movements, Skye didn't so much as shift in her sleep.

She was curled on her side, her blankets tucked up under her chin. Her eyes, shadowed with fatigue, were still beneath her eyelids. With the trailer's lack of heating, her deep, even breaths left little clouds of fog in the frigid Colorado morning.

TJ couldn't help but watch her for a long minute. There was a part of him that yearned to reach out, maybe brush his fingers over her face as he had once done or give her a casual kiss before he got going with the day.

Instead, he took a deep breath and gently turned onto his knees, so that he was on all fours. Pain sliced through him. But this time, though his spine pulled uncomfortably tight, it was bearable, and when he pushed up onto his feet, he didn't have to take those few customary seconds to fight the nausea.

Unable to emotionally process that, TJ simply started the day. He shrugged into his winter coat and stepped outside. He fed the horses and, with his promise to Skye on his mind, made numerous trips with smaller bunches of hay and alfalfa rather than haul it all at once. He gave the horses their feed and supplements and, noting that their water was icing over, broke up the ice and refilled the buckets from the trailer's sink.

When all the animals were watered and fed, he grabbed the shovel and a trash bag out of the trailer. He was just about to collapse the portable fence when Skye's voice, thick with sleep, said, 'Don't you dare.'

TJ sighed. He turned, couldn't help but scan over her as she stood in the door of the trailer. 'I feel great.'

'Unlike you, *I* read the informational packet Dr Harris gave us.' She pulled a wad of papers off the nearby counter and waved them in the air. She pointed to a random place on the first page, stated, 'It specifically says that, just because you start to feel better, that doesn't mean you should resume regular activities.'

'Jesus, I'm just going to shovel shit, Skye.'

'No. You're not. It's an uncontrolled movement with bending, twisting, and unevenly distributed weight.'

TJ slammed the shovel-head into the ground and lifted one foot to it, settling in to argue.

Skye, her temper clear, her movements filled with purpose, marched to where he stood, meeting him head-on.

She'd changed into thick sweatpants and a white, long-sleeved shirt the night before – a shirt that was ever so slightly see-through. And although she was too angry to realize it, TJ sure as fuck wasn't.

He could make out her nipples beneath her shirt, dark pink and peaked in the cold. A sharp claw of need, one he hadn't felt in *so long*, sliced through him. His hands burned to slide beneath the hem of her shirt and touch, take.

While Skye geared up to argue, her, 'We agreed you'd try,' fell largely on deaf ears.

TJ nodded dumbly. He tried to be a gentleman, tried to look away. But this was *Skye* and her fucking perfect tits, ones he'd *seen* and *touched* and *tasted.*

She frowned. 'What's wrong with you?'

Because he desperately wanted to say *Nothing* and just keep on looking, he sighed and said, 'Your shirt's see-through,' instead.

On cue, both their gazes dropped to her breasts.

'Oh, for Christ's sake,' she said, resigned. 'Why is it that the sight of boobs sends otherwise intelligent men into fits of idiocy?' She looked up at him, ready to keep tearing into him, and although he tried to hide that raging need, it was impossible.

Skye's eyes widened. Her breath left her in a surprised *whoosh.* TJ watched as his need slowly spread to her. Her irises darkened. She gnawed on her lower lip. And she didn't raise her arms to cover her peaked nipples.

'Grow up, TJ,' she said. But the command lacked heat, and instead of taking a step back, she leaned slightly closer.

TJ didn't even care that he had a semi-hard-on that was clearly visible beneath his jeans. He rasped, 'Yes, ma'am,' because he couldn't quite come down from the lust enough to think of anything better.

'You're ridiculous,' she accused.

'No.' He had to disagree with that. 'You're so fucking sexy.' He groaned, and the sound of it was pained. 'And I'm only a man.'

Her shaky inhale tore through him. Her cheeks and neck, so pale moments before, flooded with heat. Just the way he remembered.

She very quietly said, 'We need to do something about this. We can't travel together for months with all . . . *this.*' She waved one hand as if to clear the air of the thick heat between them.

TJ stilled. His heart slammed in his chest. He very carefully asked, 'What exactly did you have in mind?'

Skye turned those big blue eyes on him. 'Once. To get it out of our systems.'

'Once won't be enough,' TJ countered instantly. 'You know that.'

'Once,' she repeated.

He didn't argue further, though he wanted to point out that there were only two possibilities when it came to them: love or hate. And TJ had only ever loved her, even when she had hated him. Once might hold them over for a day or two, but it wouldn't last.

Still, he was too afraid that she'd baulk if he pointed that out. He was terrified that she'd run. So, he said, 'If that's what you need.'

'Deal.'

When she stuck out her hand, TJ took it, but because he'd never shake on a deal he didn't mean to uphold, he didn't. Instead, he closed his hand around hers, used his leverage to pull her the rest of the way into his arms.

He lowered his head, but he didn't make a move. He wanted her to close that distance between them, wanted her to need him as much as he needed her.

Skye ran her hands under his shirt, touching his bare skin, not in pity but in pleasure. She stood on her tippy toes and, without hesitating, fused her mouth to his.

The kiss was like coming home after a year on the road bull

riding. It was safe and right and good. Her taste teased him, whipping his senses into overdrive.

Unable to resist, TJ lowered both his hands and slipped them beneath the waistband of her baggy sweatpants, to find nothing but soft, naked skin. He groaned into her mouth, broke the kiss to murmur, 'No underwear?'

'I'm out. I need to go to the laundromat,' she explained breathily.

'Jesus.' He gripped her gentle curves, said, 'Don't. I like finding you like this.'

His urge was to slip his fingers around to her front and take, right there in a public park in broad daylight, but TJ resisted. He leaned down slightly, ready to pick her up, but the moment she sensed his intention, Skye said, 'Don't.'

He stopped immediately, terrified that she had changed her mind. But instead, she said, 'You're not supposed to lift more than twenty pounds outside of a controlled setting.'

TJ froze. A rusty chuckle left his lips. '*That's* what you're thinking about right now?'

Skye pouted. 'One of us clearly has to.'

His humour faded rapidly beneath the despair. It bothered him that he couldn't do all those little things. *Normal* things. Things like picking her up, carrying her twenty goddamn feet, and throwing her around a bit. Because she'd liked those things once.

Skye placed her palm on his face and turned his eyes back to hers. 'Where did you go?'

'I want to be who you need,' he said.

'Mighty arrogant of you to assume I need a man.'

TJ didn't laugh as he knew she'd hoped. 'Wanting to carry you sometimes doesn't mean that I think you're incapable of carrying yourself.'

She sighed. 'I know, TJ. But, maybe, letting go of your pride for just a little while will help you to heal in the way you need. Maybe, being humble enough to let another person carry *you* for a while is something you were always supposed to learn.' She shrugged. 'It was for me.'

'You make it so hard to argue.'

'Only because, in your head, you know I'm right. And in your heart, you want to get better.'

'I'm not so sure about that.' He thought it imperative that she know that. 'There are still moments when I'm not sure that I *do* want to get better, not sure that *I can*. But, since I saw you outside of Dave's, leaving doesn't hold the same appeal. Because, if there's nothing on the other side, logically that means there's no you.'

Skye slapped her hand over his mouth, her panic clear. 'Stop saying shit like that.'

TJ nodded slowly. But his dark sense of humour had him pointing out, 'I'm not sure that's what you're supposed to say to someone who's suicidal.'

'I don't think you really want to leave,' she reiterated. 'You just couldn't see a way out.' She turned for the trailer, and when he didn't immediately follow, she reached out her hand for his, said, 'Until now.'

TJ couldn't hold on to the hope flickering inside of him for long enough to give her back the words or make her any promises.

But he did take her hand.

And he let her pull him inside the warmth and the light.

Skye knew she was making a mistake. TJ had been right when he'd said that once would never be enough. Because even as she pulled him into the trailer, told Bandit to 'Stay' where he lay on the floor, and closed the door behind them, her hands shook with frenetic anticipation.

This wasn't just a casual hook-up or a date leading to nowhere. This was *TJ*. Her first. As far as intimacy and connection went, her only. And just remembering how it would be had her reaching for him.

Skye didn't go slow or take her time. She'd been deprived too long. She grabbed either side of his shirt and yanked, ripping the buttons off easily. TJ's abs had always been good, but now, with his new leanness, they were impossibly defined.

Skye ran her nails lightly over him, from his neck to his navel, revelling in the way his body shuddered beneath her touch.

But TJ didn't reach for her. He didn't do anything except stand there and watch her, his eyes dark with need.

'What's wrong?' Skye asked.

TJ replied, 'Nothing.' But his voice was thick with emotion. Intensity poured off of him. And when Skye stopped moving, dissatisfied with his answer, he *finally* reached for her. He enfolded her in his embrace, so that she was warmed by his hot skin. He rested his forehead against hers and sighed deeply. 'I had accepted that we'd never be here again.'

He didn't explain further, but he didn't have to. Skye felt that same disbelief and, oddly, *relief*. For so long, she'd told herself that she hadn't connected with another lover since TJ because she hadn't wanted to. And although that was partly true, the one thing she hadn't been able to admit, even to herself, was that she hadn't wanted to because she hadn't been ready to let him go completely.

She didn't – *couldn't* – say that to him. Instead, she placed both her hands on either side of his face and touched her lips to his. She whispered, 'Stop thinking. Just be here with me now, TJ.'

He nodded. A familiar wicked grin, one she'd missed seeing, spread slowly over his face. He slipped his shirt off his shoulders and let it drop to the floor. 'Do you know what it's been like – being close to you the last few days without being able to touch you?'

Skye didn't lie. 'Yes.'

'I intend to make up for it, Skye,' he warned her.

But the threat only sounded like the sweetest promise. Impatient with lust, desperate to be touched, taken, Skye hurriedly stripped.

She lifted her shirt up and off, slipped out of her sweatpants, and it was only once she stood in front of him, completely naked, that she said, 'I've masturbated to the thought of you several times since Dave's.'

TJ groaned audibly. But even as she stood there naked before him, he didn't rush. He said, 'Show me how you touched yourself.'

Skye slowly ran her hands down her own body. She paused at her breasts, cupped them as she ran her index fingers over her nipples and moaned.

TJ curled his hands into fists, almost as if to physically prevent himself from interceding. He rooted himself to the spot, encouraged her, his voice low. 'Being teased by you is my ripest fantasy come to life.'

His words spread heat through her. His eyes, glinting with challenge, excited her.

Wanting to torment him, wanting him to feel the same desperation she did, Skye dropped her hand lower. She spread herself with her fingers, ran her index and middle fingers slowly over her slick, sensitized flesh.

TJ's breath billowed. His nostrils flared. 'Fuck. Hearing how wet you are makes me want to taste you.'

Too desperate to procrastinate, even to tease him, Skye turned and walked to her lofted bed. She hopped up onto the mattress, lay back on her elbows, and let her legs fall open in invitation.

Still, TJ demanded, 'Say it. Tell me what you want.'

'I want you to eat me out.'

TJ stepped between her legs. The bed was at his belly button height, and even though Skye knew it would irritate him, she had to say, 'If your back starts to hurt, tell me.' Before that signature sadness dampened the lust in his eyes, Skye reared up, took his face in her hands, whispered, 'There are infinite ways we can be together without pain, TJ. But it might take some trial and error.'

'I don't want it here with us,' he insisted.

Skye kissed him, said, 'It's a part of you for now. And I'll take you how you come.' The words were intimate, and she wouldn't have given him them under any other circumstances. But if he was ever going to make progress, TJ needed to start learning that he had limitations but that those limitations didn't define who he was or how she felt about him.

'I don't want your pity.'

'I don't pity you,' Skye stated. 'I *crave* you.' She took his hand in hers, lifted it to where that empty ache had settled, and when TJ slipped his thumb over her, she asked, 'Does it feel like I pity you?'

TJ shook his head.

'Well then.' Skye lay back down again, opened her legs wider.

TJ braced his elbows on the bed – to stabilize his spine, she knew. And although she promised that she'd pay attention, looking for any signs of pain or discomfort, the moment he lowered his head and slid his tongue through her, coherent thought scattered.

TJ pulled back, almost instantly, his ripe, 'Fuck,' reverberating through the confines of the trailer. 'I've dreamed about tasting you again, Skye.' He spread her with his thumbs, sucked her clit gently into his mouth, using slow pulls and tugs to drive her higher.

Skye fell back onto the bed, leveraging herself as she ground against TJ's mouth, wanting more. *Needing* more.

Always so in tune with her body, TJ slipped two big fingers into her. He moved them slowly at first. His whispered, 'You're so fucking pretty, baby,' had her closing her eyes as her body drew in.

She moaned, 'TJ,' as that wave pulled her higher, begged, 'Please,' when her body hovered on the edge, refusing to let go.

TJ blew a warm breath over her, whispered, 'You know what I want.'

Skye did. And too greedy to withhold it, she said, 'Jesse. Please.'

The moment the words left her mouth, he gave her what she wanted and, lowering his mouth to her, sucked her clit hard between his lips, even as his fingers continued to work her.

Skye exploded.

Her back arched off the bed.

Her feet pressed into the mattress.

A loud cry of release left her lips with no self-consciousness.

Had she been capable of rational thought, Skye might have been embarrassed that it had only taken him thirty seconds to make her come.

TJ came up panting, his eyes wild, his face glistening with the evidence of her lust. 'I need to be inside you, Skye.' The words were said roughly, but TJ didn't move a muscle until Skye moved back on the bed, making space for him to join her.

He bent over to remove his jeans, inadvertently showing her his scar. That deep aching grief she felt every time she saw it wormed its way into her heart. But when TJ looked up at her, Skye carefully erased any evidence of it from her eyes – just not quickly enough.

TJ hesitated.

'Don't shut me out,' Skye demanded.

He chuckled dryly. 'I wasn't intending to. Not even your pity is enough to turn me off.'

This time, when Skye held out her hand, TJ linked their fingers, but instead of letting her tug him onto the bed, he turned her hand over in his and lowered his lips to her skin, imparting the gentlest of kisses. 'Being here with you again is the only thing I've dreamed about in almost two years.'

That duplicitous lick of panic reared – the one that she wasn't sure stemmed from pleasure or anxiety. Skye tried to ignore it. 'I don't need words, TJ. I just . . . I need to keep this casual.'

'Sex between us could never be casual,' TJ countered. 'But if you need me to keep my feelings to myself, then I can do that.'

'It's too much,' Skye said.

TJ nodded. 'Okay.'

With that out of the way, Skye took a deep breath. She knew that what she had to say next would irritate him, but she did it anyway, because she had promised to put his recovery first.

'I've noticed that you tend to only lie flat on your back. Is that because of the pain?'

'It helps with spine alignment,' he replied cautiously. 'Why?'

Skye didn't reply, just crooked a finger at him, and when TJ climbed up onto the bed beside her, she gave him a gentle shove, encouraging him to lie flat on his back.

TJ complied, but he was bitter about it. 'You don't have to worry about me. I can manage—'

He stopped talking abruptly when Skye gripped his hard length firmly. She gave him one long, slow pump, sliding soft skin over steel, whispered, 'I don't worry about you *managing* at all, TJ. I think you'll be just fine.'

He raised both his hands to his hair, closed his eyes, growled, 'Fuck, that feels good, baby.'

Riding on the feeling of power his words gave her, Skye did it again. TJ's body followed her movements, his hips dropping and rising slightly with the motions of her hand. His breaths, audible now, came faster. His cock throbbed in her hand, causing a resounding ache between her own thighs.

Desperate to have him in every way, Skye leaned over him. She guided him to her lips and licked from base to tip, before taking him deep into her mouth. TJ filled her, hitting the back of her throat. She closed her lips around him and drew her head back, applying enough pressure that TJ reached out and fisted one hand in her hair, stopping her movements.

'Slowly,' he warned. 'I'm out of practice, and I want to come inside of you the first time.'

His grip gentled then released. His big palm ran over her short hair and down her back to the curve of her ass. Skye repositioned herself slightly, giving TJ enough reach to slip two fingers into her.

As she tortured him, her mouth sliding slowly up and down his length, TJ tortured her. His fingers pumped into her, pushing deep before withdrawing to tease the sensitive skin around her entrance.

A second orgasm started building. Skye ground her hips against his hand, pleading for more, and when TJ just kept that slow, sensual pace, she was the one who lost her patience first.

She released him with an audible pop.

Skye scrambled off the bed, but only for long enough to fetch a condom from the bathroom cabinet.

TJ watched her as she approached the bed again. His eyes were dark with lust and filled with too many unsaid things – none of which she was ready to acknowledge. Instead, she straddled him, ripped the condom foil open and, taking him in hand, slid the condom down his hard length.

Before she could guide him to her, TJ said, 'Hold on.' He repositioned her and, with a small stretch, grabbed his black cowboy hat from where Skye had left it the night before. He plopped it on her head before lying back down. 'Much better.'

Skye managed to roll her eyes. 'You cowboys and your hats.'

But she left it on as she guided him to her centre. When she sank onto him, they released twin, shaky exhales.

His hands rose to grip her hips. His eyes drank her in. 'You're the sexiest thing I've ever seen.'

Skye *felt* the sexiest she'd ever felt. And she wasn't too proud to admit that it was him. TJ. He made her feel like a goddess.

Wanting to show him, wanting to give him some of that power back, she raised her own hands to her breasts as she rocked forward and back slowly, teasing him. 'You ready for a wild ride, cowboy?'

TJ's hands on her hips gripped tighter, as if he needed to brace himself for it. And when he said, 'Yes, ma'am,' it left his lips sounding like a plea.

Greedy for more, Skye rolled her hips, slowly at first and then faster. And faster still. She was short and a horsewoman to boot; she had all the right muscles to make good on her promise.

'Fuck, yes. That's it. Ride me hard,' TJ demanded, his voice deep and husky.

Skye started panting as her body drew in, preparing for release. But she held on, refusing to let go before him. When he raised his thumb to her clit and ran short, fast circles over the swollen nerves there, she let her head fall back, moaned, 'Oh, God. Yes!'

Her movements became shorter, her breath faster. Her back arched.

Beneath her, TJ pumped his hips, his movements matching hers. A low moan was leaving Skye's lips as the pleasure became too much to bear. And it was followed by a long, 'Jesse.'

'Again,' he commanded and pumped into her.

'Jesse.'

'Again.'

Skye opened her eyes and met his eyes as the second wave broke, taking her under. She braced both hands on his chest, rasped, 'Jesse,' breathlessly as her body tightened around him.

TJ roared as he came, spilling into her with one last hard pump. He gripped her hips mercilessly, holding their centres together as they both tumbled over the edge.

The moment he let her go, she collapsed onto the bed next to him. Her body was sated. Her mind was quiet. A pleasant hum of hormones swam in her blood. But more than the spike and crash of adrenaline to her system, her heart took a heavy hit.

For almost two years, Skye had told herself that what she'd experienced with TJ that first time had been nothing more than ignorance, virginal infatuation disguised as love. She'd even very nearly convinced herself of it.

But it had been a lie. TJ had been right: Once would never be enough.

Intimacy couldn't be forced. It was either there or it wasn't. Skye's problem – the one she couldn't avoid any longer – was that the very person she'd promised herself she'd never allow back into her heart was the only man who had the power to walk back in anyway.

And he just had.

Chapter 34

Rapid City, South Dakota – February 3, 2027

TJ stood on the sidelines as Skye and Kai took third place in Denver and then first place in the 1D at a local jackpot the following weekend. With a little money in Skye's pocket and new tyres on the trailer, they drove north to South Dakota for Rodeo Rapid City. Skye had purposefully entered the slack, taking place the day before the rodeo performance started, so that she could push north to the Bismarck PRCA Rodeo in North Dakota in time for her performance run just two days later.

It would be her first time competing in two rodeos back to back, and although TJ knew that Skye was as ready as she would ever be, telling her that didn't seem to help. Between her race schedule and her birthday, both looming on the horizon, the cracks started to show.

She was restless, edgy. When she was trapped in the truck on the road, she talked constantly, critiquing her runs and rambling on about things she needed to improve on, so that TJ had eventually lost his patience, clamped a hand over her mouth, and said, very clearly, 'You know what you're doing. Stop panicking. Take a fucking breath.'

Instead of recovering from travelling and getting the rest she needed to perform, Skye tossed and turned all night and woke up with rings under her eyes and skin so pale he could see the blue veins snaking beneath.

But it was only when she stopped eating that TJ put his foot down.

They'd booked an RV hook-up and two stalls at the Black Hills Dude Ranch, only a twenty-minute drive from The Monument, where the rodeo was being held. And because nobody could possibly know where they were staying, they stalled the horses with peace of mind before making their way over the two-hundred-acre property to their RV hook-up.

When TJ had showered, he took stock of the mini fridge, overflowing with health foods from the long list of anti-inflammatories the doctor had given Skye. He rapidly dismissed the beetroot and radish, asked, 'How about salmon and salad?'

Skye was curled on her side on the bed, wearing sweatpants and a black cotton sports bra. She didn't even raise her eyes, just said, 'I'm not hungry. But go ahead.'

TJ took a moment to check his temper, but when he said, 'You haven't eaten at all today,' it still came out tight with impatience.

'*I said I'm not hungry.*' She enunciated every word.

TJ slammed the fridge door. 'Not good enough.'

Skye sat up and crossed her arms over her chest, clearly pissed. But with her short hair mussed and her odd but sexy outfit, the effect was lost on TJ. All he could think was, *Mine.*

'I'm doing the best I can, TJ.'

'To repeat what you said to me only a week ago: that isn't good enough for me.' He walked to the bed, but he didn't touch her, knowing that if he did, he would give in and let her have whatever she wanted. He rested his forearms on the mattress, met her eyes. 'I'm doing everything you've asked of me. The physio. The diet. The sitting on my ass while you do all the heavy lifting. And it's not easy for me.' Willing to use the truth to his advantage, he added, 'It makes me feel useless. But I'm doing it because you asked me to.'

'I know.'

'I expect the same from you,' he said firmly. 'To look after yourself.'

Skye's shoulders slumped. 'I'm just tired,' she said quietly.

The tears that filled her blue eyes just about killed him. But they didn't scare him. TJ had stored every memory of her in his mind and body. He knew that the more she trusted, the more she allowed herself to be vulnerable. 'Why don't you nap?' he said. 'We can eat later.'

'I can't sleep.' She laughed bitterly, *tiredly*. She looked down at her lap, distractedly picked at a loose thread on her sweats. 'I used to have these nightmares . . .'

When she shook her head, embarrassed, TJ didn't let her get away with it. He carefully climbed onto the bed. He lay down on his back, and when she didn't move right away, he tugged her down next to him, tucked her against his side.

Skye was quiet for a long moment, her emotion clear.

TJ didn't push, just waited. Despite the fact that they had solidly ignored her 'one time' rule over the past few weeks, lying there next to Skye when she was vulnerable was almost as intimate as having sex with her.

When she started talking, her voice was quiet, almost a whisper. 'When I was little, living in the house, it was always the same nightmare. I would be sleeping, and a giant red snake would slither into my bed. It would coil itself around me, and by the time I woke up, it was wrapped so tightly that I couldn't breathe or call for help. I just lay there and felt myself suffocating.'

Her tears wet his shirt, over his heart. But TJ didn't say anything. He just held her as she spoke, as her words branded his heart with ugly, red wounds.

'The worst part wasn't the nightmare though,' she managed, her voice husky. 'It was waking up and being *so scared*, but still knowing, even as a child, that I couldn't call out, that nobody was coming to help me.'

'After we met, after I started at Hunt Ranch, I didn't have them for a long time. But since being on the road again, with everything that's happened, with my birthday approaching, they've come back.'

'Still the snake?'

'No, actually. This time, I'm not in bed. I'm back home, in the foyer. And there's no snake, just Holden's boot hovering over my face. I wake up when he stomps on my head.'

'I won't let him hurt you, Skye. I've got you.'

'It's not that I don't believe you or even think he'll have the balls to physically harm me. But he's in my head, TJ. And I can't get him out.'

TJ knew all about being so wrapped up in your own thoughts that the world passed you by. But he'd never had somebody else's voice inside his head. So, he only asked, 'What can I do to help?'

'Nothing. Just be here with me.'

'Always.'

They were both quiet for a long time, both wrapped in the intimacy of being lost and confused while wrapped safely in each other's arms with no intention of going anywhere.

It was Skye who eventually said, 'This is nice,' her voice thick with fatigue.

TJ kissed the top of her head. 'Sleep. I'll stay right here.'

Chapter 35

Bismarck, North Dakota – February 7, 2027

Skye and Kai took fourth place in South Dakota and, only two days later, they were trailered at the County Fairgrounds in Bismarck, North Dakota, waiting to run at the Bismarck Event Center a few miles away.

Although the air was clear, the temperature hovered around twenty degrees Fahrenheit, so that Skye added the freezing conditions to her ever-growing list of things to worry about.

While she showered and got dressed, TJ brushed Kai and braided his mane.

Skye looked at her reflection in the tiny mirror above her sink. Her nerves were there, alive for everyone to see. 'Get yourself together. You can do this.' The demand wasn't made just for herself but for Kai too. The horse was doing so well, and the last thing she wanted to do was stress him out with her anxiety.

She let herself out of the small restroom, pulled up short when she saw TJ leaning in the open doorway, his arms crossed over his chest.

His green eyes scanned her from head to toe. 'You okay?'

'Peachy.'

When she tried to walk past him, he gently caught her wrist.

Skye looked up at him.

TJ just dropped a kiss to her forehead, murmured, 'You'll be great. Have more faith in yourself.'

The comment, the gentle way it was issued, had her dropping her head back. 'Ugh, just once in my life, I'd like the irrational confidence of a man.'

TJ tipped his head, unoffended. 'It does make life easier.'

Skye ran both her hands through her hair as her anxiety momentarily took over. 'I still hate riding in the performance. And I'm so anxious that I feel like I'm holding Kai back.'

'Do you need me to flick your ear again?'

A surprised laugh left her lips. But Skye didn't reject the offer. 'Probably. Yes.'

'Okay.' He tugged at a short strand of her hair. 'I'll make sure to distract you before your run.'

She walked back into him, dropped her forehead to his chest, momentarily resting. 'Thanks.'

They loaded both horses and set off, arrived at the event centre an hour before her run. While TJ saddled Kai, Skye put the horse's pink polo wraps on, and by the time she was in the warm-up arena, her anxiety was simmering right below a full-blown panic attack.

Kai sensed it too. Instead of being his normal, calm self, he was spooked, and although he still ran through his warm-up perfectly, he kept arching his head back to look at Skye, as if to say *What are we worried about? Where's the danger?*

When the event staff called her drag, she and ten other girls moved their horses towards the arena. While the others rode in without hesitating, Skye waited for TJ. She needed his quiet strength just then.

He came to her immediately.

Although she didn't point it out, she wondered if he even realized that his limp was softer or that he was sleeping up to six hours a night. It wasn't that he was pain free; the daily physical therapy was still agonizing for him. But he wasn't stuck there all the time anymore.

'You ready?' he asked her. He ran one hand down Kai's neck, murmured, 'Easy,' in a low, deep voice that had Kai calming.

'As ready as I'll ever be.' She exhaled an anxious breath. 'I could use that distraction about now.'

TJ crooked his finger at her.

Skye leaned down.

But instead of flicking her ear or kissing her as she'd expected, he took her pink hat off her head and replaced it with his black one. When Skye raised both eyebrows, TJ plopped her hat on his own head.

'I would say it's disrespectful to touch another person's hat,' Skye said, laughing, 'but pink is definitely your colour.'

TJ tipped the brim up. 'It's about time everyone knew I'm your man, Skye. I'm done acting like this thing between us is ever going to go away. And if I'm going to stay, then so are you.'

Skye didn't argue. There was a lump in her throat, one she couldn't speak around. She'd always promised herself that she'd never end up back here. But it was the strangest thing to realize that, maybe, she'd always wanted to. Maybe, in a lot of ways, she'd been waiting to, waiting for him.

When she didn't reply, TJ asked, 'Is that okay with you?'

She nodded. 'On one condition?'

'Anything.'

'I want you to delete the videos.'

He didn't have to ask which videos she was referring to. 'You know, they draw in a lot of people and indirectly make me a lot of money in brand partnerships.'

Skye wished he could see how angry he still was. She wished he could see those ugly, dark videos from her perspective. 'That's my line, TJ. I won't have you monetizing your trauma by turning it into entertainment for everyone else.' She shook her head. 'Enough.'

If TJ was ever going to truly start fighting again, he needed to accept what had happened in the past and start looking towards the future. And he couldn't do that while actively branding and promoting the worst moment of his life for strangers online.

'Okay,' he said. 'You can delete whichever ones you want tonight.' He took his phone out of his pocket, said, 'Let's get a selfie to replace them with.'

Skye leaned down and, bringing her face close to his, smiled for the camera. He took the shot, slid his phone back into his pocket.

'Did that distract you enough?' TJ asked.

A sharp wolf whistle cut off her reply. Matthew Savage walked past. His, 'Looks like you got tied down, TJ! But you sure look real *purty* in pink,' was loud enough for everyone to hear.

TJ flipped him off, making Matthew howl with laughter.

Realizing that they'd attracted quite a bit of attention, Skye leaned down again and, holding the black hat on her head, kissed TJ. Not quickly either. This kiss was long and deep and intimate, so much so that people nearby started hollering and clapping.

When she pulled back, she said, 'I'm definitely going to get a fine, because this hat is not going to stay on my head.'

'Well, this one's squeezing my brains out. But we'll make do.' He took a deep breath, encouraging her to do the same. 'You ready, baby?'

'Yes.'

'So, let's fuckin' go.'

TJ stayed by her side as they entered the arena. When they came to the holding area, he gave her leg one squeeze and then waited just outside the alley.

Skye breathed long and deep as she tried to calm her – and Kai's – nervous system. She knew it was working when the horse exhaled a huge breath and licked his lips.

Down the alley, she could make out the third barrel straight ahead. The sound of the crowd blended with the throbbing music and the announcer's voice.

By the time she was called, her momentary calm had vanished. Her heart was speeding so fast that she could barely inhale around the pressure in her chest. Beneath her, Kai pulled the reins, his own anxiety clear.

Skye pushed him into the alley and stopped.

The announcer's voice boomed. 'Next up, ladies and gents, we have a rookie pair who are opening their season with a bang: Skye Marchant and Sweet Lil Bullet. Skye is currently ranked tenth in the WPRA season, and although it's early yet, we have the makings of an NFR qualifier right here in Bismarck tonight.'

'Bad Reputation,' by Joan Jett & the Blackhearts started blaring.

Skye took three long breaths.

Beneath her, Kai was completely still, his every muscle on alert.

Although TJ knew Skye wouldn't be looking up at the big screen, he was. The camera was zoomed on her and Kai, their black and pink colours flashing, their eyes facing forward. Kai stood relatively still, waiting for Skye's cue and prompting the announcer to say, 'Woohoo, folks, looks like we have a pair of cool cats right here.'

TJ held his breath. The music blared, but the sound of his heartbeat was still louder. It filled his ears. 'Come on, baby,' he murmured to himself. And when she shot down the alley, he yelled, 'Go!'

The old man standing next to him jumped, but TJ barely noticed. He watched as Skye rounded the first barrel and pushed to second, her lead change as smooth as could be. She turned the second barrel perfectly and sailed for third.

The old cowboy standing next to TJ whistled low. 'That girl of yours can jockey.'

TJ grinned. 'Yes, sir.'

Skye, a full second ahead of the next best time, didn't slow. She took the third barrel, checked a little too late so that Kai took a stumbling step off course. Skye corrected him, using her outside leg to push his hindquarters in.

For just a second, it looked like they were clear. Kai's shoulders moved past the barrel, but right before they surged down the straight, the horse's hip bumped the can. It tipped. 'Fuck,' TJ muttered as it fell.

Skye took the straight and crossed the laser line. She tugged on the bit as she tried to bring Kai down from the adrenaline high. But her face . . . it was set in a look of complete despair.

The old timer next to him commented, 'Tough luck. But even with the five second penalty, it was a good run.'

'Yeah.' TJ nodded kindly. 'Have a good one.' He followed Skye out of the arena. But he couldn't help but mutter, 'Try telling her that,' as he prepared to face her.

He knew enough about her childhood to understand *why* she put so much pressure on herself. Still, he had to reach for his patience when he saw her outside, her head hanging low, her eyes hiding under the brim of his hat. She looked like she'd failed to save a life – not, he thought, like she'd tipped a goddamn barrel over at a minor rodeo.

TJ could hate her father for just that. Her need to be perfect took so much from her, stealing moments of joy and accomplishment, moments that most people would have revelled in.

TJ went to her. He took Kai's reins, flicked the brim of Skye's hat up to reveal her face, and he said, 'Good run, beautiful. I'm proud of you.'

To his complete horror, her eyes widened and then filled. But when she spoke, she didn't point out that she'd tipped a barrel, she whispered, 'You're proud of me?'

'Fuck yes.'

'Why?' She seemed genuinely confused.

'You worked hard and consistently to get here. You adjusted when your horse got injured and made a plan to keep moving forward. You showed up today even though you were sick with nerves. And you gave it your best.'

'I tipped a barrel.'

'Yes, you did. But that's part of the game.' When a single tear slipped down her cheek, TJ brushed it aside. 'Baby, if you keep doing this, it's going to happen, and it's going to happen often, irrespective of how good you or your horse is. You know that. You watch the NFR – you see the best of the best tip them all the time.'

She seemed to consider that for a long moment, but then she nodded slowly. 'That's true.' She took her hat off and dropped her forehead to Kai's. 'I just feel like I let him down. He ran like the wind, TJ. I wish you could feel him under you.'

TJ thought that, in another life, he would have liked that too. But just then, with a bright-pink hat on his head, he didn't feel the gaping hole he'd expected, knowing that he'd certainly never run a barrel pattern again. 'You didn't let him down. You gave each other your best, and that's all you can ever do.'

As if the universe wanted to affirm his point, another rider walked past on her horse and, seeing Skye, said, 'Damn, girl, you two were hauling ass! Good run!'

Skye blushed. She raised a hand to wave, said, 'Thanks.'

Once the rider had moved past, TJ asked, 'Ready to head back, check on Smokey?'

'Yes.'

They fell into step, Kai on TJ's one side, Skye on the other. As they walked to the trailer, Skye linked her fingers with his unprompted. She let her head fall to his shoulder, said, 'I really like that hat on you, TJ.'

'Thanks. I'm thinking I'll keep it.'

'That so?'

'Oh yeah.' He squeezed her hand. 'I like the way she looks on me.'

When Skye peered up at him and asked, 'How are you feeling?' TJ didn't get angry as he would have only a week before.

He rolled his neck gently, testing out his pain level. 'I'm down to a five right now,' he said.

'I'll stretch you out once the animals are settled in for the night.'

TJ didn't argue. There'd be no point. Skye was as ruthless about his physical therapy schedule as she was about her own barrel racing one. So, he just shrugged.

Skye tied Kai to the side of the trailer so that she could untack him, and when TJ moved to help by uncinching the saddle, she hip-checked him out of the way. 'I've got it. Why don't you heat the truck up?'

TJ wasn't even annoyed. He moved behind her, wrapped his arms around her waist, leaned down, and gently bit her neck. 'You're so bossy.'

'You like it,' she shot back, and when he didn't move, just kept working his lips over the soft column of her throat, she pressed her ass back into him, asked, 'You sure you wanna start this here, cowboy?'

TJ actually looked up to check who was around, making Skye laugh. But when he saw the flood of contestants and animals going about their business, he sighed. 'I'll drive,' he said, because he knew he'd get back to the fairgrounds faster.

Skye rolled her eyes playfully.

He let her go and walked around the driver's side of the truck.

He stopped. His heart slammed hard against his ribs. His blood iced in his veins. Because there, placed on the windshield, was a single black rose with frost-tipped petals.

TJ picked it up, careful to avoid the sharp thorns. The rose was fresh. It was perfect, the bloom half-open but fat, the colour rich black with red undertones. And it was a clear threat.

A single note had been tied to the stem with black ribbon. TJ opened it, read the florist's typed letter:

Skye,

Good luck with your barrel race today. I was sad to hear about Smoking Barrel's passing; however, I trust that your replacement will work out for you temporarily. Try to remember to wear a riding helmet. I would hate if something completely avoidable happened to you.

Only a few weeks until your birthday. Your mother and I will make a point to visit.

Love,

Dad

TJ exhaled tightly. The chill in his veins warmed as rage filled him. The letter wasn't just a warning. It was a taunt. *Look how much I know. You can't hide from me. I'm coming for you.*

Well, not if TJ had anything to say about it.

He momentarily considered destroying the rose, maybe tearing the letter into a dozen little pieces. But he didn't for one reason: Skye needed to understand that Holden was escalating, and hiding the threats wasn't going to keep her sharp.

TJ climbed into the truck and waited until Skye had closed up the trailer and slid into the passenger seat next to him.

'Fuck, it's cold,' was the first thing she said. 'I thought you were supposed to crank the heat.'

'Skye—'

'Jesus, TJ – turn on the truck.'

'Hey,' he said quietly, cutting her off.

Skye, sensing his dread, fell quiet. Her eyes searched his face, waiting.

TJ picked the rose up from where he'd left it on the seat between them. For a single moment, Skye's eyes widened, but not with fear – with pleasure.

'No, baby – it's not from me.'

Her face fell. The flush of pleasure faded, leaving her bone-white. 'Holden?'

TJ nodded.

She took the rose from him, her hand shaking.

TJ stayed quiet as she read the note, and even though he wanted to shout and rage, he didn't. He wanted to be calm and strong. For her.

But, Skye, always a fucking surprise, just folded the note and tucked it into the pocket of her heavy jacket. She raised the rose to her nose, inhaled lightly. 'He's not going to use something beautiful to scare me,' she said quietly. 'Not anymore. Never again.' She grinned at him. 'I already destroyed a perfectly good saddle.'

It wasn't the response he'd been expecting. But then again, it seldom was when it came to Skye. TJ leaned over the space between them, and when she turned her head, he took her lips in a fierce kiss.

By the time they broke apart, they were both out of breath.

TJ started the truck. 'Did you read the part about Smokey?' he asked. When Skye frowned, he regurgitated the letter: '*I was sad to hear about Smoking Barrel's passing.*'

'He thinks she's dead?'

'Yup. Which means—'

'Whoever's working for him isn't telling him everything,' Skye finished.

'Ford said Smokey's wound was mostly superficial,' TJ pointed out. 'I'm not sure what we can conclude from that, but it's something to think about.'

TJ linked his fingers with hers.

Skye cranked the heat.

They turned back towards the fairgrounds, the silence between them stretching comfortably, and when they got back to their RV spot, they fell into their respective tasks without a word.

It was nice, TJ thought. Domestic – even if Holden was on both their minds.

But it was only when he let himself back into the trailer that the immensity of his feelings for Skye took him under. She'd de-thorned the rose and put it in a glass of water, so that its stem stretched up to proudly display the fat, black bloom on the end.

It took someone truly special to take such an ugly gift and nurture her own meaning from it. For the first time ever, TJ allowed himself to wonder what might have happened if he'd let Skye stay after his accident. She might have been the difference he'd needed, might have given him the fight he hadn't had for himself. She might have taken the ugly gift he'd been given and turned it into something different, something manageable. At the very least, she would have made the hard days easier to bear. He could acknowledge that, even though he was glad he'd spared her those two years.

It was no surprise then, that, with that thought on his mind, when Skye opened the trailer door and said, 'You ready for your physio?' TJ actually laughed. She turned from hanging her hat up to look at him. 'What?'

'Do you know when I first realized I was in love with you?'

Skye didn't reply. She just stood there, frozen to the spot. So, TJ went to her. He closed that space. 'It was the moment you walked out of my hospital room. I watched you go, and I realized that I didn't want you to hurt, that it killed me to know I'd caused you pain.' He thought back. 'I tried to get up to go after you, and I fell. And I couldn't stand up. So, I just lay there on the cold floor, waiting for someone to come find me. And all I could think was that it wasn't fair, to give you any more promises when I couldn't even fucking stand on my own two feet.

'But I missed you,' he said. 'I mourned for what I knew we could have been to one another had we had more time.'

'I was really angry with you, TJ,' she said quietly. 'For a long time. Sometimes, I still am. Because you didn't let me choose. You showed me what it was like to be cared for, and then you snatched it away. And even though I know it wasn't what you'd intended, it was something Holden always did. In a lot of ways, you hurt me more. Because I trusted you. I *chose* you.'

There was no point in arguing that he had done what he'd done from a place of love, not control. Maybe Skye hadn't had the life experience at the time to separate the two. And even if she had, the result was the same. It was her, floundering, wondering what she'd done wrong to be cut off.

'I'm so sorry, Skye. If I could go back . . .' He sighed. 'I don't know what I'd do. And that's the honest truth. Because the past two years have been awful, and I'm glad that you weren't there to see me drag my way through them. I'm glad I didn't burden you with that, even though I think you would have made it easier for me to carry. But I am still sorry I hurt you.'

'Okay.'

'Will you forgive me?'

'Of course. But don't do it again.'

'Hades himself couldn't drag me away,' he said, and if he thought that Holden still might, he didn't give the words life.

'Aren't you going to ask me?'

TJ frowned. 'Ask you what?'

'When I first realized I loved you.'

TJ's grin was quick and lethal, but it did not come close to reflecting the blooming pleasure that unfurled within him. When he reached for her and pulled her into his chest, his hands shook from the immensity of it. His voice wasn't quite steady when he asked, 'When? When did you first realize you loved me?'

'When you gave me that piggyback ride back to the house.'

'I remember.' He closed his eyes, thinking back. 'You said, "You're dangerously close to becoming my favourite person in the world, Jesse Jones".'

Skye smiled. 'It was the most I could give you. Even then, I was trying to convince myself it was just infatuation because you were my first.'

'And I was thinking of ways we could meet up, keep whatever we'd started alive. See where it would go.'

Skye looked up at him. 'I guess we ended up there anyway.'

TJ dropped his lips to hers, but right before he kissed her, he murmured, 'I guess we did.'

Chapter 36

Scottsdale, Arizona – March 2, 2027

They spent the last two weeks of February in San Antonio, Texas, because Skye was able to qualify for the San Antonio Stock Show & Rodeo based on her standing in the WPRA. Although the rodeo was big and loud with no slack, she and Kai progressed to the finals and took fourth place.

People started to notice.

Strangers at the rodeo would greet her and wish her luck on her next run. Several even asked to have their picture taken with her. A little cowgirl, who couldn't have been more than ten, told her, 'I'm gonna be like you one day,' and that . . . that had hit Skye deep in her soul.

For so long, she'd been running, hiding, surviving. She'd never allowed herself to dream that she'd get far, let alone that she'd build herself up enough so that a single little girl would admire her and want to be her. It was both a powerful and humbling experience.

Her rapidly spreading popularity might have worried her had she been less realistic. But after the rose and the note, Skye knew that there was no point in hiding. Holden either had her schedule or had paid whoever his henchman was to find out where she'd be going next.

But even though they couldn't do anything about the information Holden gathered, they prepared as best they could.

TJ made her reach out to her grandma's attorney, the executor of the will, and although it wasn't an easy conversation, Skye had been relieved when Mr Simcock, an ancient man with a broad face of wrinkles and bushy white eyebrows, had validated her concerns without question. Apparently, Grandma Jo hadn't held back her opinion of Holden to her attorney either. And after Holden had tried to contest the will, any last doubts of Mr Simcock's had been erased.

Together, they had drafted Skye's pre-emptively revised plans for the trust, which included cutting off her parents completely. For weight, she included a handwritten note, signed by Mr Simcock, explaining her actions and detailing, why, if anything happened to her, the trust shouldn't revert back to Caroline.

The only downside, the only catch, was that the draft document was just that: a draft. Until she actually turned twenty-five, Skye couldn't have the document witnessed, signed, and finalized, because the money wasn't yet hers to control.

Still, with Mr Simcock's assurance that he'd finalize the document as soon as possible on her birthday, March fifteenth, Skye was appeased. In fact, she was *eager*. There was a little girl in her, one who had taken all that fear and hate and built something out of it, something strong.

Now, as they rolled over the cattle grid and onto the Joneses' dairy farm, TJ warned her, 'My mom is going to cry when she sees you, so be prepared.'

'I've thought about them a lot.' She shifted in the passenger seat. 'Even when I told myself I hated you and you were an asshole, it was hard to convince myself you were the villain in my story when your parents were the nicest, kindest people I've ever met.'

TJ didn't agree. 'I think you're proof that children can turn out different from their upbringings.'

'I suppose that's true,' Skye replied. But she couldn't quite sit still. She was too full – with love and excitement and, oddly, peace. She looked out her window over the farm as they drove down the long drive.

Bandit clearly knew where they were too. The dog paced on the back seat of the truck, eager to be out. His loud whine was impatient and excited. His tail wagged a million times a minute, beating a quick tempo against the seat.

Skye laughed and told the dog, 'Relax.'

She was so distracted by him that it took a few seconds for TJ's, 'I guess my parents have guests,' to register.

She looked over at him, noticed his frown, and followed his gaze.

Everything slowed.

Except the panic. That came swiftly. Ruthlessly. The world continued in slow motion around her. The sound of her heart racing resounded in her head. Her breaths were fast but strained, rasping, as she struggled to draw in enough air.

TJ slammed on the brakes. 'Skye?'

When she couldn't reply, could only suck in the next panicked breath, he took her face in both hands. 'Hey. Hey, look at me.'

She managed to focus on his face, on those green eyes so full of confusion and fear.

'Breathe,' he demanded. 'Come on, baby, in and out.' He took his own big inhale, encouraging her to do the same.

Skye gulped down a huge breath.

'Good girl. Another one.'

She gripped TJ's wrists as he held her face. She breathed deeply, fighting the panic attack one inhale at a time. But when the worst of it had passed, when she had enough air in her lungs to speak, she only had to say one word for the panic to come back in full force: 'Holden.'

TJ's hands jerked reflexively against her face. Slowly, he redirected his gaze down the drive. Because there, sitting on the front porch with Ryan and Janey, were her parents.

TJ let her go. 'Stay in the truck.'

His voice was deep and dangerous. His movements as he opened his door were slow and controlled, like a big cat stalking prey. In her fear of what he might do, Skye tried to grab him. 'TJ—'

But he was already gone.

Skye collapsed back against the seat and closed her eyes. More than the panic and despair, the shame threatened to drag her under just then. She had imagined this moment so many times. She had played it over and over in her head. She'd imagined being fierce, maybe even reckless. She'd imagined standing up to her father, taunting him even. But now that he was here, sitting and making casual conversation with TJ's parents, she couldn't find the courage to even get out of the truck.

She was unprepared.

So, she didn't do anything, just sat and hid as TJ moved up the driveway slowly, his limp barely noticeable as he homed in on her parents.

Skye couldn't even look up for long enough to see if her mom was okay. She just sat in the passenger seat of the truck, wallowing in her own sick fear.

There was a fire in TJ that could not be extinguished. As he walked that last distance up his own goddamn drive, he promised that Holden would never put that look on Skye's face again. Christ, just remembering the way she'd gone bone-white, the way she'd struggled to draw in even a single breath, had him meeting Holden's eyes and saying, 'You're not welcome here.'

His own mom, sitting next to Skye's, gasped sharply, her shock apparent. 'TJ!'

Holden, dressed impeccably in tan chinos, a button-down and boat shoes, looked like everything he wasn't: a perfect gentleman. Even his eyes, the dark blue of calm seas, and his hair, a distinguished salt and pepper grey, made him look like an actor from some commercial that boasted sunny picnics and happy families. His voice was filled with perfectly intonated remorse when he said, 'No. No that's all right, Janey. As I said, my daughter and I have a tumultuous past.'

TJ didn't buy the bullshit, but he understood, instantly and without doubt, why nobody had ever helped Skye when she'd been a child. This wasn't some obnoxious drunk in a run-down neighbourhood, disrupting the neighbours with his domestic disputes. This was a sociopath of the highest order – a man with wealth and privilege and education on his side.

'I don't know if routinely abusing your daughter would constitute a *tumultuous past*,' TJ said tightly.

Holden sighed like he carried the weight of the world. 'My daughter told you that?' He reached for his wife's hand. As if he needed her support. As if he needed to draw strength from her.

Caroline just sat quietly, looking pale and sad. A well-trained puppet.

'I suppose my daughter forgot to mention that she was committed to in-patient psychiatric care as a teenager for the same outlandish tall tales?'

TJ didn't flinch.

It was Janey whose eyes snapped to Holden's face and darkened. 'I think it would be best if you left now,' she said coolly.

TJ put one booted foot on the first step of the porch, leaned his forearms on his raised knee, and very quietly, very clearly said, 'You have one minute to get in your vehicle and leave. After that, I will physically remove you myself. And I will not be gentle.'

Ryan wordlessly stood and came to TJ's side.

'Holden—'

Whatever Caroline had been about to say was cut off by

Holden's brutal grip on her fingers. His parents might not have noticed it, but TJ did. Because he was *looking*. Because he *knew*.

Holden shook his head. 'I was hoping to make things right with my daughter. But I can see that this was the wrong way to go about it.' He stood, pulling Caroline to her feet with that same steel grip. 'We'll just be on our way.'

TJ looked away, taking a moment to regain himself. 'I'm going to say this once: do not reach out to her again. Do not leave her any more calls or notes.'

He noticed the surprised glance Caroline shot her husband – and the fact that Holden didn't ever, not even once, look at his wife.

'If you do, you'll deal with me.'

'I hardly think that threats are necessary,' Holden replied, his apparent insult and astonishment clear. 'This was clearly a mistake.' But again, TJ noticed that Holden still had the clarity of mind to flash a pained smile at Ryan and Janey. 'I'm sorry for the drama. As I said, I was only hoping to see my daughter, to apologize.'

Holden and Caroline walked past TJ to their rental car, a silver Bentley. Although it was hard not to follow them all the way to the goddamn car door, TJ turned and watched them leave. Caroline, pale and withdrawn. Holden, perfectly playing confused and offended.

When they drove back down the driveway, TJ watched, making sure they didn't try to stop and talk to Skye.

They exited the farm without so much as slowing as they passed her truck.

The moment they had left, his dad asked, 'TJ, what on earth is going on?'

TJ turned to face his parents again. They both looked concerned, but where his dad was clearly confused by his hostile behaviour, his mom's eyes were blazing with rage.

'It was him?' she deduced.

'Holden – Skye's father – is the one who abused her. For years. Her entire childhood.' TJ looked into his dad's eyes so that Ryan knew there was no doubt. 'He's dangerous to her. Don't let him back here.'

While his dad digested that, TJ looked at his mom.

She just cocked one hip. 'I've never known a loving parent who'd brandish their child's traumatic mental health history to buy strangers' sympathy.'

'He's a snake in the grass,' TJ affirmed. But he looked back to where Skye's truck sat, idling in the driveway with her inside. 'This is going to hit her hard. She wasn't prepared.'

'Yes,' his mom agreed. But she walked to him, placed one palm on his face when she added, 'Bring her in, baby. We'll fix her up.'

'I'll see to the horses,' his dad said.

Their instant concern, their immediate and unquestionable loyalty, was stark by comparison just then. It prompted TJ to say, 'You know, I don't think I ever thanked you.'

'For what?' his mom asked.

'For supporting me in everything I did, even when you didn't necessarily understand or agree with my decisions.' He shrugged. 'For loving Julia and me so fiercely. For being good parents. I always took you for granted because, until I met Skye, that was my only experience of parenthood. I'm sorry for not appreciating that.'

His mom frowned. 'You kids are our greatest joy, TJ. You don't have to thank us for that.' She waved him off. 'Go on, now. Get your girl.'

TJ walked back down the driveway slowly, thinking over how to approach Skye just then, and settled on the direct approach because it had worked when she'd knocked the barrel in Bismarck. But the moment he opened the passenger door and saw her, so still and pale, he knew it wasn't what she needed.

Because the dog was whining, he took a moment to let Bandit

out. It said something about Skye's state that the dog only took three steps towards the farmhouse before turning around and running straight back to her. He plopped his butt on the ground outside her door and, shimmying closer, cried in concern.

Skye didn't even seem to hear him.

TJ released her seatbelt. He reached into the truck, sliding his arms beneath her thighs and her back. The fact that he could lift her out of the truck without her panicking about his back told him how truly defeated she was. He didn't address her parents' visit. Not yet. Just said, 'Come on, baby. I've got you.'

Skye didn't cry.

She didn't speak.

She just sat quietly, her eyes dry, her face bloodless, while he carried her towards the house.

Chapter 37

'Put me down.' Skye managed the words when she came out of her catatonic state for long enough to notice that TJ was carrying her towards the porch.

'Nope.'

'TJ—'

'Please, baby.' He paused for long enough to look down at her. 'I need this. Just let me hold you close right now.'

It was the one thing he could have said to soften her. And they both knew it. 'Low blow,' Skye muttered.

'Doesn't mean it's not true,' he countered, and carried her the rest of the way.

When he came to the porch, he very carefully put her down on the top step, minimizing the amount he had to bend, but he didn't let her go. He wrapped his arms around her from behind as Bandit ran forward to greet Janey.

TJ's mom had aged in two years in a way that surprised Skye. Her face was lightly wrinkled now, her hair greying at the roots, a testament to how hard the years following TJ's injury had been for her. But then she smiled, said, 'Hi, baby bug,' and Skye's walls crumbled.

She stepped out of TJ's arms, but she didn't go all the way

across the porch. She was too ashamed. 'I'm so sorry,' she rasped. 'If I'd known he'd come here, I'd have . . .' *What?* she wondered. What could she have done?

Janey took both of Skye's hands in hers, chaffed the chill out of them. 'He had us right where he wanted us before you showed up. Fed us some nonsense about you two being at odds and wanting to mend bridges. I'm ashamed to say I actually felt sympathy for them. But, honey' – Janey waited for Skye to meet her eyes – 'if I'd known the truth, I'd have met him with a shotgun instead of a lemonade.'

'I'm sorry,' Skye repeated.

Janey cocked her head. 'For what?'

Skye flung out her arms. 'F-for bringing him here! For endangering you!'

Janey looked to TJ. 'What on earth is she talking about?'

TJ shrugged. 'I have no idea. Sometimes, she just says the darndest things.'

Skye looked back and forth between them. 'You're teasing me,' she said incredulously.

'Maybe a little,' Janey said, her gentle smile taking the sting out of it.

'Why aren't you mad?' Skye didn't understand it. 'Why would you just take my word?' She fisted both hands at her side and bit down, afraid she'd let it all out if she continued.

Janey answered her anyway. 'We were there, remember – when you first showed up, nothing but a truck, a trailer, and a horse to your name? We always knew you were running, Skye. And we always knew it had to have been bad for you to choose to travel alone rather than face whatever it was you were hiding from.' Janey sighed. 'Now, the fact that you were running from your own father . . .' She trailed off and blew out a whistled breath to emphasize her point. 'I wish you'd told us that.' Her eyes cut to TJ. 'Both of you. Because if I had known, if I hadn't shot him, I would have shovelled some cow shit into that fancy rental. The smell never quite leaves, you know.'

Skye couldn't laugh, even though she knew that Janey was trying to lighten the situation. 'I don't know what to say.'

'You don't have to *say* anything,' Janey clarified. 'Well, that's not entirely true: we're dying to hear your stories from the road. We've been watching you race when it's been televised, but it's not quite the same.' She stepped back and started for the front door. 'TJ, why don't you hurry your father along with the horses?'

Before she followed, Skye turned back to TJ. Because she desperately wanted to walk back into the safety of his arms and hide, she purposefully didn't. But she said, 'This is it.'

'No.' He shook his head. 'We have ten days until your birthday. Ten days where he might escalate but wouldn't risk really hurting you. This is just his way of intimidating you. Come on, baby,' he urged. 'You *know* that.' When she didn't say anything, TJ climbed the porch steps to where she stood. He tipped her chin back, forcing her gaze to his. 'He shows up unannounced, he minimizes your history, so that when we arrive with our guns blazing, *we* seem unreasonable. He brought your mom to use as leverage against you because he knows it's the only way he can still control you. He *wanted* you to feel this way. He planned it – and you're falling into his trap.'

It was odd that, after everything Holden had put her through, Skye still had to be reminded of that. She should have known better by now. But, still, knowing it didn't diminish the anger. Or the fear.

'How did she look?' Skye hated that she had to ask, even though TJ was right – Holden had meant to bring Caroline to taunt her with.

'She looked fine. But she didn't know about Holden's contact with you.'

'It took her by surprise,' Janey affirmed from the doorway.

'I need to get her alone, to speak with her. Maybe things have changed. Maybe she's ready *t-to get out.*'

TJ nodded carefully, but he didn't stoke that hope within her. He had the luxury of rationale when it came to Caroline's situation, and he knew that sometimes – *most* times – the story didn't have a happy ending. The abuse didn't end. It just rolled on to the next nightmare. 'We'll see what we can do. For now, try to relax. It's been a long day.' He kissed her gently, right there in front of his mother. 'I'll be back in ten minutes.'

He left. Before she could stop herself, Skye shouted after him. 'No uncontrolled lifting or bending, TJ!'

He just yelled, 'I know!' without turning around.

Skye turned back to the house, but she pulled up short when she saw Janey. TJ's mom was leaning in the doorway, her arms crossed, her eyes glassing over.

'Janey?'

She waved away Skye's concern. 'The pair of us are a right mess, aren't we?'

Skye nodded. 'Yeah.'

'Wine?'

Skye laughed lightly. 'I thought you'd never ask.'

As she walked to the front door, Janey tipped her head in the direction TJ had walked off in. 'He looks better?'

Skye heard the question, which Janey asked in that cautious, hopeful tone. 'He's trying again,' Skye replied, being careful to moderate both their expectations. 'He got an epidural back in January, and it's brought his pain down a few levels, which is helping day to day. But he has a long way to go.'

When Janey nodded, the movement sent twin tears trailing down her cheeks. 'He got the steroid shot?'

'Yeah.'

'How did you convince him of that? We tried – *for so long*.'

'I told him I'd drop his butt back in Arizona unless he listened to me.'

Janey laughed, but it was watery. 'At first, we tried compassion and patience. When that didn't work, we tried fighting. And that might have been the scariest part, because TJ didn't fight back.'

'You can't help someone who doesn't want to help themself.' Skye had learned that truth at twenty-two when she'd left her mom behind. She only wished she could have given her mother an ultimatum like the one she'd given TJ. 'I don't think TJ could think clearly through the pain for long enough to realize that he was his own biggest problem,' Skye pointed out. 'He wasn't making good choices. He just wanted it to be over. Once he got the epidural and could focus again, he started taking responsibility. And now that he's starting to feel some improvement, he's starting to hope again. The hardest part for him is accepting that he has limitations.' Skye actually smiled. 'Which is why I nag him.'

'Oh, I don't think it was the epidural that got his butt back in gear,' Janey teased lightly. 'Even if it was, we still have you to thank for the fact that he got it.' She waved Skye in. 'Come on. I set up your old room.'

Skye didn't have the audacity to mention that she didn't mind bunking with TJ – at least, not to his mother. 'Thank you. I'll bring our bags in.'

'Leave them for Ryan,' Janey said.

Stepping into the house was like falling through a time portal. Nothing had changed. Even the smell – leather and orange oil – was the same. It was oddly comforting to Skye.

Until she stepped into the stairwell, because there, bolted onto the wall, was a stairlift. The sleek black leather chair and the shiny aluminum tracks didn't change how much space the lift took up in the narrow staircase. It was a bold and ugly reminder of what TJ had been through.

Skye gently touched the leather seat.

Behind her, Janey sighed. 'It took a while before he could walk again. Putting the stairlift in seemed like such a simple solution. But I'll never forget the look on TJ's face when he came home from physical therapy and saw it.' She placed one hand on the banister as if she needed the extra support. 'It was like watching a light get turned off. Just . . .' She clicked her fingers.

Skye sat down, right there on the bottom step. 'I wish I had known everything. I wish he'd told me.'

'He wanted to spare you from it, Skye. It was . . . *awful*.'

'I know that now.'

The sound of the front door opening had Skye quickly standing. She tried to paste a smile on her face, but when TJ walked in, his dad at his side, he saw straight through it. His eyes shifted from her face to the chair. His smile faltered.

'My parents refused to take it down, so that when I had a flare-up, I could get to my room.'

For one long second, nobody said anything. Skye could feel Ryan and Janey's dread, as if they'd live with TJ's anger for too long to risk continuing the conversation.

But Skye refused to be cowed by him, and she knew that TJ didn't benefit from everyone avoiding mention of his injury. What happened had happened, and they would live with that. But they could still live well.

Riding on a whim, she sat down in the chair. She put her feet up on the footplate, raised both her eyebrows at TJ. 'So, Jones? How fast does this thing go anyhow?'

TJ's grin was lightning quick. 'Oh, it's a wild ride.' He moved to the control panel by her arm, said, 'You better hold on, baby.'

Skye, feeling slightly concerned, gripped the arms of the chair. TJ turned the stairlift on, so that it hummed happily. He turned the dial to the number five, the highest speed, and asked, 'You sure you ready?'

Skye nodded. 'I barrel race for a living. I think I got it.'

He pressed the up arrow. There was no starting lurch, no quick zip upwards. Just a smooth, gliding ascent – at a snail's pace.

TJ took the steps one at a time, waiting for her to come abreast of him in the chair before moving to the next one. It was painfully slow. Skye could appreciate the mechanics of it; she could understand that, for many people, the stairlift was a life-altering piece of technology that allowed them to access parts of their houses that they otherwise wouldn't be able to. But TJ was a bull rider: a man whose idea of work had been to take on animals that weighed upwards of fifteen hundred pounds, a man who had lived for the thrill of the ride and the fear of the dismount. So, he wouldn't have seen the stairlift as a gift or a necessity. He would have seen it as a slow ascent to hell.

Skye looked up at TJ and was surprised to see that he was smiling – no, *laughing* at her. 'Enough of a thrill for you?'

Skye raised her hands in the air as if she were on a rollercoaster. She leaned exaggeratedly with the chair as it crept around the corner of the L-shaped staircase, affected a bright, 'Woohoo!'

TJ's laugh was loud. It travelled down the stairs to where Ryan and Janey stood, leaning against one another, their hands linked, tears of relief streaming down their faces.

It was only later that night, as they sat around the dining-room table sharing a meal, that Ryan said, 'If it's okay with you, Skye, I think it's time you filled us in on the situation with your father.'

Skye hesitated.

TJ saw it. He raised his hand to place it over hers on the table. 'It doesn't matter what you tell us. We're on your side. Always.'

'We just want to be prepared,' Ryan agreed. He looked to Janey, added, 'We want to help if we can.'

Beneath TJ's hand, Skye's relaxed. She started quietly, slowly. 'I can't remember the first time. It was more like . . . I don't know. Like it had always been like that. My earliest memories are of being afraid of my father . . .'

As she talked, as she recounted her childhood, glossing over the worst atrocities as if they were simply a fact of life, TJ's rage – his hatred – grew. He couldn't fathom how a father could routinely and systematically punish his own child.

He looked at Skye as she sat next to him, dry-eyed and pale, and he promised that, one day, if they had little girls of their own, he'd show her how a man was supposed to raise his children. He'd show her what Ryan and Janey had shown him all throughout his childhood: that you could get away with a lot of mistakes as a parent if your children knew that they were loved, that it was never okay to take out your own frustrations and inadequacies on anyone else, and that there was nothing a child could do that should warrant physical harm as a punishment.

'By the time I was sixteen, I knew that things weren't normal. I had been put in an in-patient psychiatric hospital for "attacking" my father.' She subtly pulled her hand out from under TJ's when she said that.

But he didn't let her add that distance, didn't let her face her past alone. He reached for her, lifted her out of her chair and onto his lap, despite her snapped 'TJ, your back.'

He just kissed her until she fell quiet, then pulled back. 'Go on.'

'The truth was that I had fought back for the first time. I scratched his face, and he knocked me unconscious. He must have panicked about trying to explain his face because he called the police. He told them that I had mental health issues and had been released from a facility six months earlier. Which was *technically* true. He said that I attacked him. And my mom took his side – not because she wanted to,' Skye was quick to add. 'Because she didn't see any other way out.'

Across the table, his own mom's face was pale, her eyes wide with horror. His dad was silent, but his eyes burned with a rage that TJ had never seen in his mild-mannered father.

'I started to hate him after that. Like *truly* hate him,' Skye said matter-of-factly. 'And in hating him, I started to play the game too. I started to retaliate.' Skye smiled, but TJ noticed that her blue eyes were flat. 'It was small things at first. Little things I knew would irritate him – leaving a single dirty dish on the kitchen counter, wearing fashionable instead of appropriate clothes, letting my grades slip a few points. When the threats and shaming didn't work, he'd get physical. But only in ways that didn't leave obvious marks. And when I just let it come, he started punishing my mother for everything *I* did. So I stopped.'

She went on to explain how she'd met Stevie and Andrea, and how they'd slowly pulled her out of that protective shell. She detailed leaving Dallas and only stopped when she said, 'And then Sheridan gave me your number, and I ended up here.' She tried to smile, but it fell flat. She was curled against him, her posture rounded, as if she were expecting judgement and wanted to shelter against it.

TJ pulled her closer, letting her take that comfort.

Skye told them about the trust, and when she had walked them through the particulars, she added things that not even TJ had heard before. 'The estate provides Caroline with fifty thousand dollars a month and lets them live in the Highland Park house rent-free. That's worth a total of seventy-five thousand dollars every thirty days. And Holden has inflated his lifestyle to match. When I take over, I fully plan on zeroing out that number, effective immediately. And it'll humiliate him. He'll be forced to downsize. He can keep up with rent on the house *if* he cuts back in every other area of his life: the lake house, the country club, the new luxury car every year.'

Ryan nodded. 'Yeah. That'll do it.'

'My only hesitation at this point is my mom. Because he will make her suffer for it.'

'How do we get her out?' TJ slammed one hand onto the table, his frustration clear. '*That's* what we've got to figure out.'

'There's nothing you can do,' Skye replied quietly. 'I tried everything. That's literally the reason I'm cutting them off; if I do, Holden will only stick around for so long. It's the period between cutting him off and him actually leaving that I'm worried about.'

'Yeah. I can see why.' Ryan leaned back in his chair. He studied his own hands, something that TJ knew meant he was deep in thought.

'What are you thinking, Dad?'

Ryan's eyes crinkled when he smiled. 'Shit, TJ. I'm a dairy farmer. I'm thinking we handle this the old-fashioned way. Some rope, a castrating knife, and maybe a branding iron.'

'Amen,' TJ said. Because, goddamn, he was desperate to sink his fists into Holden's face.

'No.' On TJ's lap, Skye went rigid. 'Nobody else is getting involved in this.'

TJ opened his mouth to argue, but his mom beat him to it. 'Sweet girl, that's not how this family works. You go after one of us, you best be prepared to take us all on.'

A shudder of emotion ran through Skye's back and into his chest, but when she spoke, her voice was firm. 'I appreciate that – more than you will ever know. But no. Nobody else is getting hurt because of me.'

'It won't end, Skye.' TJ was willing to be the one to point it out, if it kept her safe from Holden's abuse. 'Even if you change the trust, he'll keep at you. He'll keep hurting your mom. And eventually, you will give him what he wants to stop it.' He covered the backs of her hands with his, linking their fingers. 'You know that's true.'

'Just give me time,' Skye said. 'I need to speak with my mom. I need to think . . .'

Although it was hard for him to agree, TJ said, 'How about we agree to try it your way first? If it doesn't work, I get the second shot at him.'

'*We*,' his dad clarified. '*We* get the second shot at him.'

Chapter 38

When TJ came out of the bathroom after showering, dressed in jeans and an old, faded T-shirt, he was surprised to see his mom standing in his bedroom, staring out his window, a towel draped over her arm. 'Mom?'

She jumped, raised one hand to her heart. 'TJ. You scared me.'

'Sorry.' He tossed the dirty laundry he held into the hamper in the corner of the room. 'You okay?'

Instead of replying, she waved him over to the window.

TJ walked to where she stood. He looked out, and saw Skye. She was riding Smokey bareback, with no reins, only a lead rope draped over the horse's neck and threaded through the halter's throat ring. She was completely at ease, her posture relaxed, her legs dangling with no tension. Although dusk was rapidly descending, her blonde hair gleamed in the fading light. Bandit was walking at the horse's side, content to stay close.

'You know, I used to sit at this window – after my accident – and wonder where she was and what she was doing.'

His mom roped one arm around his waist. 'I remember.'

'Being with her the first time was like standing still in time and knowing exactly where I wanted my life to go. And then after . . . It felt like I had nothing left to live for – especially once she was gone.'

'There's always something to live for,' Janey argued.

TJ didn't fight her on it. She was his mom, and it was her job to fight for him. But he did say, 'I was ready. To go.'

His mom covered her mouth with her hand, but she didn't speak, just nodded as her tears streamed.

Because he hated making her sad, he pulled her into a hug. But because he needed to close the circle, he added, 'Except, every time I'd start to plan, I just felt this . . . *need* to see her one last time. I told myself it was to apologize and make sure she was safe, but I think it was also because *I* needed to prove to myself that I was done. Even after all that time, I knew that if anyone could spike through the pain and the despair, it would be her. And I wanted that for myself. I wanted one last chance to feel . . . *alive.* And then Mav reached out and asked me to watch over her, and it seemed like fate giving me that last chance.'

'I understand that.' His mom stepped out of his embrace, but only so that she could swipe her face. 'You know, TJ, I don't think you and Skye would have worked out the first time.'

'Why not?'

'She was too young, too inexperienced. Too desperate to be loved. And you were too young, too inexperienced with women like her. Too selfish.'

It hurt to hear it, hurt more to know that there was truth in it. He'd wanted Skye back then, and even though she'd taken those steps herself, he'd done everything to coax her towards him. And while he'd promised he'd never hurt her, he *had.* Not physically. Never physically. But he'd hurt her. He was man enough to admit that much.

'Maybe,' his mom continued, 'you had to lose everything you thought mattered – the bull riding, the fans, the fame – to realize what *did* matter. The people who love you.' She nodded towards the window. 'Skye.'

'I don't have anything to give her this time around.' The words were so immense that he whispered them. 'Some money, sure. But she has plenty of that. I don't have a career – just ideas, a broken back and a heart that beats for her.'

Janey just laughed. 'Baby, you have you. And you are enough. Skye knows that. You were enough for her, even with a broken back. And I think that's why it was so hard on her when you ended things. It's *you* who needed to realize that the bull riding was never what made you. The fact that you were hardworking, passionate, and gritty was what made you so good at bull riding.' She placed one hand on his cheek, patted him twice, almost condescendingly. 'Yes, it was what you loved. But there's *so much* to love in the world. Always. Sometimes, you just have to be proactive about searching for it.'

TJ knew she was right, but only because he'd had to seek out Skye to find something to love in the world, something to stay for.

His mom took the towel she had folded over her arm and placed it on the bed. 'How long are you two staying?'

'Through Rodeo Scottsdale. I don't know after that. We have a schedule, but with Holden showing up and Skye's birthday looming . . .'

His mom shook her head sadly, but TJ didn't miss the hard and unforgiving glint in her eyes. 'It curdles my blood to think about what that girl's been through. And at the hands of her own father.'

Outside, Skye let Smokey graze and lay back on her horse so that she could gaze up at the sky.

TJ was rapt. 'You wouldn't think it, looking at her. She doesn't let anything hold her back.'

'A lesson for us all, I think.' Janey moved towards the door, but she didn't leave right away. She turned to look at him, and when TJ just raised his eyebrows in question, she smiled. 'It's good to have you back, TJ. Home hasn't been quite the same without you.'

TJ ran one hand over the back of his neck. He, too, had seen what Skye had. His parents looked older, tired, worn down. 'I'm sorry, for putting you through that. It wasn't fair.'

'Parenting never is, TJ. But I still wouldn't change a thing. You and Julia are the best thing we ever did.'

Skye stood in Smokey's stall, grooming her and humming along to the radio, set to country music, but she felt the moment TJ walked into the barn. He was quiet as a cat, but her body sensed his proximity. Her heart tapped excitedly against her ribs. Her stomach swooped low.

Without turning or stopping what she was doing, Skye said, 'She's ready to get back to work.'

'She has been for a few weeks now,' TJ said. He crouched at Smokey's side to better see the faint scar. Apart from the small section that had needed stitches, most of it had already grown hair back.

Skye frowned down at him. 'Why didn't you tell me you thought she was ready?'

He pushed to his feet with a small groan. 'Because you weren't ready to hear it. And you and Kai were doing well together, so why push it?'

Skye couldn't even deny it. She ran one palm down Smokey's glossy coat. 'I just wanted to be sure she was okay. Seeing her in pain, knowing it was my fault—'

'Nope.' TJ took her by the shoulders and turned her to face him. 'You're not doing that. You're not taking blame for something that sick fuck did.'

He pulled her into his chest, and Skye wrapped her arms around his waist and nestled in. 'If it's okay with you, I'll ride Kai through Scottsdale. I need a little time to bring Smokey's conditioning back up.'

'He's yours as long as you need him. You know that.'

It was something she'd been meaning to bring up again but

hadn't found the courage to, because she thought she knew the answer already. But now, she tipped her head back to meet his green eyes, asked, 'Why did you put him in with Tia?'

TJ smiled, but it wasn't bitter. 'You know why.'

'You were going to leave him to me.' It hurt to say, to acknowledge aloud. It left her cold and scared, although she knew the worst of it had passed.

He nodded. 'It wasn't a selfless decision, if that makes you feel better. I trusted – absolutely – that you would love him and look after him despite what happened between us. And, yeah, my folks would have too, but Kai needs a job. You were the next best option.'

'Thanks for trusting me with him.'

'Of course.'

'But, TJ, we're done with that now.' It wasn't a question.

TJ dropped his forehead to hers. He closed his eyes and sighed deeply, as if he'd found his own safe space with her. 'I'm not leaving you. I just got you back.'

Hearing it settled her. Trying to tether somebody who didn't want to stay was a constantly terrifying task. It was soul-crushing, gruelling work that required encouraging, pleading, and even threatening. 'I'm not going anywhere, Jesse Jones,' she said. 'You're stuck with me.'

Skye rose onto her toes and took his mouth in a deep kiss, giving everything – all the fear and anxiety and hope she'd carried for him – back into to his care.

TJ's hands dropped her to ass and squeezed. He used his grip there to pull her up against his hard body. He broke the kiss, but only to trail his lips down her neck. 'Fuck. I can't get enough of you, Skye.'

'Who says you have to?' Skye tipped her head back, giving him her throat in a gesture that was as natural as it was trusting. That familiar, insatiable need clawed mercilessly through her. Her body was heavy, everything tightly coiled.

TJ pulled open the stall door, ushered her out, and then closed Smokey in behind them. He used his body to walk her backwards, until her back hit the tack room door. His hands dropped to the front of her jeans, but he didn't move to touch her yet, only whispered, 'You know, we walked away from an opportunity to have sex in this barn once . . .'

Skye, too desperate to worry about being caught, opened the door and stepped inside. The smell of leather and oil and feed reached for her over the sharp edge of her desperation. She looked over her shoulder at TJ, said, 'It would be a pity, don't you think, to let an opportunity pass twice?'

'Yes ma'am, I do.' TJ placed his forearms on the doorway, but he didn't come in. His green eyes were dark and focused, loving her even as he kept that torturously small distance between them, she knew, to tease her.

Unopposed to teasing him back, Skye took her hat off, but only for long enough to strip. She did so slowly, removing her clothes one piece at a time. It was only when she stood in front of him, gloriously naked, that she put her boots and hat back on.

TJ made that sound deep in the back of his throat; it zipped over her skin, pulling her peaked nipples painfully tight. His hungry gaze travelled slowly over her. 'You're fucking perfect, you know that?'

Skye raised her hands to her breasts, but she kept her eyes open and focused on him as she touched herself.

TJ bit off a pained groan. His arms dropped from the doorway. His fists clenched at his sides.

Skye could see his erection, long and hard, straining against his jeans. 'You're not gonna win this round, Cowboy,' she taunted.

TJ just grinned wickedly. 'Baby, I win this round either way.' But he gave in to his need to touch her with one last cursed 'Fuck.' He stepped into the tack room and kicked the door shut behind him.

Skye had learned how to play the game, how to accommodate

his pain without wounding his pride. So, she turned and leaned over a nearby saddle rack, resting her forearms on the leather seat of one of TJ's old roping saddles, and then, looking back at him seductively, spread her legs wider.

TJ came to her immediately. He ran his hands down her sides before gripping her hip in one hand and sliding the other between her legs. He cupped her, said, 'Fuck, baby, you're so wet,' and pushed two fingers deep inside her.

Skye tipped her hips back, taking more.

'So greedy,' TJ rasped. But he gave her what she wanted, and pumped his fingers into her, pushing her higher and higher with each thrust.

Too eager to wait any longer, Skye dropped her fingers to her clit, circling the knot of nerves with no self-consciousness, only desperation.

Her body tightened.

Her breaths became laboured.

That wave came, rising through her with destructive power.

But right as she rose with it, preparing to tumble down over the crest, TJ stopped. He pulled his fingers from her, making her whimper in protest. 'TJ, please.'

'Hold on, baby.' She heard the sound of his zipper lowering. 'You're gonna come riding my cock.'

Skye closed her eyes as moisture slicked down her upper thighs. She might have been embarrassed had TJ not slid between her legs at that exact moment, lubricating himself with her. Instead, she whispered, 'Holy shit.'

TJ grumbled in approval. He guided himself to her and teasingly eased the first inch of his penis into her and stopped.

'TJ . . .'

'Say my name.'

'Jesse.'

He gave her another inch, forcing her unbearably tight body to clench around him. 'Tell me you're mine.'

‘I’m yours,’ she panted. And because she could hear the restraint in his voice, she looked over her shoulder at him, and she said, ‘Now fuck me like you want to ruin me for anyone else.’

TJ’s head dropped back as her words unleashed the beast within him. He did not have to be told twice. He pumped into her, forcing her to reach out and grip the saddle in front of her to anchor herself against his thrusts.

He pushed her up and over the edge in seconds, so that Skye sobbed out a moan as her body greedily took him in, holding him close.

TJ wasn’t far behind. He gripped both her hips, holding her up as her bones liquified, and fucked her like he wanted to brand her from the inside out.

His breaths tore through the tack room, joining the sound of their flesh slapping together animalistically. But when he came, he didn’t say ‘Mine’ as she’d expected.

He said, ‘Yours. I’m yours.’

Chapter 39

Scottsdale, Arizona – March 5, 2027

Being back at Rodeo Scottsdale came with a lot of memories for both TJ and Skye. As they navigated the rig through the WestWorld event parking, Skye couldn't help but reach for him. She put her hand on his thigh, asked, 'Are you going to be okay – coming back here?'

TJ covered her hand with his. When he turned to glance at her, he was smiling. And it wasn't bitter or angry. It was calm, relaxed. 'It's always hard. But mostly because everyone knows who I am and feels compelled to bring it up when they run into me.' He squeezed her hand gently. 'This time I'm totally gonna use you as a distraction though.'

'A distraction?' Skye asked.

He whipped up a hand in an exaggerated stop sign, said, 'Sorry, can't talk. My girl's about to run. Gotta go.'

'The hand signal adds a certain urgency,' she teased.

'Yeah, I know.' He did it again to emphasize his point, making her laugh.

This was the TJ she remembered, the TJ she'd first fallen for. And although she loved his jagged edges too, Skye didn't feel guilty for wanting that lighter version of him – for wanting *him* to be lighter. 'You're coming back, TJ,' she said.

He nodded mock-seriously. 'What can I say? You can't keep this much charm contained for long.'

Skye scoffed. 'So modest too!'

TJ pulled into a trailer parking spot. But when Skye moved to open her door and get out, he caught her hand, stopping her. 'Thank you.'

Skye frowned. 'For what?'

'For kicking my butt when I needed it. For staying. For riding through the worst of it with me.' In a gesture that made her eyes burn, he brought her palm to his lips and placed a feather-light kiss there, before curling her hand closed over it. 'For loving me when I didn't love myself and certainly didn't deserve you.'

Skye reached forward and placed that closed fist over his heart, before opening her hand again and giving it back to him. 'Ditto.'

TJ gave her a quick kiss. He pulled back, a devilish grin on his face, said, 'Now, how about we give Scottsdale a real show?'

'Heck yeah,' she said. Although those nerves were there, Skye refused to give in to them. She would be strong for TJ today.

They climbed out the truck and moved to the back of the trailer to let Kai out. They'd left the live-in at the farm and brought the small trailer instead. Smokey was safely back at his parents' farm.

Outside, the temperature was a warm seventy-three degrees, and people seemed to be enjoying the beautiful evening. Folks laughed and chatted as they went about their business, prepping their horses for the night.

A group of saddle bronc and bareback riders walked past, Matthew Savage among them. He didn't point out the pink hat TJ still wore, only whistled loudly to get their attention and then shouted, 'Good luck tonight, Skye!'

She waved, replied, 'Thanks!' as they walked off.

As TJ got started on braiding Kai's mane, Skye wrapped the horse's legs.

'Remember, push him on the straight. Don't let him coast.'

'I know.' Once Skye was done with the polo wrap, she used tape to doubly secure the Velcro straps in place.

'Don't rush the first barrel.'

'I know.'

'And remember to keep his body under him—'

'TJ.' Skye waited until he looked down at her before repeating, 'I know.'

He slowly went back to his braiding. 'I'm sorry. I know you've got this. I just . . . I guess I *am* a bit off – being back here.'

Skye taped off the second polo wrap, but instead of moving on to Kai's back legs, she went to TJ. She waited for him to tie-off the braid, then wrapped her arms around him. 'It's okay to feel that way. Anybody would. But I've got this. I'm good at this.'

'You are.' He dropped a kiss on top of her head, teasingly said, 'Jesus, what am I going to feel like when our kids start doing this?'

Skye's body jerked involuntarily. She tipped her head back to look at TJ. 'What did you say?'

He countered with another question. 'Wait, do you want kids?'

Skye was slightly astounded. 'I don't think I've ever thought about it, to be entirely honest.' She took a step back, needing space to make sense of the emotions swirling through her.

'Well, with or without kids' – TJ pointed from her to him with his index finger – 'we're gonna make this thing between us official.'

Skye cocked one hip. She crossed her arms over her chest, half in defiance, half to steel herself against her racing heart. 'I think you're supposed to *ask* me, not *tell* me.'

'Oh, I'm gonna ask you. But I'm gonna date you first, give you all those things you missed' – he shot her a bland look – 'while you were sewing your wild oats.' Infuriatingly, after dropping that bomb, he just refocused his attention on braiding Kai's mane.

Skye refused to question him about when he planned on asking because she was embarrassed by how much she wanted to.

Instead, she moved to Kai's back legs and started wrapping them, her silence pointed and loud – but not fooling either of them.

TJ wisely hid his grin from Skye as she crouched down to finish wrapping Kai's legs. He hoped that he'd distracted her enough from her anxiety with the casual bomb he'd dropped. But because he'd meant every word, he hoped she would think about it too.

He'd give her time, because she was still so young and had things she needed to do still. And he'd ask her properly, on one knee, when the time was right. Until then, he'd try his best to be patient and let her live a little more.

As soon as she was done Skye stepped into the trailer. But just thirty seconds later, she called, 'TJ, have you seen my hat?'

'On the counter!'

'It's not there!'

He walked around to the trailer door and stepped inside, scanned the cramped space for the black hat.

'I had it yesterday.' Skye marched to the shower and yanked open the door.

'You wearing my hat in the shower now?' TJ teased.

Skye just scowled at him and kept looking.

TJ joined in.

After five minutes of searching, he was about to give up and give her the pink hat on his own head, when she said, 'Aha! Got it!' and fished it out of a top cupboard.

'Okay. Ready to haul ass?' he asked once she'd plopped it on her head.

Skye didn't reply, only nodded once, firmly.

They walked the short distance to the warm-up arena together.

TJ stood, his arms resting on the arena siding, and watched Skye run Kai through her warm-up. The horse looked good. He was calm and centred.

Across the arena, a kid who couldn't have been more than sixteen watched the riders warm up. He wasn't a cowboy. He was dressed in baggy black jeans and a black sweatshirt with the hood up. Not even his outfit, which dwarfed his reed-thin body, could hide his gleaming white sneakers, sneakers that screamed *city*. When he sensed TJ's gaze, the boy turned and met his eyes – and then quickly stepped back and hurried away.

TJ's skin prickled with unease.

'Let's get this done.'

He looked up at Skye as she brought Kai up to the arena gate. He'd been so distracted by the odd interaction that he hadn't even heard her drag get called.

He refocused, asked, 'You ready?'

'Yes.' Skye's voice was firm, her eyes calm.

As the first girl in Skye's drag ran, TJ scanned the crowd from the holding area. The rodeo was roaring. The spectators were primed, some walking around, taking restroom breaks or grabbing drinks, others chatting to their friends, all ready for a night of entertainment. He tracked the seats his parents had booked and saw them sitting side by side, their hands linked.

He wanted that one day. Not just the love and commitment, but the kids, the rodeo, the *life*. He wanted to sit in the stands with Skye and watch their children take on the world. Knowing it didn't scare him. TJ had faced death and survived – *barely*. Now, with Skye by his side and a new commitment to stay burning in his belly, life was his for the taking.

He was just about to step back when he saw them – Skye's parents. They sat off to the right in the front row, which happened to be placed immediately in front of the first barrel. Despite the fact that they both wore jeans, they still looked sorely out of place, their denim new, their boots glossy and unscuffed, their shirts ironed and starched.

TJ immediately signalled Skye. He knew how Holden worked now, and he trusted Skye's father about as far as he could kick him. He might not hurt her in so public a setting, but TJ wouldn't put it past Holden to do something Skye wasn't expecting – like cheering for her by name to try and throw her off.

Skye frowned, but she rode up to the fence that separated them. 'What is it?'

'Holden and Caroline are in the front row by the first barrel. No, don't look—'

But it was too late. Skye's gaze had snapped to them. TJ's followed, just in time to catch Holden raising his hand in what anyone else would consider a friendly – even, fatherly – wave.

'It doesn't matter.' Skye ignored her father to look back down at TJ. 'He has no power here. This is my turf.'

TJ nodded. Pride filled him. 'Damn straight. So, how about you show him what he created? Someone strong and brave and kind. Someone who can't be cowed by him.'

Skye's blue eyes lit with the challenge of that, turning ice blue. 'Fuck yes.'

'All right.' He gave her leg one last squeeze, said, 'Let's go.'

TJ stepped into the alley and joined Skye and Kai as the announcer's voice blared, 'Next up, we have Skye Marchant and Sweet Lil Bullet out of Santa Barabara, California.' The camera zoomed in on them, on TJ standing at Skye's side as they walked down the alley together, Kai pulling on the bit in his eagerness to get going.

'Looks like there's been a hat change here, folks,' the announcer teased. 'But Triple J, Scottsdale's very own *four-million-dollar bull rider*, sure looks good in pink!'

Playing to the crowd for the first time since his accident, TJ swept his pink hat off and waved it in the air.

The crowd went feral.

As if fate were aligning with them, Kip Moore's 'American Heartbreak' started over the speakers.

TJ smiled. He aimed that smile, sharp and lethal, in Holden's direction, bared his teeth when Holden didn't even blink, only stared back, his own smile cool and dangerous.

Next to him, Kai tensed up, ready to run.

TJ moved off to the side. As Skye took her moment of stillness, TJ said, 'You got this, baby!'

Skye grinned. She took a deep breath, one that TJ heard from where he stood.

When she let Kai go, TJ felt the ground shift and vibrate beneath his feet as they pounded down the alley and headed left to the first barrel. They took it fast and smooth; if Holden said anything to her, it didn't affect Skye.

She pushed Kai to the second barrel, clearing it easily before turning for the third.

It was only then that TJ noticed that something was wrong.

Skye's saddle wasn't centred; in fact, it leaned noticeably to the right, as if it had shifted during the second barrel. 'What the . . .'

He started walking down the alley, his heart pounding with fear.

The front of the saddle, held in place by the breast collar, seemed to be holding. But the seat had shifted enough that Skye felt it.

TJ held his breath as she leaned back hard in the saddle and pulled back on the reins, trying to stop Kai before the saddle slipped to the horse's front and took them both down.

Although he didn't realize it, TJ started running towards them.

The announcer's voice, filled with worry, said, 'Looks like they're having some saddle trouble, folks,' right as Kai, eager to do his job, fought through Skye's grip and took the turn anyway.

The saddle slipped off Kai's back, taking Skye with it. But it didn't detach from the breast collar. As the saddle slipped around the horse's front, Skye's foot still in the stirrup, the weight threw Kai's already off-centred balance further.

The horse fell over – and landed on Skye.

A collective gasp rang through the crowd.

The music stopped.

Everything stilled.

Chapter 40

TJ didn't think.

He ran, his back screaming in pain as his booted feet churned the thick arena dirt.

His heart raced so loudly that he could hear it in his ears. Even as he focused on Skye, the flashes of memory came.

He remembered dismounting the bull and screaming, 'Come on!' as the crowd roared. He remembered feeling like a God and wanting to see Skye's face, but instead of being greeted with her smile, he'd seen her fear. He remembered, *felt*, the bull hit him like a freight train from the side.

The thought had him moving faster, even as his limp became more noticeable.

Up ahead, Kai, in his panic, pushed to a stand, his hooves coming dangerously close to Skye's body beneath him.

The horse, panicked and in shock, started to move off, unaware that Skye's right foot was still in the stirrup.

TJ couldn't get there fast enough. He watched in horror as Skye was dragged, unconscious, over the red dirt.

The horse made it four feet before Matthew Savage jumped the arena fence and landed right in front of him. Kai spooked, but Matthew managed to reach out and grab the reins, stopping him from dragging Skye any further.

TJ was right behind. He grabbed Skye's ankle and released her foot from the stirrup, before dropping onto his knees by her side. Her eyes were closed, her body listless, her face pale. There was a long gash down her right cheek, one that bled profusely. He felt for her pulse, picked up the strong thread instantly.

A broken sob of relief tore up his throat.

Around him, the stadium was eerily quiet.

'Hey, baby.' He tapped her face gently, being careful not to articulate her neck or back in case she'd broken anything.

Skye moaned. Her eyelashes fluttered.

TJ held her face still using both hands. His eyes were dry, but his face was bloodless. When he said, 'Come on. Give me those blue eyes,' his voice was deep and hoarse.

Skye opened her eyes slowly. She blinked in confusion, said, 'TJ?'

He laughed. 'Yeah. Yeah, baby.' And when she tried to sit up, he pinned her down. 'Don't move. We don't—'

TJ's back spasmed. The pain paralyzed him.

That seemed to clear Skye's mind instantly. She broke his weakened hold and shot into a seated position. Her hat was gone, her hair covered in red dirt. Blood and sand sloughed down her face. And, still, she had the fucking gall to shout, 'If you've flared up your back after everything we've done the past two months, there's gonna be hell to pay!'

TJ could barely breathe through the spasms, but he managed a stuttered laugh and, 'Yes, ma'am.'

But the tears came, and they had nothing to do with his own pain. He reached through a violent spasm and closed his hand over hers, whispered, 'Don't ever fucking do that to me again.'

There was a moment of silence, so that when the first person started clapping, it rang through the Equidome loudly. Slowly, the crowd joined in. People started cheering and whistling.

Skye looked around, confused and disoriented. 'Oh, shit. I fell.'

'Baby, you ate it. Hard.'

'Kai.' Skye spun her torso around, but the moment she saw Kai, standing off to the side, Matthew Savage holding the reins, she placed one hand back on the dirt to support herself. 'Okay, I'm a little woozy.'

'Yeah, no shit. You were out cold.' He took a deep breath, asked, 'Any pain?'

Skye checked in with her body. 'A headache. A sprained ankle.' She raised her fingers to her cheek. 'And this hurts like a bitch.'

'Hospital,' TJ said, leaving no room to argue.

'Yeah.' Skye sighed sadly. 'Fuck, that's gonna be a DQ. I'm not gonna make the NFR this year,' she predicted. 'I'm already too far behind.'

TJ refused to laugh at the fact that a disqualification and the NFR were what she was thinking about just then. But he did ask, 'How'd a city slicker like you turn cowgirl so fast?'

Skye just reached for her hat. She put it over her dirty hair, said, 'It's just a state of mind, TJ.' And when the sports med team arrived with the stretcher, Skye waved them off. 'How about we give 'em a show?' she asked. When TJ looked unsure, she added, 'I have some pride to recoup.'

He, more than anyone, understood that. 'Yes, ma'am.' He braced, added, 'But you're gonna have to help me up.'

Skye pushed to her feet. She took a moment to steady herself and then held out one hand for TJ.

He took it and let her pull him to his feet. And when she wrapped one supporting arm around his waist and tucked herself under his arm, he didn't pull back, despite the raucous crowd. He leaned in, letting her carry him as much as she could.

Matthew brought Kai alongside them, the saddle in one hand.

On the big screen, TJ's accident replayed, this time on a split screen with Skye's. Over the speakers, the announcer said, 'And that, ladies and gentlemen, is rodeo! Cowboys and cowgirls, showing up and leaving it all on the dirt!'

The chorus of 'How You Like Me Now?' by The Heavy blared, giving them a walk-out song.

As the staff ran on to hand rake over the accident site and check the barrel's positioning, their trio walked down the alley. Once they were out of the camera's range, Skye looked up at him. 'TJ, I tightened my cinch after I warmed up. It was good.'

TJ's blood ran cold. He hadn't even had the time to think about *how* the saddle had come off. 'You sure?'

'Oh, I think we know what happened.' Matthew hefted the saddle with one hand, showing her and TJ where the leather off billet had been cut. 'Somebody sliced through your off billet.' He passed Skye Kai's reins, and the moment she took the horse, he said, 'See here. The underside of the leather, before the knot, was cut about three-quarters of the way. But this part tore.' He showed them the stretched piece of leather that hadn't been cut but had broken loose. 'Whoever did this left it attached enough for you to get through warm-up. But there's no way this would survive three barrel turns.' If TJ was surprised by Matthew's matter-of-fact recount, he was more surprised by when he said, 'And I think I might know who did it.'

'Who?' TJ and Skye asked at the same time.

TJ dared to ask, 'Distinguished-looking white guy in his sixties?'

'Nope.' Matthew hiked the saddle higher, asked, 'Either of you do anything to piss off a kid lately?'

'What?' Skye shook her head.

But TJ asked, 'A kid? Reed thin? City-type?'

'That's the one. Saw him outside your rig with the horse earlier. Didn't think much of it at first, because he was just standing there looking at him. Seemed sad as hell. But when I asked him if he was okay, he turned tail and ran – fast.'

'We didn't leave Kai alone—' began Skye.

'Except when we were looking for your hat,' TJ said.

Skye momentarily closed her eyes. 'Shit.'

Matthew stopped with them the moment they were outside the arena. 'Begs the question: what the hell did you do to him? I grew up with a lot of angry teenage boys, but none of them resorted to attempted murder until they were at least twenty-four.'

TJ managed to smile through the pain.

Skye frowned. 'What is it with you guys and your twisted sense of humour?'

Matthew just sniggered. 'Gotta have one if you wanna ride.'

TJ didn't say anything. It was Skye's story to tell, and he'd let her say as much as she wanted or needed to.

Instead of explaining, she held out one hand, said, 'Can I have my phone?'

TJ fished it out of his back pocket. She passed it to Matthew, who still held her saddle in one hand.

'Call your number so I have it. If I need you to speak to the cops, I wanna know how to reach you.'

Matthew did as she asked and then passed the phone back to her. 'I'll keep a lookout for him too.'

'If he's smart, he'll be long gone,' TJ commented.

Matthew tipped his head. 'If he has nowhere else to go, he'll hang around. The rodeo's safe. There's cheap food, lots of people, and entertainment. Besides, as far as he knows, we're not onto him.'

'Skye!'

They all turned at the voice, frantic with worry. Janey and Ryan were running towards them, their faces set in equally horrified expressions.

TJ knew from a lifetime of their concern to placate. 'She's okay. Just banged up some. We're gonna head to the hospital now.'

But Skye had no such experience, so when Janey pulled her into a tight hug and said, 'Good Lord, you scared us half to death, baby bug!' she just stared at her in bewilderment.

'Ah . . . I'm okay,' she managed. She gave his mom's back a slightly overwhelmed pat, said, 'Thanks . . .'

Ryan took Kai's reins from her hand. 'I'll get him loaded up. Janey, if you drive them to the hospital, I'll take Skye's truck home and stall Kai. Call Dr Sanchez to come look him over.'

Skye, clearly overwhelmed, started to object. 'I can do it—'

But Janey cut her off before TJ could. 'The hell you will.' Her mom-voice sent a streak of fear down TJ's spine. He was relieved to notice that both Skye and Matthew jerked to attention at it too. 'Hospital. Home – if the doctor says it's okay. Food. Bed – with alarms for concussion monitoring.'

Skye looked to TJ.

He just shook his head. 'I'm not gonna risk arguing.'

Matthew watched the Jones family walk away, Skye awkwardly supporting TJ's weight as they both hobbled after TJ's mom.

He momentarily wondered what that must be like, to have people who cared whether or not you came home after a ride . . .

When the thought settled uncomfortably between his shoulder blades, he shook it off. He pasted a cocky smile on his face and strutted back through the parking lot.

He'd already ridden for the night. He'd drawn Son of a Gun, and although the fucker had given him a wild ride, Matthew had stayed on – and he'd scored a ninety-two.

With nowhere else to go, and not really wanting to go back to the quiet hotel room just yet, he walked back towards the Equidome.

It was only when he came to the edge of the parking lot that he saw the kid hurrying towards him. The boy couldn't have been more than sixteen. He was skin and bone, with a mop of dark, shaggy hair. His baggy clothes dwarfed him.

His eyes were filled with panic. He didn't even see Matthew, just hurried past him as he looked fearfully over his shoulder.

Matthew leaned against a nearby trailer and crossed one booted ankle over the other. In less than twenty seconds, a man emerged. He wasn't a cowboy. He looked more like an oil man, all slick and moneyed. Matthew supposed this was TJ's distinguished-looking white man.

Curious despite himself, he tipped his hat down over his eyes.

The man scanned the parking lot like a snake homing in on something small and afraid.

Up ahead, the kid's black sweatshirt flashed as he ducked between two trailers.

The man was off immediately.

Matthew sighed.

He'd recognized the kid instantly when he'd seen him standing outside the trailer. They all looked the same. In many ways, he'd been that kid. Angry. Afraid. Lost. Hopping from one foster home to the next, never trusting the adults he landed with, never relaxing for long enough to risk growing attached.

He figured he didn't have to be a genius to know that the kid was in trouble – or, in the very least, asking for it. So, he flexed his shoulders, rolled his neck – and stepped into the fray.

He found them between the two trailers, the man holding the kid by the neck as he pinned him against the steel siding. 'Do you know what you could have cost me if you'd killed her?' The man spat in the kid's face.

'You said to scare her,' the kid pleaded. 'I didn't know it'd go bad.' He started to struggle as his air supply was slowly, methodically cut off. 'Please,' he gurgled. 'I've done everything you asked.'

Matthew took a long moment to cool his rage. If riding broncs had taught him anything, it was that timing mattered.

'The next time you screw up, I'm going to make sure the police pick you up and throw you back into the hole I pulled you out of. You hear me?'

The kid nodded as much as he could against the hands at his throat.

'Given that you're seventeen, I'll make sure you're tried as an adult.' The man smiled, taking pleasure from the kid's white-eyed fear. 'Do you know what happens to little boys in men's prisons?'

'Yes,' the kid whispered.

Matthew might not have made it to an adult penitentiary, but he knew what happened in juvenile hall, so could only imagine how much worse the men were. Bile slicked his throat. But he cleared it – loudly.

The man dropped the kid, who crumpled at his feet on the floor. He shifted, going from raging sociopath to calm, collected citizen in the space of a breath. 'This boy tried to pick my pocket.'

'And here I thought you were punishing him because he took your instructions a little too far.' Matthew stepped into the space between the two trailers. He was a wolf, ready – *desperate* – to attack. But he forced himself to relax.

The man's face fell. 'I have no idea what you're talking about.' He looked down at the kid on the floor, asked, 'Do you?'

The kid shook his head. But he didn't look up, didn't acknowledge Matthew in any way.

'Let me tell you how this is going to play out,' Matthew drawled. He cracked his knuckles for good measure. 'The kid's coming with me. If you try to reach out to him again, if you contact him, you will deal with me. And it will only happen once before you realize that I am your worst nightmare come to life.' He grinned maniacally, showing the man how desperate he was to have a go. 'If the police come for him at any time, I will be the first person going up against you. And I'm just going on a whim here, but I'm guessing TJ and Skye will probably join me.'

Matthew moved to stand in front of the kid, forcing the man to take a good five steps back. A subtle flash of fear zipped through his eyes.

Matthew relished it. 'I wonder what the combined weight of everything we'd have to say would do to a man like you?'

'You've got nothing! A juvenile delinquent, a lying bitch, and her crippled lover.'

'Oh, but what is a reputation when put up against even a whisper of doubt?' Matthew asked calmly.

The man froze up. He turned and walked away, but Matthew had the pleasure of knowing that the asshole tucked tail and ran because he couldn't see a better way out.

Matthew waited until he had gone, then looked down at the kid. The boy had managed to sit up against the trailer's wheel. He glared up at Matthew, spat, 'I had it under control, man!'

'Yeah, I could tell,' Matthew drawled.

The boy got up, dusted off his sweats. He took one step past Matthew but didn't get further than that. Matthew snagged him by the hood of his sweatshirt. 'Oh no. You're coming with me.'

'Fuck you!' The kid tried to struggle, but he couldn't have weighed more than a hundred and thirty pounds.

When he spun around and took a wild swing, Matthew grabbed his fist and slowly pushed it back, forcing the boy to his knees easily.

The kid looked up at him from his position on the floor, but his fight was gone, and in its place was only defeat. It was a feeling that Matthew knew too. 'What do you want from me?' he asked.

'Stop. Breathe. Think.'

He gave the kid a moment to calm before releasing him.

'I'm the only one who's seen enough to get you out of this mess. So, how about you pull your head out your ass and stop fighting me for long enough to see that.'

The kid raised those eyes, sick with hate and defeat. 'That guy – Marchant – he was my pro-bono defence attorney. If I don't do what he wants, he's gonna send me back.' His eyes glassed over. But the kid refused to cry. 'I can't go back.'

Matthew crouched in the dirt in front of him. 'If you come with me, I promise that you won't. But we need to finish this; otherwise, he's gonna hound you for the rest of your life. Is that what you want?'

The kid didn't reply when put up against that truth. He just subtly shook his head.

'You got your garbage bag with you?'

His head snapped up at that. 'You CHIPS?'

Matthew smiled grimly. He knew what CHIPS meant in the court system: Child in Need of Protection or Services. It was something he'd heard his many case workers say over the years. 'We never used to call it that when I was in. But yeah.'

'How many?'

Homes, Matthew knew. 'Eighteen. You?'

'Six. Until I got bagged.' Matthew saw the shudder that passed through the kid. 'I can't go to prison.'

'Oh, we'll think of something. But we gotta do a few rounds first.'

The kid eyed him sceptically. 'I don't do favours.'

'Kid, you ain't pretty enough to be doing me any favours.' When the kid's mouth twitched at that, Matthew stuck out a hand. 'Matthew Savage.'

The kid returned the shake. 'Rhett King.'

When Rhett took his hand, Matthew hauled him to his feet. 'Now, that's a bronc rider's name.'

Rhett actually smiled. 'Nah, man. That's a *bull rider's* name.'

Matthew just shook his head, muttered, 'Fucking bull riders.'

Chapter 41

Skye got four stitches in her face and strict instructions for overnight monitoring – instructions that Janey promised she'd see to herself. TJ refused to be seen, choosing to stay with Skye instead, but he promised that he'd get back on his physical therapy plan effective immediately.

They left the hospital at ten. By ten-twenty, they were back at the farm.

Janey drove down the driveway, TJ and Skye leaning against each other in the back seat, exhausted.

When Janey pulled up to the house, they both got out of the truck slowly, mindful of their aching bodies. While Janey disappeared inside, Skye limped around to the hood of the truck, and when she saw TJ's stiff walk to meet her, she grinned. 'We look like we just got back from war.'

'I do feel like I took on an army.' TJ roped his arm over her shoulders and walked with her up the porch steps.

'Tell me what you know about the kid?'

'Nothing. I promise. I saw him watching you warm up today. I wouldn't have thought it was that weird, but when he saw me, he ran. Like he was afraid of me.'

'Not you,' she countered. 'Holden.'

With a groan, TJ collapsed in the wicker chair. 'You think?'

'It's the only explanation, TJ. Somehow, that kid ended up under Holden's thumb.'

'Maybe.'

Skye rolled her eyes. 'The next best explanation is that *this child* is following me to rodeos, injuring my animals, slashing my tyres, and potentially trying to kill me *because* . . .?'

TJ tipped his head. 'Point taken.'

He leaned forward and grabbed her by the waistband of her jeans. When he gave her a tug, Skye went willingly. She sat on his lap, rested her body against his. She could feel the tension in him immediately. His muscles were taut, pulling tight everywhere. 'Do you need your pain pills?'

'Maybe. Let me see how I feel after physio.'

'I can give you a massage too,' Skye suggested.

TJ's arms came around her. He trailed his lips down her neck, igniting a slow burn of need in her. 'How did I get so lucky?' he murmured against her skin.

'You worked for it,' Skye replied simply.

TJ took her chin in his hand and turned her face so that their eyes met. 'I'm sorry about your run. That wasn't fair.' He placed his lips on hers gently, as if kissing away a small pain. 'What can I do?'

Skye settled back against him. She didn't want to tell him that there was nothing he could do. That time had passed. 'I think it's time to blow the lid off this thing.'

TJ nodded slowly. 'I don't think we have a choice anymore, Skye. You could have died,' he whispered.

'The most going to the cops will do is get it on record. We still have no solid proof besides videos recounting my side of the story. Holden still has my mom.' Unspeakable defeat filled her at that. 'But I can't live my entire life wondering what he's going to do next.'

The front door opened. Janey came out, two mugs of steaming

tea in her hands.

Skye took hers with murmured, 'Thanks.'

TJ protested. 'Mom, I hate that shit. It tastes like wet hay.'

Janey only continued to hold the mug out for him. 'I don't care, Jesse James Jones. It'll relax you.'

TJ took the tea, but he muttered, 'If I were any more relaxed, I'd be asleep.'

Janey took a seat in the chair next to them. She was quiet, but when Ryan came out a moment later and sat by her, Skye knew they had a purpose.

'Your father and I have been talking,' Janey began. 'And we feel that something has to be done.'

'We were just saying the same thing,' TJ agreed.

Janey's posture relaxed at that.

It was Ryan who looked at Skye. 'We'll support you in however you choose to handle this, Skye. But it's time.'

'Yeah,' she rasped. 'I know.'

'We're thinking that Ryan and I go in and get your mom.' Janey looked to Ryan, who nodded firmly. 'If we can get her out of the house for long enough to talk to you, maybe we could all convince her to leave. We'll take care of her.' Janey linked her fingers with Ryan's. 'She has a place here while you two are on the road.'

Tears clogged Skye's throat at that, and she simply nodded.

TJ's fingers trailed up and down her arm, soothing her, comforting her. 'We start fighting back. Through the legal channels at first,' TJ said. 'If that gets us nowhere, we resort to more *traditional* means.'

Skye loved that they were prepared to fight for her. But she was also terrified. Because they didn't know Holden. He'd destroy them. 'We need a plan. Something airtight.'

She shifted her eyes away as headlights turned down the driveway and cut through the night to where they sat on the porch.

'Wonder who that could be?' said Janey.

Skye tensed up at that. After the night she'd had, she couldn't face any more.

TJ tightened his arms around her, whispered, 'Relax. We won't let anything happen to you.'

'Ryan.'

Janey only had to say his name once for Ryan to understand. He went inside, and if Skye wondered what for, she didn't have to for long. Ryan came out, a shotgun in his hands. He sat back down next to Janey, casually, calmly.

The tension climbed to an unbearable level as the truck came to a stop in the driveway. Although she couldn't find the breath in her lungs to say it, Skye knew it wasn't Holden. He wouldn't drive a truck.

The headlights cut.

To all their surprise, Matthew Savage got out of the driver's side.

Skye relaxed.

He sauntered up to the porch steps, his black hair gleaming under his cowboy hat, which he swept off his head to greet them. 'Evening.'

'Savage, what the fuck?' TJ asked. 'We coulda shot you.'

Matthew's eyes glinted with humour. 'That the way you greet folks these days?' His grin was a quick flash of white teeth and wicked charm.

'After the day we've had, it holds some appeal,' TJ replied.

Matthew's grin died quickly. He tapped his hat against his thigh. 'So, look. I have the kid.'

Their collective gazes snapped to the truck. Sure enough, the kid sat in the passenger seat, looking terrified.

Beneath her, TJ went rigid. He grabbed her arms, preparing to nudge her off so that he could stand.

But Skye dead-weighted, using her small body to counteract his back strength. 'Stop,' she said.

'He could have killed you,' TJ bit off.

Matthew nodded. 'He could have. He wouldn't have meant to. But he could have.'

'Why did you bring him here, Savage?'

'I promised him no cops.'

TJ made a rough sound in the back of his throat. 'Why the fuck would you do that?'

'TJ,' Skye interceded. 'Just listen.'

'He cut your fucking saddle off!' TJ argued. 'He took a knife to Smokey!'

That just about killed her. But Skye knew, better than anyone, just how trapped a child could be by an adult who had all the power in the world over them – experience, intellect, strength, money, connections.

She raised her knuckles to TJ's face, brushed them over his scruff. 'Maybe he didn't have a choice.' When TJ shook his head but didn't argue, Skye looked back to Matthew. 'We'll listen. But that's all we'll promise.' Because whatever his story, he *had* cut her horse.

'Good enough for me.' Matthew turned. With a loud whistle and a wave, he indicated for the kid to come.

They were all eerily quiet as the boy opened the passenger door and stepped into the night. He approached slowly, his muscles tensed and ready for anything, his eyes scanning, she knew, for escape routes.

Skye couldn't even find it in herself to be angry. She just felt sad. Because she knew *exactly* what that felt like.

As the kid drew closer, TJ noticed things he hadn't from a distance earlier. The boy's sneakers were painfully white, but they were old too, the soles worn down, the laces frayed. The kid's sweatshirt and sweatpants were crumpled and dirty on the right-hand side only, as if he'd slept on the ground on that side. The very adult glint of anger in his eyes was offset by a face that hadn't even lost all its baby fat yet.

Matthew placed one hand on the kid's shoulder and propelled him the rest of the way. 'Rhett King, these are the Joneses. I think you have some things to say to them.'

Rhett's eyes flickered to Skye and dropped. He hung his head. Oddly, the first thing he said was, 'I'm sorry I hurt your horse. I didn't want to.'

'Holden made you do it?' Skye asked gently.

TJ wanted to scoff at that. There were *choices* in life. Personal responsibilities.

But then Skye got up off his lap, and she walked up to Rhett King.

TJ tensed, ready to intervene if he had to.

Skye didn't touch Rhett, only said, 'I've seen you before. At the hospital in Denver. You were in the waiting room.'

Rhett sniffed proudly. 'Got jumped by some thugs downtown.'

Skye nodded kindly. 'Look, I won't say it's okay, because it's never okay to hurt an animal. And that horse . . .' When her voice cracked, she trailed off until she'd composed herself. 'That horse is the most important thing in my life after my people. But I know, Rhett, what it's like to do things you don't want to do because someone bigger and stronger is holding all the cards.'

Rhett managed to meet her eyes at that, and TJ was mortified to see that the kid was on the verge of tears.

'My mom got me a goldfish once,' Skye continued. 'For my birthday. Because Holden didn't like pets. He said they were dirty. I forgot to clean his bowl once. *Once*. And Holden made me put him down the garbage disposal – alive. I was seven.'

TJ exhaled tightly through the fury.

Janey said, 'Excuse me, I'll go make some sandwiches,' and disappeared inside.

'He said he's gonna send me to prison. The adult one.' When

the first tear fell down Rhett's cheek, he angrily swiped it away. TJ watched as the kid forced his spine straight, pasted a cocky smirk over his fear, and said, 'I'm too pretty to go to the Big House.'

Matthew tapped him on the back of the head.

Skye smiled tiredly. 'How did you meet Holden, Rhett?'

Rhett's posture took a hit. 'He does some charity work . . .'

'He was your attorney?'

'Yeah. I got nabbed for possession *with intent*,' he added proudly. 'A kilo of white girl.'

At Skye's blank look, Matthew explained, 'Cocaine.'

'But I didn't say nothin'.'

'Anything,' Matthew corrected. 'You didn't say anything.'

'I'm no rat. Figured I'd spend a year in juvie.' He shrugged. 'Better than another foster home anyway. Regular meals.' Rhett tried for a cocky grin, but all TJ saw was pain. 'I was only in a couple of days, though. Next thing I know, my social worker's there. She says she managed to get in touch with some fancy law firm that does work for free. Community service type stuff.'

'And in walks Holden.'

'He looked like a God,' Rhett said distractedly. 'All fancy and slick. Powerful. He was nice – during our interviews and stuff.'

'And then it changed,' Skye prompted.

'The moment I got out.'

Skye sat down on the porch steps and patted the space next to her. 'What were you supposed to do?'

Rhett sat, but he kept a good distance, mistrustful of even that casual gesture. 'Scare you. Kill the horse,' he whispered. 'Vandalize.'

'Not hurt me?'

Rhett shook his head. 'I'm sorry. I . . . I panicked. I saw him – Marchant – at the rodeo. And I thought, *He's here because I haven't done enough*. But I didn't want to hurt you. I thought it would break when you got on. 'Cause the saddle kinda pulls to the side a bit, you know . . .'

'You've been watching – the horses?'

Rhett shrugged. 'They're kinda cool.'

TJ listened, and although his anger stayed at a steady simmer, he started to see a glimmer of hope.

When Rhett was done talking to Skye, TJ leaned forward. He placed his forearms on his knees. 'We have enough. To go to the cops.'

Rhett was up like a shot, his face contorted with rage. He started to walk for the truck, but Matthew just snagged him by the hoodie. 'Pipe down, King.'

'You promised!' Rhett fought. But Matthew just held on. As they tousled, Rhett's sweatshirt and T-shirt rode up, and TJ saw the dark mottles all over the kid's chest and back. Bruises the size of footprints.

'Fuck,' TJ muttered.

But it was Skye who said, 'No cops.'

Rhett started calming down. But he yanked his shirt and sweatshirt down to reveal a face red with anger and embarrassment.

Skye stared off over the farm, but her voice was calm and, if TJ heard right, excited when she said, 'We've been going about this the wrong way.'

'What do you mean?' he asked.

'We've been playing defence the entire time,' Skye said. 'But we've forgotten our biggest advantage.'

'Which is?'

Skye's grin was a little feral. 'I'm Holden Marchant's daughter.'

Chapter 42

Dallas, Texas – March 15, 2027

When Skye came out of the hotel bathroom, dressed in one of those fancy pink skirts and a matching blazer, TJ's mouth watered. She'd slicked her short hair back into some style that belonged on the runway. Her makeup was light but pristine, her blue eyes popping from between her mascaraed lashes. Strings of diamonds winked at her throat and on her wrist. The stitches in her right cheek had been removed, leaving a long scar that somehow added to the appeal. She looked like some Southern belle tossed into an action flick.

TJ stood up from where he'd been waiting in front of the TV. In his blue jeans and button-down, he felt like a cowboy in his Sunday best standing next to a princess.

He went to her but didn't dare touch. 'Damn, baby. You look like one of those little pastries that are too pretty to eat.'

She laughed and, raising her hand, patted his cheek. 'Something tells me you'll manage just fine, cowboy.'

'Bet.' Helpless to resist, he circled her waist and brought her close. But instead of kissing her, he leaned in and inhaled her perfume deeply into his lungs. It burned through his system and set everything to blazing. 'How long is this gonna take again?'

'An hour. Tops,' Skye said breathily.

'Thank God.' But he took a step back before he lost his willpower and started touching. Taking, eating. 'You ready?'

'As I'll ever be.'

'So, let's fuckin' go.' He held out his arm for her, and when she linked hers through his, TJ placed his hand on her, soothing. 'You've got this. And I've got you. Mom and Dad know their roles.'

'I know.'

The drive to the offices of Camden, Horowitz and Snow took seven minutes. They parked outside the gleaming glass tower and got out of their rented vehicle, a truck that neither of them had thought twice about selecting.

TJ craned his head back to see the top of the tower winking in the Dallas sunlight. 'Buildings like this always make me claustrophobic,' he commented. 'Just concrete and glass and bodies piled on top of each other.'

'Yeah. I never understood the appeal,' she replied. 'Even when it was expected of me.' Skye took a deep, calming breath. 'Let's do this. Before I chicken out.'

'Hey, baby?'

Skye frowned. 'Yeah?'

TJ crooked his finger at her, and when she leaned in, he flicked her ear.

Skye's hand shot up. For one second, a look of shocked outrage covered her face.

But once her brain caught up, she grinned. 'Rude.'

'But did it work?'

She nodded begrudgingly. 'It did.'

When she led the way inside the building to the front desk, TJ followed just behind her. He kept his eyes peeled, looking for Holden – just in case. This was, after all, her father's home turf.

They signed in at the sleek desk in the lobby, then used the passes they were given to scan through the waist-height turnstile to the elevator bank.

The elevator spat them out on the twenty-ninth floor. They were greeted by an aluminum sign with *Camden, Horowitz and Snow* laser-engraved on it. A large white desk sat off to the side. A pristinely turned-out secretary in a sleek business suit sitting behind it asked, 'May I help you?'

'Skye Marchant. We have an eleven o'clock with Michael Camden.'

The secretary checked her computer. She smiled, said, 'Right this way.' As she led through the immaculate offices, she asked, 'Are you related to Holden?'

Skye nodded. 'I'm his daughter.'

The secretary gushed. 'We all just adore your father.'

Skye just smiled, said, 'That doesn't surprise me.'

The secretary directed them to a waiting area with plush white leather sofas and a full wet bar. Skye's attorney, Mr Simcock, was already there, waiting for them. He heaved himself out of the sofa and came to greet them. He held out one hand and when Skye took it, the attorney closed both of his over Skye's. 'Are you sure about this?'

'Yes.'

'As your late grandmother's attorney, I have to warn you. The risks—'

'I know.' Skye smiled kindly. 'But this will work.'

Mr Simcock nodded. 'It's officially your responsibility. So, we'll do it your way.'

At that precise moment, the secretary came back. 'Mr Camden will see you now.' Her eyes flickered to TJ. 'Due to the nature of your meeting, he advises that only family and legal representation be present.'

TJ geared up to argue. There was no way Skye was facing this alone.

But he didn't have to. Skye linked her hand with his and said, 'He's family. My fiancé.'

The secretary smiled at that. She held out one arm. 'Right this way.'

Their trio started down the hall. But right before they stepped into the room, TJ leaned down and whispered, 'Fiancé?'

Skye just smiled up at him. 'It seemed more defensible than *boyfriend*.'

'At some point, we gotta make good on that lie.'

Skye winked at him, said, 'I'm just waiting for you to ask, Jesse Jones.'

Skye grinned at TJ's hungry look and stepped past him into Michael Camden's corner office. The room was large, with heavy antique furniture that was strongly incongruous with the rest of the stark, modern suite she'd seen. She sincerely hoped that the old, sturdy furniture reflected the man.

Camden sat behind his desk, his big hands linked in front of him. He was a giant with an imposing presence, but he stood when they entered, greeted all three of them with a firm shake and genuine smile, before indicating for them to take a seat.

'It's such a pleasure to meet Holden's daughter,' he began. 'He talks about you often.'

Skye smiled. 'My father was actually the one who recommended you.'

'He's been with us a long time.' Mr Camden hesitated, as if preparing to deliver bad news. 'I'm sure your current attorney has pointed out that requests like this are highly unusual.'

'Of course.'

'And given that your father contested your grandmother's will through documented channels, the risk to Camden, Horowitz and Snow can't be ignored. The conflict of interests alone—'

Skye held up a hand. 'Could we bring my father into the meeting?' At Camden's blank look, Skye affected a guileless tone. 'After he contested the will, Dad and I agreed that this is the best way forward. And we'd like to present a united front.'

'Of course.' He picked up the phone and made a call.

Within two minutes, Holden knocked on the door and stepped into the office.

Skye would cherish the moment he saw her for the rest of her life. Holden's perfect smile faltered, his face paled. Oh, he recovered quickly enough. 'What a lovely surprise.' He stepped into the room, bent over to kiss Skye's cheek. But as he came close, he whispered, 'Be very careful, little girl.'

Skye let the shiver of fear pass through her. But for the first time, she used it, hoarding the fear until it had built up to something reactive and predatory. Reckless. 'As I was saying, my father contested the will because he didn't believe that I was competent enough at twenty-five to manage such a large sum of money.' She put a little tremble in her tone when she added, 'I'll admit, the task is quite daunting. And with Mr Simcock retiring soon, I've been forced to be realistic.' She sent Holden a sickly-sweet smile. 'My dad' – she said the word even though it burned her tongue – 'and I were able to agree on a compromise.'

'Which would be engaging the services of Camden, Horowitz and Snow?' Michael Camden supplied.

'You're a firm that my father trusts implicitly. Your reputation is above reproach. And Dad has assured me that, with standard measures to ensure no conflict of interest, the trust would be safest directly in your hands, Mr Camden. After all, you're one of the most sought-after estate attorneys in the nation.'

Mr Camden looked to her father. 'Holden?'

Holden's voice when he spoke was tightly controlled. Skye wondered if anyone else could hear the restraint in it. She did. It was the tone he used when he asked a rhetorical question that led to a slap. *Do you know how much you embarrassed me today? Do you know how many Bs you got on your report card? Do you know how much it hurts me to discipline you?* Instead of saying any of that, Holden said, 'If you don't think it's for the best, Mike . . .'

'It's a lot of money. It's an account I'd personally love to oversee; Jolene MacDonald left behind quite a legacy in Dallas.' Mr Camden leaned back in his chair. 'If you trust me with it, Holden, if you can guarantee that the issues you had when you contested the will have been resolved . . .'

'Yes. Yes, quite,' Holden managed. Barely.

Skye saw how his hands shook with rage. And she rejoiced. 'Due to my dad's long-standing job here, his *loyalty* to the firm, he has also agreed to forgo my mother's monthly allowance from the trust to remove any last hesitations you might have regarding conflicts of interest.' Skye slid the revised documents, executed by Mr Simcock that morning, across the desk. 'We've agreed that removing any and all conflicts would bring any chance of further disagreements or bar complaints to zero.'

Mr Camden looked at Holden one last time. 'You realize, Holden, that by me taking this on, you would be completely removed from all firm access to the account? And that any issues arising between you and a client would put us in a completely compromising situation? One in which we'd be morally and legally obligated to side with the client?'

'Of course.' Holden's hands were fisted on his lap. But when he spoke, his voice was calm. Smooth. 'My daughter and I discussed the particulars.'

'Very well.' Mr Camden touched the fat file on his desk. 'Despite my own excitement at the prospect of representing you, Miss Marchant, I was prepared to let you down. But given this new information, I believe we can work together. Let me review this and reach back out to you next week with the official paperwork.' He stood up and came around the desk, took Skye's hand in his. 'But I hope it's not too premature to say, welcome to Camden, Horowitz, and Snow.'

Skye's entire system flooded with victory. She smiled brightly, and it was real. Victorious. 'I'm thrilled to be here,' she replied. And it was not a lie.

They left.

But outside, Skye took a seat on a nearby bench, and when TJ looked down at her, she said, 'I'll catch up with you in a minute.'

'Remember: no heroics. No baiting him. Close it.'

'Okay.'

When Holden stepped outside, TJ hesitated. Skye reached for his hand, gave it a squeeze. 'I'll be fine.'

'I'll be right over there, watching.'

The moment TJ was a safe distance, Holden sat down beside her. 'I must say, Skye, this was all very unnecessary.' His tone was sad, surprised. As if he couldn't quite believe it.

'The rent for the Highland Park house is due April first – to your boss.'

His downtrodden façade vanished instantly. 'What do you want?'

'I think I've gotten everything I want actually,' she said coolly.

'Your mother will pay for this,' Holden threatened. He covered the threat smoothly with, 'She'll be forced to live in a manner far beneath what she's used to. I'm sure you'd agree that it would be painful, *cruel* to subject her to such things.'

'Maybe. Maybe not.'

'Think about what this will do to her.'

'I am. Unlike you, I only ever think of her.'

'I've given your mother – and you – everything!' he hissed.

'No. You took her – her body, her mind, her money – and you degraded her until she had nothing left. But not anymore. She has nothing left for you to control. No money, no house.'

'Oh, but she still feels pain,' Holden threatened.

Skye's stomach sloshed with anxiety. But she didn't show it. 'I won't know about it.'

Holden seemed to buy her bluff. 'What do you want?'

'I've taken a million out of the trust. If you leave Caroline – file for divorce – it's yours. If you choose not to, you'll never see another dime of MacDonald money.'

'This is ridiculous.'

Skye laughed lightly. But when she said, 'Bless your heart, Holden,' her voice dripped Southern sugar. She leaned close, whispered, 'This is the monster you created.'

Holden didn't have anything to say to that. 'I want three.'

'You'd leave Caroline for three million dollars?' Skye asked clearly.

'She's a means to an end to me, a woman who's easy to keep in line and well-bred enough to impress at social functions. If she's a bore in bed' – he shrugged – 'the young, dumb and impressionable certainly aren't.'

His words were meant to hurt. And they did. But Skye didn't show it. 'Just for that, the offer is now seven-fifty. Take it or leave it, Holden.'

'You little bitch.'

'It'll be gone in three, two—'

'Fine. Deal.' He held out one hand.

Skye looked down at it, but she refused to shake. She just stood, said, 'Mr Simcock will send you the particulars shortly. He'll also be representing Caroline in the divorce.'

'I should have killed you when I had the chance.'

'Probably,' Skye agreed.

'Your offer is made on one fatal assumption,' he said.

Skye played ignorant. 'Oh?'

'You think your mother will agree to a divorce?' he asked. His smile was cold and bitter. 'She eats, like a starved dog, from the palm of my hand,' he taunted.

Skye took her phone out of her pocket and put it on speaker. 'Janey?'

'We're here, Skye. She heard it all.'

In the background, her mother's sobs echoed. Each stuttered cry tore through Skye. In the back of her mind, she vaguely wondered if her mom would ever forgive her for this. Hell, she wondered if she'd ever forgive herself for it.

Holden paled. But he didn't try to speak to Caroline.

Skye ended the call. 'Whether or not she decides to go through with it isn't up to me. I've done everything I can for her. The question is: how long will you stick to her once she has nothing?'

'You bitch,' he spat. 'I might just take care of you anyway.'

'If anything happens to me or anyone I love, specific things happen automatically. All the evidence I've collected – including my own and Rhett King's video accounts of abuse – go straight to your boss.'

Shock flashed in Holden's eyes. But he managed to cover it with a sneer. 'Nobody would believe you. My character, my reputation, is unimpeachable. While you . . .' He sighed sadly. 'You spent over a year in a mental health facility. You live most of the year in a mobile home. And you race horses for pennies. Rhett King is a boy in the care of the State. One who has a criminal record. One who not many people would take as a reliable witness. Optics, child, are everything.'

'Maybe,' Skye ceded. 'Which I why I've never gone to the police. After all, the last time I did, you had me institutionalized.' She tipped her head, said, 'But Holden? If optics are everything, how do you think Camden, Horowitz and Snow will react to the whiff of scandal?' She let that hang for a moment before adding, '*Were* everything I have against you to be given to your bosses, what do you think they'd do to save their firm's reputation?'

His face went from pale to red with rage.

'Firing you would be the least of it. My guess is that a bar complaint might follow. Either way, you'd be done.' Skye grinned when she saw the realization dawn in his eyes.

She stood, smoothed out her skirt. 'Goodbye, Holden. I would say have a nice life, but I wouldn't mean it. I hope that money runs through your fingers like water. And that the next woman you try to seduce puts your balls in a vice.'

She didn't look back. Only forward. But she heard her father's enraged roar.

And she smiled.

She walked to where TJ waited, his eyes focused on her, watching over her even as he trusted her to handle it herself. When she got to him, she asked, 'Home?'

And he said, 'Yes, ma'am.'

Chapter 43

Scottsdale, Arizona – March 20, 2027

Although Caroline agreed to leave with Ryan and Janey, her reunion with her daughter wasn't the big, tearful one Skye had always imagined. Her mom, numb with shock and betrayal, didn't even hug her, only stood and stared straight through Skye, as if she were a stranger blocking her view of something awe-inspiring.

Skye tried not to let it bother her. She of all people knew how long recovery took. And she knew that a person never quite recovered fully either. So, she didn't smother Caroline, simply whisked her away from Dallas before the news of her parents' divorce filtered through Dallas society.

But once her mom was safely in Scottsdale, it didn't get better as Skye had hoped. Instead, Caroline would lock herself away for hours at a time. Often, her sobs could be heard echoing down the hall.

After a week, Skye's pity grew tired as her anger at her mother increased.

TJ must have seen it, because one night at dinner, when Caroline didn't eat, just sat at the table while Janey crooned at her like a mother hen, Skye lost her temper. She slowly put her fork down. But before she could get a single word out, TJ scooped her out of her chair and carried her out of the room.

Despite her protests and violent threats of what she would do to him if he flared up his back, which had only just stabilized again after her fall, TJ just carried her to the truck and deposited her in the passenger seat.

He walked around the hood while she seethed.

But when he climbed into the driver's side and wordlessly started the vehicle, Skye simply broke.

She cried as he drove, all her anger and resentment and bitterness oozing out of her with every tear.

TJ didn't say anything, only held her thigh with one big hand.

When he came to a dirt driveway, with a rusted swinging gate sealing off the entrance, he got out and opened it.

When TJ got back into the driver's seat and pulled onto the property, Skye asked, 'Where are we?'

He got out and closed the gate. It was only when he'd gotten back into the truck that he said, 'It's a surprise.'

Confused, Skye looked out over the land. They were ten minutes or so from the dairy farm, so the landscape was the same. Dry red dirt with desert scrub. That big blue bowl of a sky so perfectly contrasting it. Up ahead, the driveway ended at a big white adobe house with a flat roof and a mud-stained foundation.

'It's like being in a desert globe, Arizona.'

'Do you like it?' TJ asked, his tone cautious.

'I do. It's really grown on me.'

He smiled, but Skye noticed that it was shaky. She looked closer, observed his pale face and sweat-coated brow for the first time. She put one hand on his arm, asked, 'How bad?'

TJ laughed shakily. 'Oh, like I'm about to have a heart attack.'

'Hospital?'

He shook his head. 'No.'

'TJ—'

He braked. Before she could keep arguing, he leaned over and stole the words from her lips with a kiss that left her breathless. Her heart slammed against her ribs once. Her hands rose to his face, taking the kiss deeper.

He broke it first, but he didn't pull back, just rested his forehead against hers, his rapid breath tickling her face. 'Before I kiss you, I always tell myself it can't be as good as I remember. But then you tear through me, Skye, and I can't wrap my head around the fact that it wasn't as good as I remember – it was better. You're like a disease of the blood, one that can't be cured, one that I can't live without.'

His words settled her. 'If you're trying to distract me from my misery, it's working.'

TJ grinned. He shucked his head, said, 'Come on,' and then got out of the truck.

Skye followed.

It was only once she was standing in front of the house that she noticed it was closed up. The windows were boarded on the outside. The front garden was somehow both overgrown and dried up.

'Where are we?'

'Well, that depends on you.' TJ roped one arm over her shoulders and pulled her against him.

Skye froze. 'What do you mean?'

'If you like it, I'm planning on buying it.'

Her head snapped back to look up at TJ's face. 'What?'

He shrugged. 'I never bought my own place because I was on the road for most of the year. But us, living with my folks and your mom is . . .'

'Smothering.'

'A little,' TJ replied. He shifted, so that he was standing in front of her. 'I know what pulling out of the season cost you.'

Skye's eyes watered just thinking about it. 'I couldn't leave my mom after what I did . . .'

'I know. And I know how much selflessness it took, especially considering your mom's not in a place to realize what you sacrificed for her, let alone appreciate you for it.'

'She's punishing me.'

'It feels like that,' TJ said cautiously. 'But I think the truth is that she just doesn't know how to function without the parameters your father always forced on her. It's like releasing a prey animal raised in captivity into the wild, Skye. She's scared and lost and has no survival skills. Give her time.'

'I resent her.' It felt good to finally say it, even though the guilt and shame that followed sank through her like a bag of stones. 'I resent her. And then I feel like a shitty person for resenting her.'

'That's normal given what you went through. You finally got your life to a point where you were going after what you wanted. And you worked so hard for so long – only to have to give it up to take care of a parent who could never really do anything to help you. Do you know how few people would do what you did?' He kissed her forehead. 'Be kind to yourself.'

Frustrated with her self-pitying mood, Skye walked off to look at the house. 'I keep telling myself there'll be other seasons, other NFRs.'

'A lifetime of them,' TJ affirmed from behind her. 'And, on the plus side, now we have the year to plan our wedding.'

Skye grinned. It had become a joke between them, only this time her, 'How many times do I have to say it? You can't tell me, you have to *ask*,' died when she turned around.

TJ was down on one knee in the dirt.

He looked around the land, said, 'I figure this way, we're far enough from my folks that we won't feel smothered. But close enough that I can still help my dad out at the farm when we're not on the road and *they* can pop by and check on things here when we are.'

Skye's heart stilled. She couldn't have known before this moment that home was not a place but a person. But as she looked at TJ, pale and sweating with nerves and pain, there was no fear, no insecurity, no flashing warning signs.

Still, she gave herself a moment to wallow in the certainty of that. She walked towards him, said, 'It needs work.'

TJ nodded. 'Most things do.'

'We'll need to build a barn, an arena, a round pen. Irrigated pastures.' She sighed dramatically. 'It'll be expensive.'

'Baby, I'll build you an indoor if that's what it'll take.'

Skye laughed. Unable to hold back, she knelt in front of him. She looked into green eyes, swimming with nerves. 'TJ, I don't care about the indoor arena.'

'I know.' He reached into his back pocket, pulled out a ring. There was no box, just a gold band with three small diamonds inlaid in a row, the centre stone slightly bigger than the others. 'It's small. But I wanted something that you'd wear all day, every day, and figured you'd prefer something that wouldn't get in the way or get damaged while you're riding or working.'

'It's perfect.'

TJ exhaled a breath of relief, and this time, when he met her eyes, his were lit with a grin. 'Skye Marchant, will you take my name?'

It was the perfect way for him to ask, the perfect reminder that she could cut the ties to her childhood and reinvent herself entirely. She leaned forward and kissed him gently, whispered, 'Yes.'

'I won't ever stop you from chasing your dreams,' he promised.

And Skye just smiled and held out her hand. 'I know. I trust you. Absolutely.'

Glossary of Relevant Rodeo Terms

- **1D, 2D, 3D, 4D:** many local and association barrel racing events use the division system, which allows riders and horses of various skill levels to compete, place and win prize money in a race. The 1D is set by the fastest rider's time within that event, the 2D half a second behind, the 3D one second behind and the 4D two seconds behind, thereby creating time brackets/divisions in which the fastest rider(s) in each division place and are paid out.
- **AQHA:** the American Quarter Horse Association is the official member organization for everything relating to the Quarter Horse breed (e.g., advocacy, events, horse bloodline/breed registration, etc.).
- **Alley:** as referenced in this book, the alley is the narrow entrance that a barrel racer and her horse enter/leave the arena by.
- **Badlands Circuit:** the WPRA's regional barrel racing circuit name for the Dakota States.
- **Barrel Racing:** a timed rodeo event where a horse and rider must navigate three triangulated barrels in a cloverleaf pattern. Scoring is time based and laser recorded at the finish line to the hundredth of a second. Knocking over a barrel results in a five second penalty.

- **Bull Rope:** a specialized, personal rope used by bull riders. The bull rope goes around the bull's shoulder and provides the rider with his grip or handhold.
- **Breakaway Roping:** a timed rodeo event where a rider must rope a calf around the neck, halt and tie the rope around the saddle horn. When the calf runs, pulling the rope taut, it releases or "breaks away," and the clock is stopped.
- **Bronc Rein:** a single, braided rope that is attached to a bucking horse's halter and provides the rider with his grip or handhold.
- **Chute:** a secure pen that is used to hold rodeo animals (typically bulls, broncs, steers, and calves) immediately prior to their event and their release into the performance arena.
- **Drag:** to ensure that the events run like clockwork, once a barrel racer has entered an event, they draw (or are assigned) a number that determines the order they run in. A 'drag', in barrel racing, is a small group of consecutive racers who are grouped together to warm up and move through to the holding area together, to keep things streamlined. Confusingly, 'to drag' the arena is also the process where the tractors come out and grade the arena after every five or so riders to guarantee fair run conditions.
- **Go-Round:** a single round of competition in a rodeo.
- **Hands:** horses are measured in 'hands' from the ground to the top of the withers (the highest point on the back). One hand is four inches.
- **NCFR:** National Circuit Finals Rodeo, the annual regional (circuit) rodeo finals held each year.
- **NFR:** National Finals Rodeo, the annual rodeo finals held in Las Vegas, Nevada, every December.
- **PBR:** Professional Bull Riders.
- **PRCA:** Professional Rodeo Cowboys Association.
- **Slack:** during those timed rodeo events with a large number of entrants, overflow competitors will take their turn(s) during the slack, designated times outside of ticketed/televised rodeo performance ('perf').

- **Team Roping:** a timed rodeo event in which two riders must work together to rope a steer. The first rider (the 'header') ropes the steer's head or horns, then turns the steer left. The second rider (the 'heeler') ropes the steer's hind legs. The clock stops once the rope is pulled taut.
- **Tie-Down Roping:** a timed rodeo event in which a rider ropes a running calf, dismounts and then 'throws' the calf and 'ties' three of its legs together. The clock stops when the roper removes their hands and places them in the air. The calf must remain tied for six seconds for the tie-down to count.
- **Turnout:** as referenced in this book, and following specific rules and fines, a turnout is the act of officially withdrawing from an entered event due to rider/horse injury or unforeseen conflicts in event schedules.
- **Turquoise Circuit:** the WPRA's regional barrel racing circuit name for the southwestern states (Arizona, New Mexico, sometimes overlapping with California too).
- **UTB:** Unleash the Beast, the PBR's main competition league.
- **WRPA:** Women's Professional Rodeo Association.

Author's Note

Thank you so much for reading *Reckless Skye*!

Although this book did deal with some tough themes, it was so much fun to write. When I first set out to write a rodeo romance, I wanted to authentically capture the experience. Not just the fun and the crowds and the cute outfits in the stands, but the athletes' grit and dedication through less-than-ideal conditions, injuries and grueling travel schedules. And, of course, their love and respect for their animals. I hope you enjoyed these behind-the-scenes snippets and that this book gave you a new appreciation for rodeo!

In choosing the rodeo setting, I knew that I needed a heroine whose trauma taught her to snarl rather than cower – and, of course, a hero to pull her out of her own mind with his cocky self-assurance and sense of humor. Skye and TJ met every challenge I set for them.

This book wouldn't have been possible without the help of my amazing editor, Grace, and the entire HQ team. Thank you for all the help – for (somehow) cutting twenty thousand words from this novel and still maintaining the heart of the story. And for catching my inconsistencies with dates, times and, really, anything to do with numbers.

Thank you to every reader who picked up this book. Most

days, I still can't believe there are real people out there who read what I write . . . I appreciate you all so much!

If you would like to stay in touch, follow along on Instagram (@author.sloane) for highly inconsistent posts. Or, if you'd like to hear from me more consistently, sign up for my newsletter at www.sloanefletcher.com.

Don't miss Matthew Savage's story, *Rebel Heart*, coming to HQ and HarperCollins in 2027.

**A hundred reasons to run.
A cowboy to make her stay . . .**

Hollywood starlet Nina Keller is searching for an escape. Arriving at Hunt Ranch after a terrifying assault, she only wants one thing: to rediscover who she is.

Maverick Hunt was never a part of that plan. But with his kind heart and unwavering patience, Nina can't help but feel safe around the strong – and undeniably handsome – cowboy. And that is worth more than he could ever know.

Enchanted by ranch life with Maverick and his young daughter, Poppy, Nina begins to imagine a future for herself in the country – in seeking an escape, she may have instead found a home.

But that dream is threatened when Nina's past catches up with her. And when an unlikely predator strikes, she and Maverick must make a choice: to let each other go or face the world together.

Two broken hearts.
One last chance to heal together . . .

Sierra Hunt never had any doubt that Benji Matthews was her person. As her brother's best friend, he should have been off-limits, but Sierra knew he was the one as surely as she knew how to ride a horse. It didn't matter that he came from nothing – to her, he was everything. And together, they were Hunt Ranch's greatest love story: the rugged wrangler and the corporate cowgirl.

Until a devastating twist of fate shattered their lives entirely.

Now they can hardly stand to be in the same room. But when Benji is left with no other choice than to step up and take the reins at Hunt Ranch, avoiding each other becomes damn near impossible. Forced to work together, the two must confront everything they've lost. In doing so, they might just find their way back to each other, and the love they thought had disappeared forever . . .